CRIME ALWAYS PAYS

CRIME ALWAYS PAYS

Declan Burke

This first world edition published 2014
in Great Britain and the USA by
SEVERN HOUSE PUBLISHERS LTD of
19 Cedar Road, Sutton, Surrey, England, SM2 5DA.
Trade paperback edition first published
in Great Britain and the USA 2014 by
SEVERN HOUSE PUBLISHERS LTD.

Burke, Declan
  Crime always pays.
  1. Islands–Greece–Fiction. 2. Noir fiction.
  I. Title
  823.9'2-dc23

ISBN-13: 978-0-7278-8375-9 (cased)
ISBN-13: 978-1-84751-509-4 (trade paper)

The extract from *The Wild Life of Sailor and Lula* by Barry Gifford
is reproduced by kind permission of the author.

All Severn House titles are printed on acid-free paper.

Severn House Publishers support the Forest Stewardship Council™ [FSC™],
the leading international forest certification organisation. All our titles that
are printed on FSC certified paper carry the FSC logo.

Typeset by Palimpsest Book Production Ltd.,
Falkirk, Stirlingshire, Scotland.
Printed and bound in Great Britain by
TJ International, Padstow, Cornwall.

Acknowledgements

Heartfelt thanks are due to: Marsha Swan, Stacia Decker, Ray Banks, John Connolly, Reed Farrel Coleman, Ken Bruen, John McFetridge, Adrian McKinty, Donna Moore, Ed O'Loughlin, Kevin McCarthy and Sarah Bannan at the Irish Arts Council.

As always, my agent Allan Guthrie is a rock of sense in a world gone mad. No, seriously, etc.

I would particularly like to thank Sara Porter, Piers Tilbury and Kate Lyall Grant at Severn House.

Finally, hugs and kisses to Aileen and Lily, whose love and support make everything possible.

Author's Note

Crime Always Pays is fiction, and takes place in a parallel universe that largely mimics the rules – gravity, etc. – of the world we are all familiar with. It is, however, a world that differs in some respects to our own, including the basic geography of some Cycladic Greek islands, the prevalence of coincidence, and the improbability of happy endings. To those readers offended by the taking of liberties in such things, I sincerely apologize.

'The best thing you can hope for in this life is that the rest of the world'll forget all about ya.'

Barry Gifford, *The Wild Life of Sailor and Lula*

WEDNESDAY
Sleeps

Rossi said he'd torque if he needed to torque, he'd just had his ear ripped off.

Sleeps allowed Rossi made a valid point, especially as the hound that tore off the ear was three parts Siberian wolf to one part furry Panzer, but thought that Rossi, with the gash in the side of his head flapping like a glove puppet every time he opened his mouth, was maybe mishearing.

'What he said,' Sleeps said, 'was try not to talk.'

It was bad enough they were holed up in a vet's surgery and down two hundred grand, Rossi minus an ear and raving about how genius isn't supposed to be perfect, it's not that kind of gig. But then the vet had started threading catgut into what looked to Sleeps like a needle he'd once seen on the Discovery Channel stuck through a cannibal's nose and sent Rossi thrashing around on the operating table, hauling on the restraints, Rossi with a terror of needles and ducking around like Sugar Ray in a bouncy castle.

The vet leaned in to squint at the raspberry jelly mess that was the side of Rossi's head. It didn't help there was no actual ear. It had been torn clean off, along with enough skin to top a sizeable tom-tom.

'If he doesn't lie still,' he said, 'he's going to wind up with his brain on a skewer.'

Sleeps sighed and climbed aboard, making a virtue of his considerable bulk by sprawling across Rossi and pinning him to the steel-frame operating table. Rossi went cross-eyed, launched into a gasping stream of profanity that sounded like a leaky balloon with Tourette's. Sleeps wriggled around, sealed Rossi's mouth with a plump hand.

The vet knotted the catgut. 'I'd appreciate it,' he said, 'if you'd point that somewhere else.'

Sleeps' pride and joy, the .22, nickel-plated, pearl grip. Enough to stop a man and put him down but not necessarily lethal unless you were unlucky. The .22 being empty right now, at least Sleeps didn't have to worry about getting any unluckier than chauffeuring Rossi around when the guy was down one ear and a fat bag of cash. He slipped the .22 into his pocket.

'OK,' the vet said, 'hold him still. This'll hurt.'

Sleeps, fascinated, watched him work. The vet, with Roman senator hair that was turning grey, the eyes grey too, giving off this unflappable vibe that Sleeps presumed came from every day sticking your hand up a cow's wazoo. Or maybe this was a regular thing for him, a couple of guys on the run stumbling out of the forest into the back yard of his veterinarian practice with wounds it might be tough to explain away at hospitals that weren't built next door to zoos.

'I'll warn you now he's going to need an anti-tetanus shot,' the vet said. 'Looks like this, ah, car door you're saying somehow ripped off your friend's ear had some serious teeth. We could be looking at rabies.'

'That's just his natural disposition,' Sleeps said, Rossi throwing in a muffled snarl or two as the vet tucked the stitches snug. 'But sure, yeah, I think we both know it wasn't a car door.'

'What are we looking at? Doberman?'

'I'm not sure,' Sleeps said. 'Some kind of Siberian wolf mix, there's maybe some husky in there. Belongs to his ex, Karen, she took it on when he went back inside.'

'I thought we said no names.'

'Right, yeah.' Sleeps, who was looking to go back inside, cop some soft time, figured it might do no harm to drop a few crumbs with the vet. 'She's a beast, though. The hound, not Karen. I mean, our friend here was driving a Transit van at the time and she shunted it off the track, came bombing through the windscreen and tried to chew his head off.' Sleeps had seen it all happen, having little else to look at on account of being stuck behind a deflating airbag at the wheel of their getaway Merc. The Merc at the time was wedged at an angle between a boulder and the bole of a fat pine near the bottom of a gully, maybe half a mile from the lake where Rossi had just heisted a two-hundred-grand cash ransom from Karen and Ray.

Rossi had pulled up in the Transit, which he'd also swiped from Karen and Ray, and called down to Sleeps, told him to hold on. Then Sleeps had heard a howl and the splintering crash of the hound going through the Transit's window. Rossi'd floored it, aiming the van at the nearest tree, but the wolf had shoved the van off the muddy track and down into the gully, at which point the hound, wedged chest-deep into the crumpled window frame, had set about decapitating her former owner.

To be fair, Sleeps acknowledged, the girl had her reasons. She was very probably the only Siberian wolf-husky cross on the planet wearing a pirate patch, this because Rossi, trying to break her in, just before he went back inside for his third jolt, had gouged out her eye with the blunt end of a fork. And that wasn't even her most recent provocation. Only twenty minutes previously Rossi had left her laid out on the lake shore, putting a .22 round in her face, point-blank.

If Karen and Ray hadn't come riding over the hill like the cavalry, hauling the hound off along with the two hundred gees, Rossi would have been crushed, minced and spat out.

'Listen, I don't mind stitching him up,' the vet said, 'but I'd appreciate you leaving out any detail that's not strictly relevant to his condition. You know I'll have to ring the police, right? Because of the possible rabies. And the less I know . . .'

'Sure,' Sleeps said, 'yeah. But if you could just give us, like, maybe an hour's start? It's been a bad enough day already.'

'It's tough all over,' the vet agreed. Then Rossi gave a yelp as the needle slipped, tried to bite Sleeps' hand.

In the end Sleeps jammed his thumb into the ragged hole where Rossi's ear used to be, stirred it around. Rossi screeched once, high-pitched, then keeled over and passed out.

Sleeps slid down off the operating table, retrieved the .22 from his pocket. 'OK,' he said, 'I'll be needing a bag of horse tranks. And whatever gun you use for putting down the animals.'

The vet sewed on. 'We don't use those any more, they're not humane.'

'Humane? You're a *vet*, man.'

'We treat them like children,' the vet said, 'not animals.'

'Nice theory.' Sleeps, who'd been hoping to bag himself a cattle-prod at the very least, gestured at Rossi with the .22. 'But what if they're a little of both?'

Karen

K aren had this little dent in her chin like a twisted dimple from the time she was fourteen years old and smashed her jaw on the porcelain sink at home, this so she could go to the hospital and tell them her father had been kicking her around ever since her mother died. Neglecting to mention for an hour or two, the nurses fussing around, that her father was right then flat-backed on their kitchen floor with a stroke, a salad fork buried deep not far off his heart.

When the cops asked about the fork, Karen told them about her mother, how she'd never realized you could beat a person to death without doing it all in one go, take years to do it. At that point Karen herself had already shipped a broken tibia, three cracked ribs and a perforated eardrum. She figured tossing the self-inflicted broken jaw in on top was, strictly speaking, perjury. But Karen could live with that.

Karen went into care. Her father got four years, eighteen months suspended. So Karen went to visit, waited until it got quiet, everyone whispering their conversations, and then she started screaming about how her father had been crawling into her bed ever since she was eight years old.

For a long time after she'd been torn between a craving to hear how the bastard had died in agony and never wanting to hear his name again.

These days Karen rarely thought about him at all, and then only to remind herself she had what it took to do whatever she needed to do. Which was, right this moment, to not collapse with exhaustion while the doctor conducted his examination.

Hunkered down beside Anna, the girl nearly eight foot from nose to tail where she lay stretched out on the shed floor, the guy looked like a child playing doctors with a bearskin rug. He listened with his eyes closed, stroking the blood-roughened fur of her chest, then unclipped his stethoscope from his ears. 'What happened to her eye?' he said, patting her flank.

'Same guy as shot her in the face,' Karen said. 'Back when he was trying to break her in, he gouged out the eye.'

The doctor winced. Karen, no point in jinxing the sympathy factor, skipped over the part where Anna had hunted Rossi through the woods after he'd shot her, gone head-first through his van window and damn near crushed his skull. 'So what's the verdict?' she said.

'Well,' he said, standing up, pressing his fists into the small of his back, 'I'm no expert in gunshot wounds in wolves. What is she, anyway?'

'Mostly wolf, yeah. Some husky too.'

'She's fabulous.'

'She is.' Karen keeping it short so the doctor wouldn't hear the wobble in her voice. 'So how's she doing?'

'About as well as can be expected after taking a .22 round at close range,' he said. 'Actually, her forehead's more or less a plate of solid bone, so the slug probably came off worse.'

'But she'll be fine.'

'If I was you I'd keep her doped for another few days, the last thing you want is a wolf with migraine. But if she gets plenty of rest she should be fine.'

'Should be?'

'It's impossible to say for sure, Karen. Head traumas can be tricky. She could well have a skull fracture, I'm really not qualified to say. Or there might be internal bleeding, clotting on the brain. All I can tell you is that her vitals are good, and she doesn't seem to be in any distress.' He looked down again at Anna, shaking his head now. 'And keep her away from the guy who gouges out eyes.'

Karen scraped up a smile. About the only thing Karen didn't need to worry about right now was Rossi. It had taken everything she had to drag Anna out of the Transit's cab, Anna still stuck in the smashed window frame when she and Ray arrived, the girl howling as she tried to get at Rossi where he'd somehow managed to squirm his way down under the steering wheel. Karen could see how the shards of glass were lacerating Anna's chest every time she heaved forward, only the thick ruff of fur at her neck saving her throat from being sliced open, Karen screaming into Anna's ear to pierce the blood-lust rage that kept Anna pounding away.

It'd been Ray, as woozy as he was after getting his arm broken in the face-off at the lake, who'd nipped around the other side of the Transit, reached in and jammed down on the horn. The shock caused Anna to rear back, the momentum allowing Karen to haul her out of the crushed window, at which point Anna had simply collapsed.

It'd been hell, with Ray pretty much out of commission, for Karen and Madge to drag Anna up out of the gully and load her into the rear seat of the car. So when Madge suggested they should probably go back down to the Transit, check to see if Rossi was still alive or was just lying doggo, Karen told Madge she was on her own if she did, Karen's priority was Anna. She further made the point that if they got down there and discovered Rossi wasn't already dead, she'd feel obliged to do something to remedy that sad fact, whether or not Madge believed Rossi was her long-lost son, and did Madge really want that on her conscience?

Madge said no, she did not. Then Ray came panting up out of

the gully toting the sports bag with the two hundred grand cash inside and said, 'He's still breathing. Let's go.'

Now the doctor packed up his leather bag, gave Karen a box of tranquillizers, enough to cover Anna for three days. 'How about you?' he said. 'How are you doing?'

Karen wanted to ask him how he'd be doing if it was his girl who'd shipped a stray bullet to the face, was sprawled on a shed floor with possible brain trauma. But the guy meant well. So she told him she was fine, just needed a three-day sleep, and saw him out. She went back around the house to the shed, checked on Anna again, made sure she was breathing regular and deep, then went looking for Madge.

She was surprised, going up the steps, to find herself wondering how Rossi might be making out, and then she realized she'd taken Ray's word for it when he said Rossi was still breathing.

Ray, who'd had his arm busted at the lake when he shipped another of Rossi's .22s.

Ray, who'd strolled away from Rossi with two hundred grand in cash.

Ray, who she'd known less than a week and only really got to know when they started planning to snatch Madge, Ray's last gig, or so he said, before he got out of the kidnap game for good.

She'd taken his word for that, too. And look where that got her.

Melody

'So if the movie gets made,' Melody said, 'or the script at least gets picked up, optioned, then I pay it back, this loan-grant that's not really a loan or a grant but somewhere in between. At, you're saying, no interest.'

'That's right.'

'But if it doesn't fly, I owe you nothing?'

'The Institute is here to encourage innovation,' the guy said, swivelling now in his chair behind the desk, fingers steepled on his pot belly. A nice view of Temple Bar behind him through the tall windows, the cobbled streets they'd laid for the Dublin set of the *Michael Collins* shoot and left down after, a gift to the city. Mel, running late, had nearly snapped an ankle on the way in, a kitten heel getting jammed between cobbles.

He smiled now, Tony, the guy with kindly pale blue eyes behind rimless specs. 'If you're worrying about how you'll pay the money back,' he said, 'you're not likely to be at your creative best, are you?'

Melody Shine liked those odds.

'I've got it all budgeted out,' she said, extracting the relevant sheaf of paper from her folder, the front of which bore the legend *The Gang That Couldn't Count Straight* in gold magic marker. 'We're talking twenty-five and change for the year. That includes research and writing, locations, some meet-and-greet funds for the—'

'Locations?'

'Sure, the eye candy. The Cayman Islands, where they shot *Into the Blue*. You've seen it, right? Shit movie, OK, but the scenery's amazing.'

'The actual Caymans?'

'The Caymans, right, where the boys have all their offshore accounts. Yes?'

'I'm just wondering,' Tony said, no longer swivelling and holding a forefinger aloft, 'if it's the Caymans you need specifically. Because if it's just an island, you might want to think about the Isle of Man, there's nice tax breaks going. Or if it's islands plural there's always the Saltees, just off the coast of Wexford. Spielberg, when he was making *Private Ryan*, he used the Saltees.'

'OK,' Mel said. 'But you're not really getting that Caribbean quality of light on the Saltees, are you?'

'That's where your post-production guys earn their money.'

'Sure.' Mel trying to decide if the guy was serious. 'Except my movie, it's set in the Caymans. What the story is *about* is what these asshole politicians get up to in, like, the actual Cayman Islands. I mean, you've read the script, right?'

'Of course,' Tony said, then eased out a cheeky smile that must have once worked for him way back when. 'At least, I read enough of it to know I want to hear the story in your own words.'

'OK.' Mel wondered why she couldn't have just wandered in off the street two years ago, or maybe just stood outside, used a loud-hailer. 'So we start with Judy, our intrepid reporter, she's flying out to the Caymans with a fact-finding junket, watching all these politicians golfing it up, swilling piña coladas, bunkering in at the local brothels. All,' Mel raised a meaningful eyebrow, 'on the hard-pressed taxpayer's time. Then she's interviewing one of them, he's poleaxed on free daiquiris, and he starts in about how they all brought their own buckets and spades, they're shovelling cash into Cayman banks. I mean,' she said, 'not literally, it's all electronic transfers these days. But the boys are in cahoots with some banker snoots back home, they're setting up this exclusive offshore scam, fifty grand minimum, a kind of trust fund for investment in Caribbean real estate.'

'So you're saying, it's political.'

'There's politicians in there, sure,' Mel said, 'but mostly it's your basic comedy crime caper flick. Judy's like a spoof of a private eye, although here she's a reporter. Anyway, she can't stop these guys telling her stuff she couldn't care less about, except here's this bunch of alpha males trying to impress the fluff in the skirt, beating their chests and slipping her state secrets. Except all Judy wants is to skip out to the beach, maybe have herself a Caribbean fling. So then she meets—'

'Just go back to these politicians for a moment,' Tony said, opening his top button and loosening his tie. 'Are they from any political party in particular?'

'Not really, it's more a loose coalition of greedy bastards. I mean, they're all the same anyway, am I right?'

Tony murmured something non-committal, then cleared his throat. 'What I'm asking,' he said, 'is if the politicians depicted in your film as engaged in a fact-finding mission represent a recognisable party in an identified government.'

'I don't follow,' Mel said.

'Well,' Tony said, sitting forward now, planting his elbows on the desk and steepling his fingers, 'are we, for example, suggesting that any of these politicians might be serving in the current administration, perhaps even in a ministerial capacity?'

'We could do, sure.' Mel with the distinct impression she was losing the guy. She forced a smile. 'But it's supposed to be, y'know, fun. Lebowski meets *Our Man in Havana*, with maybe *Showgirls* tossed in for some gratuitous flesh.'

'And all that comes through very clearly,' Tony said, riffling a few pages of the script. He sat back in the chair and favoured Melody with a grave expression that she believed he intended to come across as thoughtful evaluation, but which actually left him looking like he'd tweaked his scrotal sac in a crease of his razor-pressed chinos. 'I suppose what I'm asking is how much work it might take to give it a bit more heft.'

'Heft?'

'Serious it up,' Tony said. 'See, my problem is that the politicians all sound like morons.'

'They *are* all morons.'

'Right. But if you *play* them for morons, your argument loses its moral clarity.'

'Except there are no morals,' Mel said, 'to be clarified. I mean, it's a comedy.'

'But what if it wasn't?'

'But it is.'

'Sure. But what if it wasn't? I'm not saying,' Tony said, shooting his forefinger aloft again before Mel could answer, 'it needs to be *J'Accuse*. But say it was more like, oh, *All the President's Men*. Y'know, follow the money. Hey,' he said, 'that could be your tagline. "Follow the Money . . . All the Way to Grand Cayman!"'

Mel thought it'd look more like a travel agency ad than a movie poster. 'But wouldn't it be a bit counter-productive,' she said, 'to apply for state funding to make a film that takes a pop at the government?'

'Seriously?' Tony grinning at Mel's naiveté. 'They love that crap. Makes them look subversive and edgy, they're all about freedom of speech, yadda-ya. Not that it makes any difference,' he said, 'everyone's too busy watching *Pop Idol* on their iPhones to give a shit, couch-twerking to *Strictly*. I mean, if Simon Cowell ever parachutes Judge Judy on to his jury, it's game over. But I digress.'

Mel getting the old familiar feeling now, the mild concussion from banging her head off brick walls. Already, at thirty-four years old, Mel was staring down the long, dark barrel of a life spent behind the counter at Martin Shine & Sons' Shine travel agency with only an occasional explanation of the agency's laboured pun to leaven the monotony, in her spare time directing the straight-to-Web skin flicks she'd started in film college as a parody but had discovered were surprisingly lucrative, this on the basis that irony and bare female flesh were mutually exclusive in the average male mind.

Mel, who'd scored higher in English and Philosophy than all her other seven subjects combined in her final school exams, was well placed to appreciate the incongruity of her role in the travel agency, a frustrated movie maker facilitating the escapist fantasies of everyone who walked through the door. The fact that she was pretty much Google-searching destinations the punters could have looked up on their own computers at home only added to the soul-crushing futility of it all.

She hunched forward in her seat, tapped the manuscript sitting on Tony's desk. The pages pristine, no dog-ears, coffee stains or Post-its.

'Have you read it?' she said. 'Serious question. The synopsis, the treatment, the beat sheets and the character bible, all that stuff you had me put together, go back and rewrite like five hundred times before you'd even open that precious door over there – did anyone read *any* of it?'

Tony closed his eyes and did this thing where he pinched the corners of his eyes whilst scratching the centre of his forehead. 'Here's how it is,' he said. 'The annual budget review comes up next month, yeah? So we had a nice little informal flesh-presser last Friday night, canapés and spritzers, you know the drill. With the people, you understand, who dispense the largesse patting all the arty types on the head.' Mel, who had seen such things in the movies, nodded. 'So we're talking revenue streams and break-outs,' Tony said, 'what films we're hoping to send to Sundance, how to jam forty people into a one-bed apartment for Cannes, the usual crap. But you know what I kept hearing?'

Mel, who'd been setting it up in her head, maybe a long Altman tracking shot, the camera weaving through all these conversations, shook her head.

'White collar crime,' Tony said. 'Golden circles. Economic treason.'

'Sounds like a great party. Any chocolate fountains?'

'No fountains, chocolate or otherwise. What there was,' Tony said, 'what there *is*, is a gravy train that came off the rails. No, wait. I have enough comedy crime caper flicks back there,' he jerked a thumb at the overflowing shelves behind, 'to build every last politician in the country their own paper plane, fly them all out to the Caymans for a cameo in *The Gang That Couldn't Count Straight*. You know what I don't have? A single hard-hitting exposé about government corruption, ineptitude and institutionalised malfeasance.' He laid his hands on the desk as if he were praying, the steeple this time pointing at Mel. 'And all these guys want is that once, just once, someone would take the fact that the country's in the shitter seriously enough to go to the trouble of making a movie about how it all happened.'

'Seriously?'

'Do I sound like I'm joking?'

'That's fucked up.'

'These are not normal people,' Tony said. 'Plus they're watching all this Scandinavian crime stuff on TV, it's giving them notions.' He shrugged. 'I think it's a kind of Wildean thing, y'know, how there's only one thing worse than being talked about. Also, and unless the Black Death breaks out any time soon, they have a cast-iron majority over there, so who gives an actual fuck what the peons think.' He spread his hands. 'So what do you say?'

'I don't know, Tony.'

'You'd be paid, naturally, to rewrite the script. And you'd go straight into development.'

'Just like that.'

'Green-lit and fast-tracked, with my personal seal of approval.'

'And how much are we talking,' Mel said, 'for the rewrite?'

'Twenty grand.'

'For a rewrite?'

'As of this moment,' Tony said, *The Gang That Couldn't Count Straight* is our number one priority for the year. Although obviously,' he said, 'we'll have to change the title. Give it something with a bit of weight, a little gravitas.'

Mel reckoned they could call it *The Mel That Couldn't Get Out of Her Chair*. Mel feeling every one of her next fifty years settling down in her bones. 'So when do we start?' she said.

'Today, if you can. Right now. We have your bank details, right?'

Mel signed the contract, Tony wanting to pay five now, five on delivery and ten on final completion. Eventually they settled on twelve for a one-off lump sum.

'So we'll see you in here next week,' Tony said, shaking her hand, 'with the step outline.'

'Absolutely,' Mel said.

Twelve grand and a week's head start?

Melody Shine liked those odds.

Rossi

'Y ou think maybe the cops have their own hospital?' Sleeps said. 'Their own ER at least, it makes sense. I mean, no one wants to be flat-backed beside some perp they've just whacked.'

Rossi on edge like a guy doing, for some reason, a barefoot high-wire act on a giant razor blade. Down the two hundred grand, the side of his head on fire. Sleeps not helping, the guy rocking it sumo-style and swamping his own seat, pouring out over the hand-brake into Rossi's space, rubbing up against his thigh. And now, Christ, asking about cop hospitals.

'It was Madge,' Rossi said, 'who blew out Frank's knee. And I don't know if a husband can, like, testify against his wife, even if she kneecaps him because he had her kidnapped. So she mightn't be what you're calling a perp, technically speaking.'

'I'm pretty sure he can testify,' Sleeps said, 'even if she had enough reason to blow his balls off. The point being, she capped him while he was handcuffed to this cop, Boyle. Who he's going to be still handcuffed to when he gets here on account of you stole her handcuff keys.'

'Her name's Doyle,' Rossi said. He took a hit off the jay, holding it down while he used Doyle's handcuff keys to scratch up under the turban the vet had applied, the bandage drying out stiff and purple-black over where his ear used to be, the wound already itchy. 'I never heard of no cops' hospital,' he said.

'So then we're looking at her coming here. With you, y'know, under arrest. She read you up, right?'

Rossi flinched as the key's metal teeth snagged on the catgut stitches. 'She started to,' he said, easing the key out from under the turban. 'Then she stopped when I fired off a warning one. So I dunno if that qualifies as properly *habeas corpus*ed and shit.' He shrugged. 'What d'you want, we sit outside the cop shop 'til she shows up there?'

The problem, Rossi knew, was Sleeps was used to getting it easy. The guy on disability allowance ever since he grew out of short pants, this because he was liable to take a siesta once in a while, just drop into a nod. If Rossi was Sleeps, his only worry'd be that he might one day get up and forget to look in the mirror, go on holiday to Japan and get himself harpooned.

'Shit,' Sleeps said. 'You seeing this?'

Rossi, eyes a little weed fuzzy, squinted across the hospital's car park, seventeen rows all the way to the ER bay, where a couple of guys wearing cameras were in some kind of dispute with the bulky security guard, a lot of finger-pointing going on, verbals. The camera guys backing off now, retreating outside the big yellow box painted on the ground in front of the doors.

'The paps,' Sleeps said.

'Fuck. Y'think they're here for Frank?'

'There's every chance. Disgraced plastic surgeon gets shot in the woods by the ex-wife he had kidnapped – I mean, that's a story, right?'

'Pity it wasn't a plastic bullet. That's front page.'

They both got a bang out of that one, Rossi treating himself to a double huff on the jay. 'Hey,' he said, handing the spliff across and popping a smoke-ring out the window, 'maybe I should sell my story to the paps.'

Sleeps had a toke and let it out slow, considering. 'I can see it, yeah. The flip side to Frank's story, he has it all, gets greedy. Then there's you, coming up hard, scrapping for every little thing.'

Rossi nodding along, already rehearsing it, trying it out on Sleeps. The early years, how he'd been dumped as a baby, abandoned by this fuck of a father who'd bolted back to Sicily once he'd heard the news, Rossi getting dragged up in St Assumpta's by the sky-pilots. Although, fair dues, he'd have to acknowledge that the worst thing the nuns had done was give him his name, Francis Assisi Callaghan. Which was a good way, if that was their plan, to toughen up a small, skinny kid. Rossi taking all kinds of crap, beatings, other kids stealing his food, this until Italy won the World Cup in '82, Paolo Rossi scoring six goals, even knocking out Brazil along the way. The night the Azzurri won the Cup, Paolo poaching the first goal, Rossi had let all the other boys fall asleep in the dorm. Then he'd risen up, a Sicilian avenging angel, and gone to work with a battered aluminum tennis racket he'd snuck in and hidden under the mattress.

'And this is when,' Sleeps said, poking an invisible microphone under Rossi's nose, 'you officially take the name Rossi.'

'Correct and true,' Rossi said. 'Although not exactly officially – Sister Imelda said she couldn't go changing the birth certificate, that if she did it for me they'd all be calling themselves, like, Batman and Michael Mouse. But after that night, yeah, I never took no crap from no one.'

'Other than,' Sleeps probed, 'the cops and some parole officers, a judge or two.'

'Sure. But that was their gig, how they made their scratch. It's not like it was anything personal.'

'Right.' Sleeps handed back the jay, referred to an imaginary notebook. 'You served three prison sentences, I believe, all of them for variations on burglary, thieving and armed robbery?'

'A man needs to eat.'

'Of course. And would you consider yourself rehabilitated now, your debt to society paid?'

Rossi paused to think that one through. Truth was, his third jolt had been a life-changer, a five-year stretch that came about after Rossi was discovered trapped under a motorway median strip about twenty minutes after sticking up a chemist for product, the judge tossing in a DUI charge too, this on account of Rossi being a little too cautious for his own good, sampling the Oxy before he left the shop and hopped on his Ducati.

Five *years*. He'd bought eight months off for good behaviour but even at that Rossi thought he'd die. Of boredom, mostly. In the end he'd cracked and started reading, newspapers mostly, found himself comparing his sentence to those handed down to the guys wearing ties, were swiping millions. Which was when Rossi came up with the idea of rehabilitating ex-prisoners, a charity, the Francis Assisi Rehabilitation Concern Organisation, FARCO for short, this on the basis that charities paid no tax and could apply for all kinds of grants and shit, got free advertising. Rossi's only concern there was whether, with the name and all, the Vatican might be looking for points off FARCO.

'Except then I get out, right, and Karen's gone rogue. Swiped what they call my seed capital, this sixty-four grand I put away off a coke deal for the Galway Races, man, those fuckers like their blow. She stole the Ducati, too, went off pulling stick-ups off her own bat.' Doing it the first time, Karen had told Rossi, out of sheer frustration, to prove to Rossi it was possible to pull a job and not get caught. 'And then she blows the stash on keeping the hound at some luxury wolf-hotel, turns her against me. Next thing I know she's barging the van off the road, trying to rip my fucking head off.'

'This is the wolf, I take it, as opposed to your ex-girlfriend?'

Sleeps trying to keep it light. But the clouds were already rolling in again, thunder booming low in Rossi's head, lightning forking through his veins.

'She owes big, Sleeps. A Ducati in mint condition and sixty-four grand plus a five-year vig, which rounds up right now to the two hundred gees Karen swiped from the van, left me lying there with no ear, bleeding out.'

Sleeps settled back into his seat, shoulders slumping. 'We should be gone, Rossi,' he said.

'You're the one wants to go back inside,' Rossi pointed out, 'do soft time.'

'That was then,' Sleeps said. 'Except now there's cops involved, cops and guns.'

'And on the other side,' Rossi said, doggy-paddling his hands on an invisible see-saw, 'there's my two hundred grand and the ear.'

'The ear's gone, man. Forget about the ear.'

'For*get* about it? The bitch chewed my *ear* off.' Rossi shook his head, wincing even as he did it. 'Don't doubt it, I'm ripping the hound open, digging it out.'

'And then what – you sew it back on? After it's been in her gut? It'll be eaten away with acids.'

'You heard the vet. It's not just hearing, your balance gets screwed too. I'm looping the fucking loop over here.'

'That'll be the tranks. The guy said two every eight hours, not eight every two minutes. And what he said was, you start messing with the bandage and the inner ear gets infected, you'll—'

'Hold up.' Rossi pointed across the car park to where an ambulance had pulled in at the ER doors, was now discharging its cargo. The cop, Doyle, still cuffed to Frank, bent double at the waist until the medics extended the stretcher to its full height. Cameras flashing, Doyle making no effort to hide her face. The uncuffed hand balled into a fist and cocked on her hip, the girl just about stopping short, Rossi could tell by the way she stood, from flipping the bird at the paps.

'She's got moxy, this one,' he told Sleeps. 'I mean, for a cop.'

'Moxy?'

'Yeah.'

They watched as the medics hustled the stretcher through the ER doors, Doyle in their wake, the camera flashes reflecting off the glass, the security guard now posing for the paps.

Sleeps folded his arms, snuggled down in the driver's seat. 'Wake me up if anything happens,' he said.

Rossi found himself breathing deep, the way the prison shrink had taught him, synching with Sleeps' gentle snores. Calmer now. Thinking, yeah, Doyle. The moxy cop. His instincts had been good, those Sicilian instincts. Rossi was betting the two hundred grand that Doyle, once she got shot of Frank, would be tracking down Karen and Ray, the insurance scam loot, and then he'd—

A tattoo drilled on the car window punctured his fantasy. Rossi peered up to see the security guard's bulk blotting out most of the sky, the guy waggling a thick finger.

'What is it *now*?' Rossi groused, winding down the window.

'Sir, I'm afraid that this is a No Smoking hospital.'

'Sure thing,' Rossi said. 'But we're, like, all the way out here.'

'That is correct, sir. The new regulations cover the entire hospital grounds, car parks included.'

'You're shitting me now.'

'I'm afraid not, sir.'

The aggravation causing Rossi's stress levels to rise again. His ear, or where his ear used to be, pulsing flame.

'What if,' Rossi said, 'I roll up all the windows?'

'That would still be illegal,' the guard said, 'even if you weren't smoking an illicit substance.'

'That's medical. I got a condition.'

'Lucky you. But if you continue to, ah, self-medicate on hospital grounds, I'll be obliged to note your registration and inform the appropriate authorities.'

Sleeps sat up and stretched, yawning. 'Appreciate the advice,' he told the security guard, turning the key in the ignition. 'We'll just go and have a smoke, come back later.'

'That'd probably be best all round,' the guard said.

They drove out of the hospital gates, Rossi fuming.

'It's all there in the Bible,' he told Sleeps, 'how it's right, it's *fair*, that I get to cause Karen the kind of grief she's caused me. An eye for an eye, an ear for an ear.'

'I'm telling you now that I won't sit still for anyone laying a finger on any woman,' Sleeps said, 'let alone slice off any ears. That's a red line.'

'Not Karen,' Rossi said. No way was Rossi ever doing time again, no *way*. 'But wherever Karen is, the hound won't be far away. And I never heard of anyone pulling a jolt for offing a killer wolf.'

Karen

K aren found Madge in Terry Swipes' study, Madge sitting on the dimpled leather couch clutching a sizeable goldfish bowl of brandy like it was some kind of chalice, Terry holding forth from behind the walnut-wood desk.

'So you're not exactly devastated,' Terry was saying to Madge, 'when you hear Frank wants you kidnapped. Not exactly weeping and wailing.'

'Being honest,' Madge said, 'Frank being such a total dickwipe, I wouldn't have been entirely surprised if Karen had told me he'd organized a hit. So a kidnap, y'know . . .'

'Especially,' Terry said, nodding now at Karen as she sat down on the couch, 'when you hear it's your best friend is pulling the snatch.'

A gleam in Terry's eye like it was all one big set-up to a bizarre punchline, Terry anticipating some gut-busting laugh coming his way. Sitting there with maroon crushed-velvet curtains in the bay window behind, a green-shaded reading lamp on the desk. A benign thug, putting Karen in mind of Paul Newman, only bald. Karen, still a little shaky after all the gunplay up at the lake, found herself on edge, sensing a patronizing tone.

'It was Ray,' she said, 'who was pulling the snatch. Which was commissioned, in case anyone's forgot, by you.' Terry conceded the point but Karen went ahead and laid it all out anyway, just so there was no confusion as to who was ultimately responsible. She left out the bit about how she'd first met Ray, the guy walking in while Karen was sticking up a petrol station late one night – Christ, was it really only a week ago? – Karen pulling one of those jobs she did once in a while to keep Anna out at Pheasant Valley, these high-priced kennels that specialised in dangerous breeds. That was the night Ray told her he'd just retired from the kidnap game, this on account of some Slavs moving in, telling Terry Swipes how they'd be bankrolling his ops from now on because his previous money guy, the Fridge, had ended up like all fridges do, punctured at the bottom of a canal.

'Except then,' Karen told Terry, 'Ray hears you're doing a gig snatching Madge, and Ray knows Madge and me are friends.'

'So you're saying,' Terry said, 'Ray made a choice, no one holding any guns to his head.'

'It all would have been perfectly fine,' Madge said, helping herself to some more of Terry's brandy, Madge tucked into the corner of the couch beside a Lazy Susan laden down with about forty different kinds of hard liquor, 'if Rossi hadn't got himself mixed up in it, dragged me off before Ray arrived.'

'Rossi being this ex of yours,' Terry said to Karen, 'who shot Ray up at the lake.'

'And Anna.'

'Sure, the wolf too. What'd the doc say?'

Karen, nettled as she was, didn't want to seem ungrateful. Terry hadn't so much as blinked when Ray came banging at the door of Terry's tidy little Georgian pile out in the foothills of the Wicklow Mountains, Ray in bad shape after taking a .22 round in his upper arm, trailing Karen and Madge, Anna still comatose in the boot of the car after catching a bullet square in the face. Terry had shepherded them all inside, got some painkillers into Ray, then rung what he called his doctor for all occasions.

Karen gave them the doctor's diagnosis, how he thought there might be a possibility of trauma, blood clots, skull fracture, the guy not fully qualified to say. 'But he reckons if we give her lots of rest, keep her tranquillized, then she should be OK in a couple of days.'

'That's fantastic,' Terry said, 'a real weight off my mind. He say anything about Ray?'

'Sure. It's a clean break, six weeks in a cast. He'll be fine.'

'Could've been a lot worse,' Terry said, toasting Madge. Madge toasted him back, dropped the brandy down the hatch. 'But here's the thing,' Terry said, turning back to Karen. 'Once Ray is back on his feet, you'll need to be thinking about moving on.'

Karen nodded. 'Because they'll be looking for Anna, she tried to rip Rossi's head off.'

'Yeah, Anna. And then there's all these bullet wounds and two hundred large in cash under my roof. None of which is my idea of ideal.'

'Ray took a bullet,' Karen pointed out, 'on a job you put his way.'

'I get that, I do. Except Ray's freelance, pays me a percentage on any gig I find for him. It's not like I'm liable for his health insurance, putting him up in some Swiss chalet while he recuperates. Don't look at me like that,' he said. 'Ray knows the score.'

'Right now,' Karen bristled, 'Ray knows fuck-all, he's unconscious upstairs with a—'

'Karen?' Madge said. 'Listen to me. Remember Sunday evening, before you broke the news about the kidnap, what I told you I'd done?'

Karen stared, then shrugged and shook her head. 'Sorry,' she said. 'A lot's happened since Sunday.'

'I booked that cruise,' Madge said. 'The Greek islands. Remember?'

Karen nodding now. 'Right, the cruise. The one I couldn't go on because they had all these weird rules about no wolves on board.'

'You also said you couldn't afford it, and anyway you had a lot on.'

'What cruise is this?' Terry said.

'Well,' Madge pointed with the toe of her slingback at the holdall beside Karen, the bag bulging with two hundred grand's worth of Trust Direct's insurance ransom payola, 'I'd say you could probably afford it now. And you can't really say you've got a lot on, can you?'

'No,' Karen said. 'But there's still Anna. No way am I leaving her behind.'

Terry got up and came around the desk, filled Madge's brandy glass again, got Karen started on a little snifter for her nerves.

'So tell me some more,' Terry said, pouring a little top-up for himself, 'about this cruise.'

Frank

'Frank's actually the victim here,' Bryan told the detective, Doyle. 'You don't get that? He's been set up, dragged into some kidnap scam, had his knee shot out . . . Right, Frank?'

Frank just nodded. He had no idea of what his defence was likely to be, this because Bryan had ten minutes ago marched into the room and declared that anything Frank might say, or might have said in the recent past, would be inadmissible in court due to a temporary derangement brought on by having his knee shot out by his ex-wife.

The fact that he was still handcuffed to Detective Doyle, who was sitting on a plastic chair beside Frank's bed staring up at the ceiling while Bryan worked himself up into a jury-friendly frenzy, meant that Frank hadn't yet had the chance for a quick conflab on strategy.

'I mean,' Bryan went on, 'Frank's the one lying in a hospital bed, OK, it makes it a little easier for you to track him down, pin all this bullshit on him. I understand how it's more difficult for you to catch bad guys who're still on their feet, able to walk away, maybe run a few rings around you when they feel like a little aerobic exercise. But if you're not out of here in three seconds flat,' Bryan held up three fingers clamped together, looking to Frank like he was about to execute a Scout's salute, dib-dib-dib, 'you'll be looking at a harassment suit on top of the negligence, I kid you not.'

Now Doyle looked at Bryan. She raised her arm, the handcuffs that still bound them together ensuring that Frank's arm was hoisted aloft too.

'Hold still,' the janitor said, the guy irritable and red-faced from the effort of trying to cut through the cuffs with a blunt hacksaw.

'Sorry,' Doyle said, putting her arm down again. 'So when will he be fit to answer questions?' she asked the nurse.

'I really couldn't say,' the nurse said, tapping a forefinger against Frank's saline drip. 'Ask the doctor.'

'Where'll I find him?'

'Oh,' the nurse said, 'there's a box in the corridor marked "Doctors", we just pull one out any time we have a question. Just make sure you put him back when you're finished, OK? We hate it when there's loads of doctors running around doing stuff.'

The janitor enjoyed that one. He was twice as happy a minute later, when a uniformed cop strolled in looking for Doyle, he'd been sent over from the station with a spare key for her handcuffs.

Doyle stood up, rubbing her chafed wrist. 'I'll be back in the morning, Frank. First thing.'

'Visiting hours,' the nurse announced, 'are from eleven to three. No exceptions.'

'Can we please clear the room now?' Bryan said. 'It's imperative I speak privately with my client.'

'No problem,' Doyle said. 'Can I suggest that the first thing you speak to him about is the laptop? Because he mightn't be your client for very long after you've had that chat.'

'Christ,' Frank said as the door hissed closed, 'I've been at quieter spaghetti junctions. What am I paying Blue Riband for?'

'Technically speaking,' Bryan said, still staring at the closed door, 'medical staff have access to you at all times, it's for your own good. So what's all this about a laptop?'

'She's bluffing, Bry.'

Bryan Lawlor was Frank's current legal adviser because he was the one who'd mentioned to Frank, the pair of them tramping through knee-length rough in the out-of-bounds at the back of the seventeenth green out at Oakwood, that he'd stumbled across a tiny wrinkle in the statute books whereby Frank, even if he was barred from practicing as a cosmetic surgeon after the unfortunate incident that left Frank's client looking like Bob Mitchum on a three-day bender, could still consult, refer cases on, cream a fee off the top. Which kept Frank ticking over for a couple of years, sure, while the Medical Ethics Committee played circle-jerk.

In the last year, though, Frank's outlay had gone through the roof. First he'd hooked up with Genevieve, the former junior sales rep for a pharmaceutical company Frank'd met at a conference, the girl with a disease only retail therapy could address, and only then if the treatment was undertaken daily. Now, as a consequence of said hook-up, Frank was looking at hefty alimony for Madge, paying support for the twins, and juggling a couple of re-mortgages Doug had finessed over at Trust Direct.

So when Bryan came to Frank with the idea of having Madge snatched, then claiming on the insurance – Doug had piled on the extras to Frank's policy, knowing Frank couldn't go anywhere else, in the process including kidnap insurance – Frank had damn near wept tears of joy into Bryan's vodka martini.

Which meant, it was only occurring to Frank now, it should be Bryan and not Frank lying in a hospital bed with his knee puréed.

'Let's just say, for the moment, this Doyle isn't bluffing,' Bryan said. 'What might be on this laptop that could look bad for us if it was seen in a particular light in, say, court?'

'There might be, um, emails,' Frank conceded, 'some back and forths with various, uh, people I know, that mention a certain substance.'

'As in Nervozac?'

'Mostly Nervozac, yes,' Frank said. A trial drug, Nervozac was two parts anti-depressant to one part speed-based diet pill that worked wonders for a guy who might be having trouble with his putting, ironed out the yips. Once word spread that Frank was writing black-market scrips for one or two select friends, Frank found himself in grievous danger of being chaired around the Oakwood locker room shoulder-high any time he showed his face.

'So I'm guessing my name's in there,' Bryan said. Frank nodded. 'Who else?'

Frank rattled off a list that included three of the last four Captain's Day winners, a cabinet minister, three senior bankers, a public notary and a whole raft of legal eagles. 'But the reason she's bluffing,' he said as Bryan dry-swallowed a Nervozac, 'is there's no way she could even know where the laptop is, let alone crack the password.'

'I got a call from Genevieve this morning,' Bryan said, sitting down on the plastic seat and unlocking his briefcase. 'She was keen to have a chat. So I moved some things around, scheduled her in, because otherwise she was, and I quote, steaming straight into the nearest cop shop and blowing her wad.'

Frank closed his eyes and counted his single blessing, which was that he was currently high as a giraffe's tonsil on grade-A morphine.

Bryan extracted a single sheet of A4 paper from the briefcase and consulted it. 'She was reeking of gin when she arrived,' he said, 'so a lot of this will be approximate, but according to Genevieve you were supposed to fly out to Acapulco with her tomorrow morning. Except then, she's packing, she discovers a single ticket to Port-au-Prince in the breast pocket of your jacket. So when some people turned up at the house last night looking for you, one of whom she thinks might have been a cop, she was happy to let them in, share what she knew about Port-au-Prince. She was also happy to show them where you'd hidden the laptop and then take a flying guess at what its password might be. Apparently she guessed "belly-button" right the first time.'

'Shit.'

'I don't know about you, Frank, but I'm going to go ahead and presume that Detective Doyle is not, in fact, bluffing.' Bryan laid the sheet of paper on the bed. 'Jesus, Frank. What the fuck were you thinking?'

'They were supposed to be security,' Frank said. 'The emails, I mean. In case anyone got twitchy, started trying on some kind of squeeze.'

'You were throwing them around like jellybeans, Frank. Why would anyone need to get twitchy?'

'They'll bury it,' Frank said. 'There's a couple of cops on that list too, Christ, an assistant commissioner. No *way* that's going to trial.'

'Right,' Bryan said. 'Because that'll look better, how these golfing juicers, judges and cops and whatnot, conspired to quash their doping allegations. And don't think it won't come out. The kid who raked the bunkers, Frank – even *he* fucking knew it was going on.'

Frank caved, reached for the morphine-release doohickey, thumbed it a couple of times. He waited for the rush, then felt himself relax, ease back into the pillows.

'So what do we do?'

'I really don't know, Frank. First we'll need to see what this Detective Doyle has planned.'

'OK.'

'Anyway, we have more pressing concerns.'

'There's more?'

'Terry Swipes was in touch, Frank.'

'Terry who?'

'Terry. Y'know, the guy you commissioned to kidnap Madge.'

Frank, his brain swirling around in a warm chemical bath, explained to Bryan how the ransom, paid in cash by Trust Direct to Frank that very morning, had been hijacked by Detective Doyle as soon as he'd walked out of the building. 'Then,' he said, 'Karen and Ray took it off Doyle. Or maybe it was this guy Rossi, because he'd stepped in and snatched Madge before Ray got to her. Anyway, I don't have the money. Tell Terry he wants Rossi, or Karen and Ray.'

Bryan, surprisingly, was nodding as if he understood all of this. 'Terry's fully aware of the latest developments,' he said. 'As regards the ransom cash, at least.'

'So what's his problem?'

'Well, Terry reminded me that when you commissioned his services, you weren't in any financial position to put up a good faith down payment. Which was, at the time, twenty grand.'

'At the time?'

'The vig's twelve per cent. Per week.'

Frank, bewildered by the byzantine machinations of high finance, struggled up out of his cocoon of pillows. 'So the guy's charging me twelve per cent a week on twenty grand he gave himself because I couldn't afford to?'

'That appears to be the situation, yes.'

'But I don't have that kind of money, Bryan. That was the whole point of kidnapping Madge.'

'I did tell Terry that.'

'So what did he say?'

'He said he'll give us a week, starting from this morning when the ransom cash was taken away from you. Then, if we haven't paid off in full or at least the first week's vig, he'll be sending around a guy to give us a pedicure.'

'A pedicure?'

'That's what he said.' Bryan cleared his throat. 'Apparently we'll be needing some attention, a little pampering, Terry called it, after the guy with the nail-gun has left.'

Ray

R ay kept his eyes closed when he heard the bedroom door creak open, hoping he wouldn't hear any snuffling, the low growl Anna gave off in her throat that made her sound like a bulldozer reversing up Mont Blanc. Ray still adjusting to Anna, this one-eyed wolf wearing an eyepatch, and pretty sure he'd never get all the way there.

'Ray? You awake?'

He cranked open an eyelid, had a peek just as Karen sat on the edge of the bed. Reminding him now, maybe it was her profile, or all the drugs he was on, of a young Linda Ronstadt.

'Hey,' she said. 'How're you doing?'

'OK,' he said, hearing it raspy. Karen reached a glass of water off the bedside locker, told Ray to sip it slow. While he did she told him what the doctor had said, then laid it out, her plan.

'A cruise,' Ray said, blinking up at her. 'Me and you and a Siberian wolf named Blue, off cruising the Med.'

'Madge booked it Sunday, before we mentioned about snatching her. Remember?'

'Can't say I do. But—'

'You can still drive, right? One-armed.'

'Drive where?'

'Athens. Like, we'd be needing all sorts of documentation if we want Anna to fly.'

'You want to smuggle the wolf out of the country.'

'That's about it.'

Ray pushed out his slinged arm so that it looked like a broken wing. 'No way I'll make it all the way to Athens like this.'

'I can drive.'

'You ever driven a van before?'

'There's a first time for everything.'

'Not with me riding shotgun there isn't. What about Madge, has she ever driven a van?'

'I doubt it. Besides, she's flying.'

'Bad idea. They'll be watching the airports.'

'Terry's making, he says, private arrangements. Says he feels personally responsible for Madge's situation. What's wrong?'

'It's never good,' Ray said, 'when Terry gets personally involved in anything.'

'Well, he's hands-on with this one,' Karen said. 'He reckons if you need something done, you should do it yourself. And if that means taking a glamorous divorcée on a Mediterranean cruise, then that's exactly what he's going to do.'

'Terry's taking this cruise?'

'He's down there right now,' Karen said, 'eyeballing Madge like she's Eve playing hidey-peep with a fig leaf. Hey, listen, what's his deal – is he married or hooked up or what?'

'I don't think so.' Ray frowning, trying to remember. 'Divorced, I think. Terry likes to keep business and everything else two different things.' Ray keen to get Karen back on track. 'So Terry definitely knows it was Madge who plugged Frank, right?'

Karen nodding. 'Being honest, I think that's what clinched the deal. Guy nearly creamed himself. What?'

Fogged on too many pills, still fritzed on the shock of taking a .22 in the upper arm, the adrenaline spikes, Ray was in no state to second-guess Terry. But there was no getting around the fact that Madge had put a bullet in Frank, which meant Madge was now a magnet for cops. Going on his track record, the way he liked to keep a low profile, Terry was taking Madge on a cruise to tip her over the rail first chance he got.

'I'm just wondering,' Ray said, 'about these private arrangements Terry's making. He can't make those for Anna?'

'His responsibility, he says, is to Madge. You and me, Anna, we're on our own. But if we want he'll set us up with a van, do us a deal on an automatic he has on the books. Says all we need to do is point it and drive.'

Which was marginally better than Ray had been expecting. He heaved himself up on to his good elbow, glanced around. 'Where's the money?'

'It's here.' Karen kicked the bag she'd tucked under the bed. 'Think Terry'll still want his fifty gees?'

'That was the deal.'

'Yeah, but—'

'I already told him how Trust Direct only paid out two hundred instead of the full half million,' Ray said, subsiding on to the pillow again, 'so I don't know, maybe there'll be a miracle. But it was Terry who cut us in, him and Terry Junior, for a flat fifty. He's owed.'

Karen nodded. 'One more thing,' she said.

'Just the one?'

'I don't have a passport.'

'No?'

'Never been out of the country, Ray. Not with Anna to look after. What do you think, will that be a problem?'

'I doubt it,' Ray said. 'Not if you've got two hundred grand and Terry's taking things personal.'

Madge

'These medicinal brandies you're pouring,' Madge said as Terry topped her up again.

'What about them?'

'Let's just say I'm cured and crack on with the sociable measures.'

Terry grinned, dropped another wallop of brandy into her glass. Then extended a hand, a courtly gesture that caught Madge by surprise. She allowed herself be led across the room, out through the French windows on to the patio. Late evening by now, a couple of acres of landscaped gardens beyond the patio, a huge weeping willow in the foreground. Terry clinked his glass against hers. 'Here's to travel and good company,' he said.

Madge was happy to drink to anything Terry or anyone else might propose. Madge had had a hard night of it after being snatched by Rossi, in part because the old hut up at the lake had been lacking the basic creature comforts, but mainly because it had dawned on her, Rossi telling her about his tough upbringing in orphanages, that Rossi was short for Rossini, Frank's favourite composer on account of how it was the Lone Ranger that got Frank interested in opera, and that Rossi was the baby she'd given up for adoption all those years ago.

Now Madge flushed, remembering the histrionics when she'd told Rossi who he really was. Christ, opera? Rossi, of all people, telling Madge to calm down, she was dehydrated, running on fumes, not thinking straight. Except it had been Rossi, this morning, who'd put the gun in her hand, Frank cuffed to Doyle and helpless. Frank, who'd arranged for Madge to be kidnapped so he could cash in an insurance policy before their divorce came through Friday. Frank, who'd date-raped her at sixteen in the back of his father's Morris Minor, pumped her full of his poison and changed Madge's life forever, turned her into someone she'd never even imagined she could be. Standing over Frank this morning, Rossi's Glock in her shaking hands, Madge had closed her eyes and imagined Frank's head coming apart like an apple rotten to its core . . .

Afterwards she'd told Karen it was an accident, she'd meant to fire wide, just to see Frank soil his pants. Not true. Madge had aimed for Frank's face, not expecting the gun to be so heavy, the recoil so brutal. The first round had caught him at the top of the shin, just below the knee. The second, Madge correcting her aim, would've gone straight through his nose if the Glock hadn't jammed.

Madge, when she realized what she'd done, was capable of doing, had been horrified, felt herself pitching into some abyss, toppling into the great unknown. That hadn't lasted too long, though. Once Madge realized the world was still spinning, that gravity was doing its thing, the sky was still blue – well, *tempus fugit* and so forth.

No matter what came after, Madge had drawn a line between who she'd been and who she'd be.

The brandy, of course, was playing its part there. But Madge was pretty sure, when she woke up tomorrow, that she'd still consider today a good day's work.

Meanwhile she couldn't quite figure out Terry, this gangster who organised kidnaps. She'd been expecting someone coarse and mean. Someone like Rossi, say. Thin-faced and foul-mouthed, greasy hair, eyes shrivelled up and bitter.

Then again, Madge thought with a guilty pang, Rossi had been abandoned as a baby, just tossed away. How else could he possibly be?

'Are you OK?' Terry said.

'I'm fine, thanks.'

Terry had a nicely lined face, a little careworn, the eyes webbed with laughter lines, mischief sparkling in their faded blue. Bald, sure, but it was Madge's experience that the bald ones usually tried that crucial bit harder.

'It'd be natural,' Terry said, 'if you were feeling down. It's a common reaction. Or so I'm told.'

Madge sipped some brandy. 'So exactly what is it you do, Terry?'

'Import-export,' he said, a sly grin starting.

'What's so funny?' she said.

'Nothing.'

'No, really. What am I missing?'

Terry clipping a cigar now. 'You ever watch the Bond movies?' he said.

'Not by choice,' Madge said. Frank had been a fan. 'All that macho stuff, it's not really me.'

'Says the lady who shot out her husband's knee.'

'*Ex*-husband. The divorce comes through on Friday.'

'I guess you can kiss that alimony goodbye.'

'I'll live.'

'I'll just bet you will.'

An admiring note in his tone that bugged Madge, she couldn't help it, as if Terry was impressed at how the delicate little lady was holding up.

'There's something you should probably know, Terry.'

'What's that?'

'I have two kids. Girls. They're twins.'

'Oh yeah? I have two boys myself.'

'Sure, but you didn't *have* them. What I'm saying is, I had twins.'

Terry was getting it now. 'As in, it's not easy giving birth to twins. That by comparison, shooting Frank, coping with the fallout, is a breeze.'

Madge was, again, pleasantly surprised, this time by how quick Terry was on the uptake. 'Karen,' she said, 'I know, she's worried about me. Thinks I'm ready to freak. That I'll melt down once the shock wears off.'

'You're saying it won't.'

'She's young, Terry. I mean, she's smart, don't get me wrong, and I love the girl to bits. But she still thinks everyone should feel how she does. You know she used to pull stick-ups?'

'Karen?'

'It's how she met Ray. He walked into a place she was sticking up. He surprised her, came up from behind.'

'Lucky he didn't get his head blown off.'

'See, this is Karen all over. She never even loaded the gun.

Couldn't handle, even thinking about it, how she'd feel after putting a bullet in someone.'

'You're saying, you're handling it.'

'Put Frank in front of me now, a gun in my hand, I'd do it again.'

'But only Frank.'

'No one else ever gave me a good enough reason.'

Terry raised his glass. 'Remind me,' he said, 'never to give you a reason.'

Madge took his balloon glass away, poured its contents into her own and gave the double a swift and painless death. 'Remind yourself,' she told Terry. 'I'm long past done with looking out for everyone else.'

Doyle

Detective Stephanie Doyle massaged her recently handcuffed wrist while her boss, Superintendent Edward Sweeney, riffled through the pages of the report on his desk. Ted with an elbow planted either side of the report, chin propped on his palms and massaging both temples. Doyle only noticing now that Ted was going a little salt-and-peppery. It suited him, she thought.

He stood up and worked his shoulders, paced as far as the window and twitched the blind, glanced out into the car park, then came back across the office and slipped in behind the desk, pointed at his left ear. 'How's the hearing coming on?'

'What?'

'I said, How's your – oh.'

'Sorry.'

'This is serious, Steph.'

'I know.' Doyle considered telling Ted that she wasn't exactly desperate for confirmation of the gravity of the situation, this on the basis that she was the one who'd been handcuffed up at the lake, being shot at, while Ted had been parked behind his desk. 'Go on.'

'This is only an informal debrief,' Ted said, 'but you're still entitled to have representation here if you want it.'

'I know.'

'Want a smoke? A coffee or anything?'

'I'm fine, Ted. Really.'

'OK.' Ted scratched his stubble, glanced down at the prelim report. Doyle wishing she had her gun, could toss it on Ted's desk. Be Clint, be gone. 'So you're saying here,' he said, 'you didn't see who shot Frank.'

'I closed my eyes after *I* got shot at,' Doyle said. 'Forgot to open them again.'

'And this tinnitus you're probably developing right now means you didn't hear anything useful either.'

Doyle shook her head.

'And I'm guessing you didn't smell anything. How's your sixth sense, that female intuition?'

'That went on the blink the first night I slept with you.'

'Yeah, that happens a lot.'

Doyle felt bad stringing Ted along, Ted being one of the few good guys in the building. None of the patronizing crap about Doyle being some kind of affirmative action experiment, let's make a college girl detective, see how badly she and her shiny degree in psychology can fuck it all up . . .

Except Doyle, OK, it had taken a while, but she'd fucked up. Nine years of clean nose and regular collars, slow promotion, all screwed in ten minutes flat. Christ, Rossi had even taken the keys to her cuffs. The boys in the back office had loved that, a Pamplona charge to the phones to see who'd be first to drop the scuttlebutt on the tabloids.

Ted riffled through the report once more, cleared his throat. 'So we have Frank Dolan,' he said, 'a plastic surgeon. Except he's running a kidnap scam, juicing insurance companies. What's wrong with this picture?'

'The guy was under investigation. He's suspended, some surgery went wrong. So he branched out.'

'OK. But he sets up his *wife* to be snatched?'

'They were separated. She'll be his ex-wife by Friday.'

'Right. So Frank has this guy Ray kidnap his ex-wife-to-be. Then, he's already insured her against kidnap for half a mill, he stings Trust Direct. Except then this Ray guy comes to you looking to double-cross Frank, hang him out to dry.'

'That's about the height of it, yeah.'

'So how come you know this guy Ray?'

Doyle had been waiting for it. 'Let's just say he made himself known.'

'Just dropped into your lap.'

'Not literally, if that's what you're asking.'

'I'm not. What's Ray have to gain by blowing the whistle?'

Me, Doyle wanted to say. Or so she'd been led to believe.

'He was looking to get out,' she said. 'Reckoned he'd pull a couple of years, he was just the guy who handled the goods. I think his overall plan was to get into personal security, bodyguard stuff. He used to be an Army Ranger.'

'Poacher turned scam artist,' Ted said. 'You believe him?'

'I did, yeah.'

'And now?'

Doyle shrugged.

'OK. So this Karen,' Ted said, 'who's she?'

'She's with Ray.'

'But she's the ex-wife's friend too.'

'That's right.'

'So this Ray, he's grifting everyone.'

'Could be. I don't know. He took a bullet up at the lake when it looked like Madge was in trouble.'

Ted glanced down at the report. 'Taking one from this guy Rossi, right?' Doyle nodded. 'Where's he come in?'

'Karen's ex. Three-time loser, he's only out a week after a five-year jolt.'

'Not exactly rehabilitated, is he?'

'The way he told it, he just wanted his shit back from Karen. Except she wouldn't play ball.'

'And now he's gone. Leaving you cuffed to Frank.'

'I was the one cuffed myself to Frank, Ted. Rossi just took the key.'

'And you've no idea where Ray and Karen are gone?'

'Nope.'

'But they took the ex-wife, Madge, with them.'

'That's right.'

'Leaving you to take the rap.'

'Looks like it.'

Ted sucked on his teeth. 'Trust Direct are screaming blue murder,' he said.

'Don't, Ted. I'll cry.'

'You hear what I'm saying, though. They'll be up our crevices on the investigation. I mean, some plastic surgeon gets shot in the woods and his kidnapped wife, a charity-hound socialite, goes missing?' Ted rolled his eyes. 'Christ, it'll be front page.' He reached for the pack of Players Blue and sparked a smoke, this contrary to station regs, while he flicked idly through the report.

'What's the latest on Frank?' Doyle said.

'He's stable.' He gestured at her bloody clothes. 'By the way, in case no one else says it, you did a good job up there.'

Doyle, left handcuffed to the kneecapped Frank in the little clearing up at the lakeshore, had set fire to the Forestry Commission cottage. This because Rossi, taking Doyle's gun and the handcuff keys, had done the rounds, swiped everyone's cell phone too, chucked them all in the lake. Frank had bawled like a wind-trapped calf when she'd dragged him up on to the rickety wooden porch. Doyle couldn't really blame him. Tying a tourniquet above his knee, Doyle had wanted to puke every time she caught a glimpse of the white shards showing through the hole in his pants.

When he'd started shivering Doyle couldn't tell if it was septi-caemia or hypothermia or the guy just realizing how close he'd come. So she'd dragged him in beside the cottage's glowing embers, cuddled him close.

For nearly three hours.

By the time the first fireman came trudging out of the trees into the clearing, the guy tall and bulky in his uniform just the way she liked them, Doyle was so pissed she forgot to flirt.

'Frank's so grateful,' Ted said, 'he's suing your ass for negligence.'

'He'll hardly get fat suing this ass.' Doyle cocked a hip. Ted grinned. She said, 'So this investigation. I'm suspended for the duration, right?'

'Don't take it personal. It's for your own good.'

'With pay.'

'Innocent until proven, sure.'

'Meanwhile, you still have Frank.'

'Who's claiming he's the real victim. He was railroaded by this guy Ray.'

'Except I have Frank's laptop, and the guy kept records he shouldn't have.'

'Writing up scrips,' Ted said, riffling back through the pages again, 'for Nervozac. Black market.'

'What's important there is, one of his customers, a guy called Doug, was his insurance broker with Trust Direct. Doug also being a golf partner of Frank's.'

Ted, seeing it, nodded along. 'Trust Direct squawk too loud, we whisper inside job. I'm liking it so far. Go on.'

'You put me front and centre, I'm suspended pending blah-dee-blah. Nothing's more important than transparency, the force being accountable. Meanwhile I'm packed off to Elba with Napoleon.'

'You think this guy Ray likes the sound of Elba?'

'Fuck Ray. Rossi's the one has the money.'

'You know I can't sanction that, Steph.'

Doyle cupped a hand around her left ear. 'Sanction what, Ted?'

Ted parked his smoke on the edge of the desk, dry-washed his face, had a good long stare at the ceiling. 'OK,' he said. 'Just don't send me any postcards from Elba.' He closed the file, stood up and moved around the desk. 'C'mere.'

Doyle accepted the peck on the cheek, the comforting hug, then shouldered her bag. 'How d'you want to do this?' she said.

'Just slam the door open, leave the rest to me.'

Doyle marched away with her chin up, Ted's threats booming down the corridor behind her. Ignoring the smirks, the guffaws detonating all over the open-plan office.

Suspended with pay, indefinitely. The world her oyster with Guinness chasers.

Sleeps

'He buys a *gun*,' Sleeps said, 'steals a car.'

'What now?'

Rossi, staking out the cop shop buzzed on horse tranks and crooning some croaky Elvis, had Sleeps on edge.

'What you're singing,' Sleeps said, 'is the guy steals a gun and buys a car.'

'Sure. He tries to run but he don't get far, so he steals a gun and buys a car.'

'It's the other way round, man.'

'Your way,' Rossi said, '*their* way, that's just propaganda. They're saying the guy's a no-hoper, a clown. My way, the guy's running, OK? I mean actually running. But then he goes, "Hey, why the fuck am I running when I could be driving?" Except he's skint, yeah? So he steals a gun, heists a place, I dunno, maybe a bank, a bookies, and gets himself a poke. Then buys a car. You see what I'm saying.'

Sleeps, with a melted brain the only other alternative, let it slide.

'What you *said* was, you didn't want to hang around outside the cop shop.' Sleeps aiming for reasonable. 'This on the off-chance the guy we stole the car off picks this shop to report it, sees us on his way in.'

'Where's the last place,' Rossi said, 'the cops'll be looking for us?'

'Outside a cop shop, yeah, you already said. But—'

'She's in there now, Sleeps, getting hell from the Commissioner. She's a disgrace, the whole nine yards. But he's giving her one more chance and she better not blow it.'

Sleeps sighed. As far as he could make out, this from listening to Rossi for the last week or so, the guy's education was almost entirely built on black-and-white movies, most of them featuring Jimmy Cagney.

'It was me?' Sleeps said. 'Some guy nearly blew *my* head off? I'd be on the blower to my brief, crying post-traumatic stress disorder. Perforated eardrums, the works.'

Rossi shook his head. 'This one's tough, Sleeps. You see the way she faced me down up at the lake? I mean, even after I took her rod away, she just stepped up, gave me the eyeball. No way she's sitting back, just taking this shit. She's tracking Karen and Ray down, getting that money back. Don't doubt it.'

'Except,' Sleeps pointed out, 'as far as Doyle knows, you're the one has the money. I mean, you took it off Karen and Ray up at the lake, did a runner.'

Rossi thought about that. 'Shit, yeah. So how do we tip her off it's Karen and Ray has it?'

'Well,' Sleeps said, 'I guess I could always tell her.'

'You?'

'Sure. This Doyle, she doesn't know who I am, right?' This because Sleeps had been half a mile away at the time it all kicked off at the lake, snoozing in a stolen Merc that had slipped sideways off a muddy forest track. 'So I just stroll up to her, tell her a story a little birdie told me about how Karen and Ray heisted the two hundred grand after the hound nearly took your head off.'

Rossi nodding, liking the sound of it. Then he frowned. 'Problem there, Sleeps, is you're implicating yourself. Right? Accessory after the fact.'

'Depends on how she wants to play it,' Sleeps said. 'Worst-case scenario, I'm thinking I could cut a deal. I point her at Karen and Ray, she works it so I catch some soft time.'

'The cops?' Rossi gargling rocks. 'You're doing business with *cops* now?'

Sleeps, tuning out while Rossi went off on his latest rant about ethics, was in a bind. Rossi knew, had known from the start, that Sleeps had ambitions to go back inside, pick up some soft time, do an educational course or two and get himself qualifications more useful than a certificate for driving forklifts. He'd been drifting for the best part of two decades now, kicked out of school for all the time nodding off, no way of holding down any job when you were likely to just pass out at any time, no warning. Sleeps had tried everything the Social Welfare had thrown at him but the last time, working as a shelf packer in a supermarket, Sleeps had keeled over right there in the aisle, come down on top of a toddler. After that they told him he was a menace and shunted him over to Disability Allowance. Sleeps took a look at his first payment slip and asked if he was entitled to a complimentary cardboard cup so he could start waving it under tourists' noses. No joy. So Sleeps, rather than just lie down and slowly starve, had drifted into a little dealing on the side, weed mostly, picking up a little three-month stretch here and there that he'd come to look forward to, Sleeps warm and dry and regularly fed, no rent to worry about, no one noticing or caring if Sleeps nodded off at some point during the day.

The best part about hooking up with Rossi, Sleeps had quickly realized, was that it was only a matter of time before Rossi screwed up in a major way and went back inside, Sleeps sailing along in Rossi's wake.

Now, though, sitting outside the cop shop, thinking seriously about how he'd go about approaching Doyle, Sleeps wasn't so sure he should just take the first tumble that presented itself. Like, there was actual money out there, two hundred grand in insurance company cash, and if Sleeps could nab himself a slice of that, put together a poke for when he got out again, then maybe he could do something with himself, put in some foundations.

He tuned back in again, Rossi getting emotional now, wobbling on the high notes as he reminded Sleeps that when a man's partner is killed you're supposed to do something about it, doesn't matter if the guy's a complete plank who wants to go back inside, do soft time. Sleeps taking a moment to place it, Bogie as Sam Spade, giving Brigid the bum's rush because he had this moral code that needed to be delivered, for some reason, through his nose.

'My problem with that,' Sleeps said, cutting across Rossi's flow, 'is that I'm not any kind of partner, I'm an employee who's being paid, maybe, on the promise of a percentage of your missing stash, the sixty-four gees, if we ever catch up with Karen.'

'So?'

'So that's the first thing that's going to change. Also, I'm wondering if it's ever occurred to you, with all these movies you're always bigging up, how it's the cops who generally win in the end.'

'More propaganda,' Rossi sniffed. Then he stiffened. 'Shit, here she comes.'

Sleeps heaved his bulk forward, reaching for the keys in the ignition as Doyle exited the cop shop. 'And there she goes,' he said, slumping back in his seat as Doyle turned a sharp right into the coffee shop two doors down. 'With,' he added, 'another cop in tow. Christ, it's the *Fear and Loathing* convention over there.'

Doyle

There was a note of reverent hush in Sparks' voice as she said, 'Suspended with pay.'

Doyle, still easing her way into it, just shrugged. 'Them's the rules.'

'So what's the skinny?'

'Mainly they're wondering how come Ray just fell into my lap.'

'You wish.' Sparks, the desk sergeant, tucked a wayward strand of frizzy red hair behind her ear. 'That'll be Ted, the jealous prick.'

Doyle, sipping her latte, was surprised to realize part of her wanted to believe it. Except Ted had hooked up three or four months after he and Doyle split, got himself engaged, some tax analyst he'd met on the dry ski-slope out in Wicklow, Ted getting in some slaloms before heading away for a stag do in the French Alps.

'Ted's cool, Sparks. The shit's coming down from upstairs.'

'Because the boys can't find the kneecapping socialite.'

Doyle remarked on how the boys, her illustrious peers, wouldn't find a priest in Rome.

'Unless they bumped into one down the brothel,' Sparks said. 'I mean, it'd be all right, the ransom going west, the surgeon getting his knee blown out, if they at least had a rescued lunching lady to parade around. But she's nowhere. The boys are in a sweaty fret.' She forked up a generous chunk of triple-tier Death by Chocolate. 'You're not worried about her?'

'She left with Karen and Ray. Wherever she is, she's OK.' Doyle thought about that. 'If I was her, finding out Rossi was *my* son? I'd be unconscious on pills somewhere sunny.'

Sparks lowered her fork. 'Rossi's her *son*?'

'Long story. What's the latest on Frank?'

'They're waiting for a warrant to come through so they can search the house, officially this time. Plus they're hoping his tart on the side, Genevieve, sobers up some time this century so they can ask her a few questions.' Sparks shook her head in wonder. 'Seriously, though – Rossi's her son?'

'So she said. What about Karen and Ray?'

'The usual All Pointless Bullshit. Airports, ferries.'

'The boys think they're leaving the country?'

'That depends on whether they're dragging the wolf along. You still reckon Karen won't dump her?'

'No chance. Anna's like a child to her.'

'Then they're probably not leaving the country,' Sparks said. 'Still, we have to cover everything. By the way, the wolf? The boys are shooting on sight. We're down one Alsatian already, out at Seagrove. I wouldn't mind but it was one of our own.'

'They're shooting at Anna? But she's a pet.'

Sparks sucked chocolate off her finger. 'The vet who called in the mauling, the possible rabies? He said the guy, Rossi, was a feather off having his head mushed. And that Transit they found in the woods, the window was busted in hard enough to shunt the van into a gully. Inside it was like a bomb in a jam factory.' She forked home more cake. 'Why didn't Karen just cross a croc with a rhino, be done with it?'

'What Transit is this?'

'The van in the woods.' Sparks frowned. 'They found it in a gully, near a wrecked Merc.'

'But no Rossi. No money.'

'No money and about two pints of, they're guessing, the elusive Rossi.'

'If it was Anna,' Doyle said, wondering why Ted hadn't mentioned the van, 'she had her reasons. Rossi, breaking her in, took her eye out with a fork. It's why she wears the eyepatch.'

'Maybe,' Sparks said, 'we should tell the boys not to shoot any wolves not wearing pirate accessories.'

'They didn't get that description?'

'No.'

'How come?'

'Because I put myself in Karen's shoes. First thing *I'd* do, if I had a rogue wolf with an eyepatch? Take off the eyepatch.' Sparks tapped her temple. 'Up here for thinking, down there for dancing.'

'That's good, yeah. Although if I was you I'd probably give them both options, eyepatch and without, just in case they track her down and she's wearing the patch.'

Sparks thought about that, then shrugged and slotted home some more cake. 'So what're you going to do with your time off? You need to stick around for the investigation?'

'Nope.'

'Then take a holiday. Pack a thong, get some sun on that lily-white ass. Where's Niko these days – Barcelona? Monaco?'

'Don't even go there,' Doyle said.

'*You're* the one won't go there. I was you, had a guy calling me up, "Hey, come on over to Venice for some fun, we'll party, no strings," guess where I'd be? The Tardis, seeing if I couldn't be in like five different places at the same time, getting five different tans.'

'You have no idea,' Doyle said, 'how bad his breath stinks.'

'So tell him you've been working undercover with hookers, you don't do kissies any more. Listen, the main reason I brought it up? I've time coming. I'm due twelve days.'

'Oh yeah?'

'Plus I ran a check on one Madge aka Margaret Dolan.'

'You ever use that computer for official police work?'

'I'm police, I'm official. Anyway, the last time Madge used her credit card? Sunday, over the internet. Booking a cruise out of Athens that starts Friday night, eight o'clock.'

'It can get sunny,' Doyle said slowly, 'in Athens. She booked in on her own?'

'According to the cruise people, no.'

'They're the ones who'd know,' Doyle said. 'So who?'

'Promise to tell me about Madge and Rossi?'

'Christ, Sparks . . .'

'Karen King.'

'No Ray Brogan?'

'No Ray. No Raymond, Raphael, Rainier, Reynaldo, Raymundo . . . You find out his real name yet?'

'It's a work in progress. So she books a cruise on Sunday . . .'

'And gets herself snatched Monday. Maybe she's psychic, huh? Had herself a premonition.'

'Could be. When's she flying out?'

'Thursday evening, six o'clock. Except here's the thing. The flights are to Denver.'

'Denver?'

'Denver, Colorado, via New York. Plus there's payments to a place called Piste of Mind.'

'A ski shop?'

'You know it?'

'Let's call it a wild guess.' Doyle cocked her head. 'What d'you think, she's laying down a false trail?'

'Looks like it. But which is which?'

'With no flight to Athens, you'd be thinking Denver.'

'She look much like a skier to you?'

'I'm thinking a cruise would be more her style.'

'Me too.'

'Mainly,' Doyle said, 'because you want some sun on your ass.'

'True. But hey, you're there for Friday night when the cruise leaves, she's not on it? Just hop a flight for Denver.'

Doyle drank off the last of her latte. 'You tell the boys any of this?'

'Every last word,' Sparks said. 'In fact, I'm writing up the report right now. It should be on Ted's desk by, oh, Friday noon at the latest.'

Karen

Terry Swipes rattled off the numbers like a bingo caller speaking in tongues. 'We'll say four grand for Karen's passport. And Terry Junior gets his five points finder's fee off the gross for setting up the snatch. That's five points from both of us.'

Ray, counting bills on to Terry's desk, nodded.

'So that's what,' Terry went on, 'thirty in total? Including the van.'

Ray nodded again.

'OK,' Terry said, 'we'll call it thirty flat. I'll waive my cut.'

Ray stopped counting. 'You'll what?'

'Waive.' Terry, grinning, winked at Madge. 'What, I'm not entitled to waive?'

'Yeah, but—'

'Call it a good luck gift. From me to the happy couple.'

'Thirty grand's a lot of good luck,' Ray said. 'You think we need that much luck?'

'You're driving across Europe,' Terry swivelled in his leather chair, hands joined on his ample belly, 'with a busted arm and a wolf in the back. You packing?'

'Not yet,' Ray said. 'I'll grab the Sig from the lock-up.'

'An automatic with a busted arm? What if it jams?'

'It's never jammed before.'

'Famous last words. What about reloads?'

'I'm only ever reloading in a fire-fight,' Ray said. 'On my own? No way I'm getting in any fire-fights.'

'OK. But you're still better going with, say, a .38 Special. Never jams, manual load. Hold it between your knees, pop 'em in one at a time.'

Karen cleared her throat. 'Try this,' she said, 'just for the sake of argument. How about we bring no gun at all?'

Terry pursed his lips, glanced from Ray to Karen, then back to Ray. Ray, she noticed, didn't look at her at all.

'Uh, Karen?' Terry said. 'No disrespect. But if Ray tells me he's schlepping off across Europe with a bag of cash and no heat? I'll bust his other fucking arm right now.'

'But what if—'

'The what-ifs,' Terry said, 'is why you need the heat.'

Melody

'**B**e with you in a sec,' Melody said, looking up from the computer. She glanced over the guy's shoulder at the clock on the back wall above the rack of Far East/Australasia brochures, its red LCD showing temperatures in all the time zones. Mel noted with a pang that it was nearly ten o'clock in Marrakesh, still twenty-eight degrees.

Then she focused on the guy, hulking and slope-shouldered, the untidy shag of dirty-blond hair with a fringe falling across his eyes putting her in mind of Javier Bardem, *No Country*. 'So how can I help?' she said, flashing a smile.

'I'm looking to book a holiday.'

'Well, you've come to the right place.' She rattled a few keys on the keyboard for show. 'Anywhere particular in mind?'

'Not really. Where's hot right now?'

'Weather-hot or cool-hot?'

'You can't get both?'

'Sure. Just give me an idea of where you're thinking about.'

The guy considered, then shrugged. 'That girl who was just in here, she looked kinda hot and cool. Where's she going?'

'I shouldn't say,' Mel said. 'It's not really a service we provide to women flying alone, a potential stalker as a surprise added extra.'

The guy grinned. 'It's OK,' he said. 'I know her. She's a friend.'

'Oh yeah? What's her name?'

'Doyle.'

'You know her first name, this friend of yours?'

'We, uh, only met earlier today.'

'Love at first sight,' Mel said, trying to figure the guy. Nice eyes behind the fringe when he smiled, no psycho vibes. Big all round, the husky type, but no sense of threat with it, a gentle voice. Although maybe that was his schtick. 'Listen,' she said, 'this is a travel agency, not an information bureau. Or a dating service, for that matter.'

'I know, but—'

'Sorry,' Mel said, 'no can do.'

He held her gaze a second or two, a shaggy bear standing there with his shoulders slumped. Then he shrugged and lumbered to the door. Locked it and flipped the sign around, started back slow, tugging up his T-shirt so Mel could see the pearl-grip butt of a gun sticking out of his pants. Mel in her mind giving it a soundtrack, some doomy Rachmaninov, *Isle of the Dead.* Or Ennio, maybe.

'Look, uh, Melody,' he said, nodding at her name-tag, 'I really don't want—'

'Tough guy,' she said.

He had to think about that one. 'If I have to be,' he said, 'yeah.'

Mel, who had three older brothers, had a fair idea of how it looked when a guy was trying out tough and not making it stick. 'Is that thing even loaded?' she said.

'That's the whole point of a gun, right?'

'And if I don't tell you where the girl's gone on her holidays,' Mel said, noting he hadn't given her a straight yes or no, 'you'll shoot me. Just like that.'

'I'm not saying it'd come easy,' the guy said, 'but—'

'Bullshit.'

The guy considered that. Then his shoulders seemed to fold in a little, the tension slipping away. He grinned, one that was somewhere between you-got-me and aw shucks.

'Who're you supposed to be,' Mel said, 'Javier Bardem?'

'I was more aiming for Gosling.'

'Yeah,' Mel said, 'I can see that now, with the sleepy-eyes thing going on.'

That left them looking at one another, the guy wearing a gee-whizz grin, Mel waiting on his next line.

'So,' he said, 'this Doyle. Where's she going?'

'How come you want her?'

'You first.'

'No, you.'

The guy shaking his head. 'See,' he said, 'I could tell you, yeah, but then you'd be what they call an accessory after the fact.'

'What fact?'

'You don't have to worry about the girl,' he said. 'I mean, she's a cop, yeah. But it isn't her we want.'

'She's a cop?'

'Yep.'

'Shouldn't she be chasing you?'

'It's like, she's a friend of a friend. The friend, or friends, they've got money belongs to an associate of mine. So . . .'

'How much money?' Mel said.

'I thought this was a travel agency, not an information bureau.'

'*Touché*. But listen, uh, Ryan . . .'

'It's Gary.'

'OK, Gary.' Mel put her elbows on the counter, leaned in. 'Let's just say I tell you where she's going, Gary. How much is that worth to you?'

'That depends.'

'On what?'

'I really couldn't say,' Gary said. 'I'm the muscle, not the money-man. But you probably guessed that already.'

Madge

'I honestly don't know if I should do this,' Madge said as the red-and-white striped barrier pole went up. The car purred on to the airstrip that was basically a big field, dinky little propeller planes looming from the dusk either side, no sign of the Lear jet Madge had been half-hoping for. The headlights picking up the hangar now, heading straight for it.

'You're already doing it,' Terry said. 'Just relax, it'll be OK.'

'Please. Can we stop a sec?'

'Sure,' Terry said. 'Joe? Would you mind pulling in? Cheers.' He waited until the car rolled to a stop, then turned to her. 'What's wrong?'

'I can't do it.'

'Sure you can.'

'To you, I mean.'

'To me?'

'What if you're seen with me?'

'You won't be seen, Madge.'

'But what if I am? You'll get pulled into the whole mess.'

'You let me worry about that,' Terry said. 'All I'm doing is helping out a friend – she's terrified of this Rossi guy who snatched her. She needs a few days away until she knows the guy's been caught, it's safe to come back. So I'm making it happen.'

'Ray told Karen,' Madge said, this being the bit that had sobered her up fast before leaving Terry's place, 'that the last guy who brought the cops around wound up in four different canals.'

Terry smiled, patted her knee. 'How'll you bring the cops around, Margaret? This cop, Doyle, she told you she'd help with your alibi, right? Just after you shot Frank.'

'That's what she said *then*. But . . .'

'Look, according to Ray, this Doyle wants Frank. If the cops are going to be anywhere, it's up Frank's ass for arranging a kidnap, attempted extortion, all that. And you rang the twins, right? Letting them know you'd be away for a few days.'

Madge, being precise, had sent Jeanie a text message, not trusting herself to speak with Jeanie and Liz after the pair maxed out her credit card to pay for their flights to Denver, the deadly duo going behind her back to finance their school's-out ski-trip when Frank, yet again, failed to come through with the five grand he'd promised them. Written while Madge was still surfing the brandy buzz, the text in its entirety had read, *Break a leg, one each. See you next spring. Mom.*

She confirmed for Terry that she had, yes, let the twins know she'd be away, for a few days at least.

'So why would the cops be looking for you?'

'There's the money,' Madge said. 'The ransom.'

'Why would the cops even *think* you might have the ransom? You were the one was snatched.' Terry shook his head. 'If they're chasing anyone, it'll be Karen and Ray.'

'You think they will?'

'I doubt it. They already have Frank, and probably this guy Rossi too, Ray said the guy looked pretty bad when they left him behind in that van savaged by the wolf. And just say you're a cop, you have the ex-husband who set you up to be snatched *and* the three-time loser who did the actual job. That sounds like a result to me.'

'Except the ransom is missing.'

'An insurance company's money? No cop's busting a hernia to

find that. Besides, the insurance company's insured against losing the ransom. Stands to reason.'

'I *want* to do it,' Madge said, 'don't get me wrong. I just don't want anyone getting into trouble on my account.'

'The only way it gets hinky,' Terry said, 'is if the cops or the insurance company know where to find you. This way, flying out of here? We're into London in an hour, and from there we could be going anywhere. No one else knows about the cruise, right?'

'Just Karen and Ray.'

'Not even the twins?'

'The whole point of it,' Madge said, 'it was just me and Karen, our thing, getting away from it all, the twins included.' Madge reluctant, even now, to acknowledge that Jeanie and Liz had zero interest in where she might or might not go, or who with.

'So there it is,' Terry said. 'What're you worried about?'

'Oh, silly stuff,' Madge said. 'Y'know, fleeing the country after shooting my ex-husband, with a guy who puts people in four different canals.'

'That's just a bogeyman story,' Terry said. 'Joe? Tell the lady I never put anyone in four canals.'

'It's only a story,' Joe said, meeting her eyes in the rear-view mirror. Saying it deadpan, making Madge wonder if the truth was three canals, or five. Or that it really was four canals, except Terry himself didn't get involved personally.

'Meanwhile,' Terry said, 'I'm sitting here waiting to fly into Europe with a lady who's reminding me right now of Julie Christie, I think it's her eyes. What're you going to do, change your mind and break my heart?'

Rossi

'LeprePorn?' Rossi said, then wondered aloud if they were all midgets or just real people dressed up as actual leprechauns, the camera pulled way back so they looked small.

'LeprePorn's just the brand,' Melody said. 'Mainly aimed at snagging the Irish-American demographic.' Melody laying out her subscription model, Web-only skin flicks with an Irish angle. 'That way your distribution budget is virtually nil. *At-Quim-Two-Birds*, that's one of ours. Irish lesbians, what they call niche-niche marketing.'

Mel was in back, Rossi up front riding shotgun beside Sleeps, a fat spliff smouldering between his fingers. The lights went green. Sleeps eased the Volvo Estate forward.

'The hardest bit,' Mel said, 'I mean apart from keeping a straight face? Coming up with the names. Like, half the time you're wondering what the original guys were thinking, if they weren't subconsciously wanting to make blue movies all along. I mean, seriously – *Eat the Peach*? *I Went Down*?' She shook her head. 'We did *PS, I Fucked You One, Two* and *Three* last year. This girl, her husbands keep dying and coming back as ghosts to, y'know . . .'

'Fuck her.'

'Pretty much, yeah. In the third one, the twist is all three come back at the same time.'

'Like in a gangbang?'

'Yep.'

'Except,' Sleeps said, 'she's into it.'

'Sure,' Mel said, 'she loves these guys. I mean, she married them all. Had a thing, for some reason we never got around to exploring, for exclusively Balkan guys with big hair and fat johnsons. Take the next left,' she told Sleeps, 'then right into the housing estate. It's the third on the left, there'll be a white Fiat parked outside.'

'But now you're ready to break out,' Rossi said. 'Move into the mainstream.'

'I've *been* ready,' Mel said. 'I'm *past* ready.'

'With this story,' Sleeps said, 'it's like *Bonnie and Clyde*, except set in Greece.'

'With the twist,' Mel said, 'that Bonnie and Clyde, only they're called Judy and Jack, they're into kidnap instead of banks.'

Rossi glanced at Sleeps. Forty minutes he'd sat outside the travel agency watching Sleeps banter with the girl behind the counter, wondering when Sleeps'd get to it, find out Doyle's destination. 'Sounds familiar,' he said.

'An archetype story, sure,' Mel said. 'But there's this cop, she's tight with Jack and Judy, at least she thinks she is until they pull a switch and leave her behind handcuffed to the guy masterminding the kidnaps, then take off for a Mediterranean cruise. Not realising they're not the only Bonnie and Clyde in the picture. And this other

Bonnie and Clyde, believing the money's actually theirs, they're following the cop who's chasing Jack and Judy. She's trying to track them down, get her rep back.'

'Or,' Sleeps said, 'at this point the cop could just be suspended and schlepping off on holiday, we just don't know. Maybe doing everything she can to forget she ever met this Jack and Judy, they made her a laughing stock.'

'So where in the Med,' Rossi said, 'is Jack and Judy's cruise going from?'

'Cute,' Mel said, 'but no cigar.'

'See,' Rossi said to Sleeps, 'this is the bit I'm not getting. We're taking her with us, right? Except she's the only one who knows where we're going.'

Sleeps considered. 'About the size of it,' he said.

'That's it there, Gary. See the white Fiat?'

Sleeps indicated left, pulled in to the kerb. Rossi said, 'So you're hitting us up for points on the ransom cash if you steer us in the right direction and we nab Karen and Ray.' Mel nodded. '*And* you're tagging along for the ride, soaking it all up for this movie you're making.'

'If you were me,' Mel said, 'would *you* trust you to come back with my share, just hand it over?'

Rossi acknowledged how there might be an issue of mutual distrust. 'What I'm getting at,' he said, 'is I'm not hearing you come across. With, y'know, points in this movie you'll be making off our story.'

In the end, Rossi volunteering his services as script consultant, Mel agreed to take them on board. No way was she shelling out upfront but she was fine with cutting them in for points if she got a deal, Rossi asking twelve but settling for a back-end of five on the gross.

'That's gross-gross,' he said. 'Merchandise, the works.'

'Deal,' Mel said, reaching into the front to shake their hands in turn. 'OK,' she said, 'just give me ten minutes to pack a bag. Oh, by the way?'

'What's that?'

'If we get caught, I'm your hostage. I mean, you're dragging me along against my will, right?'

Melody

Mel went straight upstairs, pulled the fake Louis Vuitton down off the top of the wardrobe and tossed in the essentials, found her passport, packed a few books, some spiral-bound shorthand pads, a handful of blue Uniball pens with the nice flow, then dragged the LV back downstairs, bumping it on every step.

She stuck her head around the living-room door to where her father and two brothers were slumped watching a football game flickering on the TV, all three in roughly the same position, hands clasped on their midriffs.

'Hiya love,' her father said, turning his head in her direction without taking his eyes from the screen. 'Your dinner's in the oven.'

'Listen, Dad? I can't stay, I just picked up a last-minute deal.'

'Nice one. Where to this time?'

'Greece, flying out tonight.'

One of her brothers grumbled something about covering Mel's shifts. Her father shushed him, then looked across to where Mel was still standing in the doorway. 'You and Gerry, is it?' he said.

If she'd had the time, Mel might have been more inclined to tell her father that Gerry had just last week emigrated to British Columbia. Except then she'd have to tell him that Gerry had informed her of his decision via Skype, the signal a little hazy, Gerry broadcasting from a motel in Victoria on Vancouver Island, on his way to a logging camp in BC's interior.

'No,' she said, 'it's just me.'

'You're going on your own?'

'It's more like a business trip than a holiday.' Her father was the only person alive Mel hated lying to. Everyone else, she believed, was fair game, this according to Mel's philosophy, which had hardened considerably in the last week or so, of getting your retaliation in first. 'I, ah, that movie I was telling you about? The one I'm writing?'

'Yeah?'

'Well, I heard today that I qualified for what they call development funding. Gives me the green light to go scout locations, that kind of thing. Except they want me to use Greek islands instead of the Caymans, they get some kind of EU tax break.'

'Seriously? Mel, that's brilliant.' He struggled up out of the armchair and advanced with his arms wide open. Mel let him hug her, murmuring that it was only development funding, it didn't mean anything more than that.

'They wouldn't be handing out money if they didn't think you had something,' he said. 'Jesus, Mel – if only your mother could see you now.'

'I know.' Mel disentangled herself. 'Look, I better go, I've a taxi waiting.'

'Of course. You're all right for a few quid?'

'Fine, Dad. Thanks.'

'OK.' He planted a kiss on the top of her head. 'Text us when you get in,' he said. 'Let us know you're all right.'

'Will do.'

She closed the front door quickly so her father wouldn't see the pair in the car looking like Laurel and Hardy with their heads swapped around, Rossi skinny and dark, Sleeps big and fair. Sleeps got out as she came down the path, went around the back and popped the boot, took the suitcase from her and lifted it in.

'So where to now?' he said.

'The airport. Where else?'

'What I thought,' Sleeps said. 'Only thing is, I don't fly.'

Frank

F rank, finally, was having a high old time. The sunshine warm as a perfect bath, Frank with his eyes closed sensing a soft breeze wafting up from the turquoise sea to tickle the back of his bare legs where he lay outstretched on the table, the faint zephyr once in a while strong enough to set the palm trees overhead to rustling. The hands kneading his shoulders were tender but firm, causing Frank just the right amount of delicious pain every time the fingers bore down. His skin tingling, the friction setting off little depth charges in the muscles that sent gentle explosions of joy caroming up his spine. Frank, at this point, was glad he'd cut off at the second martini, any more might have desensitised him, diminished the experience.

The best, of course, was yet to come, the frontal massage that would be considerably more intimate, Frank already semi-boned in anticipation. The hands on his shoulders hauling him around now to lie on his back, although a little more roughly than Frank was expecting, Frank murmuring, 'Hey, easy on. There's precious cargo under here . . .'

'That's OK, Frank. Just relax and go with me.'

But Frank tensed up, the coarse voice puncturing his morphine-induced fantasy like they'd dropped a nuke on the Bahamian beach. Frank opened one eye, found himself staring up at a male orderly, the guy grappling with Frank's dead weight as he disentangled him from the sheets.

'Whoa,' Frank said. 'What the fuck's this?'

'It's OK, Frank. Nothing to worry about.'

'Who the fuck *are* you?'

'I'm Des, Frank. I gave you your bed-bath earlier today. Remember?'

The guy gave one last heave, got Frank partially propped up against the pillows. Now the guy stepped back and moved a wheelchair parallel with the bed, said, 'OK, Frank, over we go.'

Relieved that he wasn't about to be fiddled with in his bed while he lay there helpless, Frank nodded and edged his buttocks towards the wheelchair as best he could, wincing as fishhooks swirled up out of his knee into his femur. 'What's going on, Des?'

The orderly slipped in behind the wheelchair, got his arms around the bottom of Frank's ribcage and hauled him out of the bed into the chair. 'It's a routine drill, Frank,' he said as he clipped Frank's drip to a wheelie-pole. 'Really, nothing to stress about.'

'A drill? What kind of drill?'

'An evacuation drill.'

The guy leaning across Frank now, opening the door, pushing Frank ahead into the corridor. Outside was bedlam, red lights flashing over the nurses' station, orders being bawled, nurses sprinting down the hall waving clipboards. Des edged Frank into the river of patients shuffling along pushing their wheelie-drips ahead of them, other orderlies and porters trying to negotiate beds through the chaos.

'This is a drill?' Frank said. 'Fuck me, I'd hate to see the real deal.' This just as they passed the nurses' station, the nurse behind the desk screeching into the phone, 'No, it's *not* a drill, get her out *now*. I don't *care* if she says she's on Blue Riband, she's *out*. Everyone's *out*!'

Frank glanced up over his shoulder. 'Um, Des?'

'Yeah, OK.' Des now pressing the button to summon the lift, Frank eyeballing the sign that said the lift was under no circumstance to be used in case of fire. 'Someone phoned in a bomb threat,' Des conceded, jabbing his finger on the button. 'They're pretty sure it's a prank call, but – hold on,' he said, as the lift dinged to a stop. 'Here we go.'

'A fucking *bomb*?' Frank said as the lift doors closed. 'What kind of lunatic degenerate wants to bomb a hospital?'

'Try to relax, Frank. It's almost definitely a hoax.'

'Relax, sure,' Frank said as the lift began to descend. Already wondering if this wasn't a golden opportunity to turn everything around, have Bryan sue the hospital for post-traumatic stress syndrome. He tried to gauge how much morphine he'd need in his system to tolerate throwing himself out of the wheelchair when they cleared the building, maybe stick in a claim for physical as well as mental torture once the dust settled. Although the danger there, Frank cautioned himself, was that he might overdo the Vitamin M and forget, blissed out, all about his latest scheme.

A blast of cold air shocked Frank out of his reverie, Frank wearing the hospital-issue thin cotton nightgown that exposed pretty much everything below waist level to all four cardinal points of the compass. He was about to make that very point to Des, store away personal humiliation and psychological distress for the lawsuit to come, when he noticed they were trundling across a car park, the cars with this weird orange sheen from the sodium lights. Frank not seeing any shivering groups of patients huddled together, no medical staff setting up emergency stations.

'Uh, Des? Where the fuck are we—'

A fleshy hand clamped down across his nose and chin with enough force to punch Frank's breath back down his throat and jam a blockage somewhere at the top of his lungs. They were trundling faster now, Des grunting with the effort of steering the wheelchair with one hand. Frank reckoned that this was probably a good time, if he was ever going to do it, to throw himself out of the chair,

hopefully with enough force to propel him into a parallel
dimension.

Except then Des executed a sharp right down a row of parked
cars and Frank saw the orange-tinged Qashquai with its boot already
open, a guy on either side, waiting. One with a face like a box of
squashed frogs, the other with a shaved head and the nose of a
boxer who led with his chin.

Not good.

But what was worse, what sent the warm wetness spurting between
Frank's thighs, was the expressions on their faces, bored and impa-
tient, as Des rolled the wheelchair up to the open boot.

Frank thumbing the push-button doohickey on the morphine drip
like he was sending out Morse code, *s-s-s-s-s-s* . . .

THURSDAY
Karen

'Y ou're paying four grand for a passport,' Karen said, 'you
expect, I don't know, something more flattering than Joan
Rivers in a wind tunnel.'

'The guy turned it around in three hours.' Ray, buzzed on the
pills, had volunteered to drive while he still could. The fluorescent
orange lights gleaming weirdly on his newly blond hair. DIY kits,
Ray coming off like James Dean with the blond quiff. Karen had
gone for an electric-blue rinse. 'Anyway,' he said, 'who looks good
in their passport?'

'You do.' Karen comparing passports. 'What'd you do, get it took
professional?'

'The guy got paid, yeah, he's a pro. Anything we're forgetting?'

'Passports,' Karen said, checking off on her fingers. 'Tan oil.
Wolf. Gun. What else?'

'Money,' Ray said, nodding at the khaki duffel at Karen's feet,
the cash ransom that had fallen from half a mill to two hundred
grand to one-seventy in a little under fourteen hours. This before
Madge got her half of the fifty-fifty split. Karen having her very
own Black Friday.

'Money,' she said. 'Check.'

'So that's everything.'

'Well,' Karen said, 'I'm down the cell phone Rossi swiped up at
the lake. And then there's the whole wardrobe I'm leaving behind,
all my personal shit, y'know, photos of my dead mother. But other
than that, yeah, we're cool.'

'Doyle knows where you live, Kar.'

'I *know*. I'm just saying.'

What bugged Karen was Ray could just drop it all and go, anything
he really needed tucked away safe in his lock-up.

'You want to risk it?' he said.

'Nope.'

'You're sure?'

'Don't tempt me, Ray.' Karen wondering, Christ, when does
it end? Like, first her father beats her mother to death, taking

a slow fourteen years to do it. Then she gets tangled up with Rossi, who was in more than he was out the ten years Karen knew him.

She'd done it, though. Survived her father, got the bastard put away, then got past Rossi, put an actual life together. A life that included, OK, once in a while pulling stick-ups for chump change, using Rossi's Ducati, his .44, all this to keep Anna in kennels, the wolf-husky combo tagged a dangerous breed. A life, sure, that couldn't last. But Karen would've come up with something else when the time came. Doing it her *own* way. This? Hightailing it out of town, one step ahead of the posse . . .

'I can understand,' Ray said, 'you're concerned, starting all over somewhere strange. But take Anna. I mean, she came all the way from Siberia. Talk about not being able to speak the language . . .' When Karen didn't smile he said, 'Anna's doing OK, isn't she? Found someone to look after her, she wasn't even looking. Didn't even know how to look.'

'She lost an eye,' Karen said. 'Got a bullet in the head that could've killed her.'

'Except it didn't. She's alive and kicking. Or rather,' Ray said, 'alive and doped to the eyeballs in the back of a van. But she's making out.'

'Just about.'

They drove in silence until he turned east off the M50, heading for Dun Laoghaire, the ferry port. Down through the Sandyford industrial estate, ghostly at this hour. Just past the big roundabout Ray pulled in to the side, turned on the walkie-talkie he'd tucked into the drinks holder.

'What now?' Karen said.

'Just a heads-up.'

A burst of static, then some garbled snatches of conversation, more static. Karen hearing phrases here and there – *hospital, credible threat, evacuation*. Ray fiddling with a knob as if he was trying to tune in a channel.

Karen said, 'A police scanner?' and Ray nodded, saying *ssshhh* at the same time.

Which Karen didn't like, being reminded of how little choice she had right now. Plus she was riding around with a guy who needed to avoid the cops so much he invested in the technology. Karen, yet again, wondering who this guy Ray really was.

On the up side, she had to concede that the news from the scanner was good, any extra cops knocking around tonight getting sucked into the crazy situation at the hospital someone wanted to blow up.

'Probably the twins,' she said, 'looking to blow Frank sky high after he left them high and dry, too broke to pay for their trip to Aspen.'

'Shame,' Ray said, cocking an ear to the scanner, wincing at another blast of static.

'Five grand's worth,' Karen said. 'Madge was raging. She only found out when she tried to book the flights to Athens. I don't think I've ever seen her so bug-eyed mad. Well, apart from when she shot Frank.'

Ray looked across at her, switched off the scanner. 'She didn't get to book the flights?'

'Nope. The twins had maxed out her card. So then she has a screaming match down the phone with this bitch telling her—'

'How about the cruise? She get to book that?'

'That was already booked from the day before. Why, what's wrong?'

'You think the cops, with Madge missing, won't check her credit card transactions?'

'Maybe they'll think,' Karen said slowly, 'she's gone to Aspen.'

'They won't think it for long.'

Karen slumped back, drained. Jesus, every time she turned around it was something else. Karen wondering if maybe she shouldn't stop turning around, just for once go in a straight line. 'You think the Greek cops'll give a crap about anything to do with Frank?' she said. 'I mean, there's all that jurisdiction stuff, right?'

'It's still European Union, Kar. There's protocols, agreements.'

'So she'd be screwed.'

'Madge?' Ray nodded. 'Except we're the ones brought her to Terry and never mentioned the whole credit card deal.'

'I didn't realize,' Karen said, 'we were supposed to clue Terry in on every last thing we might or mightn't do.'

'Yeah, well, if Terry gets hauled in, aiding and abetting a fugitive from justice? Anna won't be the only one missing an eye.'

Doyle

D oyle never liked flying, especially when they served dinner. Trying to pretend cruising at thirty thousand feet was so normal there was no reason you shouldn't be eating plastic chicken too.

Then the washrooms, designed to fit anorexic dwarves. Doyle freshening her lippy while the plane jitterbugged around the sky, electric storms over the Adriatic. Doyle wondering if she wasn't overdoing the gloss. Trying to achieve a delicate balance, needing to look hot enough Niko would help her out but not so smoking the guy might take it as a come-on. She'd decided to skip the eyeliner, it was just asking for trouble, a poke in the eye, when there came a tapping on the door. The stew, telling Doyle to return to her seat, they were starting the descent.

Doyle wobbled back up the aisle, edged into the window seat and looked down on Athens, wondering how Niko'd look, two or three years now since she'd seen him last. He'd been thin then, sallow and tall. Doyle liked them tall but not as thin as Niko, the guy a greyhound, all cock and ribs. Cock, mainly. Had this habit, too, of looking at a girl from under half-closed lids over the beaky nose that he thought was sexy but made him look like a lizard with cataracts.

He'd kiss both cheeks, Doyle knew that. Long, lingering smooches. All Doyle was hoping, as she switched the big fake emerald from the baby finger of her right hand to the ring finger on her left, was Niko had remembered to floss.

Niko, he liked his *tzatziki* heavy on the garlic.

Rossi

R ossi had always imagined that if he ever made it on to the set of a blue movie he'd be a little more jazzed. It didn't help that the set doubled as the props room.

'See, he's pissed right now I'm narcoleptic,' Sleeps was telling Melody, 'a wheelman prone to dozing off at crucial moments.' Sleeps checking out his reflection in the full-length mirror, the chauffeur's cap perched at a rakish angle over one eye. 'Except I specifically told him – Rossi? – I was narcoleptic and only trained to drive forklifts. Rossi's problem was he thought narcoleptic meant I was like some kind of specialist, did wheelman on drug deals. Also, he ripped his johnson in his zipper prowling his ex's place, she surprised him taking a sneaky piss, so he couldn't drive himself.'

Rossi deep-sixed the jay, held it down for a count of ten, another tip he'd picked up at anger management class inside. 'OK,' he said. 'But let's call this a fresh start. Clean slate. Is there anything else I should know?'

'Well, I'm allergic to penicillin,' Sleeps said. 'Plus I'm borderline diabetic, on account of I'm a little big-boned.' Mel, who looked a lot to Rossi like a shrink-wrapped duvet now that she'd donned an off-white wedding dress, nodded sympathetically. 'Except when I get the dizzies I can't remember,' Sleeps said, 'do I eat sugar to keep my levels up or do I avoid it in case it blows my head off?'

'*I'll* blow your head off,' Rossi growled. 'Worry about me.'

Sleeps nodding his appreciation. 'Lee Marvin, right? *Point Blank*.' Then told Melody, 'The doc reckons it was a lack of nutrition when I was a kid, screwed my system.'

'A *lack* of nutrition?' Rossi said. 'Sleeps, no disrespect man, but you look like you ate the Michelin Man.'

'I was deprived in the *womb*. My mother, God rest her, was a juicer, drinking meth spirits, the works.'

'OK.' Rossi mulled it over while he had another toke. 'But what's any of that have to do with not flying?'

'Nothing. That's from when I went to the funfair, going up on the Whirly Chairs.'

'And?'

'They were whirly chairs, Rossi. Thirty feet up. Forty miles an hour.'

'Yeah, but . . . they crashed? What?'

'I just figured, in a plane? You're *five* miles up, doing a million miles an hour. I mean, do the math.'

'The statistical chance of being killed in a plane crash?' Mel said, fluffing out her veil. 'It's the same as being kicked to death by a herd of wild donkeys. That's a whole herd, by the way, not just one donkey.'

'Twenty-nine people died last week,' Sleeps said, 'in Uzbekistan, a 767 that didn't exactly clear the airport fence, came down tits up in a swamp. So that's twenty-nine herds of wild donkeys, at *least* twenty-nine, out there roaming the steppes.'

'You were a kid,' Rossi said, 'up on the whirly chairs. So it makes sense you got a fright.'

'At the funfair?' Sleeps shook his head. 'That was last month. I made a pact with God.'

Rossi squeezed his eyes closed, massaged his temples. 'With God?'

'There and then, in mid-air. The deal being, if I don't fly, God won't kill me in a plane crash.'

'You'd be surprised how many people won't fly since the terrorists started acting out,' Mel said.

Rossi with a pain in his ear like he'd shipped a stray bayonet. No, the hole where his ear *used* to be. 'Listen, Mel, if you don't have nothing to say that might help, I'd appreciate you keeping—'

'What I'm *saying*,' she said, 'is lots of people won't fly these days. But they still go on holiday.'

Sleeps grinned. 'The ferry,' he said. 'Of course.'

'The best part?' Melody said. 'At the port they don't really pay too much attention to passports and suchlike when you're heading out.' She squeezed past the leather couch, used her hip to bump Sleeps away from the mirror. Sleeps bumping her back, getting a grind going on. 'I mean,' she said, 'you were saying you need to get passports, right?'

'That was a private fucking conversation,' Rossi said.

'You losing an ear and all,' Sleeps pointed out, 'you've been a doing a lot of shouting ever since.'

Mel went through to a side room. Came back holding a fat envelope, from which she drew a bundle of passports.

'Holy shit,' Sleeps said. 'Are they real?'

'Most of them, yeah.'

'You get much call for passports in blue movies?' Rossi said.

'These Balkan guys we have in the movies? They want to come here, y'know, get into the EU through the back door. Except then they need to work it off, the expense of getting them here, before they get their passports back.'

'By screwing in blue movies,' Rossi said, awed. 'Christ, it's a dirty job . . .'

'What about the girls?' Sleeps said. 'They trafficked too?'

'The girls are mostly Irish. Models, like. Only in Ireland there's only enough work for about two and a half models. So they're going the other way, getting out.' Mel put the bundle of passports on the coffee table, told them to pick a wig to go with their chosen passport, she'd work on their make-up. 'Just make sure the one you pick is still in date. Don't get us screwed on some schoolboy error.'

'It's "us" now?' Rossi said.

Mel nodded. 'A full three-way split. It's that,' she added, 'or I tell you the cop's gone to the North Pole.'

Rossi, helpless, looked over at Sleeps. Sleeps just shrugged. 'A three-way split of something is at least something,' he said. 'Without Mel we got fuck-all.'

Rossi suppressed the urge to punch himself in the head. 'I got an idea,' he told Mel. 'How about we just pin you to the fucking wall and—'

'Not on my watch,' Sleeps said.

'I'm guessing,' Mel said, 'and I might be wrong here, but I'm guessing you're broke. I mean, driving into Europe, you'll need to fill up the tank once in a while, maybe eat.'

'You're going to stake us?' Sleeps said.

'Call it an investment. A straight ten per cent on my outlay. All of which comes off the gross before we split the take.'

'Christ,' Rossi said. 'Why don't you just put on a balaclava?'

'You're kidding,' Melody said, giving herself one last twirl in the mirror, flattening down her bodice, the pleated skirt billowing out in her wake. 'And ruin a perfectly good tiara?'

Ray

R ay hung up and threaded back through the tables to where Karen was sitting in a booth in the bay window. The port was busy under a sodium glare, the ferry like a tipped-over Christmas tree out along the pier. Karen was scoping for guys lounging on corners, reading newspapers in the pre-dawn chill, maybe talking into their collars once in a while.

'No joy?' she said, reading his expression.

'He's probably switched off the phone for take-off, forgot to turn it back on.' He sipped some vodka-lime. 'Listen, we need to talk about Rossi and Madge.'

'I think you're being paranoid.' Then she grinned.

'What's funny?'

'Nothing. Just something Rossi used to say.'

'What?'

'Whenever he got seriously pissed off? He'd say he was paranoid. As in, *par*-annoyed.'

'Hilarious, yeah.' Ray held up his sling-wrapped arm. 'Six inches to the left and he'd be a comic genius.'

'I'm just saying—'

'Forget it. What about the cruise?'

Karen did the thing where her lower jaw twitched, letting Ray know, even if she didn't know she was doing it, how he'd wandered up close to some line she'd drawn in her head.

She said, 'Why would Madge tell Rossi she was taking a cruise?'

Ray reminded her how Madge, in some emotional distress and possibly experiencing an extreme manifestation of Stockholm syndrome, had confessed to Rossi she was the mother who'd abandoned him way back in the mists of time. 'And if there's even a possibility she mentioned it, then taking chances is a good way to get Terry nabbed.'

'Madge too.'

'Madge, you know her better than me, maybe she can arrange for a hit from behind bars. I know for a fact that Terry can.'

'Sure,' Karen said. 'But even presuming she told Rossi, so what? The state we left him in, he's probably in ICU right now. Providing he didn't die of fright.'

Ray considered that. 'Any chance he'd tip off the cops?'

'Rossi? Tip 'em off a cliff, maybe.'

'OK, except the cops aren't even the half of it. He could sell us on.'

'Sell us . . .?'

'Say Rossi puts the word out. Who we are, where we're going. How much cash we're carrying. Then, someone hits us, Rossi gets points on the bag. A finder's fee.'

'Jesus. Whatever happened to honour among thieves?'

'It probably got thieved. Also, we don't know for fact Rossi's in ICU. And what we don't know for fact we don't presume.'

'Because,' Karen said, sounding to Ray more irritated than his caution deserved, 'that's a good way of going about getting ourselves nabbed.'

'Correct.'

'You're still coming down off those pills,' she said. 'So you're paranoid, like I said. Maybe you should just chill out, relax.'

'You want me to chill?' Ray raw on pure adrenaline by now. 'Try some guy who's not Rossi,' he said, slowing it down, keeping it simple, 'he doesn't give a fuck who you are, thinks you're carrying two hundred large, the guy's coming at you from you don't know where the fuck he's coming from. *He'll* chill me all right.' Karen staring now, dead-eyed. 'Or try an upstairs bunk, y'know, on a ten-stretch for conspiracy to kidnap, defraud and extort, with some bull dyke giving you the eye, blowing you smackers every night. Think you'd feel relaxed then?'

Karen chewed the inside of where her jaw was twisted, went back to scoping out the port. A commotion down below, a Beamer beep-beeping, white ribbons draped from its wing mirrors. Ray caught a glimpse of a bride making these wristy little waves like she was some kind of princess, a tiara sparkling under the harsh lights.

'Kar? It's only in the movies people get away. In real life they're getting away. Always. I mean, it's a constant state of getting away.'

'So we're looking over our shoulders,' Karen said, stirring her vodka-coke with a pink swizzle stick, still staring after the Beamer. 'All the time.'

'Running away,' Ray agreed, 'if at all possible, backwards.'

'Maybe we should get mirrors,' she said, glancing across at him now. 'One for each shoulder.'

'I'd say one shoulder should do it. No sense in looking ridiculous, right?'

'Just one thing.'

'What's that?'

'Don't call me Kar.' She plucked the swizzle-stick from the vodka-coke, jabbed it playfully at his right eye. 'My father used to called me Kar.'

Ray took the hit. 'OK by me,' he said.

Sleeps

'You know what I'm thinking?' Sleeps said, waving a kid-gloved hand to acknowledge the guy in the Renault letting him through, the guy tooting his horn as they filtered in ahead. 'I'm thinking this might even work.'

'It's all about the visual impact,' Melody said. 'I mean, it's already working. Am I right?'

'So far,' Sleeps agreed, 'like a dream.' Sleeps in a win-win situation for maybe the first time in his entire life. If he got caught, he was aiding-and-abetting, going down for soft time. The upside? If they made it he was driving a Beamer into Europe, its engine purring like a cat with three tails. He glanced in the rear-view, caught Rossi scratching at the foxy-looking fake beard. 'You'd want to leave that alone, Rossi,' he said. 'At least until we get on board. Then, we grab a cabin, you can take it off.'

'Two cabins,' Mel said. 'It'd look a bit odd if you were to, y'know, shack up with the honeymooning couple. Being the driver and all.'

'Yes'm,' Sleeps said, tipping the brim of his cap.

'All I'm saying,' Rossi grumbled, 'is who the fuck goes away in their wedding gear? Shouldn't we be wearing something casual for the ferry?'

'We're running late,' Mel said, adjusting her veil. 'After the ceremony? It was raining when we wanted to take the photos.'

'Plus,' Sleeps said, 'you got that visual impact you're talking about.'

'Exactly.' Mel gave a preeny little wave out the window. 'Even before we get there they've jumped to the conclusion, we're just married.'

Sleeps nodded up the line of cars. 'They're waving everyone through, Rossi. I haven't seen them stop anyone yet.'

'Law of fucking averages,' Rossi groused. 'You're guaranteed they'll stop us.'

'To congratulate us, maybe,' Mel said. 'Take some pictures.'

Sleeps said, 'Mel? This might be a good time to tell us where we're going. In case they ask.'

'OK,' she said. 'The good news is we're going to Sicily. Palermo.'

'You're shitting me,' Rossi said. 'Sicily?'

'Why, is that a problem?'

'Are you kidding?' Rossi thumped a thumb into his chest. 'I'm half-Sicilian.'

'You are?'

'Absofuckinglutely. Tell her, Sleeps.'

'He's half-Sicilian,' Sleeps confirmed. Rossi with this fantasy how his father was some Mafia guy, had to bunk off back to the motherland after knocking up Rossi's mother, Interpol halfway up his crevice. Sleeps had asked around. The word was Rossi's old man was the son of a guy owned an Italian chipper up around Rathmines, got Shirley, this simpleton who was still working the canal on weekend nights, up the pole back in the day. 'So what's the bad news?' he said.

'We need to be there Friday night, eight o'clock.'

'That's what,' Sleeps said, closing one eye, checking the clock on the dashboard, 'forty-odd hours? You want me to drive to Sicily in forty hours?'

'Think you can do it?'

'A normal guy,' Sleeps said, 'would need to sleep, what, sixteen hours between now and then. So that cuts you down to twenty-four.' He honked the horn in response to a toot-toot from a Volkswagen bus alongside. 'And I'm narcoleptic.'

'I know a place,' Rossi said, 'we can pick up some good crank. Crystal meth.'

Sleeps started whistling 'Tulips From Amsterdam', then checked his uniform was buttoned to the throat, rolling up now to passport control. 'Just out of curiosity,' he said, meeting Mel's eye in the rear-view, 'the chauffeur, in *Drilling Miss Daisy*? He was the one did the drilling, right?'

'He did his fair share,' Mel said, holding Sleeps' gaze a second or two before glancing away to smile a demure one at the tubby Customs guy beaming down at her, his hand out for their passports.

Madge

Madge lay awake listening to her tummy's gurgling drown out the drip-drip of the tap in the bathroom, the dull buzz of a moped crossing the empty square, the yawn and stretch of a city slowly waking to another day. She'd known, last night, that she'd suffer the consequences of eating lobster so late. But what was a girl to do? Terry had rung ahead, arranged it all, had the hotel set them up with a table in the room, candles flickering. The place not far from the Spanish Steps, overlooking a square – no, a piazza – with a fountain big enough to wash a polo team, horses and all.

It hadn't looked much from outside – discreet, Terry'd assured her, boutique – but inside was a whole different world, the lobby looking vaguely Edwardian to Madge with its pillars and Turkish carpets and potted palms. Madge, if she squinted, could imagine herself taking the Grand Tour, Henry James skulking in the undergrowth sniffing some young girl's bloomers. Or was that Joyce? Madge could never remember.

She groped on the bedside locker for her watch, frowning as she tried to make out the time, then wondered about the time difference, was she an hour ahead? Or behind? Or, wait, was there even a time difference? Not that it mattered, she was awake now, needing something to settle her stomach, a nice creamy latte. She slipped out from under the sheet, watching Terry all the while, not wanting to wake him – not that she had any regrets there, Terry with a lot going for him even before he crawled into bed beside her, smelling rosy fresh but spicy, this after taking a shower, whispering, 'Hey, if you're tired, y'know, I'm kinda tired too. Like, what's the hurry, am I right . . .?'

No, Madge just wanted to savour the moment on her own. The early stillness, the sense that the whole of Rome, the Eternal City, was out there poised, holding its breath. Waiting for Madge to come out to play and make it perfect.

She decided she'd shower later, she wouldn't be gone that long anyway. Dressed casual, light sweater and slacks, a low heel on the strappy sandals in case she had to walk any distance. The guy on Reception was as helpful as he could be speaking Italian, Madge's knowledge of the language extending as far as Gucci, Armani, Fendi and Prada – still, she got the gist from the way he waved his arms around like a helicopter going down in flames. Out the front door, angle left across the piazza, cut a hard right down the second street she came to.

She was brisk going across the piazza, loving the echo of her heels on the air that still had a crisp chill to it, and was surprised to discover that the coffee shop, finding it first try, was already half-full. Professionals mainly, with their power suits and gleaming leather satchels, glowing tans, hair perfect, the kohl and blusher subtle but perfectly applied. And that was just the chaps. Madge, wishing now she'd at least glanced in the mirror on the way out, slunk down the back and found a high stool at the counter running along the rear wall. The vibe smug, like a gang of cats plotting to hijack a milk-float. Christ, even the middle-aged women looked to Madge like Sophia Loren's nieces. As for the satchels, the staccato chatter into headsets . . . Madge, with a pang, wondered how'd she fare in their world, cutting deals, making and shaking at, what – she glanced at her watch – Jesus, six-thirty in the morning. Or was it seven-thirty? Five-thirty?

Didn't matter. This time of the morning, generally speaking, and for the past ten years or so, Madge would usually be turning over for her second sleep, giving the hangover some me-time, vaguely aware of Frank through the fuzzy dullness as he banged drawers and cursed a missing sock.

Madge sipped her latte, grinning. Frank, the useless waste of space, wouldn't be needing any more than one sock for some time to come.

The coffee was good but the joy didn't last. Hating herself for feeling guilty, she took her latte up to the guy behind the counter and mimed making a phone call, asked for some change. He pointed out a booth to the right of the door and mimed sliding a credit card into a slot. Madge tugged the folding door closed behind her, balanced her latte on the narrow ledge. Then, taking a deep breath, she dialled Jeanie's cell.

The plan being to leave a message, hoping Jeanie was somewhere over the Atlantic, or had her phone switched—

'*Hello?*'

'Jeanie?'

The girl sounding so doleful, probably still coming down from last night, that Madge couldn't tell which twin it was.

'*Moms?*'

'Jeanie,' she guessed, 'how many times do I have to tell you, don't *call* me—'

'*Have you seen him?*'

'Seen who?'

'*Dad, who else?*'

Madge tried to remember the last time either of the twins had called Frank anything paternal and decided they'd probably still been dressing identical back then. 'No,' she said, 'I haven't seen your father. Have you tried all the hospitals?'

But that, apparently, was the problem. With one hospital being evacuated after a bomb threat, and most of the others swamped with the overflow intake, it was proving impossible to track Frank down.

'Jeanie?' Madge said, interrupting the girl's doleful monologue about how Bryan had called Liz just as they were about to board the flight to Denver, Bryan wanting to know if they'd heard from Frank, or if Frank was maybe right there with them in Terminal 1, Frank packing a single ski. 'Back up a sec,' Madge said. 'What's all this about a bomb threat?'

Jeanie told her what she knew. The bottom line being, Frank was MIA, the only patient still unaccounted for.

'*Moms?*'

'What?'

Jeanie sounding very small now, far away. '*Liz saw something on Sky News about how you shot Dad out in the woods.*'

'I'm losing you, Jeanie.' Madge hissed into the phone, made a sucking sound. 'You're breaking up. What'd you say?' Then hung up.

Melody

M el came awake fast, aware of the cabin's confines, the weird pressure that goes with sleeping beneath the water-line. Then heard a soft knockity-knock at the door. 'Hold on,' she called. She tossed back the sheet, padded across the cabin. 'Who's there?' she whispered.

'It's me. Sleeps.'

She opened the door a crack. 'What's wrong?'

'We'll be docking in half an hour. I just wanted to make sure you were up.'

'OK, thanks.'

'You need a hand with your bags?'

'No, that's OK.' He turned to go. 'Hey,' she said, 'have you got a sec?'

'Sure.'

Melody opened the door, let him in, closed it quickly behind him.

'Nice PJs,' he said.

Mel wearing a white silk nightie dotted with little honey-bees, each with a speech-bubble saying *Beeyoutiful*. Sleeps back in civvies now, wearing a baggy T-shirt that said, *Cops Uncouth to Youth*.

Mel said, 'Listen, Gary? About Rossi.'

He held up a hand to stall her. 'You don't have to worry about him, Mel. He talks a big game, but . . . I mean, he shot Ray, OK, but the way Rossi tells it, he was firing off a warning and Ray was running, he slipped, fell into it. Complete fluke. Anyway, Ray shouldn't have got involved. The shit was between Rossi and Karen, she stole his stuff, he just wanted it back.'

'See,' Mel said, 'this is what I don't get. It's all on Rossi but you're saying, correct me if I'm wrong, you'll do his time for him.'

'It sounds what you might call defeatist, sure. But I got a plan.'

'That involves, you said, going to prison.' Mel a little concerned that Sleeps' modest ambitions were screwing with her story arc.

'Doing time,' he said, 'yeah, it can be a bitch. Specially if you go in with the wrong frame of mind. Except the worst bit? Like, once you get past sharing a cell with three other blokes, the shit food, being locked down twenty-three hours – it's the boredom.'

'That and the gang rape in the showers.'

'I'm not saying,' Sleeps shrugged, 'it doesn't happen.' He gestured down at himself. 'But I'm no one's idea of Brad Pitt. Or Angelina Jolie. I got an ass, someone wants to stick something in it, they better be packing about twelve inches, y'know?'

Mel, who erred on the statuesque side herself, felt a pang of empathy. 'Beauty's only skin deep, Gary.'

'Skin deep and a mile wide.' He brushed it off. 'Anyway, the boredom? I got that plan. Taking courses and shit, get me an education. On the outside? No one's letting me into any college. And anyway, there's the fees, all the books.' He shook his head. 'Inside? They're *throwing* books at you. Christ, they get one guy a year they can point to, say look at him, he's rehabilitated, that's their grants for next year looked after. Then, when I'm not reading and shit? I've got the narcolepsy, I'm snoozing left, right and centre.'

'Reading and sleeping,' Melody said, considering. 'Maybe that's not such a bad plan.'

'Like, the whole point of hanging out with Rossi is the boy's done three jolts already, it's only a matter of time before he goes back inside.' He shrugged. 'Except when he goes, Mel, he'll take everyone around him down too.'

'You're worried about me?' Mel said. 'But I'm your hostage. If Rossi gets—'

'When.'

'When, OK. *When* Rossi gets caught, I go back home.'

'Because you'll just explain how Rossi kidnapped you, took you along.'

'Exactly.'

'You speak French? Italian?'

'I don't follow.'

'I'm just saying, wherever we get caught, they probably won't speak a lot of English. What they call the nuances will probably get lost in translation.'

'So we call the consul.'

'Or maybe the ambassador.'

'Well, whatever.'

'Because guys like that, they're just sitting by their phones hoping some low-life somersaults into the crap, needs bailing out.'

Melody thought that over. 'OK,' she said. 'I'll take that one on board. But how do I know you're not just angling to get back to a two-way split with Rossi?'

'Two-way, three-way, who gives a rat's ass? There's no *split*, Mel. I mean, Rossi's chasing this cop 'cos he thinks she's chasing Madge, on the basis Karen's with her. Except the cop's probably on holiday. This is even supposing,' he said, 'Karen's hooking up with Madge. Or that she'll have the cash with her if she does.'

'The ear,' Melody murmured. 'You're forgetting his ear.'

Sleeps nodded. 'You got a guy, OK, he's upstairs right now in a fucking tux and fedora, a false beard, he's missing an ear and drinking Woo-Woos on top of goofballs enough to stun the US Marine Corps. I mean, Mel – this is a guy whose all-time hero is Napoleon 'cos the guy was Italian and small.'

Mel's fingers were twitching to shape themselves around a pencil. 'So what're you suggesting?' she said.

'You need to duck out. Soon as we dock, turn around and take the next ferry home.'

'Just run away,' Mel said, 'from what I'm thinking might be my last decent shot at getting out from under.'

'There's worse things than being under.'

'There's better things too.'

He stared. Mel didn't blink. 'Well,' he said, hauling himself upright, 'you can't say you weren't warned.' Standing over her now, his bulk sagging, resigned to it. 'And when the shit hits the fan, I'll do my best, say how we dragged you along. But no one's ever listened to me my entire life. No reason they'll start now.'

Mel gestured for him to sit down again, then leaned forward to take his hand. 'Gary? *I'll* listen to you. Anytime you want to talk, I'm here.' She let go of his hand and reached the notepad and pen off the bedside locker, saying, 'Why don't you start with this FARCO thing. What's all that about?'

Karen

'That's him all right,' Ray said, adjusting the rear-view to watch Rossi cross the forecourt, flares flapping. Rossi headed for the Beamer parked off to the side of the petrol station. Karen, arms folded, watched in the wing mirror. 'You think I wouldn't know Rossi? Even wearing a beard?'

'Who's the big guy?'

'No idea.'

'His muscle?'

'How would *I* know, Ray? I never seen him before.'

'I'm only asking.'

'OK. Only next time? Ask me something I might know.'

Ray sipped some coffee and chewed lightly on the rim of the cardboard beaker. 'Know what I'm thinking?' he said.

Karen nodded, grim. 'We go over there, drag him out of the fucking car and put a round in each knee.'

'Tempting,' Ray said. 'But first let's see if there's other options.'

'Like what?'

'Like how this doesn't actually change anything.'

'Are you insane? The sick fuck's sitting right there.'

'He's not over here. Not pointing a rod at your face, wanting the money. I'm saying,' Ray said, 'he doesn't know we're here. And there's no way he can know what we're driving. We could spin all the way down to Athens behind him, keeping an eye on the Beamer, he wouldn't think twice about it. Like, he reckons we got a jump-start on him, right?'

'So now we're following him,' Karen said, 'following us?'

'This way we know where he's at. And until I can raise Terry on the blower, we still need to hit Athens.'

'I can't believe Madge told him about the cruise.'

Ray had nothing to add to that. They watched as the big guy got out of the Beamer and lumbered back across the forecourt, went to the Ladies' restroom. From the rear of the van came a rumbling sigh that sounded a lot like a sabre-toothed tiger contemplating a mammoth. Ray flinched, ducking his head into his shoulders. Without looking, Karen reached back over the seat and patted Anna's shaggy head. 'Not now, hon,' she murmured. 'Just give me five minutes, OK?' Then, her eyes still on the wing mirror, 'You were saying, about this island.'

Ray sipped some coffee. 'Ios, yeah. Time I was there, where I was staying, the guy had a hound he said was Rottweiler mixed with some Alsatian. To me it looked more like a bear crossed with a bigger bear but I'm no expert. Anyway, the guy says the dog was for gypsies, blacks and guys in funny hats. Seriously, funny hats.' Karen gave Anna's ear a gentle tug, Anna growling sleepily way down in her throat. He said, 'You're living remote on the islands? They'll expect you to have a dog. Bigger the better.'

'So that's Anna looked after,' Karen said. 'What about me?'

'You'll buy a place,' he said, 'for forty, fifty. Nothing flash, you're not talking pools and wet bars. Then, you ride bikes, you can splash out for a Harley or some shit. Although in the islands, they mainly ride mopeds.'

'Mopeds?'

'Scooters. Anyway, your choice.'

'And I'm working as a waitress. In a cocktail bar, right?'

'Staying incognito,' Ray said, missing the reference. 'For a while, anyway. Until you decide what you want to do.' He glanced across. 'You've worked waitress before, right?'

'Never, no. But you're saying, I look the type.'

'No offence,' Ray said. 'I thought all women, at some point, work waitress. Like, part-time. When they're kids, during the holidays.'

'On my résumé,' Karen said, 'if I had one, which I don't, but if I had? It'd say, "Taking care of bastard father".'

'Cooking, cleaning, serving him dinner. Same deal, right? And the living's cheap, especially on the islands. So you've still, even after buying the place, thirty, forty gees in the mattress. That buys you, even not working, a couple of years to work things out.'

'We'll have eighty-five,' Karen said, 'once we split with Madge.

Then, after *we* split, that's forty and change. That's before I go buying any ranches.'

'So if we don't split,' Ray said, 'you've still got eighty-five.'

Karen watched the big guy give up knocking on the Ladies' door, do a quick sketch left and right, barge through. She said, 'If *we* don't split or if we don't split the money?'

'Either or,' Ray said.

'Because what I'm thinking,' Karen said, 'is that kind of living – I mean, remote on an island? Working in bars? It doesn't sound like your kind of living.'

'Hold on, here he comes.'

The big guy crossed the forecourt again, a suitcase under one armpit, the girl now in a two-piece suit, jacket and slacks, a silk scarf knotted at her neck, tottering along on kitten heels in the big guy's wake. Ray lit a Marlboro and waited for the Beamer to pull off, the Beamer veering from the left-hand lane into the right when a Ford Focus came tearing towards it flashing its lights, honking its horn. 'Don't sweat the details, Karen,' he said. 'Living's living.'

They pulled out of the service station and got on the road. Karen dug out her bottle of pills and leaned over the partition, fed one to Anna, shushed her to sleep. Then she filched one of Ray's Marlboros, cranked open the window an inch or two.

'So what happens,' she said, 'we get to Athens, you still haven't heard from Terry?'

Ray scratched the plaster-cast below his elbow. 'I guess we make a new plan.'

'Another one?'

'Plans are cheap,' Ray said. 'Plans come free.'

Doyle

'The Acrockolis?' Sparks said. 'That anywhere near the Acropolis?'

'Right next door,' Doyle said, 'just there behind the Acrapolis.' She switched the phone to her other ear, perched a buttock on a smooth rock that might have been just a rock or yet another ancient altar, Christ, Doyle afraid to step on dog turds in case they turned out sacred.

'Ingrate,' Sparks said. 'That's three thousand years' worth of culture you're looking at there.'

Doyle, who'd found it hard to sleep in the muggy heat, felt like she fit right in with all the ruins. 'It's hot up here, Sparks. Plus they take your bag away in case you smuggle out a temple or two, maybe. So I forgot to bring any water.'

'Details, girl. What's it like?'

Doyle shaded her eyes and looked up the dusty hill towards the Parthenon, the vast blue dome of sky behind. 'Right now,' she said, 'it's infested with Yanks and Japs, it's Iwo Jima with Nikons. And the temples are all covered with scaffolding, so it looks a lot like a building site for the world's biggest sauna.' She pulled her clammy T-shirt away from her belly, the jeans sticking to her thighs. 'So what's happening there?'

Sparks cleared her throat. 'Frank's gone.'

'He died?'

Sparks explained about the bomb threat phoned in to the hospital, the evacuation. How they'd checked the CCTV footage, eventually getting around to the cameras installed in the overflow car park to enforce the new No Smoking regs. Which was when Frank was spotted being transferred from a wheelchair into the trunk of a Qashquai, three guys, no fuss.

'And no sign of him since?' Doyle said.

'Nary a sign.'

'We get the Qashquai's number?'

'The plate's covered in mud, it looks like. But we took some screen-grabs, blew them up. Got a flag on one of the guys.'

'Yeah?'

'Charlie Byrne, he's a bouncer by trade. Known to us for occasional nixers doing shit-work for Terry Swipes' crew – collections, evictions, enforcing, what have you.'

'What's Terry Swipes want with Frank?'

'Right now,' Sparks said, 'we have no proof Terry wants anything to do with Frank, or even knows he exists. If he still does. That said, we all know how Terry's a bad baker, has his fingers in all these pies. So it'd be remiss of us not to at least consider the theory that Terry's the guy behind the snatch operation, he's tidying up Frank as a loose end.'

Doyle, feeling none too proud about it, found herself hoping Frank'd turn up dead, thus transferring the heat from Doyle to someone – anyone – else.

'What's Ted's take?' she said.

'Right now, nothing, mainly because he has Frank's lawyer crawling up his fundament with a six-foot probe. I mean, the guy was already squawking about negligence, how you're the biggest fuck-up since . . .' Sparks paused. 'Actually, he reckons you're the biggest fuck-up ever. But don't take it personal, he's just building a case.'

'What about Madge?' Doyle said. 'What's the read on her?'

'Madge kneecapping her ex-husband-to-be,' Sparks said, 'isn't so much a priority right now, given that the rest of Frank is now as missing as his knee. Which is, I guess, a stroke of luck for Madge.'

'I guess it is.' Doyle dragged a wrist across her forehead, felt the sweat dribble down her forearm. 'So where am I in all this?'

'Ted wants you back. Yesterday.'

'What'll that achieve?'

'My guess is he's planning to drape you across his desk like Linda Carter, have you deflect that big fat bullet heading his way with your funky bracelets.'

'Fuck that. He doesn't know where I am, right?'

'Nope. But the boys finally got around to checking Madge's credit card records. So he knows about the cruise.'

'They know about Aspen?'

'That was the twins, her kids were supposed to fly out on a ski holiday. Aspen's a non-runner.'

Doyle felt that tightening in her gut, she got it once in a while, not often but sometimes it played out – the instinct, the hunch, starting to pay off. 'So there's a pretty good chance she's already here.'

'Except,' Sparks said, 'there's no record of her leaving the country. None for Karen or Ray, either.'

'Karen won't be sticking around, Sparks. Not after Anna savaged Rossi. And if they were smuggling out a Siberian wolf . . .'

'They could be anywhere, Doyle. You're hoping they're in Athens, or heading there, just because you're there. You want my advice? Come home. No way is Madge letting her kids go through all this shit on their own. Then, worst-case scenario, you're in court with your record of competence and shit, the model cop, you're keeping your head down. Meanwhile the jury's looking at Mad Madge McMad, the socialite who popped a cap in her husband's knee.'

Doyle watched a tiny lizard crawl up the side of the stone, its bluey-green iridescence reflecting back the sun in a million glinting sparks. 'So Karen and Ray, they just skate out free?'

'What do you care? Right now you need to think about you.'

'See, that's just it. I come home now, the best that happens is I get a pat on the head for not screwing it *all* the way up. And that's presuming they don't follow through on Ray and me, start asking what the deal was there. Maybe start wondering where the money's gone.'

'You think it'll look any better if you *don't* come back?'

Doyle thought about that. She said, 'How's this? We can't know for sure they're not taking that cruise until Madge shows up back home. She does, OK, I come home too. That buys me a couple of days to maybe nail Ray.'

'Ray?'

'He's the one, he told me himself, pulled the snatch together. I get him, the money, I don't have to worry about keeping my head down, in court or anywhere else.'

'OK,' Sparks said. 'But are we talking about nailing Ray or, y'know, *nailing* him?'

'If we find Anna—'

'Big if.'

'OK, but a Siberian wolf, she's noticeable, y'know? And *if* we find her, we have Karen, and wherever Karen is, there's Ray. A guy like that, she's not letting him walk away now. I mean, he took a bullet for her. You ever known a guy you could've said he'd take a bullet for you?'

'I've known a few,' Sparks said, 'I wouldn't mind volunteering for the role.'

Melody

'FARCO?' Johnny Priest said.

'The Francis Assisi Rehabilitation Concern Organisation,' Rossi said. 'For short? FARCO.'

'And you're saying, it's like AA for ex-cons.'

'Perxactly.'

'Putting cons back on their feet,' Johnny said. 'Giving them a helping hand.'

'It's a charity,' Rossi said. 'So we'll be getting tax breaks, grants, free ads on TV, all this.' Rossi held up his balloon glass, twirling it slowly so the tawny liquid caught the light. 'This Napoleon brandy,' he said. 'Y'think they call it that 'cos it gets you thinking all strategic and shit?'

'But it's nothing to do, with the Colombians?' Johnny said.

'The FARC fuckers? Christ, no. Like I say, it's a charity. Only everyone gets to what they call pool their resources. Networking, all this.'

Johnny Priest showed good teeth in a quick grin, seeing it now. 'A co-op for ex-cons? Christ, it'll be unions next.'

Mel making mental notes every three seconds, the front of her brain a yellow wall plastered with Post-its.

Rossi laid an arm along the back of the booth and took a sip on a joint that was no bigger, Melody judged, than a bicycle pump. 'You want in, Johnny, I'm talking ground floor, just say the word. You being based here in Amsterdam, we could get what they call an international dimension going.'

'Appreciate the offer, Rossi.' Johnny, Mel was disappointed to admit, wasn't exactly her idea of a gangster. Softly spoken, clean shaven, some old acne scars making him craggy but with neat strawberry-blond hair. Sitting back now in the circular booth to consider Rossi's proposal with an ankle propped on his knee, wearing faded denims and penny loafers, no socks, a pale blue shirt open at the neck showing a tuft of blond. 'And I'm grateful, don't get me wrong, you took the time to look me up. But things have changed since we celled, man. This,' he gestured around at the low-ceilinged club, Vatican Too, empty now at mid-afternoon, smelling faintly of stale beer and ammonia, 'this is where I'm at now. It's small, yeah, but it's mine and I'm not looking over my shoulder every three seconds. Y'know? So no disrespect, but the last thing I need is hooking up with ex-cons, charity or otherwise.'

'I hear you,' Rossi said. 'No harm done, right? I'm just letting you know it's there.'

'Much obliged.' He leaned in past the gently snoring Sleeps to accept the joint from Rossi. 'Good shit, right?'

'Not bad, yeah. What's this one called?'

'THX-1176.'

'OK. What was the first one again?'

'Purple Craze.'

'Bit trippy, that. Not so sure I'm up for flying monkeys this early, y'know?'

'It's what they call,' Johnny said, sipping on the joint, 'value for money. You're chilled, you're tripping, you're covering all the bases. Mel? Want to try this one?'

'No thanks, Johnny.' Mel was half-stoned already, just sitting there, Johnny on a sub-committee assessing the long-list for something called the Cannabis Cup. 'Right now I'm high on life.'

'No pressure,' Johnny said. 'It's there if you want it. Don't feel you need to ask.'

'I won't.'

Johnny nudged Sleeps' knee, offering the joint when Sleeps half-opened one eye. Sleeps just shook his head, closed the eye again. Johnny shrugged, handed the joint to Rossi. 'So you're driving all the way to Sicily,' he said, jerking a thumb at Sleeps, 'with the human dynamo here at the wheel. This is why you need the crizz.'

'Can you do it?'

'I can make a call, sure. No guarantees, mind, I'm not really moving in those circles any more. So I wouldn't be able to vouch for the quality either.'

'Even your basic Billy will do it. I mean, it's that or we find him a barbed-wire cushion.'

'I'll see what I can do,' Johnny said. 'So what's happening in Sicily?'

'I probably shouldn't say, man. You being clean and all, the less you know the better.' Rossi winked, tapped the side of his nose. 'Loose tips sink fish, right?'

'Sure thing,' Johnny said, scratching his jaw. 'OK, I'll make some calls, see if I can raise anyone.' He stood up, gestured at the low table. 'Make free with the samples, let me know what you think.'

'Will do,' Rossi said. Johnny moved off, went through a door behind the bar. Rossi grinned at Mel. 'Nice guy, huh?'

'Seems to be,' Melody said. 'Listen, Rossi – you think you should be smoking so much dope? I mean, with all we have to do?'

'Mother's milk,' Rossi said. 'Anyway, what's with this "we" shit?'

Melody counted to ten. 'We've been through this,' she said. 'I'm the one staking you, so I get equal say.'

'How about,' Rossi said, 'and I'm just having my equal say here, you was to be dragged down an alleyway, slapped around a little?'

'I'm out of shape,' Sleeps mumbled, his eyes still closed, 'but I'm a big man. You don't want me sitting on your head too long.'

'Much as I hate to admit it,' Mel said to Rossi, 'I'm about forty pounds heavier than you are. And what, four inches taller?'

'Maybe three,' Rossi said.

'I also have three brothers, just in case you're wondering if I've any experience in putting guys flat on their back when they start acting out. Anything else you need to know?'

Rossi had a toke thinking it over. 'So it's OK for you to go slapping someone around, but not me.' He turned his head to exhale, keeping his eyes on Melody's. 'How's that work?'

'Self-defence doesn't count.'

Johnny came through the door behind the bar and crossed to the booth, eased in past Melody. 'You're in luck,' he said, rubbing his hands.

'Yeah?' Rossi said. 'Crizz?'

'Yep.'

'The good shit?'

'You can tell me. The guy's bringing it over, he'll be here in a couple of hours. You don't fly, you don't buy.'

'Sweet. Hey, Sleeps? Guy's coming here with the crizz.'

'Gorgeous,' Sleeps said.

'Fuck's the matter now?'

Sleeps opened one eye. 'Narcolepsy's a condition, Rossi. It's not like I get tired, y'know, take a power nap. The shit's hard-wired. Except *you* want to pump crizz in, jolly it all up, see how it goes.'

'How else do we get to Palermo on time? You won't fucking fly, now you're bitching about driving . . .'

'So why don't you drive?'

'Because,' Rossi said, making an effort to restrain himself, Melody could tell, in Johnny's presence, 'you're the one took me to a vet after the wolf ripped half my head off, which is why I'm taking horse tranks. So I'm driving goofed to the eyeballs or blind with agony. That what you want?'

'Why don't I drive?' Melody said.

Rossi's eyebrows shot up. Johnny coughed. 'Rossi? Sorry to interrupt, man. But there's just one thing.'

'It's the dame who's paying, Johnny. Like she keeps saying, she's the one staking us.'

'It's just, this guy who's on his way? Maybe I shouldn't have said, but I told him where you were headed.'

'Shit, Johnny. What'd we say about sinking fish?'

'I know.' Johnny held up a hand. 'Anyway, I told him about FARCO too.'

'Oh yeah?'

'He's got a proposal.'

Madge

'Y ou got a good brief?' Terry said.

'He's OK, I guess. I mean, for handling a divorce. But for something like this?'

'See, what you're doing right there is thinking guilty. And until someone proves different, this is nothing like anything. I mean, sure, you blew his knee out. But no one's dying from a capping, not unless it's deliberate.'

'I knew exactly what I was doing, Terry.'

'I'm talking about after. Like if he was just left there, no one puts in a call. Then, yes, you're talking shock, blood loss, hypo-thermia . . . Anyway,' he said, clocking the expression on Madge's face, 'Frank was cuffed to this cop when the actual shooting happened, right? And she'd know your basic emergency procedures, what Frank needed. The fact that the guy didn't even make it to ICU, was in his own room when it happened, means he was doing OK. He'd probably never have walked right again, sure, but he was off the critical list.'

Madge stirred her martini, chasing the olive around while she watched the tourists stroll arm-in-arm in the warm early evening, couples smiling, murmuring sweet nothings. Somehow she'd always imagined the conversation over a digestif on the terrace of a trattoria on a side street off the Piazza di Spagna being a little more romantic.

'I shot him, Terry.'

'No one's disputing that. Except, between then and him going missing he was in the hands of the cops, the doctors, for what, twelve hours?'

'Closer to fourteen.'

'He wasn't even in ICU, Madge. If he had been, they wouldn't have been able to get to him.'

'*Get* to him?'

Terry paused while the waiter slipped sideways between their table and the low railing, the guy young and slim, whip-crack taut. Madge feeling old beyond her years, a heaviness inside like her bones had fossilised.

'We're agreed,' Terry said, keeping his voice low, 'Frank probably didn't experience any miracle, just stand up and stroll out of that hospital of his own free will.'

'You're saying,' she picked her words with care, 'someone might have taken him?'

'Maybe, maybe not. But that's not your problem. All you're concerned about right now is the post-mortem putting blue sky between you shooting out his shin and him being gone. That's all you need, reasonable doubt. Worst-case scenario, it comes down to it, you need an actual alibi for where you were at the time . . .' Terry reached across the table and took her hand, patted the back of it. 'I know of a guy, Madge, a brief, he's had some experience in cases like this. He'd stroll this one, eyes closed. You might have to bark once in a while, roll your eyes, froth up at the mouth when Frank's name gets mentioned. But this guy'll seal the deal.'

'If you're so sure, why aren't we headed for the airport?'

Terry, with a final pat, released her hand. 'Flying back,' he said, 'like the dutiful wife, the good mother.'

'Actually,' Madge said, unwilling to add hypocrisy to her claim to infamy, 'it'd be more like I have nothing to fear, so I'm not running away.'

'That's one way to look at it,' Terry said. 'You're calm, you're rational. You're innocent, right?'

'According to your brief I am.'

'Except it'll look better in court if you panic a little first.'

'Panic?'

'Let's just say Frank turns up dead.'

'No, Terry, let's not say that.'

'Sure, yeah, but listen. If there's a chance they might be charged with second-degree murder, they've already put a bullet in the corpse? Most people, by which I mean a jury of your peers, they'd be inclined to shit themselves a cartload. So, you should panic a little.'

Madge prodded gloomily at the olive. 'It'll look bad if I don't go back, Terry. If only for the twins' sake.'

'See, this is how panicked you were. Except it's not your fault, it's evolution.'

Madge raised an eyebrow. 'Evolution?'

'What they call fight or flight. Yeah? And you can't fight it, all those cops, so your instinct is to take off. But only for a few days. Then, you get a chance to think it over, it's the twins that bring you back.' Terry warming to his theme. 'Even though there's a chance you might be wrongfully convicted, you're taking that chance so they don't have to suffer on their own. That's even supposing it goes to court.' He cocked his head. 'Hey, did you even know the gun was loaded? I mean, obviously it was, we know that now. But when this guy Rossi handed you the gun, did you know for sure it was loaded?'

'Well, I . . .'

'How could you? You didn't *see* him load it, did you?'

Madge shook her head. 'I don't even know where it came from. One minute I was looking at Frank, the next—'

'Whoa. Don't even *go* there, Madge. The trauma? You've blocked it all out.'

Madge was a little overwhelmed by Terry's being so au fait with the amount of wriggle room in what seemed to her a cast-iron case. 'Terry? I don't mean to sound ungrateful, you being so supportive and all, but there's one thing I need to ask.'

'Fire away.'

'Well,' Madge said, 'I'd hate you think I was complaining, but how come you're being so supportive?'

Terry gave a quick grin, clinked his glass on Madge's. 'What am I going to do, leave a damsel in distress?'

'It's a bit more than that, Terry. You're offering your brief, an alibi . . . I mean, people will ask about you, won't they? What you're getting out of it.'

'They'll take one look at you and know exactly what I'm getting out of it.'

'That's sweet, Terry, but seriously – aren't you taking on a lot here that you don't need to?'

Terry picked up his silver cigarette case, offered it to Madge, then took one himself when she declined. He lit up, waving his hand through the smoke so it wouldn't drift over to Madge's side of the table. 'I'm clean, Madge. The thing with Frank? Unless you want me to say different, I hadn't even met you before you blew a hole in him. Fact is, or far as anyone can prove, the first I ever heard of Frank is from you telling me you used him for target practice.'

'But won't they investigate you? Dig around, see if we had any motive for wanting Frank dead?'

'Let 'em. It's not like we were having an affair, sneaking around behind Frank's back, especially seeing as how you were separated, Frank already with a new tart on board. And then, you're saying Frank was broke, the guy re-mortgaging and shit – I mean, that's why he was having you snatched, right? He was brassic.' Madge nodded. 'OK,' Terry said, 'so what motive could I have? Anyone wants to look at my accounts, I'm in pretty good shape. And you were already getting divorced. So what do I gain from messing around with Frank?'

'Nothing, I guess.'

Terry signalled the waiter, spiralled his forefinger for two more martinis. 'So there it is. We hop a flight tomorrow, get into Athens nice and early, maybe see a few—'

'Athens?' Madge stared. 'You're still taking the cruise?'

'Naturally. This is how panicked you are, how screwed your thinking is. So we arrive at the port, they pick us up there, maybe. Or, they haven't twigged yet you're taking the cruise, we give it a few days, see some sights. Then you make a call, say you're coming home.'

'It's that easy.'

'Hey, you've already paid for the cruise, right? Might as well get some value for it . . . Only thing is,' he said, sitting back to allow the waiter to place the martinis on the table, nodding his thanks, 'we'll need to let Ray know the score. Best they don't get involved and complicate things. You have a number for Karen, right?'

Madge, distracted as she thought dolefully about how Frank was making her life even more of a misery now that he was missing, possibly dead, just nodded. Terry sat forward. 'Madge? Don't worry about it.' He raised his glass, toasting her. 'Here's to panicking,' he said, 'in the lap of luxury.'

'To panicking,' Madge said, forcing a smile. But when Terry went to the bathroom the dread crept back in, this prickly sensation calcifying the walls of her gut.

Madge, her whole life had been shaped by Frank ever since the bastard date-raped her that night in his father's car, got her pregnant, Madge sixteen years old. Now she stared across the street at the haughty mannequins in the shop window opposite, trying to remember a single kindness, a gentle touch or generosity that didn't eventually reveal itself as a means to an end. The end being, inevitably, Frank's gratification.

He had ruined her life like sea on rock, wearing her down by imperceptible degrees.

And now he was dead, or maybe not. Madge didn't really care much either way. All that mattered was that Frank, dead or alive, still had the power to drag her back, drag her down.

Rossi

The guy finally arrived, Johnny making the introductions, the guy, Jochem, breaking out the crizz straight away. Exactly three minutes later Sleeps was primed to hijack a submarine, take it all the way to Sydney.

'So Johnny,' Jochem said, 'he tells me about the FARCO.'

Rossi, feeling his eyes the size of golf balls, nodded tersely. 'Johnny says you got a proposal.'

'Is the cruise,' Jochem said. The guy with less presence than Rossi'd expected. Thin and wiry, a scruffy black toothbrush moustache, dark and wary eyes. 'Where will it going?'

Rossi glanced across at Mel. 'Oh,' she said airily, 'y'know, the usual. Egypt. The Holy Land. All around.'

'The Greek islands?' Johnny said.

'Sure,' Mel said. 'Some of them, sure.'

'What about Ios?' Johnny said.

'Definitely.'

'And when does it get in there?'

'Without the itinerary,' Melody said, 'I couldn't say for sure, it's back in the car. I mean, I could—'

'What's the gig?' Rossi cut in.

Johnny glanced at Jochem, who nodded. 'OK,' Johnny said. 'So the deal is the Greeks are death on your recreational chemicals. You've seen *Midnight Express*, right?'

'That was in Turkey,' Sleeps pointed out.

Rossi snorted. 'Greeks, Turks, South Sea fucking Samolians. What's the job?'

'Jochem here,' Johnny said, 'reckons there's a famine out in the Greek islands, the Cyclades. Some guys who really shouldn't are experiencing a cash-flow issue, which means a lot of party people are coming up short on their holiday quota of snow.'

'I'm guessing,' Mel said, 'we're not talking about skiing.'

'Gak,' Johnny said. 'Although,' he looked to Jochem for reassurance, 'nothing too heavy. Just a couple've of keys, already stamped. All you have to do is hand it over to a man who'll be waiting when the ship docks.'

'On this Ios,' Rossi said.

'What's in it for us?' said Mel.

Johnny consulted with Jochem in Dutch. Jochem shrugged, said something that sounded to Rossi like he was gargling marbles. 'Ten gees,' Johnny translated. 'Throwing the crizz in on top.'

'Sounds fair,' Rossi said.

'That's generous,' Sleeps said, 'for two keys.'

'Jochem needs a man,' Johnny Priest said, 'can be trusted to do the hard thing the simple way.'

Rossi nodding along. 'We can do simple,' he said. 'So where's this gak?'

Ray

Ten hours out of Amsterdam and they were still only passing Munich. Ray's eyes burning. Even wearing shades, the headlights of the oncoming traffic were lasers.

'So where's next?' Karen said.

'Milan,' he said through clenched teeth. Wondering if it was just exhaustion or if lockjaw was in the post, tetanus. 'Through the Alps, down into Milan. That's another six hundred clicks. Then, Milan to Rome, eight hundred. About the same to Bari, maybe a little more. How're we doing on the happy tabs?'

Karen rummaged in her bag, passed one over. Ray dry-swallowed the pill, lit a cigarette. 'Any chance,' he said, 'of changing that CD?'

'You don't like Tom Waits?'

'Sixteen times in a row? I wouldn't even want Scarlett Johansson sixteen times in a row.'

'Seriously?' Karen flicked through Ray's CDs. 'How about these guys, The Jam?'

'"Going Underground",' Ray said. 'Appropriate.'

Karen switched CDs. Ray, nodding along to 'That's Entertainment', said, 'I'm not going to make it.'

'No?'

'Not a chance. The arm's fucked, I'm numb to the shoulder. The not-good numb.'

'Shit. So what do we do?'

'Plan B.'

'There's a plan B?'

'Always.'

'Do we still get to see the Alps?'

'We'll be mostly skipping the Alps,' Ray admitted. 'At least, they won't be getting any bigger than they are now.'

'They're pretty big now,' Karen said, craning her neck to look up at the snow-capped peaks. She said, 'Hey, Ray? Know what I like best about you?' Ray wasn't so tired he didn't catch the needle in her tone. 'It's how you're spontaneous,' she said. 'Flexible. You're not the kind of guy, he makes a plan and that's it, has to stick to it after his feet catch fire.'

'Life's too short for sticking to plans.'

'How about keeping promises?'

'A plan,' he said, 'is a theory. A promise is people. It's like abstract and actual, and you can fuck with abstract. Actual's different.'

'So what promise did you actually make to Doyle? I mean, Stephanie.'

'None,' Ray said.

'You told her,' Karen persisted, 'you'd do time. That you'd stand up in court, be her fall guy. So she could put Frank away for all the kidnaps, Frank instead of Terry Swipes. With you doing, I think you said, a two-year jolt for aiding and abetting.'

'Telling's telling. I didn't make any actual promises.'

'You lied to her, Ray. This is what I'm saying about the spontaneity. You said one thing, did another.'

'You're saying I lied?'

'You *did* lie.'

'I'm pretty sure I said I'd do the time if you got the money.'

'We *got* the money. All two hundred grand of it. Now, after deductions, one-seventy or thereabouts.'

'Only because we ran off with it,' Ray said. 'Doyle, you didn't see it? She had other plans. And if we'd stuck around, I'd have gone for a tumble and you wouldn't have seen any cash. Bang goes the cottage at the lake, the three acres for Anna to run around in.'

Karen staring out into gathering gloom. 'They have many lakes on the Greek islands, Ray?'

'Hey, you're the one said you had to flee the country. That's the word you used, right? Flee.' Karen, chewing her lip, nodded. 'Because,' he said, 'if we stuck around, Anna'd be put down for mauling Rossi. Correct me if I'm wrong.'

Karen, grudging it, nodded again.

'Right,' Ray said. 'So I took that on board, made the suggestion – a suggestion, mind – that the Greek islands might suit Anna, the Greeks being pretty cool about homicidal hounds doing the whole *Born Free* bit. Even agreed, this with a busted fucking arm from shipping a bullet, to drive her there. Except now I'm flat out fucked, can't do it all the way down through Italy, all I'm talking about is diverting a little out of the way, make it easier on everyone.'

'This being the latest plan. Another one.'

Ray with these odd quivers in the small of his back, the strain, the constant pressure. He knuckled his eyes. 'Just say it, Karen. Whatever it is you're brewing up in there, just—'

'You made plans with Doyle.'

'You're still worrying about Doyle.'

'You made her look ridiculous. This after she specifically told you, and I quote, not to leave her looking a total fucking blonde.'

'Christ.' Ray shook his head. 'I thought it was men had problems with pride.'

'There's pride,' Karen said, 'and there's looking ridiculous.'

Ray, bone weary, flipped his smoke into the breeze. 'What're you saying, she'll come after us?'

'You,' Karen said. 'I'm saying, she'll be coming after you.'

Doyle

Watching him now through the mist as he paced the street arguing on the phone, Doyle had to admit Niko had changed. Still tall, sure, but filling out in all the right places, shoulders and chest, leaving him slim through the hips, rangy now even in the suit and open-necked shirt, the guy could easily have passed for Italian if it wasn't for the snakeskin calf-length cowboy boots.

She wondered if it was a woman on the other end of the line, Niko dropping her at short notice to hook up with Doyle, bring her to this cute little restaurant where they could sit out on the veranda with water streaming down off the awning overhead like a curtain against the dead heat, a cool mist blowing in against the patrons. Athens in mid-September, Christ, sultry like a Tennessee Williams fourth act. Doyle, she had a straw, was sure she could've sipped the air.

Niko ducked in through the curtain of mist and strode to their table, folded himself carefully into the chair. 'Sorry,' he said, 'but that was unavoidable.' He turned off the mobile phone and tucked it away into the breast pocket of the jacket hanging from the back of his chair. 'There,' he said with a wide, easy smile. 'No more interruptions.'

'Don't worry about it.'

His face had filled out too, the olive skin taut now over a fleshy fullness, the dominant nose giving him a patrician look. Plus, Doyle'd forgotten, he had eyes like warm liquorice. He picked up his fork. 'So where were we?' he said.

Something else Doyle had forgotten, was thrilling to now, was Niko's accent, rich and slightly guttural.

'The girl's about my age,' she lied, 'thirty-one, thirty-two. Has this weird twist to her chin like she busted her jaw one time. She'll be the one driving because the guy stopped a bullet.' She prodded her upper arm with her fork. 'Then, the wolf has only one eye, the other one being covered with an eyepatch.'

'Like a pirate.'

'A were-pirate. We'll be needing silver bullets.'

'So if we locate them, identification shouldn't be a problem.'

'I wouldn't have thought so, no.'

'Of course, the finding, this is the difficult part.'

'You get many wolves in Athens? I mean, this late in the season.'

'September is a busy time here, Stephanie.' Doyle with an involuntary shiver at how Niko packed about six syllables into her name. 'September is when Italy closes down, everyone goes on holidays. They come over like ants. Piraeus gets crazy this time of the year.'

Doyle, having hit the glass ceiling a little earlier than she expected, had found herself with a lot of time on her hands career-wise. So she'd broadened her horizons, started taking courses to get her out of the office for a week at a time and put some points on her pension. Marksmanship, hostage negotiation, community policing for ethnic minorities – Doyle had done the lot. Then Ted took her away for a long weekend to Barcelona, a junket on policing electronic frontiers, cops swapping tips on how not to look like total muppets while the bad guys ran the show. Doyle'd caught on fast, all those free lunches in Prague, Florence, Berlin, Madrid – Doyle had seen them all at her leisure, all expenses paid.

She believed Prague had been her favourite. The worst had been Athens, dirty, dusty and noisy, the buildings imported wholesale from some Kiev industrial estate. Worse, Niko had taken a shine to her, Niko the official interpreter for the group, not long back from his secondment in London and keen to impress with his Oxford English. A greyhound chasing her all over town, tongue lolling from this inane grin Doyle had wanted to put her fist through.

She was glad now she'd held off.

'All I'm asking,' she said, 'is you keep your ears open. Someone mentions a wolf with an eyepatch, you let me know.'

'Of course. Consider it done.' He sipped some wine, patted his lips with the napkin. 'But what happens then? Unless the woman, Marge—'

'Madge.'

'Madge, yes.' He gave one of his exquisitely careless shrugs. 'But unless she makes a statement saying she is a hostage, then there is nothing we can do. Not until an official request comes through the channels, at least, and we would have no reason to hold them long enough for that to happen. You know how long it can take.'

Doyle, who'd neglected to mention Frank's untimely disappearance, and believed the issue of her suspension was news to be doled out on a strictly need-to-know basis, said, 'Sure, yeah. But all I'm asking is you tip me off as to where they are.'

Niko nodded. 'Just so long as you remember,' he said, waggling his fork at her, 'you have no jurisdiction here.'

'Who said anything about jurisdictions?' she said. 'I'm on my holidays, Niko. Here to have some fun.'

Niko popped home some *kalamari*. 'Fun, huh?'

'Absolutely. Take a ferry or two, see some islands.'

He held up a warning forefinger. 'It's not safe in the islands for a beautiful woman on her own, Stephanie.'

'Safe's for back home, Niko. And I'm on my holidays.'

FRIDAY
Sleeps

'W hen Hannibal crossed the Alps?' Sleeps said. He pointed through the windscreen in the general direction of where the snow-capped peaks had been before night came down. 'He lost sixteen elephants.'

'How does anyone,' Melody said, 'lose sixteen elephants?'

'One would've been unfortunate,' Sleeps said, flexing his hands on the steering wheel, enjoying the pay-off. 'Sixteen? That's just careless.'

'Oscar Wilde,' she said. 'Right?'

Sleeps nodded, getting a shivery tingle that had nothing to do with the crizz. Over the hump now, the first blast like being plugged into a tiny sun, hair crackling, muscles taut and skin humming. He glanced across at Melody, who was fiddling now with the stereo, trying to find a station that wasn't cranking out guttural death-metal. OK, the girl was flat-out loon, Sleeps was hoping they didn't encounter any full moons on the high seas, but he had always liked the larger girls and Melody had those Botticelli curves.

In the end she switched the stereo off. A gentle snoring purred in from the rear, the combination of crizz, Woo-Woos, Purple Craze and horse tranks finally catching up with Rossi somewhere around Stuttgart.

'Think we'll make it?' she said.

'It's do-able. I mean, thirteen hundred clicks in what, sixteen hours? I stay awake, that's do-able. And we've got that extra hour. They're an hour ahead in Palermo, right?'

'They would be,' Mel said, 'if we were still at home. But I think we've caught up with the time zone now.'

'Shit. Really?'

'I'm not sure. We're still in Germany, right?'

'Long as we're heading in the general direction of up, we're still in Deutschland. Then, we get to where it's all heading down, we're into Italy. Freewheeling all the way to Sicily.'

'Yeah.' Mel nibbled a thumbnail. 'Listen, Gary? There's something you should know.'

'What's that?'

'We're not going to Sicily.'

'No?'

'The cruise, it's leaving from Athens.'

Sleeps digested that. 'So why'd you say Palermo?'

'I thought Rossi might try to dump me, swipe my credit card.'

'Smart thinking, yeah. Perceptive. Except why wouldn't he have dumped you when he heard it was Palermo?'

'It was a test. If he tried, I'd have told him it wasn't Palermo.'

'Makes sense, I guess.'

'You're not mad at me?'

He glanced across. 'I'm here to drive, Mel. All I have to do is point this baby until we get caught or we don't. Athens, Sicily, Outer Kazakhstan, it's all the one to me.'

'What about Rossi? Y'know, with him being half-Sicilian and all.'

Rossi being about as half-Sicilian as melted igloos, Sleeps just shrugged. 'I won't tell him if you don't.'

'How d'you mean?'

'When we get to Athens, there won't be these big signs, "This Is Athens". Right?'

'But they'll be speaking Greek.'

'To Rossi, Italian would be all Greek.' Sleeps shrugged. 'If he twigs, we just tell him the truth.'

'And then what?'

'He'll vent a bit, sure. Probably mention Napoleon, how the little guy was never backstabbed by his troops, all this. Then he'll have a toke, a dab of crizz, remember something else he's pissed about.' Sleeps made a spiralling gesture with his forefinger. 'And the circle of life turns on evermore.'

Melody fell silent. Sleeps drove on into the darkness, wondering if driving on the wrong side of the road, the wrong side being actually the right side, was some kind of omen for where his life was headed. Then caught his first glimpse of the Alpine tunnels, brightly lit orange beacons in the blackness, their round mouths putting Sleeps in mind of sawn-off shotguns. So he got off the whole omens thing.

Mel, whispering now, said, 'You ever think about dumping him?'

'Nope.'

'Seriously?'

'Yep.'

'The thought never even occurred to you?'

'Why don't you just put it out there, Mel? Get it off your chest.'

'Well,' she said, 'it makes sense, doesn't it? The guy's a liability. I mean, you're the driver, I know where the cruise is going from. Why do we need him?'

'You just told me where the cruise is going from. So why do I need you?'

'Maybe I lied.'

'I was kind of presuming you did.'

'You don't trust me?'

'Don't take it personal. It's just best all round when no one trusts anyone, keeps everyone on their toes.'

'I thought,' she said, 'back on the ferry, you and me had a connection.'

'No disrespect, Mel, but you're a straight, a civilian.' Sleeps flicked his head in the general direction of the low drone buzzing from the rear. 'Who's now driving through Europe in a stolen car with two fuckwits and a stash of stamped gak in the trunk. That kind of desperate measure, it makes me wonder what kind of desperate times you got going on you're not telling anyone about.'

'I told you, I'm making this movie.'

'Sure. Butch Cassidy and the Zorba Kid.'

'You don't believe me?'

'I'd like to. Really, I'd love to think you were on the level.'

'If it's good enough for Rossi—'

'Rossi doesn't give a shit, Mel. You think he's a moron, he believes all this movie crap'll pan out?' He shook his head. 'Right now you could tell him, I dunno, you're the reincarnation of Maria Callas off to marry Onassis all over again, the guy'd play along, ask you to sing him 'The Wild Colonial Boy'. Rossi wants Karen, the money, and you're putting him beside her. That's as far as it goes for Rossi.'

'But not for you.'

'I'm not so worried about the money. Being honest, it'll be a miracle if we ever catch up with Karen. So I'm along for the ride, just enjoying the buzz, the drive.' The crizz glowing deep down in his system. 'Know what'd spoil that? If I got the impression I was the one being taken for a ride.'

'By me.'

'Rossi, I know why he's here. And I'm the one driving him. That leaves you.'

Melody stared out into the darkness, her face blue-tinged from the glow of the dashboard lights. The glare of oncoming headlights splashing her yellowy once in a while. 'You want the truth?' she said, so quietly Sleeps barely heard her over the snoring, the hum of the Beamer. 'I can't write for shit.'

'That's probably a good way to be thinking,' Sleeps said. 'You were to tell me you were terrific all the time, I'd be worried, wondering if you weren't a bit deluded. But look, those guys at the Institute you mentioned, they wouldn't have given you, what, two grand, to write a movie if they thought you weren't any good.'

'They didn't even read the script,' Mel said. 'They just liked the idea, how it had politicians in there.'

'Right.'

'See,' she said, 'you're writing porn scripts, there's not much call for real people, what they call character development. It's like, "Do we go wham-bam thank you ma'am, or just wham-ma'am?"'

'I always prefer a bit of bam,' Sleeps said.

'Sure. But take the new story. Right now the script has Jack and Judy,' Mel said, 'heading for Greece. Yeah?'

'Go on.'

'Well, that's just it. They're heading for Greece. Like in a straight line, A to B.'

'No bam.'

'So I'm wondering, what if Jack was thinking about dumping Judy. Or vice versa.'

'Get some sand in the Vaseline,' Sleeps said.

'Conflict, yeah. Like,' Mel said, 'Judy thinks she's being dumped? How's she going to react?'

'And this,' Sleep said, 'is why you're asking me to dump Rossi. See what I say, if I play along. Hoping for some bam.'

Mel nodding. 'Only now it's too late. Now you'll be thinking, "How's this going to sound in a movie?" Trying to come up with a snappy line, instead of just saying it.'

'You want to know what a real bad guy might say, he got that kind of proposal.'

'I don't know any criminal types, Gary. You're the best I've got.'

Sleeps nodding along. 'All I can tell you is what *I'd* say, Mel. And right now Rossi owes me five gees, my cut off the stash Karen stole from him, this whether or not he finds Karen. Plus, this FARCO thing ever takes off, he's promised me president for life. Being honest,' he shrugged, 'I've a pretty good idea I'll be seeing no five gees, no president for life. Only right now I'm cruising Europe in a Beamer with a decent chance of going down for soft time.'

'See,' Mel said, 'that right there is screwing with the story. Like, who's interested in watching a movie about a guy who *wants* to get caught?'

'You're saying, where's the bam?'

'Well . . .'

Sleeps licked the tip of his forefinger and dabbed it into the foil wrap on the dashboard, snorted a pinch up each nostril, rubbed the remainder into his gums. 'How about this?' he said. 'How about, you wait 'til I'm having a snooze, you mention to Rossi about dumping me? Maybe tell him I was the one suggested dumping him.'

Mel considered. 'You're not worried he'd freak?'

'That's the whole point, right? But I warn you now, you do it and you'll have all the bam you can handle. You'll be up to your tits, pardon my French, in bam.'

'You think?'

'A-wop-bop-a-loo-bop,' Sleeps said, 'a-wop-*boom*-bam.'

Ray

'So that's Trieste we didn't get to see,' Karen said. 'And now you're saying we won't see Corfu either.'

Up on deck smoking, leaning on the rail, Ray guessed the occasional glow here and there was Albania, its huge dark bulk rearing up into the Balkans, stars glittering if he craned his neck all the way back.

'Right now,' he said, 'the priority is to make the cruise. Then, we know for sure no one's getting screwed, specifically Terry, we can go anywhere we want. Maybe even come back and see Corfu. Either way, we're seeing that ferry off.'

'And then making our getaway.'

'That's the basic idea.'

'Except you already said, there's no getaway as such. We're *getting* away. All the time worried about Doyle sharking you.'

'You're the one who's worried about Doyle.'

'Right now,' Karen said, 'I'm actually more worried that you're not.'

'Doyle didn't strike me as the kind to hold a grudge. I mean, she was hacked off, OK. But she's a cop. She'll be practical.'

'This is how well you know her. You can predict how she's going to react, and for how long.'

'Doyle's the same as anyone else. She has her limits.'

'And you know what they are.'

'I can make an educated guess.'

'I'm all ears.'

'I'm thinking the Caribbean might be a jump too far for her.'

'The Caribbean?'

Ray jerked a thumb in the general direction of Albania. 'I served in there,' he said. 'Way back in there. When I was with the Rangers, a peace-keeping mission in Kosovo. Six-month tour. Anyway,' he said, 'this guy I served with, he's out now, running an op in the Caribbean based out of Haiti. Has the security franchise for an internet provider set-up, they're expanding into the Caribbean, Central America. Said he could always use a guy could handle himself.'

'You're thinking,' Karen said, 'about going to the Caribbean.'

'I'm saying it's an option. One that's probably beyond Doyle's limits, even if she ever found out where I was.'

'And where's that leave me?'

'The issue,' Ray said, 'far as I understand it, is me and Doyle. You being worried about how I'm not worried about her.'

'While you're still with me and Anna, sure.'

'This is what I'm getting at,' Ray said. 'If I'm gone you don't have to worry about Doyle no more. Or about me not worrying about Doyle.' He sparked another Lucky, no Marlboro Lights on the ferry. 'Or am I missing something here?'

'Like what?'

'Like I don't know. Maybe something about Doyle and me, you haven't gotten around to saying it yet.'

'I just said it.'

'Not this horseshit,' Ray said, 'some outside shot about Doyle maybe prowling me.'

Karen, eyes hidden away behind mirrored shades at four in the morning, the electric-blue hair glowing weirdly in the moonlight, said, 'You ever listen to jazz, Ray?'

'Not by choice.'

'What they say about jazz is, if it has to be explained you'll never get it.'

Ray sucked on the Lucky. 'So now it's jazz. It's jazz, it's Doyle, it's Madge. It's Anna.' He exhaled hard. 'You see it?'

'See what?'

'It's never *you*, Karen.'

'It's never me how?'

Ray flipped the Lucky, two in a row too harsh after the Marlboro Lights. He said, tasting the tar, 'We get into Patra? There's a train overland to Athens.'

'You told me this already.'

'The train'll get you into Piraeus, the port, or damn near.'

'We've been over—'

'Then, the ferries take you out to the islands.'

Karen folded her arms. 'Your point being?'

'To get this far, to Greece, you needed a driver. Except now you don't need a driver.'

'You're bailing?'

'Now I've got you here, I'm a liability.'

'I'm asking,' Karen said, 'if you're bailing out.'

'Let's say it's more in the way of letting myself be pushed.'

'Don't try and fake me, Ray. I don't fake.'

'It's another six, seven hours,' Ray said, 'to Patra. Gives you plenty of time to think it over. Then, you want to find me, I'll be easy found.'

Karen getting the twist in her jaw again. 'You want to be found,' she said, 'you better be lying out somewhere so's I trip over your legs.'

Ray dug in his pocket, came up with the van's keys and laid them on top of the ferry's rail. 'Your call,' he said.

Madge

Madge wasn't sure if she was rehearsing an alibi or making a confession. Telling Doyle – an imaginary Doyle, the detective sitting at the cute hotel room table taking notes – how, being honest, she'd sometimes fantasized about what it'd be like to have Frank at the business end of a gun. 'Or maybe,' she said, 'tucked into an iron maiden.' Except the likelihood of that ever coming to pass had

always been size zero slim, a thing you read about in magazines but
only ever happens to the lucky few, the insanely dedicated. 'But then
it's Frank himself who starts the ball rolling. Has me snatched, we're
married twenty years, we have *twins* for Chrissakes, he puts me in a
place where this guy's handing me a gun, Frank's helpless in handcuffs.
Like, what's a reasonable woman to do?'

Madge, suffering night sweats and hot flushes, pacing the hotel
room with dawn in the post, couldn't decide if she was finally
coming menopausal or just suffering a bad case of the guilties.
Although guilty, she clarified for Doyle's sake, only in the technical
sense. As in, legally. The way Madge was seeing it, if anyone was
guilty for Frank being missing presumed dead, it was Frank. No,
not guilty – responsible.

She filched one of the sleeping Terry's cigarettes and went out
on to the balcony. Stood there smoking and gazing out over the
piazza, wondering what the difference was, legally speaking,
between guilty and responsible. Not really caring, though.
Everything felt a bit conceptual right now, theoretical. It was like,
she thought, being caught in a bubble looking out at the world
carrying on as normal, Madge watching it turn, interested but not
particularly engaged, like drinking a coffee on some terrace, curious
as to what people were wearing, why they were wearing it, how
in Christ's name they thought they could get away with knee-high
boots and three-quarter-length jeans with fat turn-ups over calf-
muscles they'd swiped off a baby hippo. The Italians, Christ, all
fashion, no style.

She felt weirdly immune, emotionally dislocated. But in a good
way, for maybe the first time in her life. Knowing, sure, the long arm
of the law could come reaching out across the horizon any minute,
knock on the bubble's door, crook a finger – except, if it did?

Then it did. And she'd deal with that if it happened.

Her problem right now, she told Doyle, was the twins. Only it
was in the past couple of hours, Madge pacing and thinking back
over the last two decades, that she had come to the conclusion that
the twins had *always* been the problem.

Like, how probable was it Madge would've stuck with Frank for
twenty years if it hadn't been for Jeanie and Liz? And for what?
So they could grow up to watch *Jersey Shore* like it was *Open
University*? Madge had done her best by them, at least until their
teens, before the twins got sucked into the race to become the

skinniest twit on YouTube and Madge turned to nurturing her preferred deadly duo, the old Prozac-and-vodka one-two.

But really, what did she owe them?

Wrong question, Madge told herself, crushing the cigarette butt on the balcony rail. She slipped back into the room, luxuriating in the sensation of the heavy velvet curtains sliding across her bare arms and shoulders. Round about now was when the twins, old enough to jaunt around the world, educated to the point where they were on their way to college, needed to realize how much they owed the woman who'd been ripped open giving birth.

Madge was hoping they'd do the maths and come up owing her nothing. No demands, no more whingeing, an absolute moratorium on constant, low-level grief about clothes, hair, boys and money.

Madge, OK, was the one responsible for bringing them into the world. So sure, she'd done the crime. But she'd done her time too. And the least she was entitled to, the very least, was to walk away free and clear, debt to society paid.

Terry, she thought, looking down at him now where he lay humped over in the bed, wanted to take a cruise, live the high life, then take her home, he said, to face the music. Madge imagining a whole orchestra lined up in a row, a firing squad.

She shrugged. Maybe because Frank had been such a nut for Rossini, was always playing opera like it made him some kind of half-assed intellectual, Madge had never been a big fan of orchestras, all that classical horseshit. Terry, on the other—

The thought arrowed into her mind so fast she felt herself recoil. And then its enormity struck her, thunder arriving in the lightning's wake. Afterwards, huddled on the toilet, still shivering, she wondered if the reason she hadn't seen it was because it was so big, so obvious.

How Terry'd had it all arranged.

Frank, the fool, bringing the heat down on everyone, Karen and Ray first but then Terry too, Terry the man behind Madge getting snatched, the guy who'd brought it all to Ray.

She wondered if Terry had made Frank disappear because he was a potential witness or just to make an example of him – this is what happens when you fuck with Terry Swipes.

Not that it mattered now. What mattered now was, Terry wasn't Madge's alibi.

Madge was Terry's.

Melody

'What is he?' Mel said. 'A cop?'

'Dunno,' Sleeps said.

'A soldier?'

'Could be.'

'That's some weird marching he's got going on there.'

'I'm guessing he's drunk.'

'Oh.' Mel leaned forward to peer into the wing mirror. 'Think he fell asleep?'

'If he did, he's sleepwalking this way.'

'Rossi, I mean.'

'Sssh. Let me do the talking, yeah?'

The cop, or maybe soldier, the guy wearing dusty fatigues, weaved across the tarmac towards them, one hand upraised as if telling them to stop. Except they'd been stopped twenty minutes now, Rossi coming awake fast with a look of fright on his face, bawling at Sleeps to pull *over*, he was touching cloth, the turtle showing its head.

So Sleeps pulled in on to the apron of a little supermarket, the place still closed this early, the sky lightening to a dull maroon over the crest of the hills rising sheer on their left. It was, Mel had decided, the most idyllic setting she'd ever seen for a supermarket, tucked neatly into the elbow of a bay that opened up on the other side of the road, rowboats moored and bobbing gently on the metallic glimmerings of the Adriatic half-glimpsed between the pines. Even the sight of Rossi shambling away across the tarmac into the scrub, one hand jammed between his buttocks, hadn't spoiled the view entirely.

And then this guy had come stumbling down off the hill, out of the darkness into the orange glow of the supermarket's forecourt.

Sleeps wound down the window, leaned out. 'How's it going?' he said.

The cop, or soldier, held up his hand again, peering now at the registration plate, the tax and insurance discs. Late twenties, maybe, but grizzled with it, stubble running to grey. A hard, strong jaw, eyes dark under the peak of the forage cap. Mel, noting the leather strap running diagonally across his chest that suggested he was carrying some kind of machine gun, felt a frisson tingle up the back of her thighs.

He came around to Sleeps' side and grunted.

'Sorry,' Sleeps said. 'We're tourists. Don't suppose you speak English?'

The cop, or soldier, growled this time, then hawked a gunger that gurgled in his throat before he spat it out. He held out his hand and made the universal gimme sign.

'Passports?' Sleeps said.

The guy shook his head.

'Driver's licence?' Sleeps hazarded.

The cop, the soldier, was taking it personal now. He straightened up, lurched backwards half a step, then tugged on the leather strap so the machine gun slid around into view, leaving it high on his hip. He jabbed a finger in the general direction of north, muttered something guttural.

'That's right,' Sleeps said. 'We've just come from Split. Heading down into Dubrovnik now. Looking forward to seeing that old city, man. Hey, don't suppose you were around when the Serbs were—'

The cop, the soldier, punched the door with the side of his fist. Wriggled his shoulders and jabbed his finger north again, then made a lifting gesture.

'You want to look in the trunk?' Sleeps said. 'Sure thing, no worries.' He made to open the door, get out. The guy slammed it closed again, then pointed down towards Sleeps' feet, made a jerking motion this time. Sleeps held up both his hands, palms out. 'OK, man. Relax.' He reached down, tugged on the trunk-release. 'There,' he said. 'It's open.'

With one last growl, which even Mel could interpret as a warning to stay put, the guy staggered around to the back of the Beamer, hauled on the trunk. Up it came, blotting out their rear-view vision.

'What if he finds the package?' she whispered.

'Then he finds it,' Sleeps said, sounding grim. Melody glanced across, then felt a more intense frisson, one that knifed into her guts, Sleeps with the little gun, his .22, holding it flat against his right thigh.

'I thought you said that wasn't loaded,' she hissed.

'Sssh. He'll hear you.'

'But—'

'Oh-*ho*!' croaked the guy from the rear.

'Fuck,' Sleeps said. Gently, very gently, he eased the door-release towards himself until it clicked. 'Get down,' he said. 'Get *way* down.'

'Don't *do* it, Gary. The guy's got a—'

There came a high-pitched yelp from the rear, swiftly followed by the Beamer rocking on its springs. A number of dull thuds. Then a bang as the trunk slammed down.

Rossi slid into the back shaking one hand out, the knuckles skinned and bleeding. But looking at his other hand, eyes fixed on the machine-pistol that gleamed blackly in the dim light, a mix of metal and plastic that Melody wanted to believe made it a toy.

'An Uzi,' he breathed. 'Sleeps? It's a motherlovin' *Uzi.*'

'Looks like it,' Sleeps said, reaching forward to replace the .22 in the glove compartment.

'What d'you think, is it a sign?'

'Is he . . .?' Mel swallowed. 'Where's the guy?'

'In the trunk.'

'Is he OK?'

'The best,' Rossi said, using his sleeve to polish the Uzi's barrel.

'He's not dying or anything, is he?'

'Nope.'

'Or, like, already dead.'

'I barely tapped him, Mel. The guy just collapsed.'

Sleeps put the Beamer in gear, indicated right, rolled off the apron. 'You ever shot an Uzi before?' he asked Rossi.

'Never, no. Remind me to make a wish before I blow some fucker away.'

Mel tried to clear her throat and made a sound like a strangled budgie. Sleeps looked across. 'Now'd be a good time to walk away, Mel. We drop you off, you take a holiday in Dubrovnik, then head for home. No one's any the wiser.'

Mel had a flash on herself standing behind the travel agency counter, Gary lumbering through the door doing his Javier Bardem schtick. The time to walk away, she realized now, had been when he'd lifted his shirt to show her the pearl-handled .22. When she didn't scream or run out the back of the shop, just stared him down, hoping to hear some bona fide gangster patter, the die had been cast.

Now things were getting a little intense, Rossi waving around an Uzi, a guy bundled in the trunk. But Mel believed that if she held her nerve just a little bit longer, she could ride back to Dublin with a big bag of cash, enough to repay the Institute and tell them to go fuck themselves all the way to the Cayman Islands, Mel with a story like no one would believe and enough seed capital to get the wheels rolling herself.

'That's fine, Gary,' she said. 'I'm just wondering if the guy's bleeding hard. I mean, that's a genuine reproduction Louis Vuitton I've got back there.'

Doyle

Niko saw Doyle off at the airport, Doyle taking the short hop out to Santorini, Sparks booking all the way through with a quick turnaround in Athens and due in to Santorini on an afternoon flight. This after Niko put his foot down. No way was he having Doyle, unaccredited and on holiday, hanging around Piraeus and getting herself spotted waiting for Karen and Ray, maybe starting a fire-fight that'd get Italian tourists massacred, as tempting as the prospect might seem just talking about it.

She'd be forty minutes away, he said. First sight of a pirate wolf and Niko'd be on the phone, get Doyle back in for the good stuff, the paperwork.

Doyle said no way, Karen and Ray were crafty fuckers, she was staying on it, camping out in the ferry port until they came through or they didn't.

'Crafty, huh?' Niko said. 'And you never heard about Greeks bearing gifts?'

The point being, apparently, that the Greeks had basically invented world literature by being the sneakiest bastards on the planet. Which Doyle didn't find very reassuring. 'Ray,' she said, 'he'll burn down your Trojan horse and then ride off on it into the sunset. I'm serious.'

But so was Niko. Doyle was on his patch and he wasn't letting her put herself or anyone else in any danger. Her options were Santorini or a one-way ticket home.

Besides, if Karen and Ray were as smart as Doyle seemed to think, it wasn't just Piraeus she had to worry about. Niko'd need to send descriptions to Thessaloniki, Patras, Pylos, Corinth . . . basically, half the ports in Greece, or so it sounded to Doyle.

The other thing, he said, if Ray really was as sneaky as she made out, Santorini – Niko calling it Thira – was the island hub for all the cruise liners. If Karen and Ray came into Greece worried about getting caught, and snuck through, they'd have loosened up by the time they made Santorini, more likely to make a mistake. 'And you're right there,' Niko said, 'calling me.'

If they didn't show up, he said, he could take a few days off later in the week, come join Doyle and Sparks in the islands. But that was his best offer.

Doyle'd had worse offers.

She went through the departure gate backwards, fluttering her fingers at him, specifically the finger with the fake emerald. Doyle had told him the night before, Niko walking her back to her hotel, how the ring wasn't an engagement ring per se, more of a promise from this guy she was seeing, Ted. Niko just shrugged. Doyle had seen movies with less in them than that shrug.

The flight was all take-off and landing, took two minutes more than the forty Niko'd said. Doyle taxied down from the airport high on a plateau and winkled out a place to stay in Fira, then set off to rent a moped.

Found a beach down the coast, a shack that served beers and ice cream, club sandwiches. Ordered a frappé, then changed her mind and had a cocktail, a Tequila Sunrise, it just seemed right, sitting out on the veranda overlooking the beach under a wide umbrella, the Aegean like a vast sapphire sparkling up new. A narrow spit way off to the right edging out into the sea, a tiny white church perched at the very end. The breeze still balmy, although Doyle could smell it on the salty air, the heat that'd be bearing down any time soon.

Except just when everything was coming up Doyle, this professor type gets in her space. Fifty-ish, a narrow head shaved tight to the sides and bald up the middle, the bald bit red and peeling, sunscreen glistening, like he was trying to sauté the bare flesh. Wearing horn-rimmed specs, pushing them back up his sweaty nose all the time, the guy was sponging his brow every three seconds with a damp white handkerchief.

'Of course,' he said, droning on like some massive four-eyed insect, Doyle itching to just swat him, 'most people think it was the eruption that destroyed the Minoan civilisation, whereas it was actually the Myceneans invading from the north.'

'Kicking the crap,' Doyle said, 'out of these half-drowned Minoans.'

'In a manner of speaking, yes. But by then their civilization had run its course. They were already in terminal decline.'

'So the Mycenaean guys did them a favour, putting them out of their misery.'

'That's one way of looking at it, certainly. Although the Minoans might not agree.'

'They probably wouldn't,' Doyle agreed, 'being drowned three thousand years and all.'

The guy not really listening, the Adam's apple trapped above the buttoned-up shirt working hard as he made his play. 'If you'd like to see the remnants of the volcano while you're on Santorini,' he said, 'I'd be delighted to be your guide.'

'Sorry, but looking into holes in the ground isn't on my list of priorities right now.' Doyle with no plans beyond her second Tequila Sunrise and a vague intention of meeting Sparks off her flight.

'It's actually an island,' the guy said. He pointed out over the tiny white church at a clump of black smudges visible in the horizon's haze. 'Santorini is just part of the rim of the ancient volcano.'

'No shit.'

'There's a boat tour,' he said, scraping his chair closer. 'You get to see all the islands and walk up on the volcanic one. At the top they'll let you hold some rocks, feel how hot they are.'

'Because this is why I've come on holiday. To fondle coal.'

'Then they'll dig into the earth so you can see the steam emerge. Most people think it's smoke,' he smiled, 'but it's actually steam.'

'The ground is steaming?'

'It's live. The volcano, I mean. I didn't mention that?'

'No one,' Doyle said, 'mentioned that.'

'Amazing, isn't it?'

'What, that there's lunatics who want to live next door to a volcano?'

The guy got a bang out of that one. 'The balloon isn't likely to go up any time soon,' he said. 'And even if it was, there's an early-warning system in place. We can read volcanoes now, we know when they're going to erupt.'

'This,' Doyle said, 'by comparison with the dopey Minoans, who didn't know volcanoes from pigshit.'

'It certainly would have helped their cause if—'

'I have my own early-warning system.'

'Oh?'

'Yeah. Someone tells me a volcano is live, I hop a plane.'

The guy chuckling. 'I really don't think there's any need—'

'A guy shot at me,' Doyle said, 'three days ago. So you can see how I might feel about unnecessary risks.'

Doyle feeling these strange tremors in her shoulders, maybe in sympathy with the ancient volcano. Tapping into its memory, the after-shocks still buried in the island's subconscious. Realising, now, why she'd kept herself so busy the last few days, flying here, scooting there, chasing Madge, then Ray . . . Doyle, fourteen years on the force, had never been shot at before. Now, for the first time in her life, she knew for sure she was going to die, and not in theory, some Buddhist grand-scheme bullshit. She *felt* it, a sucking black hole in the pit of her stomach, how she was already dying.

Doyle and the Minoans, in terminal decline.

One time Doyle had lain back in the bath after pulling the stopper and let the water drain away the deliciously light floating, feeling her body get heavy and awkward again, the walls of the bath closing in like a porcelain coffin. Doyle'd never done it again.

The guy looked a little green now under the sunburn. '*Shot* at you?' he croaked.

'With a gun.' Doyle pointed her forefinger, cocked her thumb. 'It's why I'm here, on the run.'

'You mean he's still . . .'

'Yep.' Doyle snapped down her thumb. 'Bang, you're dead.' Then drained her glass, the last of the Tequila Sunrise sliding down smooth. 'So,' she said, beaming a bright smile, 'when did you say that boat tour is leaving?'

Karen

'What'll I do with the key?' Karen said. 'I mean, just leave it in the ignition? What?'

Karen unloading the khaki duffel, her sports holdall with the few essentials she'd picked up in the ferry's shops. Then she got back in the cab again and filched the Tom Waits from the glove compartment. Wondering if she should leave the van unlocked or lock it up and hide the key somewhere, the parking bay cavernous in the bowels of the ferry, everyone revving their engines despite the signs that said not to, making it hard for Karen to hear herself think.

In the end she left the key behind the front wheel on the driver's side, Ray'd find it or he wouldn't. *His* call, she thought, making her way forward.

'See,' she said, 'if he can say that, how it's never about me, he just doesn't get it. I told him straight off, soon as we met, I had priorities. One, me. Two, you. Except,' she said, scratching Anna's forehead, 'not necessarily in that order, they're just two sides of the same thing. And if he doesn't get that, he's not the guy I thought he was.'

Anna growled, a puzzled-sounding note in her coarse timbre.

'I know, hon.' Karen could sympathize, Anna drugged up for two days straight, coming around in a dungeon full of noise with a hangover to beat all. The front of the ferry clanking down now, light streaming in around the edges. Anna growling against the revving engines, someone back there honking because he was stuck behind the van, no one arriving to pick it up.

Karen tugged on Anna's ear and stoically accepted a lashing from her bushy tail. 'What he's saying is, it's never about *him*. Am I right?'

Anna barked short and hard, rammed her flank against Karen's leg.

'Yeah,' Karen said softly, 'I liked him too. But c'mon, the guy has to fit in around us, he knows that. He doesn't, what happens to you?'

The front of the ferry clanged down on the dock, the port bustling with delivery trucks, buzzing mopeds, guys like admirals in their white suits shouting orders that couldn't be heard over the revving engines, the ferry's rumble. Karen bent down, hugged Anna to her. 'What happens to you,' she whispered, 'is you get abandoned, maybe wind up with someone even worse than Rossi.'

Anna stiffened, then threw back her huge head with a violence that sent Karen stumbling backwards, catching her heel on a metal stud and slamming down hard on the floor, right on her ass-bone. The murderous howl, magnified in the cavernous parking bay, drowned out everything, the ferry's rumble included.

When Karen got back on her feet again all she could see was these tiny little black Os, every mouth in the port wide open.

Rossi

'Sicily's an island now?' Rossi said, crossing the observation deck, the breeze billowing out the fatigues so he flapped like an old sail. 'Since when?'

'There was, um, an earthquake about two years back,' Sleeps said, looking to Mel. 'That right, Mel? Two years ago?'

'I think it was three,' she said.

'You being inside,' Sleeps said, 'you probably didn't hear about it. Anyway, it broke off from the rest of Italy, damn near sank. Terrible, it was. Millions dead.'

'They tell you nothing inside,' Rossi groused. 'I mean, I probably lost actual family, cousins and shit.' Elbowing in at the rail now, flashing some dead-eye to the guy about to complain, this asshole in a straw sunhat. Letting him know, fair warning, you don't fuck with Rossi Francis Assisi Callaghan. Backed him off a little, got some elbow room, talking space, then plonked down Mel's Louis Futon, put a knee on it and leaned his elbows on the rail. The others huddling in close, Mel in the middle smelling like, it was the only way Rossi could describe it, the Arabian Nights. He up-jutted his chin at the approaching port. 'And this earthquake's why Palmero looks like Calcutta's evil twin.'

'That's not, um, Palmero,' Mel said. 'Not as such.'

'No?'

'It's Palermo's port. The actual city is way back in the hinterland.'

'The what now?'

Rossi was feeling beat down, the buzz from the Uzi draining out fast. First all the crap at Dubrovnik, Sleeps bollocking on about it was Italy's world-famous mediaeval city, how it was traditional, you were going to Sicily for the first time, to ferry down the coast from Dubrovnik. Then Mel, gipping on about the blood on her Louis Futon – although Rossi was wondering who'd sleep on a pull-out bed from a bag that size. Plus they were running low on crizz, Sleeps being narcoleptic and hoovering it up.

And if that wasn't enough, Melody starts in about him smoking in the car, how she's getting half-stoned. Rossi was tempted to ask her to pay for half the baggie. He tried it hanging out the window and got in one good draw but the blifter went off like a Roman candle at 120 kph and Rossi nearly inhaled the flaming tip, sparks singeing his eyelids.

'The hinterland,' Sleeps explained, knuckling his bloodshot eyes and then waving vaguely in the direction of the mountains, 'being the way-back-behind. We get into Patras, the port, we still need to go cross-country to, uh, Palmero.'

'The cruise isn't leaving from this Patras?'

'Patras,' Sleeps said, 'is where the industrial stuff goes in and out. Oil tankers and whatnot. For cruise liners? It's Palmero.'

'Fuck.'

'We still got nine, ten hours,' Sleeps said. 'Plenty of time. Right, Mel?'

Mel nodded.

'OK,' Rossi said to Sleeps, 'so the Beamer – I say we booby-trap it. Wire the fucker up to the gas tank so it shorts out when they turn the key.' He gave a wristy twist. 'Ka-*boom*.'

'And fry someone,' Sleeps said. 'Start a manhunt.'

'What, I'm a moron now? I'll be ringing it in, Sleeps. Fair warning.'

'This making it a booby-trap everyone knows about. Besides, you issued many bomb-warnings in Italian lately?'

'You got any better suggestions?'

'Sure. We leave it sitting where it is. Walk away.'

'And get us nabbed on forensics?'

'Forensics?'

'One eyelash'll do it,' Rossi warned. 'You think you're free and clear, then bang, they've matched a sweaty spot to the crack of your ass and you're looking at five-to-ten, hard time.'

Sleeps made goggles of his fingers, stretched out his eye sockets. 'First they'd need to know it was us driving the Beamer,' he said. 'This being a motor we boosted the other side of the continent. Then they'll need enough reason to chase us into, y'know, Sicily. Which I think is like a foreign jurisdiction for Italy.'

'We got one of their Uzis,' Rossi pointed out. He adjusted the forage cap so it sat low on the turban, angled rakish over one eye. 'Plus, a uniform.'

'Sure,' Sleeps said. 'But that's not exactly something that'll get them swearing out extradition warrants. More likely they'll want to keep quiet about that one.'

'I'm just saying, we don't want to take any chances we don't have to.'

'Other than, say, abducting a cop, or a soldier, we're still not sure which he is. Then smuggling his assault rifle across the border, this while we're muling enough gak to chill the Foreign fucking Legion. With,' he inclined his head at Mel, 'a volunteer hostage in tow.'

'I'm talking about taking chances,' Rossi said with quiet dignity, 'not what they call adapting to circumstance.'

'Which reminds me,' Sleeps said. 'The guy in the trunk – we booby-trapping him too?'

'The fuck's the point in that? The car's already wired. Like, he's *in* the fucking thing.'

'Sure. But you're tipping 'em off, remember? So no one gets hurt, they don't call in any choppers, send an aircraft carrier steaming up from the gulf.'

'Meaning,' Rossi said, seeing it now, 'the guy survives, he can identify us, right? In a line-up.'

'On the remote chance we get ourselves caught, yeah.'

'Be just like a copper,' Rossi said, 'to squeal.'

'It's not so much squealing when you're a cop,' Sleeps said, 'as it's gathering evidence.'

'This is how bogey a cop is.'

'It's his *job*, Rossi. How he gets paid.'

'You're saying he'll do it.'

'See if it was me, I was due a rocket up my hoop over some tourists swiped my Uzi when I was blind drunk some night? I'd say whatever I was told.'

Rossi, just one of those things, he did his best thinking with a finger in his ear. Now he dug all the way in there, rooted around. 'We can't just dump him over the rail,' he said. The port already close enough to make out cranes, gantries, the ant-like chaos of the docks. 'We'd be seen.'

'Probably, yeah. And besides, if you're going that radical, you could just leave him in the trunk, wire the car, tip nobody off. Except we're not doing corpses today.'

'I'm just ruling out options.' Rossi examined the tip of his finger, rolled a little orange ball between the tip of thumb and forefinger, then flicked it into the breeze. 'I say we blind him.'

'*Blind* him?' Mel said.

'Cuts out the wondering if he knows us. Doesn't matter, he can't see us anyway. We could be the Stooges, he's pawing our faces trying to work out who's Curly.'

'I bags Iggy,' Sleeps said.

'Blind him how?' Mel said.

Rossi had a good tug on his lobe. 'Battery acid? Or, y'know.' He held out his thumbs and twisted them upwards, scooping.

Mel put a hand to her mouth.

'Now you're thinking lateral,' Sleeps said. 'But I got an idea, it's a bit more lateral, where no one has to go blind or get dumped over any rails or burned up.'

Rossi squinted so hard trying to work it around he got a burning sensation where his ear used to be and still came up with only one option. 'You want to let him walk away? A cop?'

'Or soldier,' Sleeps said. 'And it's more that he drives rather than walks.'

Madge

'Still no joy,' Terry said, frowning at his phone, Karen's number ringing out again.

'There won't be,' Madge said, scanning for culture through the cab's window. Any culture at all, Madge wasn't fussy. Anything other than half-built high-rise apartment blocks, the only relief an occasional splash of graffiti, reds and yellows mainly. Although, that being in Greek, it wasn't much help. 'I was there when Rossi threw all the phones in the lake,' she said, trying to remember how many times she'd said it now, 'and Karen didn't go after hers. No one did, none of us being kitted out with scuba gear at the time.' She closed her eyes, pinched the bridge of her nose. 'Ray hasn't been in touch yet?'

'I told you, this is a burner phone.' Terry had explained last night, in detail, how it wasn't such a bright idea to bring your own phone on a trip, leaving a record of how you were taking calls in strange places.

'I know it's not your phone,' Madge said. 'What I'm asking is if he's been in touch back home, left a number you can call.' Like any reasonable person might, she didn't add.

Terry grunted. 'Ray's a bit brighter than that.'

'He's bright,' Madge said. 'And we're bright too, not leaving any traces.' Terry nodded. 'So how come everyone's in the dark?' she said.

Terry glanced across. 'You OK?'

'I'm fine, Terry. Really, you don't have to keep asking. If it does get to the point where I'm not fine, you'll be the first to know. Like, who else would I tell?'

'All right then.'

'Although,' she said, 'there is something I've been wanting to say.'

'Yeah?'

All morning she'd been wondering, it being Friday already, when exactly it was that her divorce kicked in. First thing in the morning, office hours? Or noon, for some weird reason? Or was she officially divorced since one minute past midnight, something like that?

She said, 'Let's just say, hypothetically speaking, that Frank didn't just wander off from the hospital, roll down a hill in his wheelchair and fall in a river. That Ray, just for an example, thought Frank might be a loose end that should be dealt with. Or it might even have been Rossi. Or someone we don't know had a grudge.'

Terry studying her now, the cab pulling up in front of the hotel. 'This is what's bugging you,' he said.

'Well,' she said, 'if that's what happened, and I admit it's a big if, but if that *is* what happened, then whoever made Frank disappear basically dropped me in it from a very great height.'

'Madge. We've been through—'

'That's not the point I'm trying to make, Terry. Just let me finish, OK?'

'Sure.'

Madge, the bellhop coming down the steps now, this other guy dressed like a Swiss general opening her door, had an instinct to keep moving in a straight line for the rest of her life, just keep on circling the globe, repeating nothing. Mistakes, especially. 'I guess what I'm trying to say,' she said, holding up a hand to the Swiss general, pulling the car door to again, 'is that if I had the person responsible for Frank being missing in front of me now, I think I'd want to tell him it was worth it. Even knowing that I'll have to go back home and act like a loon to try and get off on temporary insanity, wind up all over the front pages, I'm some kind of rabid Black Widow.' She shrugged. 'It'd still be worth it.'

'It would, huh?'

'I don't know if Ray happened to mention it,' she said, 'but Frank date-raped me when I was a kid, sixteen years old, got me pregnant. Then, when it all came out, he agreed this deal with my father, how we'd have the kid adopted and Frank, once he finished his studies, became a doctor, he'd swing around again and marry me. So, and I don't know if you can understand this, but it was like every time we, y'know, it was like being raped all over again. I mean, it's horrible to think of them this way, but I can't help it . . .'

'The twins,' Terry said.

'Exactly.'

'I had no idea,' he said.

'No reason you should. But maybe you can appreciate now why everything that's happened might be worth it, no matter what goes wrong from here on in.'

'I'll bear that in mind,' Terry said. He reached across and patted the back of her hand. 'So what do you want to do?'

Madge considered. 'Right now, we have a couple of hours to kill, I wouldn't mind seeing the Acropolis.'

'No, I mean—'

'I know exactly what you mean, Terry. And I want to see the Acropolis.'

'I'll get directions,' he said.

'That's OK, I hear they put it on top of a hill.' She lifted his hand off hers, then held it for a moment and patted it gently. 'I'll find it on my own.'

Karen

K aren wondered what you might call a bad miracle, what the actual word for it was. Wondering too, Rossi with the brains of a pigeon, if he didn't have their homing instinct as well. For Karen, like. She peeked around the corner again, half-hoping she'd hallucinated him, bone-tired and spending way too long in paranoid Ray's company . . .

Nope. Rossi and the big guy, his muscle, and the girl, right there halfway down Platform 1, standing in the middle of a pile of luggage made it look like they were playing forts. Rossi jabbing a forefinger at the girl, making some point, wearing, Christ, some kind of *army* gear now? Karen couldn't keep up, Rossi quick-changing like Cher at Vegas.

She ducked back around the corner and hunkered down beside Anna, the girl curled around the khaki duffel under a wooden bench, her bushy tail covering her snout. The options being, one, find a cop, a security guard, start a rumour about Rossi smuggling dope. Karen didn't know for sure he was carrying but it was a safe bet, Rossi without dope was a pigeon on one wing. Except that way Karen'd be pulled into it too, making statements, how'd she know Rossi had the dope, getting into it with Greek cops, in Greek.

Or, two: use the milling crowd for cover and make a break straight across the platform on to the train, hoping Rossi didn't spot Anna.

Or worse, Anna spot Rossi.

Except then? Karen didn't like the idea of hiding out on a train to Athens for four or five hours praying Rossi didn't stumble across them, there being no good way to explain to the relevant authorities why your pet mostly-wolf has ripped out the throat of another passenger, mostly-rat though he might be.

She had another peek around the corner, making sure the brave defenders were still inside their little Alamo, then had a rummage through her bag, found Anna's muzzle. Anna whining as Karen strapped it on.

'I know, hon. But it's for your own good. Trust me.'

She sat on the bench with her chin on her palm, trying to work through it. At least now she knew Madge had told Rossi about the cruise. Ray, OK, had got that much right at least. Except Rossi was chasing Karen, the money. Which meant he had no issue with Madge. And Madge being with Terry, and Ray probably turning up to warn them off the cruise, Madge would have a nice little bodyguard detail to keep Rossi away from her.

Unless Terry took it bad, blamed Madge for Rossi turning up with his entourage in tow, Elton John in combat fatigues. Karen trying to get a read on Terry from what Ray had told her, trying to guess which way Terry'd jump. Karen's impression was the guy was a looker not a leaper. Ray'd said, 'To you, yeah. The guy's a pussycat you're not fucking him around. But Terry, he has the horror bad.'

'The horror?'

'Doing time. Some guys get it worse than others. Terry, maybe it's claustrophobia, some shit like that, I don't know, he doesn't like to talk about it. But anyone likely to put him away? Terry'll cut 'em out like that.' He'd snapped his fingers. 'I seen him do it, Karen.' Ray, solemn, placing the tip of a finger in the middle of his forehead, just above the bridge of his nose.

So just skipping out, jumping a ferry to the nearest island and lying low until Rossi got himself nabbed, it was only a matter of time, that wasn't a runner either. Karen, patting Anna's flank now, the girl getting restless in the confines of the noisy station, the heat oppressive, believed it was typical – the one time you actually need a guy around, just to bounce some ideas off, he's gone, taking off without so much as a sayonara. Trying now to put herself in Ray's frame of mind, wondering how he'd play this one out. He'd be cool, she knew that much, looking for ways to slide around the problem, not meet it head-on. One thing Ray was good at, she allowed, was getting his head up, looking out beyond the horizon. Giving off, it wasn't so much attitude as altitude. Like he was above all the crap until he took the decision to get involved.

She got up and peered around the corner again, wondering if Crockett and Bowie had been massacred by Santa Anna yet, or if she should just send in her own Anna, be done with it. Then heard, turning back to the bench, the penetrating growl like a tank on rumble-strips that Anna gave off when the girl was particularly pleased with herself.

The guy hunkered down beside the bench, tickling Anna under the muzzle, had a greying ponytail hanging loose between his shoulders, a red bandana up top, faded Ramones T-shirt, beige duck pants with zip pockets down the sides. Anna straining her throat so he could get right in there at her chest. The guy, Karen in her mind calling him Dee-Dee, smiling up at her now, slow and easy, nice even white teeth, the brown eyes warm.

He patted Anna way back on her head. 'Timber wolf, right?'

'Part husky,' Karen said. 'But she's mostly Siberian.'

'Russki, huh?' Pronouncing it 'Rooski', the drawl rolling out the word so far you could've pinned it down, mapped the Mason-Dixon line. When he stood the hems of the duck pants rose up and Karen could see he was going around barefoot. 'Can't say as I've ever met a Russki wolf with an eyepatch before.'

'Something I can do for you?' Karen said.

The guy, Dee-Dee, said, 'She's suffered some hardship. But I'm guessing, I've been watching you with her, it wasn't your doing.'

Karen, she was fritzed, the guy had the drawl going on, those warm brown eyes, a way with Anna she still wasn't sure she believed she'd just seen – anyway, she jerked a thumb in the direction of Platform 1. 'He's over there,' she said.

'Looking for you or her?'

'Me.'

'But you don't want to get into it with him right now.'

Karen, thinking how all she wanted right now was a long, deep, warm bath, just nodded.

'OK,' the guy said, taking a seat on the bench. 'So what're your options?'

Sleeps

'The train?' Rossi sweating hard out on Platform 1, flushed from carrying the Louis Vuitton, Rossi designated because he was the one wanted to keep the Uzi in there, Johnny Priest's gak packed away under what Melody called her skimpies. Although, Sleeps had noted, they were more skimpy by name than nature. 'You expect me to take the *train*?'

Mel said it was only four, five hours to Palermo. Which'd get them in with time to spare, the cruise not leaving until eight.

'All I'm asking,' Rossi said, 'is if I look to you like the Little Loser That Can.'

It had taken a while to sort out the soldier, some kind of Croatian reservist, a National Guard-type, but he finally got it – the Beamer for the Uzi, everyone's a winner. The guy drove a hard bargain, even hung-over, sitting there in his skanks in the bowels of the ferry with Rossi waving the .22 around, Rossi adamant he was keeping the fatigues. Eventually Mel had agreed to buy the guy's ticket back to Dubrovnik to seal the deal. Then down off the ferry into the port, Rossi for some reason pushing the suitcase rather than pulling, one of the little wheels gone wonky. Rossi steering it all over the port like he was divining for water. Puce even before they made the gate, inventing a whole new language, like he'd seen the Rapture and got Tourette's rather than the gift of tongues.

Once they made it outside, the possibilities, Mel rattling them off from the guide book, opened up more or less straight away – on the right the ferry terminal for the Ionian islands, with the bus station farther along the other side of the street. The train station opposite that, backing on to the sea. The place, when they got in, bristling with energy, engines ticking over, a PA crackling. And, man, *hot*.

'The next one,' Mel said, consulting the timetable that wasn't just a foreign language, Sleeps intrigued by a whole new alphabet, 'goes in ten minutes. From here, Platform One.'

'I'm leaving,' Rossi said, 'no fucking place from no platform fucking anything. You ever see Michael take a train?'

'Michael?' Mel said.

'Corleone,' Sleeps clarified.

Mel rolled her eyes. 'We could always cab out to the airport,' she said, 'take a flight.'

'Because,' Rossi approved, patting the suitcase with the Uzi nestled inside, 'there'll be no customs or X-ray machines on internal flights.'

'I don't know about that,' Mel said. 'But that way? We don't know for sure what time we get in to Palermo. On top of that, once we touch down, we still have to get from the airport out to the cruise port.'

'And even internal flights,' Sleeps said, 'go a lot higher than whirly chairs.'

'Eight minutes,' Mel said.

Rossi kicked the suitcase.

'There's always the bus,' Sleeps said.

'The bus?' Rossi, shocked, stared at Sleeps. 'The fucking *bus*?'

'You don't want to take—'

'Why don't we,' Rossi said, 'just start hitching lifts? Or walk it? I mean, am I right? All we're doing is sharking two hundred grand, muling a little coke, trying to get a connection set up. You see what I'm saying. Johnny Priest says, "So how'd you get to Palermo?" I say, "It was sweet, man. We took the bus".' He spat. 'The guy'd bust a fucking gut.'

'Why would he have to know?' Sleeps said.

'*I'd* know.' Rossi thumped a thumb into his chest. '*Me*.'

'Six minutes,' Mel said, drowned out by the droning PA that was, Sleeps supposed, saying the same thing as Mel, only in Greek. Sleeps, OK, was buzzing on the crizz, a little lightheaded from being up thirty-six hours. But intoxicated too by all the newness, everything fresh no matter where you looked.

'Um, excuse me?'

Rossi whirled around on the guy wearing the bandana, the Ramones T-shirt. '*What?*'

'You guys taking the train?'

'Who wants to know?'

'Uh, me,' the guy said. Exaggerating it, Sleeps could tell. Enjoying his own joke.

'I fucking *know* it's—' Rossi began.

'How can we help?' Sleeps cut in.

'I'm just wondering if you know what time the next train leaves for Athens.'

'Dunno,' Rossi snapped, turning away. 'We're for Palermo.'

'Eventually,' Mel added. 'But the next train, it goes from here. Platform One.'

The guy shook his head. 'They're saying that one's delayed,' he said, 'or maybe cancelled. But everyone's talking Greek, so I don't know when the next one's going.'

'It's all, er, Greek to us too,' Mel said.

Rossi, fuming, mopped sweat off his forehead with the cuff of the fatigues. 'If I'm not on my way to Palermo inside the next hour,' he said, 'other than on any fucking trains or buses, I'm stabbing some fucker in the heart. I'll *do* it, Sleeps.'

Sleeps heaved a sigh. 'I'll see what I can do,' he said.

Ray

Ray, like practically everyone else in the Peloponnese, had heard Anna howl. Then, from across the street, watched Karen march out of the ferry terminal and turn right to where the train station was right there, convenient, practically on the docks. Karen staring straight ahead in case she might see Ray somewhere and have to admit she was maybe looking out for him. Everyone giving her a wide berth, one girl and her wolf. One thing Ray didn't have to worry about, Karen wouldn't be mugged for any khaki duffels while Anna was around.

He cut diagonally across the street, angling towards a café beside the bus depot, a place he could watch the train station and see Karen coming out if for some reason the Greeks objected to transporting a wolf on their rail network. Took a seat in the shade, ordered a *frappé* and asked for ice in it, sparked a Marlboro light. An oily heat from the traffic shimmering the air, the sun high and fierce.

For a while he toyed with the notion of hopping the ferry to Italy, one due in from Bari in an hour or so. Ray liked good pizza. But the idea of going back on board so soon after an overnight from Trieste was too much, and Ray wasn't fully convinced as to why he should be the one, Karen coming off all prima donna, to leave the country.

This was when he saw Rossi playing sherpas, pushing a suitcase along the other side of the street, Rossi togged out like a soldier now, his ragtag platoon dandering along behind him in civvies having a ball pointing stuff out to one another, hey, lookit that, it's a cute little train station. Ray holding his breath, willing them to keep going . . .

No go. A brief discussion outside, Rossi jabbing his forefinger around like he was conducting a mini-orchestra, and then they all trudged into the dark maw.

So Ray had to decide fast, twist or stick. Except, twist and Karen'd know he was watching over her, Karen the independent type, none too keen on guys lurking in the shrubbery with her best interests at heart. Sticking, that all came down to one thing, whether Rossi was liable to try something in a public place, witnesses all over.

Ray, if he was Rossi, he'd have sat tight, watched Karen off the train in Athens, tailed her from a discreet distance. Except Ray wasn't Rossi. And what Ray knew of the guy, this coming from Karen, who was biased, sure, but Rossi was on his best day unpredictable. It comes to Rossi, she'd said, you need eyes in the back of your eyes.

Then there was the last Ray'd heard from Rossi, up at the lake, Ray down for the count and still in shock after shipping the round that broke bone, Rossi hunkering down to say, '*Don't try and find me, Ray. No kidding. You won't even see me coming.*'

So there was that, too. Ray and threats a bad mix.

He eased his arm out of the sling, packed the sling away in the holdall. Pulled the shirtsleeve down over the cast, buttoned it tight, tucked a five under his *frappé* and shouldered the bag, zigzagged through the traffic across the street. Still no idea of what he was going to do. But pretty sure he'd have enough, busted arm or otherwise, to face down Rossi. This being the plan until he made it to the front of the station and the big guy, Rossi's muscle wearing a T-shirt with a big pink daisy, came ambling out. Ray had a quick

scan to make sure Rossi wasn't toddling along in his wake and
said, 'Hey.'

The big guy paused. 'Yeah?'

'Don't suppose you know,' Ray nodded at the station, 'what time
the next train goes to Athens?'

'The one that was supposed to go now,' the guy said, 'that's been
delayed. Or maybe cancelled. Anyway it's not going.' He shrugged.
'Don't ask me when the next one goes.'

'Not waiting for it, huh?'

Whatever the guy said was drowned out by a mournful blare, a
long hiss, the unmistakable shunting of rolling stock. The guy
looking back at the station now, frowning as he scratched his jaw.

'Thought you said it wasn't going,' Ray said.

'Was what a guy just told us,' the big guy said. He shrugged
again. 'Must be for someplace else.'

'Probably, yeah.' Ray wriggled his shoulder, getting the bag
comfortable. 'You in a hurry,' he said, 'to get to Athens?'

The big guy blinking at him now. 'Why?'

'We could rent a car,' Ray said. 'You and me. Split it two ways.'

'There's three of us,' the guy said. He jerked a thumb over his
shoulder. 'Two more in there.'

'Better still,' Ray said. 'A four-way split. That'd make it about
what we'd pay on the train anyway.'

'I dunno,' the big guy said. Working the angles, Ray could tell.
Trying to nail the scam. He said, 'I don't have any, y'know, credit
card or nothing.'

'I'll rent the car,' Ray said, 'you can sort me out with cash. Yeah?
Meet you back here, say half an hour. Are we on?'

'Yeah, OK. Half an hour.'

'Or thereabouts. I'm late, don't go running off, stiffing me for
the whole car.'

'No worries,' the big guy said. He put out a hand. 'I'm Gary, by
the way.'

'Jerry,' Ray said. They shook. 'Nice to meet you, Gary.'

'Same as that.' The guy hesitated. 'Listen, there's just one thing.'

'What's that?'

'You pick us up, any chance you'd mind pretending we're on
Sicily, headed for Palermo?'

Karen

'Most people,' Pyle was saying, 'they've got a camera these days, they're happy with photographs, nice little keepsakes to jog the memory. Others, they want more, maybe they got engaged, fell in love. Something they can hang on the wall over the fireplace.'

He'd come over from the States in 'seventy-five, twenty-one years old, to serve his year in the Greek army, help keep an eye on the perfidious Turks. Stayed in another couple of years, then took another year bumming around making sketches, landscapes mostly, he never did have an eye for people.

He was fairly fluent, courtesy of his father, from long before he arrived in Greece. Pyle being bilingual, he kind of fell into tour-guiding, week-long excursions into the islands. Bringing the sketchpad along. People started to notice, offered to pay for his drawings, the roughs. Wasn't long before he had his own shop, a one-room gallery up a side street off the waterfront on Paros. 'I was never going to be rich, but I was living in the islands, all that sun, the people. And the light, Christ. Ever see that *View over Toledo*, El Greco?'

Karen nodding along, then shaking her head. The baked earth through the windows shimmering like hot biscuits, enough to dry out her eyes just looking at it.

'Man, that's a picture. They got it in the Met, in New York, it's a force of fucking nature. It's Spain, yeah, but the light's more or less the same. And El Greco, the Greek, he was from Crete originally. Although, my own favourite? *Laocoön*, with the nude guys fighting snakes.'

'Nude?'

'What'd be the point of fighting snakes in togas? It's art, for Chrissakes.'

'And people email you their photos, is that it?'

'Telling me where they took it, all the details, what date. Even what time of day, if they can remember. So I can get the right angle, the light.'

'And off you go, easel under your arm.'

'Hi-ho, hi-ho,' Pyle grinned. Lying back in the seat opposite, the khaki duffel on the seat beside him, Anna's head resting on that. Gazing up at the guy now, her soulful brown eyes unblinking while he scratched between her ears.

'You don't just paint them from the photograph?' Karen said.

'Such cynicism from one so young and cynical.' He shrugged. 'I like the islands, Karen, being free to travel around. Anyway, a photograph? It's like one tile in a mosaic. I go where they were, I get to see what they saw, the whole vista, see if I can't give them more of a sense of it all. More the way they remember than how they saw it.'

'So what have you got on now?'

'Coupla things,' Pyle said. 'I generally let them build up, four or five, then take off for a month. One's up to the Acropolis, although a little different than usual, looking down into the amphitheatre, a nice sunset kicking in from off to your right, the west, the sky's a lovely bluey-green, like mouldy turquoise. Then there's the monastery over on Amorgos, you ever been?' Karen shook her head. 'Beautiful place,' Pyle said. 'Very peaceful. You can see why the monks hang out there. That movie, *The Big Blue*? They shot a lot of the exteriors there.'

Anna batting her tail against Karen's legs, making these squirmy whines way back in her throat. The girl responding, Karen believed, as much to Pyle's honeyed Southern drawl as his fingers scratching between her ears. He was easy on the eye too, greying but still cool, claiming one-half Greek, a quarter Spanish, one-eighth Cherokee. What she liked best was how he didn't give her the third-degree about who she was running away from back in Patras. Just rolled with it, leaving it to Karen whether she told him or not.

'I should tell you,' she said, 'I've never seen Anna react like this before. Usually you'd be missing an arm by now, at least an arm. I mean, the girl's a killer twice over.'

Pyle grinned, chucked Anna under the chin. 'Pop was a park ranger,' he said, 'although originally a keeper at Athens Zoo, before the Nazis came in. Anyway, when I was a kid? I wanted to be a park ranger too. Y'know, like Old Smokey?' Karen shook her head. Pyle shrugged. 'What I'm saying is, I always got on fine with the animals. Pop got posted to Alaska one time, Christ, we must've been the only Greeks in Alaska. The bears'd come in raiding the garbage, I'd be out there waving like they were Yogi and Boo-Boo. I never got this close to a wolf, though. Saw some from a helicopter once, Pop tracking these good ol' boys on Alaskan safari, so loaded they couldn't even hit their own fucking helicopter from the inside. Basically, they chased the poor bastards to death.'

Karen, a first time for everything, found herself wishing she was twenty years older, just for one night.

'So this gallery,' she said. 'Who takes care of it when you're away?'

'The gallery,' Pyle grinned, 'is a bit like its owner. It doesn't take an awful lot of taking care of.'

'I'll just bet,' Karen said.

Doyle

First thing Doyle said to Sparks after kissing her cheek was, 'We're leaving.'

'But I only just *got* here.'

Doyle took one of Sparks' bags and marched off across the tiny terminal, out into the blinding glare to the cab she'd had wait right there at the front entrance. 'It's a volcano,' she said when they were in. 'The entire island, it's a live volcano. They've lost whole civilizations here.'

'Like, thousands of years ago.'

Doyle stared. 'You knew about that?'

'You didn't?'

Doyle was always the last to know. 'I checked,' she said. 'Last time it went up was nineteen-fifty. Which, with my luck lately, means it'll probably blow again tomorrow, if not tonight.'

Sparks shrugged. 'So where're we going?'

'First place that doesn't have cataclysmic destruction.'

'What about Niko and this friend of his you'll be persuading him to bring along?'

'He said he'll ring later.'

'What if he rings the Santorini code?'

'Then we find ourselves a new Niko.'

Sparks left it until the cab dropped them off at the port. With an hour or so to kill, they took a couple of coffees over to the edge of the dock, sat with their legs dangling. 'You all right?' Sparks said.

'I don't know.'

'What's up?'

'Ever been shot at, Sparks?'

'Nope.'

'Me neither. Not 'til Tuesday.'

'You're feeling it?'

'It's bubbling up, yeah.'

'So let it go.'

'I'm thinking I might. Soon as we're on the ferry.'

'Fine by me.'

Doyle held on until the ferry cleared the rocky point that marked the last of Santorini. Then bawled. Going into it deep, barely aware of Sparks rubbing her back. The hard bubble in her chest taking a while to puncture, then easing out slow, one heave at a time. Coming out of it she heard Sparks say, 'Yeah, morning sickness. She's pregnant to some gypsy guy, he ran off last night. It's a real tragedy. I mean, the guy was seriously hot.'

Doyle came up laughing through more tears, snuffling snot and wiping her eyes. A middle-aged Greek waiter was standing there agog, tray dangling. Sparks said, 'While you're there, I'll be having a mojito, heavy on the mint. Doyle?'

So they had a nice buzz on by the time the first island hove over the horizon. Early evening, like walking into a giant warm sponge coming down the ramp, Doyle oozing a slow sweat in the small of her back. They skirted the knot of hawkers with their day-glo signs promising swimming pools, A/C, asses' milk in the bath. Crossed the square and found a vacant table at the first café they came to, ordered cheeseburgers and beers. The square was lined on two sides with cafés, hostels, tourist bureaus. A life-size greeny-bronze statue on a roundabout of dusty white marble. The place quiet now the ferry had gone, the port officials in their white uniforms strolling back to base, the hawkers dispersed. Some backpackers, the stragglers, still wandering around, dazed by the heat. Across the way, in the middle of the yachts moored against the dock, was one mocked up like a pirate ship, Jolly Roger and all, below that the Swiss flag. Doyle liked the combo.

'Money with a slow wink,' Sparks agreed. 'Speaking of which – Trust Direct put up a reward.'

'Oh yeah? How much?'

'Ten per cent.'

'Of the ransom.'

'Correct.'

'On what they paid or what's recovered?'

'On what they get back, I guess.' Sparks chugged some beer. 'In theory, just call me curious, how much would you keep?'

'How much would you?'

'Depends on what's left. And who's around when you're counting it.'

'Yeah.'

'You going to tell Niko? About the reward, I mean.'

'Niko's on need-to-know right now.'

'So what does he know? Just so I don't screw you, say the wrong thing.'

'Keep it social, Sparks, and you won't go far wrong.'

'You tell him about Frank?'

'Not all of it, no.'

'But he knows you're suspended.'

'He thinks I'm on holiday.'

'Busman's holiday. Chasing bad guys in between cocktails.'

'I say too much, Sparks, especially about Frank, Niko'll walk me on to the plane home himself.'

'And you don't want anyone getting to Ray before you do.'

Actually, Doyle was wondering if it wasn't Rossi she wanted after all. Put the skinny prick against a tree and pump a round into the wood about an inch from his ear, see how he coped with the fallout. She believed he'd probably cry too.

Doyle starting to see things from Madge's point of view, why she'd pulled the trigger on Frank.

'What?' she said.

Sparks repeated her observation, which amounted to a warning that the Greek economy was in the toilet, and that if any of the locals stumbled across Trust Direct's cash, Doyle could kiss goodbye to any ten per cent.

'And then,' Sparks needled, 'there's the whole Ray issue.'

'Fuck the money, and fuck Ray.'

'Sounds like my kind of party.' The waitress, Jade by her name-tag, with wheat-blonde hair, deeply tanned, was wiping down the next table along. 'Do I need to bring my own Ray or are they, like, on tap?'

'There's only one,' Sparks said. 'He's durable, though.'

Doyle said, 'Hey, there's no volcanoes here, right?'

The girl shook her head. 'That's Santorini.'

'Santorini we know about. What about here?'

'Back home, in New Zealand? We have volcanoes. I come away for the summer, the last place I'm going is where they have volcanoes.'

Doyle nodded. Sparks said, 'So what's there to see?'

The waitress tucked her rag into a back pocket, sat down and shook a cigarette free from a soft pack of Marlboros. 'There's Homer's tomb,' she said, biting softly on the filter lighting up. 'A Venetian castle. Some monasteries, and there's windmills up at the top of the Chora. It's not what you might call culture central.' She nodded at their bags. 'You get somewhere to stay yet?'

'We're just in,' Sparks said. She held up her bottle. 'First beer.'

'You looking for a pool?'

'That all depends on your quality of cabana boys. I mean, I generally lean more towards willing than sculpted back home. On holidays? I'm thinking I'll treat myself to some architecture.'

Jade grinned, then pointed out across the square to where Doyle could make out a beach curving away to a headland maybe quarter of a mile distant. 'Most people stay up in the village or around at Mylopotas, wherever the bars and clubs are. If you're not looking to be up all night every night, though, you'll want Yialos. There's no pool, but it's quiet day and night and the beach is right outside your front door. I stay there, so I can vouch for it being clean, daily sheet and towel changes. None of which has anything to do with the fact that if you book in using my name, I get commission.'

'Nice hustle,' Sparks said.

'It's a cool place. Cheap and laid-back.'

'Sold. What's it called?'

'The Katina. Just take the shore road; it's about three hundred yards past the ESY, the health clinic. Make sure and tell them Jade sent you.'

'We'll do that. I'm Sparks, by the way. This is Doyle.'

Jade stubbed her smoke, checked her big Mickey Mouse watch. 'If you go now, you've a couple of hours to grab a nap, get your disco pants on.'

'I don't dance,' Doyle said.

'You don't *dance*?'

'Her and all the other tough guys,' Sparks said. 'Me, I like to dance. What are we talking, acid house? Will there be poppers and shit?'

'Christ,' Jade said, getting up. 'When's the last time you were in a club?'

'It's been a while, yeah,' Sparks said. 'So what time are we hooking up? I mean, you're taking us out, right, showing us the town. Our treat, looking to get blitzed. What d'you say?'

'Appreciate the offer but I'm already out tonight. Although,' Jade said, 'we'll be getting together in the Blue Orange, you're welcome to come along. Just ask in the village where it is. Any time after eleven, we'll be there.'

'It's a date,' Sparks said.

Ray

'You're a sneaky prick, Ray, I'll give you that.' Rossi nodded a grudging approval. 'Except what I'm wondering is if you're being sneaky-sneaky or, y'know, super-sneaky.'

'Is that even loaded?' Ray said.

'That's perxactly the gamble,' Rossi said, waggling the .22, 'you're looking at right now. It's like—' He glanced across at Gary. 'What's that one with Walken?'

'*Things To Do in Denver*?'

'That's Andy Garcia. The other one.'

'*True Romance*.'

'The fucking Vietnam one, man.'

'*Deer Hunter*,' Ray said. 'Walken sweats years of Russian roulette and then De Niro turns up, Bobby the jinx.'

Gary driving, Rossi riding shotgun but twisted around to face into the back to keep the .22 on Ray.

Ray's plan, originally, had been to rent the car, then watch from up the street for Gary to bring everyone out front, so Ray knew Karen wasn't with them, Karen or the duffel. If she wasn't, Ray planned to keep them waiting on the street, buy Karen some time.

Except then, it was only the three of them. Ray reconsidered. Wondering if it mightn't mean less heartache in the long run, with Rossi heading for Athens, under the impression he was Palermo-bound, for Ray to be inside the tent pissing out. So he drove up the street and pulled in, picked them up. Rossi gawping like a slapped fish until he remembered he was packing the .22.

'So this is what you need to decide,' Rossi said. 'Like, is this baby loaded or not?'

'Not,' Ray said.

'Just out of curiosity,' Melody said, 'how come you're so sure?'

Melody with a vanity case propped on her knees, the lid up. Ray could see a notebook in there, the girl scribbling notes with an eyeliner pencil.

'The safety's off,' Ray said.

''Course it's off,' Rossi said.

'Except,' Ray said, 'you never *took* it off. So it's been off since before you whipped it out all Billy the Kid-like, this after I'd watched you patting your pockets trying to remember where you'd put it. And only a moron would walk around with the safety off on a loaded gun, even a .22.'

Mel paused in her scribbling. 'That's what you're banking on? That he's not a moron?'

'What I'm banking on,' Ray said, 'is how hard it is to keep someone hostage. At least one person's got to watch over them all the time in case they try something bogey. Then you're untying them, bringing them to the bathroom, tying them up again, cooking three times a day . . . I mean, kidnap's a full-time gig. Rossi, am I right?'

'Fucking A,' Rossi said, glum.

'I mean, you can do it,' Ray told Mel, 'I'm not saying it can't be done. But there's techniques, y'know? In the Rangers there was whole courses you could do, how to manage prisoners of war.' Ray glanced up at Rossi. 'Point being,' he said, 'you can't depend on Mel here, and Gary's got his hands full driving. Hey, I got another one,' he said to Sleeps. 'Kasparov.'

Sleeps nodding. 'The state capital of Indiana, that's Gary too.'

'So that leaves you, Rossi,' Ray said. 'Hostaging me with an empty gat.'

'Gat?' Mel said.

'Rod,' Rossi said sourly. 'Roscoe.'

'Roscoe?'

'Ray,' Rossi said, 'one pro to another, this isn't a you-me issue. It's about justice. Ethics, Ray.'

'So it's not about the two hundred gees. Which, I should point out, is now down to around one-seventy or so, less change. With Madge still to get her split.'

Rossi lowered his head, began butting his forearm. 'That's my gelt, Ray.' The voice coming muffled from the crook of his arm. 'I have it coming. I'm *owed*.'

'Possession's ten-tenths. You know the drill.'

Rossi, an idea brewing, looked up. 'How about I have Sleeps sit on you?'

'I'm sitting on no one,' Sleeps said. 'You think that's fun, some guy's nose up your crack?'

Rossi swore.

'I'm the one's owed,' Ray said. 'For renting the car, like.'

'I shook on that,' Sleeps reminded Rossi. 'Gave him my word.'

'This was before,' Rossi said, 'you realized he was Karen's guy.'

'I shook on it,' Sleeps insisted.

Rossi poking at his good ear with the muzzle of the .22. 'Karen swiped my stash,' he told Ray. 'You know this, right? When I was inside, she ran off with sixty gees, my Ducati motorcycle and the .44, which she chucked in the lake. You were half-unconscious at the time after I shot you, so you might've missed that last bit.'

'I heard, yeah.'

'So I'm calling double-bubble.'

'Fine by me. But you better call it loud, so Karen hears you. No point telling me.'

'Double-bubble?' Melody said.

'On the inside,' Ray said, 'you get in hock to a guy for a pack of smokes? You have to pay back double.'

'I'm willing,' Rossi said, 'to forget the Ducati, the .44. But the sixty-grand stash goes double-bubble. That way Karen walks away with, what, fifty grand clear. Except,' he pointed at where his ear used to be, 'the wolf? She goes double-bubble too. She's dead.'

'Rossi, man – how many times? Karen dumped me, ran off with the loot. For all I know she's in fucking Tibet.'

'She'll be hooking up with Madge,' Rossi said. 'Somewhere along this cruise there'll be a big reunion, fucking cake and candles.'

'This is presuming Madge even makes the cruise.'

'This Madge,' Mel said to Rossi, eyeliner pen poised, 'being the woman you kidnapped who thought she was your mother.'

Rossi glanced across at Sleeps. 'Let's try keeping the personal shit personal,' he suggested. 'Let's just try that, see how it works.' Sleeps shrugged, kept his eyes on the road. Rossi came back to Ray. 'I'm seeing that cruise off anyway. Just to be sure.'

'We saw you on the ferry over,' Ray said, 'watched you getting into Amsterdam. So Karen knows you're on your way. Still think she's going to make that cruise?'

'Put yourself where I am,' Rossi said. 'Down two hundred large. Would you see that cruise off?'

'If I was sure Karen wouldn't blow the whistle, have cops waiting for me at any specific piers, then maybe, yeah.'

'Rossi?' Mel said. 'I'm thinking we should cut our losses, head straight for Ios.'

Rossi glared. '*Our* losses?'

'For as long as I'm still owed my ten thousand,' Mel said, 'plus expenses, then they're our losses.'

'That's agreed from way back,' Sleeps said.

Rossi put the muzzle of the .22 to his temple and pulled the trigger, click-click-click. Then said, to Ray, 'You think she'd do it?'

'Would who do what?'

'Karen. Sic the cops on me.'

Ray shrugged. 'I only knew the girl a week, Rossi. You've known her what, ten years? You tell me.'

Madge

B ack when Frank's lawyer Bryan approached Terry Junior to have Madge snatched, the first thing Terry Senior did was have Frank audited.

'And you can just do that,' Madge said.

'You can pay enough,' Terry said, 'you can do anything, Christ, order up a Middle East invasion.' He caught the look on her face. 'Generally, though, it's the client provides the details, a good faith gesture as part of the deal.' He checked his watch again, third time in two minutes. 'No way they're making it now,' he said.

Early evening, still balmy but with a hint of chill up on the liner's observation deck, the breeze flapping at Madge's headscarf, Madge with big round shades on, the whole Jackie O schtick.

'So you're saying,' she said, 'this life insurance policy runs to a million and a half.'

'Correct. The payout, if anything happens to either of you, going to the twins, with the surviving parent in charge of the spending until they turn twenty-one. Frank never told you this?'

'No,' Madge said, neglecting to mention how she'd never asked. 'And the house is mine?'

'The mortgage was in Frank's name from when he remortgaged his own home to buy you yours. So that goes null and void. The bank, for once, gets screwed.' He slapped his bicep, punching the air an uppercut. 'Up the workers.'

'But what about the circumstances? How he died.'

'You get charged, it goes to trial, then yeah, it'll get complicated. But the money is the twins', not yours. So someone'll have to – this presuming worst-case scenario and you pull a short stretch – administrate your estate on their behalf, at least until they're twenty-one. But that's not even an issue.' He turned away from the breeze, pulled his lapel up to light a cigar. 'You want to know what I think?' he said after some ruminative puffing. 'I think they'd all be happier if you never came home.'

Madge felt hollowed out, sipping a Bellini on the observation deck of the *Patna*, scanning the chaotic port below for a Karen- or Anna-shaped ant. Athens beyond the port rising on three sides, a shallow white bowl washed now in delicate mauves and violets, the sun virtually gone.

'Either way I'm screwed,' she said. 'If I go back I can't touch the money. And if I don't go back, I can't touch the money.'

'That's one way of looking at it.'

'There's no other way, Terry. I can't touch the money.'

'Sure. *You* can't touch it.'

'I'm not sure I follow,' Madge lied, Madge with a fair idea she was starting to see it now, Terry's plan all along.

'What you need,' Terry said, puffing on his cigar, 'is someone you can trust to do the right thing. By you *and* the twins.'

'You're talking about someone administrating the estate,' Madge said, 'on my behalf.'

'Exactly.'

'In which case it wouldn't matter where I was, back home or Bongo-Bongoland.'

'It'd probably be better if you were somewhere in the EU zone,' Terry said, 'for the sake of convenience, so everyone's singing off the same legal hymn sheet. But, in theory, yeah.'

'I don't know.' Madge aiming for a Little Bo-Peep vibe. 'It sounds awfully complicated.'

'That's partly a benefit,' Terry said. 'You open up a few shell companies, siphon off a little here, divert a bit there. Pretty soon it's a jungle a guy'd need a machete to get through.'

'What happens when it's all sucked dry?'

'Generally you'd sue whoever was taking care of the estate, this to prove your own innocence.' Terry peered at his watch, tapped the face. 'Eventually it goes to court, none of the principals turn up. So the judge throws it out.'

'And where's the money?'

'Wherever you want it to be. If you're smart, lots of different places, preferably washed through investment portfolios, the blue-chip shit. You'll get low returns but it's safe until you need it. You want my advice, I'd say plunge on Chinese cement, take a punt on some radical energy, maybe nuclear power. But it's your money. Hold on, is that them?'

But it was only a family of immigrants, the cops wading in, batons drawn. 'I don't have anyone I can trust that way,' Madge said, reclining on the deckchair again. 'No one who's that clued in legally, I mean.'

'Not a problem. You want, I'll put my guys on it.'

'Yet again,' Madge said, 'that's incredibly generous of you, and very sweet.'

'Don't mention it.'

'But it sounds to me,' she went on, 'that something like that, it'd be expensive. Lawyers' fees and what have you. I'd be afraid the money would be gone by the time it's all over.'

Terry grunted. 'I've seen it happen,' he said.

'Which'd put me back to square zero. Not even on the board.'

'If I were you,' Terry said, 'what I'd do is get my guys to outsource. Y'know? Find some young firm, new and keen, get them to hump the coal up the hill. Then, it all falls apart after, you're flat broke, you've got the added benefit of knowing some lawyers got screwed too.' Another bicep-slap. 'Anyway,' he said, 'there's no way you're falling off the board. You're officially divorced now, right?' Madge nodded and toasted Terry with the Bellini. 'I was you,' he said, 'on a tub like this? I'd spread the word. Looking the way you do, I'd be surprised you didn't walk away from the cruise with about ten proposals, maybe even from the captain himself.' He raised his eyebrows. 'You know they have a shop on the third deck specialises in engagement rings?'

'I honestly don't know if I'll ever get married again,' Madge said, parrying his clumsy lunge. 'Besides, it's far too early to—'

'Who's talking about getting married? I'm saying engaged, having fun, Christ knows you deserve it. Meet some new guys, let 'em buy you shit. Scrapping to impress you, tossing one another overboard.'

'You wouldn't be one of them?'

'Fuck no. I've *been* married, got the T-shirt, it didn't fit. But don't worry about me, I'll keep a low profile. You want me gone, I'm gone. Or I can stick around, make sure no one gets any notions he shouldn't. It's up to you.'

The liner sounded its klaxon, a mournful blare that shuddered through its entire length, sounding to Madge like the lady had a cold coming on.

'That's final call,' Terry said, 'they're definitely not making it now. What'll we do, stay or go?'

Sleeps

'Rossi? I'm getting a little yawny over here.'

'Tough shit, you've had all the crizz.' Rossi slumped in the passenger seat, arms folded, cheesed off ever since he sparked a doobie and Mel, halfway through her second warning, puked across his shoulder into his lap. 'Stick your face in the breeze,' he said.

'One, we're stalled in a tailback. Two, it's humid enough out there to boil eggs. You want me to nod off?'

'Whaddya want *me* to do? Magic up some fucking crizz?'

Things were a little tense in the van, the cruise gone twenty minutes ago if it was leaving on schedule, traffic log-jammed on the outskirts of Athens. Everyone was edgy, the stench of stale puke not helping. 'What I'm getting at,' Sleeps said, 'is Johnny's, y'know.'

'You've a Bob hope. That fucker stays sealed. Johnny said, being specific on it, how the load gets through intact.'

'But only saying that on the presumption you'd be dipping in. Making sure you didn't party it up, just tried a taster.'

'What're we looking at?' Ray said. 'Coke?'

'Never you fucking mind,' Rossi said.

'In the Rangers,' Ray said, 'for night sorties? They'd pass out the speed. Even in training. Guys were volunteering to go out. Queues to sign up, all this.'

'You had any common decency,' Rossi told Ray, 'any sense of fucking shame, you'd be bringing something to the party, not sponging dabs of coke off us.'

Sleeps glanced at Ray in the rear-view. 'You being in the Rangers, you'll have done some work with machine guns. Right? The heavy shit.'

'Sure.'

Rossi glaring across, not getting it. But then started to see, nodding along, as Sleeps said, 'So you could clue us in if we had, say, an Uzi.'

'Your Uzi's as straightforward as it gets,' Ray says. 'Just point and fire, you can't go wrong.'

'You'd think so,' Sleeps said as Rossi opened the door and got out, 'wouldn't you? Except none of us have any experience, never having been to any war zones or Miami Beach.'

Rossi slammed down the trunk of the car then hustled back into the passenger seat again. Started fumbling with the catches on Mel's suitcase. 'The fuck's with the Fort Knox?' he said.

'There's a combination,' Mel said.

'And what, I'm supposed to guess?'

'It's, erm, double-o seven.'

'Sweet suffering Cheez-Its.' Rossi sprung the locks and opened the case, holding the lid sideways so no passer-by could glance in, spot the hardware. Then gave Ray the nod. Ray scooched up so he was peering down over Rossi's shoulder, holding his nose against the waft of puke. 'Nice, yeah. Where'd you pick it up?'

'Under the machine-gun tree. So what's the skinny?'

'First off,' Ray said, 'it's not your actual Uzi. It's a copy.'

'A fake?'

'An Uzi rip-off. The stock's wrong, it looks like some kind of local adaptation. The Ingram, maybe?' Ray thinking out loud. 'But it'll do the same damage as an Uzi, don't worry about that.'

'So how's it work?' Rossi said.

'Work? You pull the trigger, bullets come out. How d'you think it works?'

Sleeps put the car in gear, rolled forward a few feet. 'Just presume for a second,' he said, knocking the car out of gear again, 'we're complete morons here, we never handled an Uzi before. Start at the start.'

'I could do that,' Ray said. 'Except, I get you tooled up, you'll point it at me and tell me take you to Karen.'

'I thought you said,' Mel said, 'you don't know where she is.'

'This is my problem.'

'I give you my word,' Rossi said.

'Rossi, no offence, but you've shot me once already.'

'Yeah, but that was a fluke.'

'OK, but from there? With an Uzi? Even you couldn't miss.'

'Hey, Ray?' Sleeps said. 'Take a good look at me, man. I look to you the type that'd do good time in a Greek prison?'

'I don't know,' Ray said, 'if there's actually that type. Greek time, what I'm hearing, it's a tough stretch.'

'This is what I'm saying.'

Ray shrugged. 'See that catch,' he said to Rossi, 'left side, just behind the trigger guard. Pull it back, you'll get the mag out.'

Rossi slipped the magazine out, handed the Uzi back between the seats. Ray hunched over, the gun in his lap. 'Looks like it might be the Ero,' he said. 'The Croatians ran some Uzi knock-offs back in the early nineties, this could be one.'

'Fuck the history,' Rossi said, 'and make with the geography.'

'It's your basic Uzi,' Ray said. 'Sturdy, safe, reliable, the Israelis make good guns. Doesn't have many working parts, so it's easy to clean. You've got full, semi and single-shot options with the three-way safety. On full you're looking at, I think, sixteen, twenty rounds a second, some shit like that. The mag holding anywhere from twenty-five to thirty-two rounds, depending, the ammo nine-millimetre, Parabellum, you'll pick it up anywhere. You want panic, just close your eyes and blaze away. You want accuracy you'll need to unfold the stock, tuck it in here,' he patted the hollow just below his shoulder, 'and get yourself set solid. Anything else you need to know?'

'Where's the safety?' Rossi said.

'Right, yeah. This is a feature, why the Uzi's so safe. See here?' he said, picking up the gun, patting the ball of his thumb against the back of the pistol grip. 'You need to be squeezing that while you're pulling the trigger. A bit of practice, you can do it with the first joint of the thumb, you're not even thinking about it.'

'Which one's the single round option?'

'This,' Ray said, making the adjustment. 'Anything else?'

'Nope, that should just about do it.'

'That's what I'm hoping,' Ray said, sitting back, elbow tucked into his side, the Uzi pointed at the back of Rossi's seat. 'OK, new plan. Sleeps? We're going to Crete.'

'Crete my hairy hoop,' Rossi said. 'Gimme that.'

'Take it.'

'Christ!' Rossi hunched himself up, twisting around to reach into the rear.

'First though, you'll need to be sure it isn't loaded.'

'The fuck're you talking about?' Rossi holding up the Uzi's mag. 'I got the bullets.'

Sleeps hearing it like Jimmy Dean, Jimmy tumbling out of the planetarium, Sal Mineo riddled on the steps.

'Sure you do,' Ray said. 'But now what you're dealing with, the gamble you're taking, is whether the Croatian guy left one up the spout. He was drunk, right?'

Karen

Pyle was staying over in Athens so he could sketch up at the Acropolis next day, so Karen left Anna with him in a little public park near the docks and went on down to the quay.

The liner was a horizontal skyscraper all lit up and festooned with balloons and ribbons. Eight, maybe nine stories high. Karen asked at the booking office and was told the cruise was running behind time as per usual but had already boarded. No, there was no message for Karen King. Ringing the ship, yes, that could be arranged.

The operator on board put her through to Madge's cabin but there was no answer and no answering service. Karen was in the phone booth watching the floor show outside, a horde of Albanians busting out of a van and sprinting in all directions, cops and port officials in hot pursuit. This on top of bedlam anyway, buses, scooters, delivery vans. Karen couldn't work out how the Greeks, having first dibs on the set-up, hadn't made mayhem an Olympic sport.

She hung up, went back to the desk.

'Would you mind checking,' she asked the guy, portly under a waistcoat and dicky-bow combo, oily hair, 'if there's a ticket booked for Karen King?'

The guy consulted the computer, found her name. Went to print off her details. 'Hold on,' Karen said, 'I'm hoping to book another place. What's the policy on pets?'

The policy was flexible, depending on the kind of pet. For dogs the liner had kennel accommodation down in the hold.

'Cool,' Karen said. 'Put me down for one space.'

The guy went to say something but was drowned out by the liner's klaxon, this blaring moan. Karen waited for it and wasn't disappointed, Anna's howl echoing faintly through the port as the klaxon died away. The guy telling her she needed to get to the ship fast, it was pulling out in ten minutes, he'd ring ahead and tell them she was coming.

She jogged back through the port, dusk thickening now. Into the little park, hearing a murmur of conversation even before she got all the way round the shrubbery to the bench facing out over the ornamental lake, the little fountain. Then realized, coming all the way around, it wasn't a conversation as such. A tall guy, skinny, flicking these amber beads and asking Pyle where the wolf's owner was while Pyle spoke in low tones to Anna, one hand on her collar. Anna had a baleful glitter in her one good eye.

Karen breezed by the Greek, saying, 'Hey, you're looking for me?'

The Greek turned, adjusting his stance so he could keep Karen and Pyle in view. Except Karen went straight to Pyle, the bench, patting Anna as she hunkered down at the khaki duffel, unzipped it. She said, over her shoulder to the Greek, 'You mind if I ask you something?'

The guy shrugged, frowning now.

Karen came up holding the .38, aiming it two-handed at the guy's groin. 'What's the worst idea you've ever had?' she said.

'This one, probably.' The guy cool, still flicking his beads.

'Back up,' she said, advancing. 'Keep going,' she said when he came up against the shrubbery. He ducked his head reversing into the loose foliage, pushing back until they emerged into the little clearing, the soil dusty brown. 'Sit down,' she said.

'In this suit?' the Greek said, a dry leaf trapped above his right ear.

Karen cocked the .38. The Greek shrugged, pocketed his beads and folded himself up, the guy like an ironing board going down. 'Grab your ankles,' Karen said, then went around behind, patted him down. Came up with a stubby black automatic he had holstered under his left armpit. 'Heckler and Koch nine millimetre,' she said, 'the P-7.'

'You know your guns,' he said.

'It says it on the side.' Karen tucked the gun into her waistband and patted the guy's breast pocket, found his wallet, worn leather, hefty. 'You shouldn't carry that in your breast pocket,' she told the Greek, backing away. 'Good suit like that, you'll ruin the cut.'

'I'll remember that,' he said.

'Remember I know where you live now. What's your name?'

'Niko.'

'OK, Niko, the snazzy little holster's telling me you're a cop. Except, this was an official gig, you'd have back-up. How come you're on your own?'

'Maybe I'm not.'

'I saw your guys just now,' Karen said, 'when the Albanians made their break. So I'm guessing your Greek cop is about as patient as cops anywhere else, as subtle. You had a partner, he'd have shot me dead by now.'

'I heard a dog howling,' Niko said, 'it sounded like a hell of a dog. So I came to take a look.'

'Bullshit.' Karen on an adrenaline buzz, trying to figure the guy's accent. 'Where's Doyle?'

'Doyle?'

Karen, still behind him, placed the muzzle of the .38 against his exposed neck. 'Just so we're clear,' she said. 'Everything in the world I care about is right here. It looks like anyone's taking that away, you won't get to see it happen.' She forced his head forward so it hung down over his chest. 'I won't ask again. Where's Doyle?'

'I don't know.'

'But she's here in Athens, right?'

'She was, yes. Now she's supposed to be on Santorini.'

'Supposed to be?'

'She was there. She's gone now.'

'And you don't know where.'

'No.'

Karen considered. 'I got two options here,' she said. 'One, you promise to behave, I can take you along. Or, it looks like you're going to start causing problems, I can do you right here.'

Niko shrugged. 'I was asked to do a friend a favour,' he said. 'That's all I'm in for.'

Karen called, 'Pyle?'

'Uh-huh?'

'There's some pills in the front pocket of the duffel, a bottle of water. Mind bringing me them?'

Karen made it a double dose of Anna's pills, just to be on the safe side. Twenty minutes later, Niko prone under the shrubbery, she was tucking the guy's Heckler back into the holster, wiped down, the wallet into his hip pocket. The liner's lights still visible, just about, when she stepped out of the laurel.

'Sorry you got involved,' she said.

Pyle shrugged. 'Looks like you missed your cruise.'

'I'll catch it up.' She consulted the itinerary. 'It gets into Paros tomorrow morning, first stop.'

'You think that's smart?' Pyle said. 'I mean, I don't know what's going on but you just doped a cop, waving a gun around. Think they'll let that slide?'

Karen thought about that. Realising now, with the cruise gone, she hadn't thought much about what'd happen after she hooked up with Madge again.

'What d'you suggest?' she said.

'Skip the cruise, that's first. I was you, I'd go to ground, get Anna here squirrelled away safe. Pick an island, any island. Just so long as it's not Paros.'

'Except it doesn't matter if I skip the cruise,' Karen said, 'when I'm booking Anna on board. First thing they'll ask when they're checking the booking offices is where'd the wolf go.'

'So don't book her on.'

'I'm not leaving her behind, Pyle. She's the whole point I'm here.'

Pyle shook his head. 'You're not seeing it. You need to rent a van, something spacious. Then book it on, you and me, Anna's hid away. Although,' he said, 'it'd probably be better if I was the one rented the van, did the booking.'

'You and me?'

'If I'm not sticking in where I'm not wanted.'

'I thought you had to paint the Acropolis.'

'It's been there thousands of years,' Pyle said. 'Where's it likely to go?'

Rossi

'But how could there be no cops?' Rossi said, hardly daring to believe it.

'Not all over,' Ray said. 'I mean, there's cops, Crete's a

big island. But down on the south coast, the south-west? People basically look out for themselves.'

'Man, that's beautiful. I mean, it's a thing of fucking beauty.'

'And makes it all the more likely,' Ray said, 'Karen'll talk a three-way split. I mean, who's she squawking to?'

'Three ways,' Sleeps said.

'Karen gets some,' Ray said, 'I get some, you get some.'

'There's three of us,' Sleeps said, 'including Mel.'

'So you're splitting your split.'

'Which is how much?' Rossi said.

'About fifty-odd grand.'

'Each?'

Ray shook his head.

'Shit,' Rossi said.

'By the time this is over,' Sleeps said, 'we're going to wind up owing money.'

The rear door swung open and Melody climbed in. She distributed the tickets, sullen, still pissed at Ray for ratting out Karen.

'So what time do we leave?' Ray said.

'Half past midnight,' she said. 'Getting into Heraklion at eleven-forty tomorrow.'

'When can we board?'

'Any time.'

'Good,' Ray said. 'Sleeps?'

'Where to?'

'Dock seven,' Mel said. Sleeps eased along the quay, turned in at dock seven, waving back at the guy guiding him up the ramp.

'You don't think Karen has enough grief in her life?' Mel asked Ray.

'Karen thrives on grief,' Ray said, as Sleeps drove up to the end of the orange-lit parking area. 'Grief's what keeps her going. Anyway, in the long run? She'll be better off knowing she can relax, Rossi won't turn up some day she's not expecting him.'

'She didn't rip me off in the first place,' Rossi said, 'I wouldn't be chasing her nowhere.'

'That's a point,' Ray said. 'Gary? You want to get tight against the wall, man. Last thing we want is someone clipping the car, insurance details being asked for, drawing down heat.'

Rossi, grudging it, had to admit Ray had style. Real cool, this one-armed bandit holding a cannon on Rossi but still thinking ahead, worrying about insurance details. Now using, Rossi couldn't help but notice, his busted arm to unzip the holdall.

'Hey,' Rossi said. 'I thought your arm was broke.'

'Arm's busted,' Ray agreed. 'The hand's fine, though.' He pulled the strap of the holdall over his head, placed the Uzi inside. Then opened the door and stepped out of the car. 'See y'all up on deck,' he drawled, closing the door.

'The fuck's he going?' Rossi said, shoving his door open. Then heard it clang against the metal wall.

By the time he got Sleeps out of the driver's seat and crawled across, chased up the steep metal steps, found his way out on to the top deck, Ray was already at the rail with the holdall dangling from his shoulder at waist height and pointed at Rossi.

'She isn't on Crete,' Rossi said, 'is she?'

'I told you, she ran out. She could be anywhere. And that's far enough.'

Ray raising the Uzi out of the holdall a little, so Rossi could see his finger on the trigger. Except, up here, in full view of the quays? Ray was shooting no one.

He kept going. 'You know I'm right, Ray. I'm owed.'

'Karen tells it different.'

'Karen who ran out on you.'

'Don't do it, Rossi.'

'Do what?' he said. 'All we're doing's talking, right? It's a parley.'

Ray backing off now. The space behind him narrowing between the rail and the big black funnel. Rossi giving away fifty, maybe sixty pounds, three or four inches in height. But Ray had that busted arm.

Rossi measuring the distance. Another two, three steps . . .

He felt a rumbling beneath his feet and made up his mind – fake left, dive right. He put his hands up, palms out, said, 'We can sort this, Ray. One pro to another. We can do a deal here.'

'What kind of deal?'

'Fifty-fifty split. She's fucked you, she's fucked me. So we fuck her back.'

'I'm all fucked out,' Ray said but Rossi was already lunging. This as the klaxon blared, the funnel juddering. Rossi aiming for the holdall, the Uzi and Ray's bogey arm, the one he'd have trouble swinging up fast enough to—

But he was still only halfway there when his sucking gut told him, shit, he'd guessed wrong. Ray the ex-Ranger quicker than Rossi would've believed.

The Uzi's barrel swinging up to meet his lunge, Rossi so close the muzzle-flash blinded him.

Then his head blew up.

SATURDAY
Ray

'There's fink,' Ray said. 'Fink, rat, squeal, snitch.' He thought about it. 'Finger, peach and stool. How many do you need?'

Ray had a nice buzz building, four or five vodka-cranberries down the hatch, heart still pumping hard from dragging Rossi's dead weight one-armed. The rush easing off now, chilling into what he could only describe as a mellow exhilaration.

'One'll do it.' Melody sniffed. 'The one that sums up how you feel about Karen.'

'Then definitely fink. F for Friday, I for ink.'

'I know how to spell fink, Ray.'

The ferry's bar quiet, only a few hardy souls still drinking this late. Or, Ray trying to focus on the mirror-clock behind the bar, this early. Most of the plush velvet seats, the semi-circular booths, taken up with prone backpackers, rucksacks piled every which way.

'What you might find interesting,' Ray said as Mel bent to her notebook again, 'is that they're all verbs that used to be nouns.'

She checked her notes. 'It's possible to peach?'

Mel with the idea Ray was some kind of gangster, hard-boiled. Ray hated to disappoint the ladies. 'Nothing sweeter than a juicy peach,' he said. He sipped on his highball and leaned in along the polished counter of the bar. 'Hey, can you keep a secret?'

'That all depends,' Mel said, edging closer.

'It only has to be a secret from Sleeps. Otherwise you can tell whoever you want.'

'Even Rossi?'

'Why would you want to tell Rossi?'

'No reason. I'm just checking.'

Ray tapped a finger against his nose. 'Karen isn't gone to Crete,' he said.

'No?'

'Nope.'

Melody flipped back a page or two, scratched out a line. 'So where has she gone?'

'Ah.' Ray waggled a forefinger. 'That's a different secret.'

'It's all part of the same secret, Ray.'

'Actually,' Ray said, considering, 'I haven't the faintest idea where she's gone. For all I know she's headed for Crete.'

'But you just said—'

'I just picked an island,' Ray said. 'First one popped into my head.'

'So why Crete?'

'It's a big place. Wild in spots. You want to hide away, you and your wolf, there's plenty of room.'

'So *you'd* have gone to Crete,' Mel said.

'I had a wolf, yeah.'

'Did you tell Karen that?'

'About Crete?' Mel nodded. 'I don't know if I mentioned Crete specifically,' he said. 'Why?'

'Because if you did, it's the last place she'd go.'

'She knows I won't be chasing her.'

'You just broke up with her, Ray. Think she's taking your advice on anything now?'

'I'm not entirely sure,' Ray said, 'it was me broke up with her.'

'So she dumped you. Same difference.'

'Being honest, and technically speaking, I don't know if we were together long enough to break up. It was barely a week.'

Mel, the tip of her tongue poking from the corner of her mouth, scribbled another note, underlined it twice. 'So what'll we do about the ten grand?' she said.

'What ten grand?'

'The ten we're owed by Rossi and Sleeps. For their passports.'

'We?'

'I'll cut you in for two. Get it back and there's two in it for you.'

'Sorry, Mel. I'm retired.'

'Three. Three's my final offer.'

Ray heard himself tell Mel how much he had stashed in a safety deposit box. How little he needed three grand, no offence, thanks all the same.

Mel, eyes huge, licked her lips. 'You're kidding.'

'Don't believe the hype, Mel. Crime pays. Ask Marx.' He drained his highball. 'Anyway, I've a notion Rossi won't be following through on that deal he'd planned. I'd say your ten gees are gone.'

Mel put her pen down and stared gloomily into her Shirley Temple, stirring it with the big pink swizzle stick. 'Not really up to speed on the whole knight in shiny armour bit, are you?' she said.

'You're white,' Ray said, 'you speak English, you have a credit card. There's about three billion people who'd think they'd died and gone to heaven they had half your chances.'

'So much,' Mel said, 'for chivalry.'

'What can I tell you?' Ray said, signalling the barman for another round. 'I'm a peach.'

Sleeps

Sleeps woke to gnawing panic, already reaching for the steering wheel, shit, his worst nightmare, falling asleep at the—

Then realized, relief flooding through, the car was parked, still deep in the guts of a ferry. He knuckled his eyes, hauling himself upright, saying, 'Sorry, I must've dozed off. What were you saying?'

Except she had gone. Leaving a note on the dashboard, '*Gone to freshen up, back soon. x Mel.*'

Not saying, no surprise there, what time she left.

Sleeps, fiddling with the stereo, getting only static, snatches of Greek gabble, wasn't sure if he should be worried. On the one hand, Rossi'd been gone for hours. On the other, Rossi gone missing for hours tended to reduce the stress rates wherever he wasn't.

Sleeps, feeling a little guilty about it, was more worried about Mel. Rossi could handle himself, mostly, but Mel was a bit more delicate. Not to look at, sure, the girl was built like a gingerbread cottage. But there was something Sleeps liked about the fragile way she thought. Ideas that went off at tangents, looped around, tied her up in knots. Sleeps, dozing off one time, tried to imagine what one of Mel's thoughts might look like as an arc and was so impressed he woke up dizzy. Or maybe he was so dizzy he woke up impressed.

The girl asking him, not long after Rossi took off after Ray, 'How come you let Rossi call the shots?'

'The guy's happier,' Sleeps'd said, 'he thinks he's the one running the show.'

'OK, but what about you? When do you get happy?'

Sleeps had to think about that one. 'I always thought,' he said, 'I was a coward for not wanting to go to war. I mean in theory, no one's letting me in any man's army, right? But, you think about it, going

off to war and shit, you're thinking, no fucking way. I used to say I
was a pacifist, like it was a philosophy, not wanting someone to blow
your head off. Especially as it's always some other fucker's war, some
bastard sitting in an office ringing up some bastard on the other side,
saying, "Hey, I got a surplus on rockets over here, want a war?"'
Sleeps glanced in the rear-view. 'How come you're not taking notes?'

'It's, um, all up here,' Mel said, tapping her temple.

'Anyway,' Sleeps said, 'I didn't realize, you go off to war even
though you're crapping it, not because you're some kind of hero.
Most guys, you'll find, they're not heroes. And then, most soldiers
make it back. They didn't, you'd run out of soldiers fast, one way
or another.'

'Right. But what's that have to do with Rossi ordering you around?'

'I've seen a movie once,' Sleeps said, 'you had this ordinary guy,
a private, and his sergeant or corporal, can't remember which, but
the dude gets shot by a sniper. So the ordinary guy, he radios back
to base, he's told, "You're promoted, congratulations". So the guy,
it's bad enough he's in the middle of a fucking war, in the jungle,
he has to take charge. Making sure everyone else makes it out too.
I mean, most soldiers make it back, like I said. But lots don't.'

'So you're saying,' Mel said, 'it's a lack of ambition.'

'That's one way of looking at it, I guess. Plus, I go on the nod.
You go back through history, look at the achievers: Alexander, Khan,
Ali, Rossi – there's not many narcoleptics in there, y'know? Or,
say they were even prone to the anytime siesta, no one's hailing it
as any kind of unfair advantage they had over everyone else.'

'I wouldn't,' Mel demurred, 'have necessarily put Rossi and
Alexander the Great in the same bracket.'

'Valentino Rossi. You never heard of him?'

'Can't say as I have.'

'The Doc, yeah, greatest motorbike rider in history. So good he
was planning to race cars, he was bored winning on bikes. The
guy's Rossi's hero, the reason he picked the name Rossi. Although
he'll tell you too it's for Paolo Rossi, the footballer, won the World
Cup for Italy. Depends on his mood.'

'Rossi isn't his real name?'

'So he says.'

'So what is it?'

'Dunno, he never said. Anyway, the Doc, he wasn't given to forty
winks whizzing through any chicanes, y'know?'

'Isn't there any kind of treatment you can take?' Mel said. 'For the narcolepsy, I mean.'

Which must have been the point where Sleeps dozed off. Now he wondered if he shouldn't go take a look-see upstairs. Rossi, taking off after Ray, had said to stick with the car, but Sleeps couldn't see what he was achieving by staying put. Plus his sugar levels were dropping, he hadn't eaten in five, six hours, this on top of the big black hole opening up where the lake of crizz used to be. A crash in the post, Sleeps'd been there before, a plummet like a suicidal lemming.

Not pretty.

He locked the car, leaving the key behind the driver's wheel in case Mel came back down, and got up on deck just as the ferry docked at some port, reversing in. Sleeps hung on the rail watching the folks beetle up on to the orange-lit dock, shivering now in his shorts and pink daisy shirt. It was only then it occurred to him that Rossi and Mel, either or both, might have already jumped ship.

He went back down to the car, opened the trunk. No fake Louis Vuitton. He pulled up the trunk's floor and hauled out the spare tire, expecting Johnny Priest's parcel to be gone too. Except that was there. He wondered if she'd forgotten about it, or couldn't find it, or if it was just, the girl checking out, she hadn't wanted to give them any reason to chase her.

That one gave Sleeps a pang, an empty feeling it took a chocolate malt and three cheeseburgers to fill again. *So you're saying it's a lack of ambition.* Munching steadily, dribbling hot sauce on to the pink daisy, Sleeps realized he was going to have to meet Mel halfway.

So he filched the rucksack of the biggest guy he could find, the guy snoring on a bench behind the self-service restaurant, found himself a quiet restroom and dug in. Came out wearing baggy denims, a white tee under a V-necked short-sleeved blue shirt, navy Caterpillar trainers that pinched a little at the toes so Sleeps had to dump his socks. He bought a shaving kit at a restroom vending machine and scrubbed up, even laced some gel through his hair. Then stepped it out, heading first for the ferry's bar, and saw, soon as he stepped through the doors, Mel at the bar with Ray's arm around her shoulders, Mel close enough to suck out Ray's fillings and not need a straw.

Sleeps let the door swing to, went back up on deck and made his way to the stern. Spent a while looking down into the ferry's wake, the black sea churning up greeny-white, the phosphorescence hypnotic. Sleeps tempted to go face-first into Johnny's parcel, do all the coke in one snort. Fritz up his works with one lightning bolt to the brain.

Sleeps squidging his bare toes in the new trainers with an empty ache inside that a sack of cheeseburgers wouldn't fill.

Karen

Pyle put the carton of orange juice down on the bedside locker, the half-pint of vodka, two ham-and-cheese paninis, a jumbo bag of crisps. Pyle calling them chips. He went in the bathroom and came out with the toothbrush glass. 'This guy Ray,' he said. 'You were saying he has an Elvis quiff, right? Only blond.'

'Elvis, 'fifty-six,' Karen said through a mouthful of crisps. 'Why?'

'He's upstairs in the bar.'

'Shit.'

'Draped around some girl,' Pyle said, pouring the vodka, 'looks a lot like Elvis, 'seventy-seven.'

'There's a girl?'

'Woman enough for two,' Pyle said approvingly. He tossed off the vodka-orange, poured one for Karen. 'So what's this mean?' he said. 'We doping him too?'

Karen waved away the vodka-orange. 'He isn't chasing me,' she said. 'He's got no reason.'

'Hell of a coincidence, though, him just turning up like that. I mean, there's a lot of ferries leave Piraeus every day. And he just happens to take the one you're on.'

'There was a girl with Rossi,' Karen said, 'coming off the ferry into Amsterdam, she looked built to model mosquito nets for four-poster beds.'

'Then that could be her, sure.'

'So what the fuck's Ray playing at?'

'Pat-a-cakes, it looked to me.' Pyle chugged another vodka-orange. He said, 'The guy left you most of the money, the .38 so you'd be safe. Why should he turn on you now?'

Karen went into her spiel, her experience with men. Starting with her father, who she'd forked in the chest and got put away. 'I had to bust my own jaw to convince them,' she said, thumbing just above her chin, the twist where the bone hadn't fused properly.

Pyle winced.

Then, Karen went on, Rossi, the guy who'd mutilated Anna, a rogue loser gene in his DNA. And now Ray, who, there was a good chance, had been scheming with this cop Doyle behind Karen's back. Except, when the heat came on? Ray'd run. And was now, by the sounds of things, hanging out with Rossi's crew.

'What I'm saying,' she said, 'is if you stick with a guy long enough, he'll turn on you. Ray, it took him a whole week.'

Pyle sipped his vodka-orange. 'I've known you what, ten hours? Twelve?' Karen shrugged. 'In that time,' he said, 'you've done a bunk from this guy Rossi, then disarmed a cop, doped him to the eyeballs. All the while running around with a bag of cash you're saying you scammed from some insurance company, a .38 tucked in there too. A bona fide wolf in tow, with this cop, Doyle, possibly on your tail.'

'What's your point?' Karen said.

'You're not at any point wondering,' Pyle said, 'and I'm just asking here, just throwing it out, if maybe any guy who's not Superman mightn't think you're a little high maintenance?'

Doyle

D oyle and Sparks arrived at a beach to watch the sun come up, a bonfire down to embers, crates of Amstel in the tide keeping cool. Some Aussie guy strumming a guitar, Crowded House songs, Doyle never could stand Crowded fucking House.

Sparks copped off around dawn, one of two Aussie guys, strapping, they played footy for the same team back home. On a gap year, working their way around Europe. Except Doyle'd lost interest when she learned her guy, Jamie, was just three months older than exactly half her age. The guys horsing around, asking Sparks who she'd thrown her knickers at, John or Paul, when the Beatles were still touring.

'They're just kids,' Doyle warned.

'Like, duh.' Sparks touching up her mascara in the compact

mirror, putting Doyle in mind of a guy shovelling sand on to lava flow.

'I mean, we're just their older woman story for when they get back home.'

Sparks packed away her stuff, put out her hand and shook Doyle's. 'Hi,' she said, 'I'm Miss Happy-Ever-After.'

So Sparks'd headed off with Ron, linking his arm going up the beach, telling him how her favourite tae kwon-do move was the old bassai dai with a yama tsuki combo, asking Ron if he'd ever seen a guy who'd had his nose cartilage jammed up into his brain. Leaving Doyle behind, tired and cold. Sand in her skimpies. Doyle wondering if island life was all it was cracked up to be.

When Jamie, blond dreads and wearing an ironic tie-dyed Deadhead tee, ambled across and sat down, offered Doyle a joint, Doyle had a toke and then told him she was a cop working undercover. The guy thinking this was hilarious until Doyle dug in her bag and showed him the badge she shouldn't have been carrying, being suspended.

Three minutes later Doyle was alone with the joint, the bonfire and two crates of Amstel, no idea of where she was or how to make it back to the Katina.

So she smoked the joint slow, the first in a long time, and watched the sun slide up around the headland, the greens and violets burning off, the sea hardening to petrol-blue and then softening to azure. The headlands either side bright orange like new brick and dotted with dusty scrub. A fishing smack bumbling along way out to sea, its foamy wake a brilliant white. Doyle felt a long, long way from home.

The buzzing of her phone woke her up.

'Hey,' she said, untangling her tongue from the web some spider had built in her throat, the lesser-spotted musty sock spider. 'What's up?'

'You all right?'

'Fine, yeah. You still hanging out at Ron's cradle?'

'It's crib, Doyle. Get with the programme.'

'I said cradle, I meant cradle.'

'Listen, where are you?'

'Still on the beach, I fell asleep.' Doyle dry-washed her face with her free hand, wondering if she should try to open her eyes sometime soon. 'What time is it?'

'Nearly nine. The reason I'm ringing, a ferry's just pulled in and a wolf got off.'

Doyle came awake fast. 'It's Karen?'

'Karen I've never seen. But there's a girl, yeah, she has this wolf on a chain leash. A guy with her looks like Johnny Depp's dad.'

'Ray,' Doyle said, 'looks nothing like Johnny Depp. More like a smaller Morrissey, has a quiff going on.'

'OK, yeah, I see him now. He's the one the wolf's attacking.'

'Sparks? What's happening?'

'Ray's down. The big girl with him, she looks worried.'

The big girl? 'Where are you, Sparks?'

'The port. Place called Ios Burger, they do a nice Irish fry, three sausages, beans on top. Good coffee, too. So who'd you want me to follow, Karen or Ray?'

Melody

Ray said, 'Karen, meet Melody. Mel, Karen.'

'I've heard so much about you,' Mel said.

Karen ignored Mel's outstretched hand. 'Ray, this is Pyle. Pyle, Ray. Anna you probably remember.'

''Course. Hey, Anna.' Which was when Mel realized Ray was drunker than she'd believed, Ray hunkering down to pat Anna and getting a head-butt that knocked him clean out of his unlaced trainers. Pyle helped him up. 'So this is Ios,' Ray said. 'I was expecting, I don't know, less wolves.'

'Although,' Karen said, 'I hear they have a big rat problem. So you should feel right at home.'

Ray leaned on Pyle's shoulder, pulling on his left trainer, then the right. 'Is it the rats that're big,' he said, 'or that there's loads of 'em?'

'He told Rossi,' Mel said to Karen, 'you were going to Crete. When Rossi had a gun on him.'

It wasn't easy when she was already sweating, the sun like a laser clearing the village on top of the hill, but Karen did her best aiming a frosty eye at Mel.

'What I'm saying is,' Mel said, 'I thought he was a rat too.'

'Was the gun loaded?'

'No, but we didn't know that until after.'

'Cojones, man,' Pyle said. He held out a fist. Ray, at the second attempt, managed to touch knuckles, then staggered a little. Mel starting to realize Ray was sweating harder than he should be, the guy pale, pinching now at his eyes.

'This being the dude,' Pyle said, 'shot you in the arm?'

Ray closed his eyes. 'That was a fluke.'

'I wouldn't,' Pyle said, 'I was you, give him another opportunity. Three's the charm, man.'

Ray looked directly at Karen. 'Rossi won't be trying again,' he said. It was the way he said it.

'Because,' Karen said, 'you sent him off to Crete.'

'The south coast,' Mel confirmed.

'In a box,' Ray said.

The ferry blew a long wail going out around the headland. Ray turned to watch it go and then his shoulders sagged and one knee went. He fell forward on to the other knee, half-twisting to protect his broken arm.

'I could do,' he said over his shoulder, 'with some hospital.' Then he pitched face-first into the dirt.

Madge

What bugged Madge was Terry, sprawling poolside on a sun lounger on a Mediterranean cruise, had no problem paying over the odds for outrageously priced cocktails but stiffed the waiters on their tips. The kid trudging off with a phone on his tray as Madge arrived, Madge calling him back, rummaging now in her canvas sun bag.

'Now you're just embarrassing him,' Terry said without looking up from his portable DVD player.

'I'd say he'd rather be embarrassed and tipped than pissed off and not,' Madge said, placing a twenty on the tray. The kid, he couldn't have been any older than Jeanie and Liz, gave Madge a jaunty salute, one finger to his temple, and sauntered off.

Terry paused his movie, shading his eyes as he looked up at her. 'Having a good morning?' he said.

'Not so's you'd notice,' Madge said, lighting one of Terry's cigarettes. 'The all-you-can-eat buffet is actually inedible. Then, sunrise up on the observation deck? You're observing nothing but fat asses, this scrum all pointing cameras at the sun coming up. I wouldn't have minded so much but they were all Japanese, from the Land of the Rising Sun. So I went for a swim and this guy came along, had that whole white socks under sandals thing going on, baggy shorts, he hunkers down on the edge of the pool flashing me some of his undercarriage. Wants to know if I want to play giant chess, except what he means is giant chest, he's about to topple over into my cleavage. On a rescue mission, maybe, taking the chance that that's where his self-respect disappeared to.'

'I didn't know you played chess,' Terry said.

'We didn't make it to the chess. He's helping me out of the pool, I haul back harder than I should, he goes in over my head. This is the shallow end, mind. Comes down on top of this three-year-old wearing inflatable armbands, a little Donald Duck rubber ring. So now the guy's being treated for concussion and I'm banned from the pool.' She stubbed the cigarette. 'How's your movie?'

'Good, yeah.' He jerked a thumb after the kid with the tray. 'Listen, Karen rang. Says she's on Ios. If you want to swing by, pick up your cut, she'll be there a few days.'

'What'd you say?'

'I told her if you weren't game, I'd meet her myself.' He put the DVD player to one side. 'No offence, Madge, but—'

'Would it make sense to rent a helicopter?' Madge said.

Ray

Ray woke up to find Doyle standing beside his bed with some chubby girl had the contours, to Ray's mind, of a punctured beach ball. Doyle wearing a short-sleeved 'FCUK FASHION' pink tee and short denim skirt, the chubby girl in a leopard-print bikini top and sarong combo. He drank down most of a glass of water from the bedside locker and said, 'Y'know, Stephanie, in one way I'm kinda hoping you're not a hallucination.'

'The word you're looking for is vision. This is Sparks, by the way.'

'Hi, Ray.'

'Hey.' The ward a four-bed, Ray the only patient. Windows open, so he could hear seagulls, mopeds, someone somewhere playing the Stones, 'Paint It Black', the driving percussion, that snaky sitar. 'So, Stephanie—'

'Where's the money, Ray?'

'I don't have it.'

'I know, I checked.' Doyle held up the black holdall that had held, the last Ray'd heard, the thirty grand kicking-around money he'd taken from his lock-up, Ray not knowing when he'd see the lock-up again. 'So where's the two hundred grand?' Doyle said.

'Last I saw it,' he conceded with a shrug, 'Karen's bag, when she got off on Corfu.'

'Try again. We know she's on Ios.'

'Karen's *here*?'

'Ray? Sparks saw you on the dock, before you fainted.'

'Blacked out.'

'Whatever. Where is she now?'

'How would I know? I've been in a coma.'

'If you want, we can just sit here and wait 'til she comes back.'

'OK by me. Will you read me a story? I mean, in case you get bored sitting there all week.' Ray waggled the empty glass. '*War and Peace* if you can get it.'

Doyle poured him some water, saying, 'Why should I believe she isn't coming back?'

'Because me and Karen, we're done. And anyway, Stephanie, if you're here on business you're out of your jurisdiction. If it's pleasure, you should relax.'

'How about I tell the local cops, as a professional courtesy, that they're harbouring a wanted criminal, a snatch artist. What would that be, business or pleasure?'

'That'd be spite.'

'So you're saying, pleasure.'

'Pity I'm not hooked up to something. You could pull the plug or stand on my air-pipe. Cut out the middle-man.'

'Help me and you help yourself. Otherwise, I wash my hands.'

'You came a long way,' Ray said, 'just to wash your hands.'

Karen

P yle warned Karen to stay abreast once they left the asphalt road or one of them would be eating grit for a week. Pyle being a hippy, he was happy enough renting a scooter, a silver Vespa with red piping. Karen on a royal-blue Kawasaki scrambler, no way she was riding any toy bikes. Anna still a little groggy from the pills but doing fine, loping awkwardly alongside.

They dipped first into a wide, shallow valley dotted with lemon trees, then turned off the asphalt road on to a rutted dust track angling up towards some mountain peaks. Karen waving Pyle down every ten minutes, stopping to give Anna water.

The third time, in the bend of a long U scored into the cliff face, Pyle cut his engine and took off his helmet, pointed back the way they'd come. Olive groves in the foreground, the village perched on the hill above the valley, a milky-blue haze to the horizon.

They smoked a cigarette between them, Anna prone and panting hard, tongue lolling. Cicadas *zizz-zizzing* from the scrub, the heat strong and dry. 'I can see why you might want to paint that,' Karen said. 'I mean, to catch all that in one frame, that'd be something.'

'With landscapes it's not what you put in, it's what you leave out.' Pyle dragged hard on the Marlboro, handed it across. 'See,' he pointed from one end of the horizon to the other, 'there's enough there but not too much. Any less, or any more, it wouldn't work. What you have to do is decide how much it needs to make it work.'

'You're saying, leave out a mountain. Or the village.'

'Not exactly.' Pyle chewed the inside of his lip. 'I read this thing once, it blew me away.' He closed his eyes, concentrating, then opened them again. 'OK, I can't remember the exact line. But, basically? If the universe had been bigger or smaller by one part in a thousand billion the split-second after it started? It wouldn't have started.'

Karen tried to fit it all in but couldn't make it click. Then a fly buzzed her nose and Karen, brushing it away, saw it up close against the vast backdrop. 'Jesus,' she said, shivering despite the heat.

'Bearing in mind,' Pyle said, 'we're dealing with infinity here, that's a hell of a lot of shit to come out of a microscopic piece of whatever the fuck it was.'

'And you're looking to find this it. When you paint.'

'Maybe not *it*, exactly. But yeah, something that gives the impression.'

'You don't make it easy on yourself, do you?'

'With the painting, no. Otherwise?' He grinned. 'I cut a lot of slack all round. What do you think, is Anna good to go yet?'

Ten minutes later they topped a ridge. The sign pointing to the right said 'Homer's Tomb' in Greek and English but Pyle waved Karen on through the left fork into a high-sided canyon that sloped down and away. The canyon gouged out of an orangey-red rock, the sides ridged like a grated cheese. When they made it through the canyon and out on to an escarpment, he pulled over. Karen took her helmet off and said, 'Oh, wow.'

Pouring water into her palm for Anna to lap at, she said, 'Jesus.'

Wondering where Rossi was, she said, 'How fucking glorious is that?'

Pyle nodded, crisscrossing the road trying to get a signal on his phone so he could let the hippy artist commune-types know he was coming in. The escarpment dropped away sharply, opening out into a wide plain that looked to Karen like the edge of the world. She'd never seen so much blue in her entire life, Karen trying to drink it all in but drowning in the perfect blend of sea and sky, the sun up there in the corner blazing away like a spoilt child trying to get her attention.

In the end Pyle sent a text. He lit a smoke and sat on a rock beside Karen's and said, 'You mind if I say something personal?'

'Depends what it is.'

'Leaving the guy behind like that? That was cold.'

'Who, Ray?' Karen sniffed. 'Ray's the kind that makes out.'

'Looks like it. Facing down this guy, what d'you call him, Rossi? The guy holding a rod on him?'

'Ray hadn't run out on us,' Karen said, tugging on Anna's ear, 'he wouldn't have had to face anyone down, rods or no rods.'

Karen, being honest, and hating herself for it, was more worried about Rossi. Ray, sure, he'd been half-delirious in the port. Drunk, too. But Karen didn't like the sound of that Rossi-in-a-box crap he'd pulled. And then, what was frustrating, collapsing before she could quiz him on the details. Karen had to admit she didn't know

Ray so well she could say for sure how he'd react in any and all situations, especially a one-on-one with the guy who'd put a bullet in him.

What she did know, realizing it outside the ESY, the one-storey health clinic, smoking and looking across at the scooter rental place wondering if they had any proper bikes, was if she stayed to watch over Ray, made sure he recovered, then Ray would always have the whip hand, would know Karen'd come through for him no matter how many times he walked away, ran out.

'One strike and you're gone,' she said.

'This is what I'm saying. Cold.'

'Most people don't even get one, Pyle.' Saying it without any edge, just letting him know in advance. 'Listen, how much further?'

Pyle pointed down at a ranch-style jumble of whitewashed buildings on the plain about half a mile from the sea, rows of blue boxes radiating out in semi-circles. ''Bout three clicks.'

'Think we could crack on?'

'You don't want to sneak up on these guys. They like their, uh, privacy. It's one of the rules, what they call commandments, no one turns up unannounced.' His phone beep-beeped. He checked the message. 'OK, we're set.'

Karen straddled the Kawasaki, kicked the bike to life. Called to Anna, pointing her down at the wide plain below, the blue haze beyond. Thinking, yeah, maybe Ray got that much right at least, life lived remote on a Greek island might have one or two things going in its favour.

Doyle

D oyle sat on the low stone wall across the way from the ESY in the shade of a scrubby beach oak, the wall separating the road from the umbrella-dotted beach, bodies glistening like new toffee. Doyle could see the Katina the other side of the horseshoe bay, shimmering now in the haze, a mirage promising sleep.

'How come,' Sparks said, prone on a sun lounger, the lounger angled so she faced Doyle, 'you didn't ask him about the big girl got off the ferry with him?'

Her toes aimed either side of Doyle, so Doyle couldn't help but notice Sparks had been in for a wax.

'Because this way,' Doyle said, 'he thinks we don't know about her.'

'What does that achieve?'

'Not one damn thing.'

'So why didn't you ask him?'

'Why didn't *you* ask him? You were there.'

'I thought you had a cunning plan.'

All Doyle'd had was an overwhelming urge to crawl between the crisp sheets of one of the ESY's spare beds. 'Next time,' she said, 'and until you hear otherwise, presume different.'

'That doctor wasn't much help,' Sparks observed.

'Someone came in to visit a patient of mine,' Doyle said, 'saying they were his friends, and then asked to see his passport? I'd be wondering why too.'

Sparks sat up, dipped her shades. 'You all right?'

'Just tired, Sparks. Hung-over. I haven't slept right since Tuesday night.'

'And there was me thinking it was the shock of Ray saying he and Karen were done.'

'I'm going to bed,' Doyle said, standing up.

Sparks lay back on the lounger. 'I think I'll stake out the clinic for a while. See if Karen comes back. Or the big girl.'

'What I like best about you,' Doyle said, 'is how you're always volunteering for the dirty missions.'

'I wouldn't ask anyone to do anything,' Sparks said, sipping some banana daiquiri through a straw, 'I wouldn't do myself.'

Sleeps

Sleeps, from the top deck of the ferry, had watched Melody and Ray disembark, Mel lugging the Louis Vuitton, Ray with the busted arm in no shape to help out. Ray with a spazzy shuffle going on, like he was afraid to lift his feet, the world might fall away if he did.

Sleeps knew that feeling.

He'd tucked Johnny's parcel under his arm and clanged all the way up the metal steps to the top deck, along the gangway to where it narrowed running past the funnel, the breeze whipping through. Not the smartest place in the world to snort coke, Sleeps conceded, although only if you were worried about some blowing away. Sleeps, planning a face-plant into Johnny Priest's snow, Al in *Scarface*, wasn't too worried about what came after that.

So he got himself comfortable on a whitewashed slatted bench containing life jackets, Johnny's parcel on his lap, noticing, contrary to what he would've believed were the safety regulations, that the lid of the box was tied down at its front corners by what appeared to be a pair of sneaker laces. This was when he felt his ass being kicked, faintly, through the slatted bars of the bench.

Sleeps had a moment when he considered walking away, finding another bench. Except there came another kick, a muffled squawk.

He knelt down and peered through the slats and met a wildly staring eye, bloodshot. Beyond that, half-shadowed, Sleeps could make out the side of Rossi's head, a sticky mess of black-looking blood running down out of the turban from roughly where the wolf-savaged ear used to be.

He said, 'Ray, right?'

'Dead man walking,' Rossi snarled.

Ray

'He's coming straight at me,' Ray said. 'Like, what am I supposed to do, jump overboard? This being a scumbag,' he added, 'who's already shot me, three days ago.' He took a drag off his smoke. 'Fuck that, he got warned.'

'You sure you should be out of bed?' Sparks said. The girl with frizzy red hair, pale skin, not far off hibernating in the shade under the beach umbrella. 'That sun's pretty fierce.'

Ray dragged his sun lounger into the shade. 'You want the truth?' he said. 'I never shot down on anyone before. Not even in the Rangers. Never wanted to, never did.' Ray trying to work out if it was the drugs had him high or the adrenaline rush, seeping through now the shock had dissipated, Ray buzzed after his long sleep. He'd waited until the doctor clocked off and then went looking for his clothes, his valuables, the nurse reluctant to let him go but having no real choice in the matter, Ray demanding to see some form he could sign to absolve the clinic from responsibility. 'Anyway,' he said, 'I squeezed one off.'

'Except at this stage, you're saying, you're not sure if there's one up the spout.'

'You ever handled an Uzi?'

'I work the desk,' Sparks said. 'Me and guns, even allowing for the whole phallic thing, we just don't mix.'

Ray nodded. 'The joy with your Uzi,' he said, 'is it's so safe you can run around with one in the hole. Drop it, hit the fucker with a hammer, it still won't go off. So I'm presuming, without checking, there's a round ready to go.'

'You could've killed him.'

'Not unless he grew three feet in a split-second, and he was already ducking in low.'

'And no one heard the shot?'

Ray shrugged. 'I'd say loads of people heard it. Whether they knew it was a gunshot, though . . . Most people, they hear a gun go off, they're hoping it's not what they think it is, y'know? Looking around for a back-firing van.' He scratched his nose. 'Anyway, I clonked him here,' Ray said, pointing above his ear, 'with the barrel of the Uzi.'

Sparks grimaced. 'This the same ear the wolf ripped off?'

'It wasn't like I was aiming for it. I just swung, one-handed, it was dumb luck I got him there. And I don't even know if he felt it, he went down that fast.'

'Don't tell me you chucked him overboard,' Sparks said. 'I'd have to testify under oath.'

'It was the Uzi went overboard. Rossi I dragged across to the bench.' Ray shook his head, remembering. 'Ever try to drag an unconscious man?'

'Seduction, some of us call it,' Sparks said. 'So what then?'

'I stuck him in this box where they keep the life preservers.'

'And no one said boo.'

'There was no one around, we were early getting on the ferry.'

'Leaving him comfortable in there,' Sparks said, 'on top of all the life preservers.'

'I thought he'd enjoy the irony.'

'I know someone who'll get a bang out of it. Mind if I ring her again?'

'Work away. But if she's sleeping, she's sleeping.'

Sparks rang Doyle. Ray lit a fresh smoke and tried to decide, again, who was most likely to have swiped the thirty grand and his passport, Karen or Mel. When Sparks was finished leaving her message, he nodded across the road. 'And you're saying, the guys in the scooter rental gave Doyle nothing.'

'She was fed up, hung-over. Only asked the once, where's the girl staying who rented the blue Kawasaki, Karen King. The guy got pissy, he couldn't speak English, so she just walked out again.'

Ray smoked on. 'How d'you think she is?' he said.

Sparks shrugged. 'She looked happy enough to me. That guy she's with, he's cute for an older guy.'

'Not Karen,' Ray said, 'Doyle. How's she making out?'

'Doyle?' Sparks shaded her eyes looking across. 'I don't know. She says she's tired but it's more than that.'

'Like how?'

'She's just not herself. Maybe, she was saying yesterday, it was the fright she got, being shot at. You were there when it happened, right?'

'I was already shot by then.' Ray crushed his smoke in the sand. 'Listen, I'm grabbing a beer. Want another one of those?'

'Sure. Only make it a strawberry one this time. Banana's a fattening fruit.'

'There's nothing less sexy,' Ray said, getting up, 'than too skinny.' He stepped over the low wall, crossed the road and went into the roadside bar, Baywatch, ordered an Amstel, a strawberry daiquiri. Then, while the guy went out back hunting fresh strawberries, Ray rolled down his sleeves and strolled next door to the scooter rental, slipping a credit card, the gold one, out of his wallet.

'*Yassou,*' he said. '*Kalimera.*'

'*Kalispera,*' the middle-aged guy behind the counter said, smiling. 'How can I help for you?'

'Looking to rent a bike, something decent. For a week.'

'You have the driver licence?'

'Sure.' Ray got out his wallet, laid the licence beside the credit card. 'I was here last year,' he said, 'you won't remember, but you rented me a sweet blue Kawasaki. Any chance it's still around?'

'Ah, but no.' The guy copying out Ray's details, liver spots like a join-the-dots game on the crown of his bald head. 'This is not possible. This bike, she is rented.'

'That's a shame,' Ray said. 'The guy rent it for long?'

'A woman. She rent for one week also.'

'Maybe I'll see her around,' Ray said. 'Persuade her to swap.'

'Perhaps.' The guy bobbing his head. 'But where she stays, is not a very good place to see her.'

'Oh yeah? She's staying up in the village?'

The ice had melted in the daiquiri by the time Ray got back to the beach. Sparks said, 'Any joy with the rental guy?'

'Nope. Unhelpful bastards, aren't they?'

'Who's that, the Greeks or just men in general?'

'Miaow,' Ray said.

Karen

U p close the ranch-style building was more in the way of an old bus garage converted into a dormitory, the whitewash dulled pinkish from the orange dust. Pyle led the way through the double gates into a gravelled courtyard with a round dry fountain in the middle, the high walls topped by dinky little battlements that got Karen thinking, again, maybe it was just her frame of mind, of the Alamo. A red-brick barbecue over in the corner built into a recess under an olive tree. Karen liked the look of the bleached-wood picnic tables.

The dorm was another matter. Twelve beds curtained off, not all of them taken. Pyle said Karen could rent one of the rooms built on if she wasn't cool with the set-up. So that's what Karen did, choosing a room for its balcony looking on to the courtyard, a view of the Aegean beyond the battlements, Karen seeing the sea as a vast moat, liking the notion. She'd never seen Anna this placid, and wondered if it was all the open space or just the girl hung-over from too many pills.

Or maybe it was Pyle. He had his feet up on the balcony wall, a beer on his midriff. A comforting rumble to his voice, Karen feeling safe for the first time in she couldn't remember how long, the commune being so remote. A guy, George, out on the road watching for strangers. She said, 'That George doesn't talk much, does he?'

'It's better when poets don't talk out loud.'

'He didn't look much like a poet.'

'The best ones don't.'

Karen grooving on the scene, people wandering aimless through the courtyard, stopping off at balconies to shoot the shit, gathering around the picnic tables. Beefheart filtering out from the dorm, 'Her Eyes Are a Blue Million Miles'.

When she tuned back in, Pyle was talking about his time in the army, the special forces training he'd had.

'Ray used to be in the Irish Rangers,' Karen said. 'He said it was like the Marines.'

'Ray of the Rangers?'

They both got a bang out of that one. Pyle said, 'I'm guessing he's a good man in a tight spot.'

'When he's not running off, sure.'

Anna whining at the sound of Ray's name, raising her head to look around. Pyle chucked her under the chin.

'Pyle? No offence, but I have to ask. I mean, about the duffel bag. How safe it is.'

Pyle shrugged. 'We have writers, painters. George the poet. One guy, he's a fire-eater. Another one's putting together a symphony of shell sounds and seagulls. Not exactly your criminal mastermind types.'

'I know, but—'

'First off, no one knows what's in the duffel. Second, Anna. Third, one of the commandments, it's actually a commandment, the Biblical kind. Around here no one steals from anyone else. You finished with that?'

Karen sloshed around the inch or two of beer in her bottle. 'Just about.'

Pyle got up, went inside. Karen tapped along to a new Beefheart number and then realized it wasn't Beefheart, it was Elvis Costello, a tune Karen didn't recognize. She put her feet up on the balcony wall and tried to figure out how to play Pyle.

Karen wondering, again, if it all mightn't be a whole lot simpler if she was older, didn't need that buzz she got from Ray, Christ, even from Rossi – how they let her feel it was OK, just once in a while, to get animal, forget everything except the right here and now, who she was, who she always needed to be . . .

He came back out with two bottles and a saucer, poured some of his beer for Anna and set it down in front of her. Anna sniffing, curious, then lapping at it cautiously.

'One thing I should mention,' Pyle said.

'What's that?'

'They'll need to think you're some kind of artist, you're working on a project. Otherwise they'll be asking why you're here.'

Karen thought about that. 'Me and Anna,' she decided, 'we're running away from the circus. Working on a new act.'

'Sounds good.'

'Pyle, you have no fucking idea.'

Melody

Mel went Spartan for accommodation, low-key, no sense in drawing attention to herself, but was still a little disappointed to realize the wardrobe in her room was just a smidge narrower than she was herself.

She sat at the table out on the balcony overlooking the port and opened the notebook. Time to recap. Except the glare of the setting sun on the blank pages reminded her of Ray in the ESY, so drained he was a jaundice stain on the crisp white sheets.

Ray, who should be waking up any time now.

Mel hoped he'd get back on his feet and presume she'd hopped the next ferry out, the logical thing to do when you've ripped someone off for thirty grand, the guy flat-backed, unconscious with exhaustion. The doctor wanting to know how Ray had busted his arm.

'Before my time,' Melody'd said. 'I met him on the ferry, thought he looked sickly. What do you think, is it heatstroke?'

Telling the doc Karen and Pyle were just off the ferry too, generously offering to help haul Ray out of the port around to the ESY. Mel dropping in a reference to Blanche DuBois, the kindness of strangers.

The doctor had nodded along, dubiously, then said Ray would

be fine once he got to the other side of about two days' sleep. Although, he'd be running some X-rays on the arm once Ray woke up, make sure it was healing right, wasn't part of the problem.

'Super,' Mel had said. 'I'll drop by tomorrow, see how he's doing.'

The doctor quizzing her about travel insurance, stuff like that.

'No idea,' Mel had said. 'Like I say, I just met the guy. All I know is his name's Ray and he looked poorly.' Mel arriving in the doctor's office via a visit to the restroom with Ray's holdall. She'd given the doctor the bag. 'You want to rummage around in there,' she'd said. 'Maybe you'll come up with some of the details you need.'

Then left and dragged her bags around to the port. Hailed a taxi, directing the cabbie up the hill to the village. Looking out at the pubs and clubs they passed, Melody wondered which one was Johnny Priest's, where Rossi and Sleeps were supposed to drop off the coke. Asking herself, a direct question, if she had the audacity, she ever found out which bar was Johnny's, to just walk in and ask for the ten grand she was owed. Thrilling to the idea, the daring. Actual tingles, like some dark electricity, when she pictured it for the script – Jack, cool and roguish, an older guy, Judy with that big-girl style going on, packing heat and demanding the ten grand she was owed . . .

Write what you know, they said. Every time, every single writing course, Mel shelling out good money to hear the same damn thing fifty different ways – write what you know. Mel was always tempted to raise a hand, ask how that worked for ghost stories, or you wanted to write a movie about spacemen. If John Milton, say, had stuck to the facts.

What Melody mostly knew was how little she knew.

Until, OK, now. Mel's idea being to write who she was, what she'd do . . .

The plan, if Ray was to catch her up, ask about his money, was to say she'd been keeping it safe for him, no sense in leaving all that cash lying around, a temptation to the overworked, underpaid nurses.

As for Rossi and Sleeps, if they tracked her down wanting to know where Johnny Priest's package was at, Melody figured the same ploy would work there too.

Rossi

'So I says, "Ray, we can do a deal here."'

'How'd that go down?'

'*I* went down,' Rossi said. 'We're in parley, yeah? But he cracks me one with the Uzi anyway. Ow, Jesus. Go easy.'

This last was to the nurse sewing the fresh wound. Which was at least a step up, Rossi had to concede, from getting stitched by a vet.

'He had a go during a sit-down?' Sleeps said.

'This is what we're dealing with, Sleeps. A moral degenerate. Next thing I'm waking up in the box.' Rossi skipping how he'd thought he'd been buried alive, sliding past the bit where he'd had himself a quiet weep.

Rossi, in a bad week to start with, was having a long day. Shot at, knocked unconscious, dumped in an early grave, then jumping ship on Santorini, ferrying back the way they came, a couple of hours each way. Rossi traumatized by his experience and anxious to share. Except Sleeps was catatonic the whole time, only perking up when they made it back to Ios.

'It gets worse,' Sleeps said. 'He's swiped Mel too.'

'Fuck *Mel*. Ow.'

'Please to sit still,' the nurse said.

'First off, I want that Uzi back,' Rossi said. 'You still have the mag, right?'

'You're the one had it. You must've left it in the van.'

'Crap.'

'Seriously, Rossi, I'm worried about Mel.'

'You're worried about *her*? Sleeps, give that girl six months and she'll be running the white slave trade out of Hong Kong.'

'Last I saw her,' Sleeps said morosely, 'she was with someone who'd shoot down on an unarmed man. The kind of degenerate, you called him, who'd whack a man during parley.'

'Except,' Rossi said, 'she's more likely the one who swiped Ray. Jesus! *Ow!*'

The nurse staring at him, the needle poised. 'Your friend is Ray?' she said.

Karen

Karen reckoned the best thing, in case Pyle took any notions when he got back, the guy with a couple of beers on, was to be gone at the time. Pyle being smart enough, or experienced enough, to take the hint. Or so she hoped. The last thing Karen needed right now was another guy telling her he could solve her problems, the first step being to take off all their clothes.

So she left Anna snoozing off her beer buzz and grabbed a sweater, the night turning chilly. Strolled out into the silvery-grey world beyond the walls, on down towards the shore along a tyre-rut track that wound through a grove of desiccated trees, Karen giving a wide berth to the little blue boxes Pyle'd told her were beehives. Ios honey, he said, being famous for its hint of oregano. Karen only realising then what it was she'd been smelling all day.

Truth be told, Karen had been more than a little relieved when Pyle mentioned the oregano, because she'd believed, on and off, that she'd been smelling weed. Well, not actually smelling it, but psychosomatically – the way she'd woken up one morning, four or five years ago, to the sickly-sweet stench of rotting flowers, a rank whiff that only disappeared at lunchtime when Madge rang to ask how Karen was coping with it being the anniversary of her mother's funeral.

And that had been it. Karen had never experienced the sickly-sweet smell again. Nor had she ever forgotten the anniversary of her mother's funeral.

Karen, sniffing the tang of weed on the warm air earlier on, had thought she was having some kind of olfactory reaction to the idea of Rossi tracking her out to the islands, Rossi being fond of a toke in the way a fish was fond of water. To be fair to the guy, she couldn't fault him when he argued he was self-medicating, that a good smoke took the edge off, kept him calm – Rossi with a lot to be angry about, given that his life as a kid had been pretty much that of a pinball ball, ricocheting from one slapping to another – although there were two things about that. One, Rossi's idea of calm was most doctors' definition of catatonic. Two, on those rare occasions when he wasn't pole-axed on the trippiest shit he could get his mitts on, Rossi could be truly vicious, like the time he'd gone mediaeval on Anna's eye with the blunt end of a fork.

Even now Karen could sense her mind shying away from imagining Anna's pain, the girl's terror as the metal scraped into the eye socket. She wondered if Rossi had felt the same way when Anna was ripping his ear off, and not in any eye-for-an-eye way, Anna trying to crush Rossi's skull flat.

She strolled on, cicadas *zizz-zizzing*, lizards rustling in the dry scrub. A tinkle-tankle of goat bells. She heard a self-satisfied rumble and saw a faint plume of dust way off to her left, ghostly in the moonlight. Someone coming down off the escarpment, arriving late to the commune. A chainsaw juggler, maybe, or a seaweed sculptor. Pyle, OK, seemed to know what he was doing, talked a good game. But the rest were artists of the bullshit variety. One guy, eating vegetarian barbecue for Chrissakes, had told her with a straight face he was writing a ballet for trees.

She picked her way down a steep ravine, careful not to slip on the loose shale, maybe twist an ankle, and got herself perched on a still-warm boulder overlooking a sheltered bay, a faint breeze funnelling up the narrow channel to cool her face. She lit a cigarette but mainly she inhaled the night, the quiet, the impression of comforting distance that went with looking out across a placid black sea. The cicadas, the whish-shushing waves, somehow part of the silence. The night damn near perfect except for the bee that'd tracked Karen all the way to the shore and was whining now somewhere up to her right, invisible in the dark.

Except then a boat rounded the near headland, its outboard motor buzzing, and angled down the channel.

Karen slid backwards off the boulder as a spotlight blazed, turning the cove bright as day.

Madge

"'Deliver Israel, O God, from all his tribulations,'" Madge said. 'It's from the Psalms, Psalms twenty-four.'

'You wanted to call the kid Israel?'

Madge nodded. 'The nuns said to take something from the Bible. So, if I'm handing him up, the least I can do is give him a name that means something. Like a prayer, a blessing he'd carry all his life.'

'Nice thought,' Terry said. 'But for an Irish kid? Patrick was probably the safer bet.'

'Don't sweat it,' Madge said. 'Frank got involved, Frank the fucking wannabe intellectual, the opera freak. A *big* fan of Rossini. Mainly,' she added, tapping ash, 'because of the Lone Ranger.'

'So you're saying neither of you was particularly worried about how the kid might fare in the playground.'

'I was seventeen, Terry, just after having a baby. I mean, this was a couple of hours after being ripped open. Just trying to do the right thing.'

'And still trying now,' Terry said, 'even though the guy, you're saying, reckons you're wrong.'

She'd seen Rossi on Santorini, Madge and Terry disembarked from the cruise ship and waiting to board the next ferry out to Ios, Madge perched on their luggage while Terry sorted the tickets. Not recognising him at first, just idly scanning the faces of the milling crowd, then noticing the bloody turban, some guy seriously pissed about something, waving his arms around, a big guy – Sleeps, who'd been so good to Madge, given her his jacket for a pillow the time she fainted up at the lake – Sleeps nodding patiently while Rossi vented.

Fate, she reckoned. Surprising herself at how quietly she accepted it, all her effort taken up with suppressing the urge to go to him, take a cool cloth to his bloody face.

'He's in denial,' she said, Terry leaning back to order another couple of beers from the barman, Mr Baywatch. Madge's gaze riveted to the entrance of the health centre, Rossi'd been in there over an hour now. 'Like, he's been told all his life his mother was some slapper worked the canal, his father a pizza guy over from Sicily. This is what he's being told by the other kids in the orphanage. But he's the right age, Terry. The right *name*.'

'It's perfect,' Terry agreed. 'So perfect he steps in and snatches you right out from under Ray's nose. This Rossi-Rossini being the reason,' he added, 'everything fucked up. Why you're right now a fugitive from justice.'

Madge thought about that. 'Maybe,' she said, the barman placing a tray with two beers, frosted glasses, on the table, 'if I hadn't dumped him all those years ago, he wouldn't have been just out of prison and so desperate for money he'd cut in on Ray and Karen. How's that sound?'

'Like you're still a fugitive from justice,' Terry said, sucking some froth off his upper lip, 'only this time it's natural justice.' He considered. 'Except sounding, to me, like you're thinking of turning the tables, going off to hunt down natural justice. Make it all well with Rossi again.'

'You could just as easily have said that,' Madge observed, 'without the sneer.'

'All I'm saying is, you've got enough problems without—'

'If Rossi's here,' Madge said, 'then it's Karen he's after. The money she owes him.'

'And you're going to help him,' Terry said, 'nail Karen. This guy who shot Ray.'

'Ray seems to me like a guy who can see the bigger picture.'

'Ray thinks twice,' Terry admitted, 'for sure. It's one of his strong points. But asking him to go splits with a guy nearly killed him? That's a big ask.'

'Who said anything,' Madge said, peering into the gathering gloom at the ESY, 'about asking?'

Ray

Ray had never ridden any bikes with a busted arm before and wouldn't be in any hurry to try it again, especially not at night along some dirt track felt like he was cruising railway sleepers. Ray wondering if he should've listened to the doc, stayed between the sheets. And then, just as the worst was over, Ray coming down off the escarpment and crossing the plain towards the lights, some guy ambles out of this tumbledown cottage and plants himself in the middle of the track. Ray, he wasn't doing four miles a fortnight on account of the arm, would've run him down.

The guy motioned for Ray to switch off. Ray left the engine idling. 'Yassou,' he said.

'Yassou, friend.' The guy was heavy, face like a mushroom pizza, these shoulders he'd swiped off some unwary bear. Ray waited. The guy scratched his stubble, sweat stains showing in the armpits of the rumpled shirt. 'Is there a problem?' Ray said.

'No problem.' Sounding harsh, maybe Nordic. 'You just took the wrong turn.'

'That's the commune down there, right? Where the hippies hang out.'

'That's private property.' No menace. If anything, the guy sounded bored.

'OK. But I'm looking for a friend.'

'Aren't we all?'

'Sure. But—'

The guy jerked a thumb over his shoulder. 'People come out here for peace and quiet. That's what they pay for.'

'What if I went down on tippy-toe?'

'What if you turned around, went back the way you came?'

'That way I wouldn't get to see my friend.'

'If you tell me where you're staying, I'll pass on a message.'

'I haven't got a place to stay yet.'

The guy shrugged.

'How about,' Ray said, 'you ring down ahead, see if she wants to talk.'

'No visitors, friend.'

'How about Pyle? He take calls?'

'Pyle?'

'Pyle, yeah, with the ponytail.'

'Why'd you want to talk to him?'

'Ask him after we're done. He wants you to know, he'll tell you.'

The guy thought it over. Then he reached in over the handlebars and turned the key, tugged it out and went inside. He came out with a phone, dialling up. Waited a moment or two, listening, then handed the phone to Ray.

'Pyle?'

'Who's this?'

'Ray.'

'Ray?' A beat, then, 'Fuck're you doing out of bed, man? You trying to kill yourself?'

'Just looking for Karen.'

'Same thing, right?' Pyle chuckling. 'Listen,' he said, 'she's not here right now, she must've gone for a walk. You want, I'll get her to buzz you when she gets back.'

'Appreciate it. Only I don't have a phone.'

'Where're you staying? She can call there.'

'I'm not staying anywhere yet. I couldn't just drop by, wait 'til she gets back?'

'No can do, buddy. Like George says, rules is rules. You'll get me kicked out. Hey, you were really in the Rangers?'

'She told you that, huh?'

'She mentioned it in passing. Tell you what, man – I'm busy here for another hour, then I'll come meet you, we'll grab a beer. If Karen's back by then, I'll bring her along. How's that?'

'I kind of need to sneak up on Karen at the moment, Pyle.'

'I hear you. Still want to grab that beer?'

'Where?'

'There's a place called Baywatch, I shit you not, it's down on Yialos beach out back of the port. A little cantina operation. Might be they'll sort you out with a place to stay too. Ask for Kosta.'

'An hour.'

'Thereabouts.'

Ray hung up, swapped the phone for the ignition key, kicked the bike to life and walked it around in a semi-circle. 'George,' he said, climbing aboard, 'it's been beautiful.'

'For you, maybe.'

Doyle

'All I'm saying,' Doyle said, 'is you shouldn't have accepted any invitation from Ray, not on my behalf.'

'I thought you'd have said yes.'

'Maybe I would, maybe I wouldn't.'

'*I* would,' Sparks said.

'You *did*,' Doyle pointed out. 'Invited yourself, then turned up. On time, too.'

'If I hadn't,' Sparks said, 'you'd have no one to take it out on. Ray not showing, I mean.' She sucked up some spaghetti, dabbed her napkin into the corners of the mouth. 'Still no word from Niko?'

'Not since he left that message.' Niko saying he'd been delayed, he'd keep her posted. Short and a long way from sweet, the guy sounding seriously hacked off.

The restaurant starting to empty out now. Doyle watched one couple pay their bill and take their Metaxas across the road to the beach to sprawl on sun loungers under the stars. The restaurant open-fronted, a cool breeze wafting in off the bay.

'Maybe Ray arrived,' Sparks said, 'saw you and left again. Expecting it to be me on my own.'

'And maybe he never planned on coming.'

'He said he would.'

'Ray's a liar. Compulsive.'

'Looks good doing it, though.'

'He kidnaps people, Sparks. I mean, this is how he earns a living.'

'I thought you said he was retired.'

'I'm talking about his character. How lying, to Ray, comes second nature.' Doyle, despite taking a shower, lowering a couple of frizzies, was still lethargic after her eight-hour siesta.

Sparks slurped up some more pasta. 'You're just pissed because he left you in the lurch.'

'The *lurch*? He left me, after being shot at by Rossi, cuffed to Frank in the middle of the woods.'

'Some lurches,' Sparks conceded, 'being worse than others.'

'See, this is what's bugging me. You knew all this before you let him ride off.'

'Sure. But this was after he was asking about you.'

Doyle forked some moussaka around the plate. 'What'd he say, exactly?'

'He was asking how you were, were you all right. Sounding concerned. Genuine.'

'Ray'd sound sincere reading a shopping list.'

'I know. What is it, his eyes?'

Doyle in no mood to talk about Ray's eyes. 'He say anything about Karen?'

'*I* thought he was asking about Karen. When he was asking about you.'

'I mean, where she might be.'

'Nope. He tried the bike rental place too. No joy.'

'This is what he told you.'

'Why should they tell him and not you?'

'Maybe he asked the right way.'

Sparks pointed at Doyle's moussaka with her fork. 'You want to change that? Something wrong?'

'It's fine. I'm just not hungry.'

Sparks closed one eye, adding up. 'Let's see,' she said. 'No appetite. Symptoms of withdrawal. Irritability. Obsessive behaviour. Any nausea?'

'Leave it, Sparks.'

'Look at the facts. You're pregnant, in love or you've picked up cholera.'

'Maybe I just want to be left alone.'

'You and Garbo. Another actress.'

'Mention Ray once more, Sparks, and I'm gone. Seriously.'

'OK. You want dessert?'

'No, thanks.'

'Me neither. Not really.'

Sparks had the chocolate fudge, Doyle a slice of strawberry cheese-cake. Ray arrived in time for coffee. Sparks said, as Ray pulled up a seat, 'There's a rule for a good-looking guy, how he's never actually late, just running behind. You're not gorgeous enough to qualify.'

'Yeah,' he said. 'Sorry about that. I'm not staying, either.'

Looking straight at Doyle while he apologized. Doyle shrugged it off, letting him know, but doing it cool, she didn't expect any better.

'I have to meet a guy now,' he said, 'but just for a beer. How about a drink after? My treat.'

'Why don't you bring your friend here?' Sparks said. 'The treat'll be all mine.'

Doyle kept her eyes on Ray. 'Where?'

'I don't mind.' He nodded across the road. 'The beach?'

Sparks winced. 'You're not worried about friction burns?'

Karek

From behind the boulder Karen couldn't be sure what was in the bales being unloaded off the motorboat. But at getting on for midnight, on a deserted beach, Karen had a good idea they weren't trafficking Tupperware.

So she backed away, keeping the boulder between her and the beach. Aiming for the ravine, testing each stone before she put her full weight on it. Breathing shallow and fast, blood roaring in her ears.

Then heard a click like there's no other click, felt something solid and cold against the nape of her neck.

A hand on her shoulder, turning her around. Karen had time to notice three dark holes, one the snout of the gun, the other two being cavernous nostrils under a vulture-beak nose. The gun whipped back then came in fast again, lashing Karen across the face.

After that, all she saw was velvety black.

Ray

Pyle cracked a gag with the barman on his way down to where Ray was sitting on a stool at the corner of the L, then slid through so he was looking past Ray out on to the road, the beach beyond, the port a blaze of golden lights away to the left.

'I'm hoping you're not on any medication, man. Booze and pills, it's a bad mix.'

'Karen didn't make it?'

'Still haven't seen her. Can I freshen that?'

Ray stayed with rum-and-coke. Pyle had a Mythos in a frosted glass, chugging half in one go. He wiped his mouth with the back of his hand. 'I guess,' he said, amping up the Southern-fried accent, 'this is where I ask if your intentions are honourable.'

'Towards Karen or the money?'

'The money's Karen's, man. They don't get separated.'

'I'm the one left the money with Karen,' Ray said. 'I know whose it is.'

'Cool. So why d'you want to see her?'

'Make sure she's all right.'

'She says she's fine.'

'Karen says a lot of things.'

'She says she hardly knows you. Or she only knows you ten days, something like that.'

'We've been through a lot.'

'She said that too.'

'This is what I'm talking about. Who knows what she's saying?'

Pyle drank off his beer. 'A woman doesn't change her mind once in a while, she's probably dead.'

Ray called another round, leaving his credit card, not the gold one, on the bar. 'It's not the money,' he said. 'I don't need the money.'

'Says the man buying drinks on plastic.'

'Temporary cash-flow glitch. Money's not the issue. Although,' he said, the barman, Kosta, setting them up, 'I wouldn't mind getting my passport back.'

'Karen took your passport?'

'It was her or Melody.'

'How come?'

Ray wasn't sure. 'They both got reasons for wanting me gone, but one doesn't want me to leave.'

'You're betting it's Karen?'

'I don't gamble, Pyle.'

'So I hear.' He toasted Ray with the fresh beer. 'Karen mentioned the snatches, how you'd pull them off. Sounds like a neat trick.'

'I'm retired.'

'This is where I'm coming from. You're looking for a new challenge. Also, you're ex-Rangers.'

'Yes to the ex-Rangers. Thanks but no to the new challenge.'

Pyle sucked froth off his upper lip. 'You just haven't heard yet,' he said, 'how challenging it is.'

Sleeps

'We already came this way, Rossi.'

'Fuck.' Rossi, after an hour spent wandering around the village, the Chora, had a face like a burst ulcer. 'You sure?'

'From the other direction. That tree with the pink flowers? We already passed that coming down.'

The village a maze of alleyways, crazy-paved. Sleeps getting snow-blind from the whitewashed walls, the windows and doors trimmed in blue. Trekking up steps, ducking into tunnels, the alleys curving away around corners to intersect like so many rollercoaster rides. Sleeps resigned to, at some point, meeting himself coming back.

Rossi turned another corner and stopped dead. 'Shit – is this the fucking square *again*?'

They found a space on a low wall circling a tree and had a couple of Singapore Slings to take the edge off. Rossi pinching out the crease in his strides, at this point dressed head-to-toe in Italian as a result of his larcenous expedition on the ferry back to Ios, wearing a coal-black suit, no socks, Gucci loafers for the finishing touch. Sleeps in beige chino shorts and a white tee, XXL, untucked.

'Why don't you just ring Johnny?' Sleeps said. 'Ask him to get his guy come meet us.'

'Amateur hour,' Rossi said. 'Giving them the giggles back in Amsterdam.'

'You could play it like you were being cool,' Sleeps said. 'Taking no chances, a neutral venue, all this.'

'Making it sound like we don't trust Johnny.'

'I don't trust Johnny.'

'Because,' Rossi said, 'you never did serious time. Don't appreciate the bond between guys celled together. Besides, I been doing some research.'

'Research?' Sleeps said.

'Multi-tasking,' Rossi said. 'Like, how long have we been walking up and down the village?'

''Bout an hour, maybe more.'

Rossi nodding along. 'And I haven't once, not fucking *once*, had even a whiff of a toke.'

'Maybe they do their smoking at home,' Sleeps said. 'Private-like, so's they don't, y'know, get nabbed by the cops.'

'You even seen a cop?'

'Not yet.'

'I rest my case.' Rossi lifting Johnny's parcel, putting it down again, to make his point. 'What I'm saying,' he said, 'is there's a niche here. You see it? Johnny's piping in coke, yeah?'

'Not if you believe Johnny. According to Johnny he's just doing this guy Jochem a favour.'

Rossi winked. 'This is Johnny's cover. Operating on a need-to-know basis.'

'So you're trusting him even though he doesn't trust you.'

'What're you spraffing about, man? He gave us the coke, didn't he?'

'Yeah, but—'

'Ask no questions, Sleeps, hear no lies. You ever move up, get to some place there's responsibility involved, you'll see that's how the big boys run it. Nudge-nudge, know what I mean?'

'Running it like a Monty Python sketch.'

'A what now?'

'Forget it.' Sleeps scanned the crowd that filtered out of the alleyways to mill around the village's main square like it was a vortex sucking them in, Sleeps still hoping Mel might wander by. The square fronted by four or five bars with tables outside, each bar with speakers blasting out different tunes, the effect being roughly that of Russian sopranos on a spin-dry cycle.

Everyone passed through the square at least once every night, the nurse had said. The girl concerned for Ray, the guy out of bed too early, glad she'd met friends of his who might persuade him to take it easy, maybe come back in for a check-up tomorrow morning. Telling them how the girl Melody had gone off alone, abandoning Ray in the bed, unconscious. This leaving Sleeps and Rossi to decide, once Rossi'd been patched up again, whether Mel had pulled a scam on Ray. Or if Ray had just worked a diversion, faking a black-out to let Mel get away first, then following on to hook up with her later. Maybe, this being Rossi's suggestion, with Karen behind it all, pulling strings.

'Business,' Rossi was saying, 'it's all about what they call identifying a niche, yeah? So I'm saying, Johnny looks after the coke end, maybe even your pills, gets the punters up and buzzed. Then we come in, take care of the chillin'.'

'The chillin'.'

'Perxactly. That way there's no conflict of interest. We kick a sweetener upstairs to Johnny, everyone gets well.'

'And where're we getting the smoke?' Sleeps said.

'First thing,' Rossi said, 'is we impress Johnny. Deliver this baby,' he patted the parcel, 'all ship-shape and brisket fashion. Then, we're on the in, we put together a proposal.'

'Bristol,' Sleeps said. 'And then what – we go to work for Johnny?'

'*For* him? Fuck no. We come in equal partners, what they call pawning our resources.'

'What about FARCO?' Sleeps said. 'I thought you were going legit.'

'This *is* FARCO, Sleeps. You see what I'm saying? Johnny's helping us out, we're helping him . . . I mean, FARCO was never going to be, like, a hundred per cent legit. You knew that, right?'

'I was kind of hoping,' Sleeps said, 'it might be mostly legit. Or at least partly.'

'We could do it that way,' Rossi said, sipping on his Sling. 'Like, we could wander around the village a little more until we find a magic door into another fucking universe, where guys like me and you, came up in a home, had to hustle a little once in a while, we don't get the bum's rush every time we stand still. Y'know? A place where they say, hey, here's a guy needs a break, let's not bust his balls this once, see how he works out. Instead of saying look at this guy,' Rossi nodding now at a group of well-fed teens, all perfectly gelled hair and swagger, braying so loud they even drowned out the Russian sopranos now and again, 'this guy's who's had it sweet all his life, college and shit, guy's got money falling out of his hole, so let's give him more money, see if he can't wedge *that* up his hole and stop all the other money falling out. You see what I'm saying.'

'Sure. Except we got no resources to, um, pawn with Johnny.'

'The fuck're you talking about? We got ten grand coming from Johnny we hand over the snow. Then, we nail Karen, nab the loot, we're coming in with,' he shrugged, 'shit, whatever's fucking left. But a hundred gees clear, minimum, or I'm selling Karen's kidneys. Plus,' he said, tapping the table with a dirty forefinger, 'the Uzi. I'm going nowhere without the cannon.'

'You think Karen's still here?'

'The nurse seen her go off on a bike with this other guy, the ponytail guy. So I'm guessing, yeah, she's around, no one rents a bike then brings it back and fucks off. And once we find Ray, we find Karen. So,' he said, drinking off the last of his Sling, 'tomorrow morning, bright and early, we're back at the ESY for when Ray comes around to see if his passport wasn't filed in the wrong place and shit, like the cute little nurse said.'

'You seriously think he'd give Karen up? I mean, the guy's been looking out for her all along, man. Why would he stop now?'

'He's got one arm, we got four. Do the math.'

'I told you already, Rossi, I don't do muscle. I'm a pacifist.'

Rossi crossed his eyes in frustration. 'OK,' he said, 'so you're a spacifist. How's Ray supposed to know that?'

'Mainly,' Sleeps said, 'because we didn't muscle him the last time, when we had the chance. And whatever happened to honour among thieves?'

Rossi pointed at his freshly bandaged ear. 'The man broke a parley, means he's gone rogue.' He stood, shot his cuffs, picked up the parcel. 'From now on it's Rossi's rules.'

'Which are?'

'Need-to-know, Sleeps.' Rossi tapped the side of his nose. 'You'll know 'em when you hear 'em.'

Doyle

'So this guy,' Doyle said, 'you won't tell me his name, wants you to snatch some guy.'

Ray nodded. 'That's about the height of it, yeah.'

'He notice you've a busted arm?'

'I imagine he was too polite to say.'

'I thought you'd retired.'

'I did,' Ray said. 'I am.'

'And you told him this.'

'Yep.'

'But he's still asking. I mean, this guy you've only met once, he's persistent.'

'I've met him twice, briefly. But yeah, he's offering top wedge.'

They were down on the beach opposite Doyle's place, the Katina, sprawled on loungers under an umbrella facing the port across the bay. The night still warm, stars sparkling, tiny waves nibbling the sand. Doyle thinking how it was all just one willing guy off perfectly romantic.

'He tell you why he wants this guy snatched?' she said.

'I didn't ask.'

'But you're thinking of doing it.'

Ray lit two cigarettes, passed one over. 'He said he liked Anna,' he said.

'Anna's a dote.'

'He likes her for a guard dog.'

'She'd do a damn fine job.'

'Except the only way Anna's doing guard dog for anyone else,' Ray said, 'is if Karen's out of the picture.'

'So you think it was a threat.'

'Maybe.'

'So it mightn't be a threat.'

'It's a threat,' Ray said.

Doyle starting to see it. 'You're not so worried about the threat,' she said, 'as who's making it. I mean, if it's this guy or Karen who's behind it, wanting you to think she's in trouble. Again.'

'Karen can be tricky,' Ray said. 'Y'know,' he said, 'one thing I like about you, a man can assume a lot straight off, just get to the point.'

'I thought you and Karen split,' Doyle said, wondering if Ray, with the compliments, telling her earlier how starlight was good for her eyes, she should think about becoming an astronaut, was working up to making a pass.

'We did,' he said.

'So how come you're still involved?'

Ray shrugged. 'If you're in, you're in.'

Doyle thought about that, then swung her legs off her lounger and crossed to Ray's, hunkered down and took his face in her hands and kissed him, long and luscious.

Ray, pressing his lips together, tasting her strawberry balm, watched her go back to her lounger. 'What was that for?' he said.

'Why's it have to be for something?'

'It generally is.'

'I'm on holiday. On a beach, with the moon up. A guy just sitting there.'

'A waste,' Ray said, 'not to smooch him.'

'You know what's a waste? You running around after Karen, she's trying to screw you.'

'You're not trying to screw me?'

'It's my *job* to screw you. Professionally speaking.'

'I thought you were on holiday.'

'The way you're retired, thinking of snatching someone.'

'I never said I was thinking of doing it. I'm just wondering why the guy wants it done.'

'Or why Karen wants it done.'

Ray made to sip some beer then decided against it, pressed his lips together again, snaked the tip of his tongue into the corner of his mouth.

'Try this,' Doyle said. 'I mean, as a theory. Say Karen has this guy screwing you over. What do you owe her?'

'If it's her that's behind it.'

'That's the theory. If it's her, what d'you owe her?'

'Nothing.'

'OK. So why not play along?'

'What's that achieve?'

'We let Karen tie herself in knots. Then we add a little pink bow, hand her up.'

Ray grinned. 'You're serious.'

'It's self-defence, Ray. If she's screwing you.'

'We don't know she is. And even if she is, no.'

'No?'

'No.'

'What would it take,' Doyle said, 'for you to hand her up?'

'Karen has plenty to worry about right now. And the one thing she doesn't have to worry about is me ratting her out. So let's just leave it that way.'

'You're thinking I want Karen for my score. Bring her home, hand her up, close the case. But if I do that, you're going down with her.'

'The thought had occurred.'

'What if I'm asking you to make a gesture?'

'A gesture.'

'For me.'

'I owe you,' Ray said, 'about as much as I owe Karen.'

'You left me in the middle of a forest handcuffed to Frank. While you ran off with the loot and Karen.'

'Point taken. But you're asking too much.'

'A gesture's too much?'

'Depends on the gesture. You're asking me to fuck Karen over.'

'Only because you're thinking she's doing the same to you.'

'Even if she was, two wrongs don't make a right.'

Doyle asked for another cigarette. Ray lit two from the butt of the old, handed one over. 'Noble's one thing, Ray. Blind stupidity's another.'

Ray mulled that one over, then said, 'You never had anyone wouldn't rat you out like that?'

'Other than family?'

'Family's family. Family doesn't count.'

'Then no, I've never had anyone wouldn't rat me out like that.'

Ray got up and went over to her lounger and sat down straddling it. Doyle pulled her knees up to her chest. Ray scooched up the lounger, put his beer down on the sand, leaned in with her knees against his chest. This time the kiss went on a little longer, a lot deeper.

'If I stitched up Karen,' Ray said, tasting strawberry, 'then you'd always know I could do the same to you sometime.' Then ducked in again for another lingering smooch Doyle felt in her toes. She pushed him back, got him upright again.

'What're you guaranteeing me here?' she said.

'There's no guarantees, Doyle. You get down into it, all the way down, down past the atoms into the quantum level? Everything, and I mean the whole damn universe, is based on probability and uncertainty.'

'A girl needs a bit more than lectures on quantum physics, Ray.'

'You'll laugh every day.'

'I'd settle for a pension plan.'

Ray sat back and reached for his beer, took a sip. Eyes on hers, he said, 'This gesture you're talking about. You have any joy yet with my name?'

'Nope.'

'What'd you try?'

Doyle went through the list: Raymond, Raphael, Rainier, Reynaldo, Raymundo, Rumpelstiltskin . . .

Ray said, 'You didn't try Israel?'

'*Is*rael?'

'It's biblical,' he said.

Rossi

'Seriously, yeah. He's sitting in front of me right now.' The English guy, Roger, behind the desk on the phone to Johnny Priest. 'Yeah, Rossi Callaghan. Says he's half Sicilian, half Dirty Harry.'

Rossi winked at Sleeps. Roger saying, 'Why would I kid you about this? He's here, the other side of the desk. Looking for some ten grand he's owed.'

Rossi was more than a little disappointed with the poky office over the Blue Orange, just enough room for a battered desk, a filing cabinet, an empty water cooler. A mousetrap in the corner by the skirting board. Rossi'd been expecting something plusher for Johnny's Greek island hub.

Roger, a peroxide surfer-type wearing a T-shirt that read 'Everything Rhymes With Orange', said, 'I don't know. Ask him yourself.' Then handed Rossi the phone.

Rossi sat forward clearing his throat. 'How're they hanging, Johnny?'

'Rossi?'

'The one and only. What's new?'

'You made it?'

'Mission accomplished, man.'

'Yeah . . . Any, y'know, trouble on the way?'

'I don't do trouble, Johnny.' Rossi poking a finger in his good ear. 'The right thing the simple way, man, that's how it gets done Rossi-style. Anyway, if you'll just authorise your man Roger here to kick free the ten grand, we'll be—'

'Hold up,' Johnny said. 'Roger there's just looking after the bar. Jochem's guy is on Crete, won't make it to Ios 'til tomorrow. Some problem, he said, with flights to Santorini.'

'Crap.'

'You on your own? Everyone make it?'

'No man left behind, Johnny. You know the drill.'

'Let me talk to Sleeps.'

'Sleeps? How come?'

'I just want to be sure everyone made it. That way I know there was no fuck-ups.'

'There was no fuck-ups. We're here, aren't we?'

'Let me talk to Sleeps.'

Rossi, fuming, handed the phone to Sleeps, who said, 'What?'

'None of your fucking business,' Sleeps said.

'Like I give a fuck,' he said.

'You and whose army?' he said.

Rossi snatched the phone back. 'Johnny? Don't mind him, he just gets antsy when he's tired. It's been a long trip.'

'Put Mel on.'

'She's, ah, she's not here right now.'

'Where is she?'

'Back at the room. Minding the stuff.'

'What stuff?'

'The stuff. Luggage and shit.'

Static on the line. Then, 'Where're you staying?'

'Place in the village,' Rossi said, not willing to mention they hadn't sorted a place to stay yet, concerned it might sound unprofessional.

'Whereabouts exactly?'

'I dunno, man. That village, there's no street signs, it's a fucking maze.'

'OK, but what's the place called?'

'Something Greek,' Rossi said. 'The name right now escapes me.'

Rossi listened to static. Then Johnny said, 'Come back tomorrow, Rossi. All three of you. I want to know there's been no fuck-ups. Say noon-ish, Jochem's guy'll be there by then. Once he knows everything's kosher, he'll sort you out. Put Roger back on.'

Rossi handed Roger the phone. Roger listened, then said, 'No chance.'

He said, 'I pull beers and count the money.'

He said, 'Yeah, that's the way it is. And that's the way it's staying.'

Then he looked at the phone, shrugged and hung up. 'Sorry, boys. Johnny says I can't take the package.'

'*Try* and fucking take it,' Rossi growled.

Roger looking puzzled. 'I just said, I'm not touching it.'

Sleeps said, 'Rossi? Let's roll.'

Downstairs the low-ceilinged bar looked like two living rooms with a wall put through. The walls roughly plastered, whitewashed. A pool table to the right of the door, a dartboard near the bar. A smattering of customers huddled in dark corners. A guy behind the bar, headphones on, wearing a T-shirt that said 'Human Jukebox'. Don Henley's 'Boys of Summer' a mellow hum with occasional kerrangs.

Rossi bellied up to the bar and ordered two Singapore Slings from the cute Scottish girl, then asked for the darts. Drank off his Sling in one go, told the girl Johnny'd said they were on the house and walked out, pocketing the darts.

'See,' he said, as they strolled away down the narrow alleyway, the parcel tucked under his armpit, 'this is the kind of crap you don't get when you're an independent, unaffiliated. You see what I'm saying.'

Sleeps said, 'Rossi? I think we need to take a look-see in Johnny's parcel.'

Madge

I f anyone ever asked Madge about the twins she'd say they had hearts of gold. Meaning, hard and cold, buried miles down. So she figured, even if Rossi kept up his act, playing hard to get, she'd had plenty of practice digging.

'Here they come again,' Terry said, drinking off his beer. 'You ready?'

'Let's not just jump in there,' Madge said. 'He's like a half-wild cat, y'know?'

Madge and Terry sitting at the front window of a restaurant that was, Madge was guessing, someone's front parlour in the off-season, the window looking out on to the alleyway. The Blue Orange across the way, the sign in blue-and-orange neon above a little window seat, a low-lintelled stable door with the upper half open. Rossi and Sleeps strolled away down the gentle incline towards the heart of the village, arguing. Rossi, Madge had been surprised to notice, looked dapper, very businesslike, in a suit and tie, nice shoes.

'I can appreciate,' Terry said, 'how you're worried about being rejected again. Can't be nice to be denied, it's your own flesh and blood. But if we don't stick tight to this guy, we'll lose him.' Terry was impressed with Rossi's strategic thinking, the way he'd criss-crossed and double-backed earlier on, coming up through the village, Rossi covering the angles, watching for spotters, tails. 'The least we need to know,' he said, 'is where they're staying. We get that, we can relax. Maybe, tomorrow morning, touch base by phone first, break the ice easy. Set up a meet.'

They stayed well back winding down through the village, Sleeps' bulk hard to miss even if Rossi was swallowed up in the thronged streets.

'You think I'm crazy, don't you?' she said.

'Yes, I do.'

'You can't see it?'

'Anyone giving away money's crazy to me,' Terry said. 'After that, you're asking if I can see the logic of a three-way split, Rossi and the twins, then yeah, I can see it. Although,' he said, 'you want to push the logic, it'd make even more sense to cut the twins out, they've had all the breaks so far. Rossi's had none. So he's got a lot of ground to make up.'

'Maybe I should give him half,' Madge said, 'let the girls split the rest.'

'I was Rossi,' Terry said, 'that'd sound just about right to me. Hold on, here we go.'

They watched Rossi and Sleeps disappear into a pension, the Triton, then took a seat on the low whitewashed wall overlooking a weed-choked parking lot, a floodlit basketball court at the other end. Twenty minutes later the pair reappeared, Rossi now with his shirt open at the neck, no tie. No sign, either, of the parcel he'd had tucked under his arm.

'C'mon,' Terry said, taking Madge by the hand and leading the way across the street, up the steps to the Triton's foyer.

A young guy, early twenties, was behind the desk watching football on a TV bracketed high in the corner over an archway. Terry said, 'Hey, how're you doing? You speak English?'

'Well enough,' the guy said. 'How can I help you?'

'We're supposed to be meeting up with some friends, a guy called Rossi Callaghan, he said he'd be staying here.'

'That's correct,' the guy said. Attractive erring on the side of pretty, Madge decided, with a glossy sheen to his olive skin, thick black hair, dark and sullen eyes. 'They checked in half an hour ago. We serve breakfast only, so they've gone out to eat.'

'That's a pity,' Terry said. 'You mind if we leave a note?'

'Of course.'

'You got a pen, some paper?'

While the guy hunted up the necessaries, Madge whispered to Terry, 'You think *we* could stay here? I mean, we still need some-where to stay, right?'

'If you're OK with that,' Terry said. 'You don't think it'd freak Rossi out.'

'I'll stay out of the way,' Madge said. 'Let you meet him, like an intermediary. It's a lot to ask, I know, but—'

'Not a problem,' Terry said. He said to the guy behind the desk, 'You got any rooms free? One with a balcony? A kind of suite vibe to it?'

'Certainly.'

'Great, we'll take it.' He held up a hundred folded in two between fore and middle fingers. 'One thing, though. We left our luggage down at the port, it's in—'

'Allow me,' the guy said, 'to take care of that.'

'Nice,' Terry said. 'I appreciate the gesture.' He tucked the hundred back into his breast pocket. 'Now,' he said to Madge, ignoring the Greek guy's glare as he picked up the pen, 'what is it you want to say in this note?'

Melody

The phone book being in Greek, all the operators speaking Greek, it took Mel ages to get the right number. It didn't help that the phone booth was a head-and-shoulders affair across the road from a nightclub, Sweet Irish Dreams, and right beside a souvlaki vendor that had a generator buzzing, a transistor radio with a semi-hysterical football commentary dangling from a strut on an old leather dog-leash.

Mel twitching every three seconds, glancing left and right, on the off-chance Ray might wander out from the hordes of drunken tourists flooding by, singing. One group so blitzed they were doing 'Fairytale of New York', maggots and lousy faggots and bells ringing out for Christmas Day.

But she got through in the end, went straight into her spiel. How Rossi'd forgotten the name of the bar, was too embarrassed to ring himself and ask for directions. She'd had to sneak away so he wouldn't know she was calling.

'Is that a fact?'

'Rossi's really the shy type when you get to know him. As most Sicilians tend to be, I find. Don't you?'

'I don't know if I've ever met any. Italians, though, I wouldn't as a rule describe them as bashful.'

'You're so right. So where can we, um, find it?'

'It's getting late, Mel. You just relax there, kick back. If you do find the Blue Orange, just get them to run you a tab, I'll fix it up when I get in. That's about noon or thereabouts, so I can take you to lunch first, then show you around.'

'Super. But I should warn you, there's a bit of a hitch with the ten grand.'

'A hitch?'

'See, I'm owed for the passports.'

'The passports.'

'The ones I got for Rossi and Sleeps. Like, they owe *me* ten grand. So now that I've got the package, you won't need to meet with them at all, really. Will you?'

'I don't suppose I do. Not really. It's still sealed, right?'

'Absolutely.'

'OK. Can you meet me off the Santorini ferry, the hi-speed? It'll be in around noon.'

'Should I wear a carnation?' Mel said, being of the opinion, it was a philosophy she generally adhered to, there was no such thing as a wasted flirt.

'That's OK,' Johnny Priest said. 'I've got a good memory for faces.'

SUNDAY
Sleeps

'What's it say?' Rossi said, shovelling home a forkful of bacon.

Sleeps flattened the note with his elbow while angling a slab of toast into his mouth. '*Dear Rossi,*' he read, chewing. '*If you'd like to have a chat about some money you're owed, meet me for lunch at noon at Sally Baba's. Yours, an Admirer.*' He swallowed the toast. 'There's also two x's on the end, I think they're kisses.'

'Sally fucking Baba's?'

'What it says. Who d'you think it's from?'

'Johnny?' Rossi hazarded.

'Signing off with two kisses?' Sleeps said. 'Besides, we're already meeting his guy later on, back at the Blue Orange.'

'So who?' Rossi said. 'It can't be Mel, she thinks we're the ones owe her.'

'And Mel,' Sleeps pointed out, 'wouldn't be going into print as a big admirer of yours.' He speared half a fried tomato, slotted it home. 'Karen? Looking for a parley?'

'Possible,' Rossi said. 'Maybe even a full, y'know, makey-up.'

'That'd explain the kisses, yeah.'

'What'd the guy on the desk say?'

'Something about being owed a tip, a hundred.'

'For delivering a *note*?'

'Times are hard here in Greece. Man's got a living to make.'

'Maybe it's Johnny's guy,' Rossi said, 'getting in early from Crete and keeping it in code. That make sense?'

'Maybe. Think Johnny had us tailed here?'

'You'd be disappointed,' Rossi said, 'a pro like Johnny, if he didn't.'

'So he's still not trusting us. While we're trusting him.'

'No way we're opening that package, Sleeps. We do that, the ten grand goes bogey.'

'How's he even gonna know?' Sleeps said. 'Hey, you eating those eggs?'

Rossi passed his plate across. 'How about this?' he said. 'You're the one wants it open, so we say, there's any grief after, you're the one opened it. While I was asleep or some shit. You're a coke fiend, can't help yourself.'

'Hanging me out to dry,' Sleeps said, wiping a dribble of yolk off his chin, 'for looking out for your interests.'

'That's perxactly how it lies,' Rossi said. 'Your call.'

Three minutes later they were staring down at a hefty pile of Mel's none-too-skimpy skimpies, the package unwrapped on Sleeps' bed. Arriving at the consensus that they were Mel's via the guess that Johnny Priest, if for some reason he wanted to double-cross Jochem, probably wouldn't have had a heap of what Rossi referred to as dwarves' ponchos lying around in Vatican Two.

Rossi, outraged, went hunting out the darts, raving about how he was planning to harpoon himself some beached whale right through the fucking eyeball.

'No personals,' Sleeps said. He bundled together the delicates. 'Let's keep this one strictly business. The way Mel's playing it.'

Karen

K aren woke up with a head full of scrapy cellos. Skull pounding, a metallic taste in her mouth, stale and damp from sleeping in her clothes. Pyle perched on the edge of the bed, shaking her ankle. 'Hey,' he said. 'How're you feeling?'

'Not good.' She gave him her symptoms, Pyle nodding along.

'Concussion. Here.' He handed her a bottle of water, some pills. 'These'll help.'

The room was cool, the A/C humming. Doors and windows closed, so their slats threw fat shadow-ladders across the tiled floor. Karen sat up, trying to ignore the bile bubbling in her gut, and gulped down the pills, feeling the water filter through her body one parched cell at a time. 'Who found me?' she said.

'I did. You must've slipped off a rock, clonked your head.'

'I slipped off the rock on purpose. The clonking came after.'

'You fell?'

'You'd have fallen too, someone cracked you with a gun.'

Pyle frowned. 'A gun?'

'That cop from Piraeus? He's here.'

'Shit.'

'There was a boat,' she said. 'They were unloading some bales, I couldn't see what they were.' Karen looking past Pyle, to where the khaki duffel was propped against the other bed. 'Then he just popped up with the gun, and bam.'

'Bastard.'

The room quiet apart from the A/C hum. No snuffling or deep-chested growls, no nails clickety-clicking on the white tiles. Karen stifled a yawn, wincing as her nose wrinkled. 'Where's Anna?' she said.

'Anna's fine. You worry about yourself for a change.'

Karen drank some more water. 'You worry about you,' she said. 'Start with how this guy found me, just happened to be here on the same beach at this place you told me we'd be safe.'

'You think *I* tipped him off?'

'It damn sure wasn't Anna.'

'If you think I had anything to do with that,' he gestured at her face, 'you're crazy.'

'OK,' Karen said. 'But what I'm wondering is how come he found me.'

'I doubt he was even looking for you,' Pyle said. 'Just got lucky.'

'In all these islands? No one's that lucky.'

'Maybe it was you,' Pyle said, 'who just happened to be unlucky. Wrong time, wrong beach.'

'I don't follow.'

'It's a long story. C'mon, I'll tell you over breakfast. You think you could eat something?'

'No, thanks.' Even the idea of food made her nauseous, pain throbbing now from the bridge of her nose down through her upper jaw. 'How's it look?'

'Not great. I think he broke your nose. When you're ready to move I'll take you in for an X-ray, make sure there isn't a fracture of the actual skull.'

'I'm ready now.'

'The health centre doesn't open till noon.' He stood up. 'Anything else I can get you?'

'Just Anna.'

'Will do. I'll check back in a while, bring her along.'

She waited until he had gone, then crossed to the other bed and hunkered down beside the duffel, guts boiling up hot and greasy.

The money was there.

The .38 had gone.

She went in the bathroom and stared at the huge bruise on her forehead, the blackish swelling under both eyes. Then she purged the vomit, got undressed and stepped under the shower. The icy blast made her gasp but she couldn't shake the torpor. Realizing the pills were kicking in, she towelled off and went back in the room to lock the door, except Pyle had already locked it. The window shutters rattled but were hooked on the outside.

Karen trudged through deep treacle to the bed and collapsed. She drifted off trying to remember if she'd brought the .38 along, the night before, just going for a stroll on the beach. Pretty sure she hadn't.

Doyle

Sparks was out on the balcony sunbathing topless, her breasts the bluey-white of halogen headlights. Doyle sat on the other lounger averting her eyes from the glare.

'Dirty stop-out,' Sparks said.

'He took a room down the hall. So it wasn't really a stop-out as such.'

'And?'

'It's complicated.'

'When is it not?'

'He's thinking of doing another snatch.'

'Christ.' Sparks dipped her Mickey Mouse shades. 'You're serious?'

Doyle filched a cigarette from Sparks' deck.

'And you can't stop him,' Sparks said.

'I think he wants me to help.'

'Now that *is* complicated. I thought he was retired.'

'He is.' Doyle lit up, sucked hard on the smoke. 'But he thinks Karen's in trouble.'

'He wants *you* to help him save Karen?'

'Sort of, yeah.'

'He doesn't know much about women, does he?'

'Not much.'

'So what're you going to do?'

'Think about the little,' Doyle said, popping a smoke-ring, 'he does know.'

Ray

'If you gotta go, man, this is the place to be buried. Am I right?' Ray was looking out from Homer's Tomb to some islands nesting in the horizon's haze, the sea and sky a blue so huge it hurt his eyes trying to fit it all in. Off to his right a deep ravine wound down to the sea. Beyond that, some drystone buildings that might have been goat shelters or German pill-boxes from the war. Ray heard seabirds *skee-yar*, goat-bells clunking. A lone cicada like a one-stroke hyena.

'This is where it all started, man,' Pyle said. 'Gods and heroes, Troy in flames. What I like about Homer? Three thousand years of culture, kick-started by a guy who was blind.'

'There's caves in the Sahara,' Ray said, 'that have paintings go back to the Neolithic.'

'Oh yeah?' Pyle undid his red bandana, mopped his neck and throat. 'You like wall art?'

'Murals.'

'The Sistine Chapel, man. Am I right?' Ray nodded. 'So maybe you'll get it,' Pyle said.

'Get what?'

Pyle waved back towards the commune, the white buildings shimmering in the heat-haze down on the plain. 'This guy, he's making what you might call a hostile takeover bid.'

'On a hippy commune?'

'Not us, exactly. The place. See that crack in the shoreline, looks like someone knocked out a chip with a hammer? It's a natural harbour,' Pyle said. 'A sheltered deep-water. So this guy's planning a hotel, the exclusive kind. Water-skiing, wind-surfing, scuba-diving, you name it. Then, for culture, he has Homer's Tomb on his door-step. A Venetian castle just over at Paleokastro. Some nice pieces in the village, various eras, even some Ionic.'

'And you think a spooking will put him off?'

'Depends on how he's spooked. I'm thinking about leaving him overnight in a room with Anna, see how he's talking next morning.'

'I just snatch them, Pyle. I don't do fantasies.'

'So Karen said. But Ray, I should tell you, Karen got clonked last night.'

'Clonked?'

'Some guy, she said, smacked her over the head with a gun.'

'Shit. She all right?'

'He bust her *nose*, man. I'm thinking, this guy might need some clonking himself.'

'Where was Anna?'

'Sleeping off a hangover from the pills. Karen went for a walk, ended up down at the cove. Then this guy comes out of nowhere, smacks her. Warning us off.'

'She see a doctor?'

'Right now she's sleeping. I'm bringing her in later to get some X-rays done, make sure there's nothing serious.'

'And this guy just strolled in past George.'

'Karen said they came in a boat.'

'They?'

'The guy's protected, Ray. I'm hearing rumours he's a coke guy from Amsterdam, looking to run a pipeline into the islands.'

Ray grinned. 'You're serious?'

'Sure. Guy called Johnny Priest, he's well known in—'

'No, Pyle. I mean, you're serious about wanting me to snatch a guy fronted by muscle with guns.'

Pyle reached under his shirt, tugged a .38 from his belt, walnut grip. 'He's arriving today,' he said. 'Like for a sit-down? Last thing he'll be expecting is some hippy crew to be tooled up, put a gun in his face.'

'I'm a hippy now?'

'Honorary.'

Ray thought it over. 'Say you snatch this guy, spook him. What's to stop him coming back, next time with an army?'

'He's a businessman. So we present him with a better proposal.'

'What's that?'

'How it's better being a businessman than some dead asshole used to have an army. Maybe teach him a little geography. How there's all these other islands that don't have killer wolves.'

'Karen's sticking around?'

'What she says. Karen, you probably noticed, she doesn't take kindly to orders. And she reckons it's perfect out here for Anna.'

Ray lit a cigarette. 'Where'll I find this guy?'

'He's coming in at noon, the hi-speed from Santorini. He owns a club up in the village, the Blue Orange, you'll need to hit him before he gets there. Get tight in the crowd, stick the gun in his ribs.'

'Dial back, Pyle. I'll have a look at it, see if it can be done. If it looks OK, then maybe.'

'Karen's nose isn't maybe busted, Ray. It's busted.'

Ray thought about that. 'This guy's moron enough to walk off the ferry with no muscle around, you won't need me. He's smart enough to bring muscle, they're tooled, there's fuck-all I can do.'

'I'm telling you, man, he's expecting acid-fried hippies. He won't be packing.'

'Says the acid-fried hippy packing Karen's .38.'

'What's that supposed to mean?'

'I'm not hearing you volunteer for back-up, Pyle. Not even volunteering George, anyone else looks like they might be useful.'

'We get seen, man, the guy'll know something's going down.'

Ray thought it over finishing his smoke. 'What I'm feeling,' he said, crushing the butt dead in the reddish dust, 'is there's way too many variables. But I'll have a look, see this guy off the ferry. You keep Karen on at the ESY after she gets her X-rays, I need to drop around there anyway. You don't see me by twelve-thirty, it means it was do-able, he's taken.'

'Sweet.'

'But it probably won't be. And it might be better, this guy's coming in for a sit-down anyway, to hold off, do him somewhere you can scope out first, cut down on the what-ifs.'

'Uh-huh.'

'Meanwhile,' Ray said, 'you might want to start drumming up a few volunteers. Starting with you.'

Pyle didn't like the insinuation. 'What d'you think this is for?' he said, holding up the .38. 'An ornament?'

'We've all got balls,' Ray said. 'Using them, that's a whole other thing.'

Melody

'Say some guys owed you ten grand,' Mel said to the skinny waitress as she placed a latte on the table, 'and you had a chance to get it back. Would you take it?'

'What would I have to do?' the waitress said. Jade, by her name-tag.

'Meet with a friend of theirs who says he'll honour the debt.'

'And that's it?'

'That's it.'

'You're sure?'

'That's what this guy says.'

'Then I'd meet him. Ten grand is ten grand.'

'It is, isn't it?'

'Absolutely. Can I get you something to eat with that?'

'That's fine, thanks. I'm being taken to lunch.'

'Lucky you.'

Melody watching the hi-speed ferry make a long turn around the headland and roar in towards the near dock, foam churning as it slowed. She took a twenty out of her purse, held it up, then tucked it under the latte.

'Um, Jade? Mind if I ask you a favour?'

Rossi

'The guy doesn't give me what you might call an itinerary,' Roger said. 'Maybe the hi-speed was late, how would I know?'

'It's unprofessional,' Rossi said, 'is what it is.'

'It can get choppy out there when there's a wind. And the hi-speed doesn't sail in what they call adverse weather conditions.'

'A wind?' Rossi, wondering if black was really the way to go in the islands, loosened the knot in his tie, opened the silk shirt a couple of buttons. He compared Roger's baggy shorts and sandals with his own suit and shoes, Rossi's bare toes swimming in sweat just sitting on a cane-weave chair at a three-legged metal table in the alleyway outside the Blue Orange, sipping a tall iced tea. Roger sweeping out and picking up litter. The air dead, stifling. 'There hasn't been a puff of breeze,' Rossi said, 'in two whole days. And you're talking about adverse fucking conditions?'

Roger shrugged. 'No point giving me grief. All I do is—'

The tinny sound of 'We Are the Champions' came muffled from Rossi's breast pocket. He dug out the cell phone. 'Sleeps? You see him?'

'Yeah. He just got off the boat.'

''Bout time. OK, stick tight, see if he heads for Sally fucking—'

'Rossi? He might be a while yet.'

'What's he doing?'

'He's taking Mel to lunch.'

Rossi went cross-eyed trying to picture it. 'Mel's with Johnny P?'

'And, it looks like, some Greek-looking guy met Johnny off the ferry. His guy in from Crete, I'm guessing.'

'Christ. The girl can't help herself, can she? What're they saying?'

'I'm in a phone box, Rossi. Because you wouldn't splash out for two mobile phones.'

'Fuck. OK, hold on there, I'm on my way down.'

Rossi hung up and said, 'Johnny's playing a dangerous game.'

Roger leaned on his broom. 'What's that, Naked Twister?'

Rossi rose above the sarcasm. 'First rule of business,' he said, 'is you take care of your staff, your staff'll take care of you. And Johnny, it looks like, is taking care of staff, they're not even on the payroll.'

'You want to put a complaint in writing? Meet the union rep, maybe?'

'I don't get my ten grand,' Rossi said, 'just like that it goes up to twenty. What they call the double-bubble. You tell Johnny that. He wants to haggle, he knows where to find me.'

'Where's that?'

'The name escapes me right this second,' Rossi said with no little dignity. 'But it's the place his guy already found me with the note.'

'Right you are.'

'You tell Johnny,' Rossi said, 'he's thinking of fucking me around, I got a package with his mitts all over it.'

'And you've been carrying this package around,' Roger said, intrigued, 'coming from Amsterdam, using gloves all the way. Is that right?'

'Anything happens to me,' Rossi went on, 'Johnny goes rogue, then my man's got strict instructions to take the package to the cops.'

Roger raised an eyebrow. 'So your guy'll go to the cops with a package that'll get Johnny in the shit. Putting himself,' he said, 'in the shit alongside Johnny.'

'Let me ask you this one question, Roger.' Rossi drained the iced tea, stood up. 'How probable is it you'd take a hit, do time, for Johnny?'

'I couldn't say for certain,' Roger said, considering. 'Is there such a thing as a negative value for probable?'

'See,' Rossi said, 'what I got, what Johnny don't, is my guy'll do time for me. Guy's already put himself in the frame.'

'Your man *wants* to do time?'

'Believe it.' He forked his fingers at Roger's eyes. 'You tell Johnny, he's dealing with Sicilians now.'

Madge

'**M**aybe,' Terry said, shading his eyes looking up at the sign, Sally Baba's, 'we should try saying ala-kazaam, some shit like that.'

'Now isn't the time for facetious,' Madge said.

'I asked the kid,' Terry said, 'the name of a restaurant, somewhere out of the way where it's good to eat. Presuming, sure, maybe I shouldn't, but presuming your average restaurant on a tourist island would be open for lunch. Who could've known?'

'Maybe you should have given him that tip you promised.'

'He jumped to the wrong conclusion. It's my fault he's greedy?'

Madge uncapped her water bottle and had a sip. 'What if Rossi was already here,' she said, 'found the place locked up and believed he was being taken for a ride?'

'The good news there,' Terry said, 'is it was an anonymous note. So he won't think it was you stringing him along.'

'What time is it now?'

'Ten past.'

'He might still arrive.'

'He's the smart type, Madge. He'd have got here early, casing the place. Making sure it was all kosher.'

'So what do we do now?'

'I'm thinking lunch, a siesta, another note at reception. This time signing it, so there's no confusion about who's admiring him from a distance.'

'And this time backing it up with an actual tip.'

Terry smiled at three tanned teens sashaying by in flip-flops, denim mini-skirts, all three combined wearing less than Madge. 'You want my advice?' he said, gazing after the trio, head bobbing in time to the rise and fall of their pert butts. 'Put a number in the note. Mention this inheritance, three-quarters of a mill. Guy'll break your door down.'

'I don't want to make it sound like I'm trying to buy his love,' Madge said.

'I thought that was the plan.'

'Well, sure. I just don't want it to sound that way.'

'He starts to quibble, hears anything other than ker-ching,' Terry said with a wistful note as the trio disappeared around the corner, 'I'll round it up to the full mill myself.' He seemed to shake himself as he turned back to Madge. 'Let's try the port for lunch, some seafood. God's own Viagra.'

Madge led the way.

Karen

What woke Karen up was she rolled over in bed and there was nothing to stop her rolling, no Ray. Then she came fully awake, remembering there was no Ray any more. She chugged some water, wondering where Anna was, and then her nose began to throb, a sharp pulsing that caused her to squint, her eyes to water. She went for the painkillers on the beside locker and then realized she was more worried about getting pills down her neck than finding out where Anna was.

Karen, the idea filtering through slow, started to wonder if she hadn't spent the last twelve hours or so doped, Pyle for some reason keeping her knocked out.

A cold shower blasted her out of sluggish mode. She was half-dressed when the idea occurred to her, Karen noodling it around, seeing how it could maybe work. So she stripped the bedsheet, started wrapping it around her waist, winding it up around her torso. Then she dipped into the duffle, took a packet of bills and tucked it snug against her ribs.

Once she was finished and fully dressed, she began banging on the locked door, then got up on the bed beside the window to karate-kick the shutters.

Feet scraped up the steps on to her porch. 'Cut that shit out *now*.'

'I'm starving,' Karen called. 'I haven't eaten since yesterday.'

'I'll bring you a sandwich.'

'And coffee. Black, no sugar.'

'No problem. Just take it easy, yeah?'

The feet scraped away down the steps. Karen, eyes watering again at the thought of it, glad she was still semi-doped, went in the bathroom and found the toilet roll, put it in her mouth and bit down hard. Bent over the sink, grabbing a good hold of each side. Then, on three, she bounced her nose off the rim.

Ten minutes later the feet scraped back up on to the porch. 'Move away from the door.'

'I'm on the bed,' Karen shouted.

A key grated in the lock and the door pushed open. A stocky guy peered in, the crew-cut who was composing the ballet for trees, although right now playing waiter, a tray in his hands. Then, seeing Karen on the bed, her bloody face, the front of her T-shirt a sticky red mess, he swore and hurried across the room. Karen held off until he bent down to place the tray on the bedside locker, then twisted and scissor-kicked from the hip, booting the tray into his face.

Sandwich and coffee flew, mostly into the guy's face. He reared back, leaving himself wide open, allowing Karen to re-scissor and put her instep deep in his crotch. He groaned, staggering backwards, then went down on one knee like someone about to leave church, genuflecting. Karen rolled off the bed, ducking down a little to jam the heel of her hand up into his nose. A dull crunch, the guy's head rocking. Karen took a half-step back and then booted him in the groin like she was kicking a conversion from two counties over. He folded, hinged at the hips, a faint whimper as he toppled on to his side.

Karen hunkered in and patted him down, came up with a snub-nose .32. Karen, OK, she didn't know too many ballet composers, but she was pretty sure carrying guns wasn't part of the job description. She crossed to the door and locked it, then checked to make sure the .32 was loaded. Went back to the groaning lump between the beds and clicked off the safety beside his ear.

'Where's Anna?'

The guy mumbled something. She tried again, but the guy was off in tree-tops, composing. Karen snibbed the safety on again and cracked him across the temple, hard, not particularly worried about how much damage she did. Then tucked the .32 into the front of her jeans.

Heard Ray again. How she'd never get away, she'd always be getting away.

But Karen was done running.

Melody

J ohnny Priest, the sea breeze ruffling his blond hair, asked Mel if she'd mind if he ordered for the three of them, and chose a crisp, fruity white to go with the seafood platter. Then leaned in, once the waiter had gone, and laid the tips of his fingers on the back of her wrist.

'What can you tell me about our mutual friend Rossi?' he said.

Given that Johnny was buying lunch at an upmarket restaurant facing on to the harbour, their table under a fringed awning catching that nice breeze, Mel believed he deserved a little value for his ten grand. 'What do you want to know?' she said, snaffling a shrimp.

'Who's he with?'

'You met him. Sleeps. Although his real name,' Mel said, 'is Gary.'

'Right. But who's Rossi working *for*?'

'You,' Mel said. 'He's delivering the package from Amsterdam for Jochem. To, y'know, you.'

'Bullshit,' Niko said.

Mel was already irritated by the Greek's presence, not least because he sat with his head back scanning the port so Melody couldn't help but see up the hairy caverns of his nose while she nibbled her kalamari. 'Excuse me?' she said.

'See, we have reason to believe,' Johnny cut in, 'that Rossi is working with someone else. Maybe for, maybe with. She's got a wolf, that much we know.'

'Karen?' Mel shook her head. 'Karen and Rossi split *way* back. She's been through Ray since Rossi.'

'Ray?'

'Except Rossi isn't with Ray either, if that's what you're thinking. Ray sent Rossi to Crete in a box.'

'Is that a fact?'

'I can only tell you,' Mel said, spearing a prawn, 'what Ray told us.'

'Us?'

'Me. I mean, he told me and I'm telling you. Us.'

'Let's just go *get* the fucking thing,' Niko growled.

Johnny waved him off. 'See,' he said to Mel, 'what's worrying me about Rossi, the guy's hard to pin down. I mean, Jochem said Ios was where he wanted the package dropped off, but then Niko thought it might be better if Rossi handed off in Athens, cut out the messing around getting out here. Only Niko got, uh, intercepted by this Karen you're calling her. So now we're wondering if Rossi isn't pulling some scam.'

'Far as I know,' Mel said, 'he only ever wanted the ten grand you were paying. Which,' she added, 'is actually mine, for the passports.'

'Sure thing. Only Roger, Jochem's guy here on Ios, is telling me Rossi dropped by an hour ago, talking up twenty grand.'

'Rossi's *here*?'

'Saying,' Johnny nodded, 'if I didn't play ball on the ten grand, he'd get the fat guy—'

'Gary's chunky, not fat. More husky, I'd have said.'

'Sure thing. Anyway, Rossi says the big guy'll take a tumble for him, go back inside, if I'm not onside with paying twenty.'

'More fucking bullshit,' Niko said.

'Actually,' Mel said, 'Gary says his life is crap on the outside. So he's hoping Rossi'll screw up so bad he'll get to go to prison again.'

'Christ,' Niko said, 'that's all we need. A suicide bomber.'

'There's no chance of *that*,' Mel said. 'Like, just *try* and get Gary up on a whirly-chair even.'

'What about Rossi?' Johnny said. 'He looking to go back in too?'

'God, no. Rossi's off to Sicily.'

'Sicily?'

'Where his family are from. Originally, I mean. Although Rossi,' she smirked, 'the last I heard, was under the impression he was already home.'

Johnny swore softly, glanced across at Niko. 'I knew it,' he said. 'The fucker's hooked up.'

'It was only a matter of time,' Niko said. He hawked and spat. 'Fucking Sicilians, they want it *all*.' Then he stiffened, stared hawk-like across the port. 'Shit,' he said, getting up.

'Where're you off to?' Johnny said.

'Be back in a minute,' Niko said, striding away. Johnny, mopping the back of his neck with a napkin, watched him go.

'Y'know, Johnny,' Mel said, 'I didn't want to say anything in front of Niko, but I think you've got bigger worries than Rossi.'

'How's that?'

'I'm wondering, how well do you know Jochem?'

'He's a guy I know. Why?'

'It's just . . .' Mel hesitated, then plunged in. 'You know how he gave Rossi,' she lowered her voice, 'cocaine to bring to Ios?'

'Yeah?'

'Well, there was no cocaine in the package.'

Johnny groaned. 'He opened it? Rossi?'

'Um, Rossi, yeah, he was the one opened it. Anyway, you'll never guess what he found.'

'Just taking a flyer at total random,' Johnny said, his eyes glazing over, 'I'd say it was a CZ 99, nine-millimetre Parabellum. Recently fired, two rounds missing.'

'Jochem told you about it?'

'He, uh, yeah. That's why,' Johnny patting beads of sweat from his upper lip, 'Niko wanted to catch Rossi in Athens, let him know a mistake had been made.'

Mel nodded. 'I presume Jochem'll be wanting it back then,' she said. 'A perfectly good gun like that.'

'I'd say he would,' Johnny said. 'Soon as possible.'

Mel snaffled another shrimp, dipped it into the garlic sauce. 'Because,' she said, 'missing bullets, and smelling the way it does, that nasty cordite whiff, I'd imagine it's hotter than Ryan Gosling right now.'

Johnny, working on his goldfish impression, just stared. Mel popped the shrimp home.

'Could you do me just the tiniest little favour,' she said, chewing, 'and let Jochem know it'll cost him twenty grand to get it back? You do that,' she added, 'and I'll wipe out the original ten you owe me. Do we have a deal?'

Doyle

'You never told me,' Jade said, putting the Diet Coke down, tucking the chit under the ashtray, 'that you were a cop.'

'It's not something you advertise,' Doyle said. 'Especially on holiday.'

'That I can appreciate. But Jamie hasn't been seen for like two whole days. People're starting to worry.'

'Jamie being the asshole,' Doyle said, 'offered me a spliff on a public beach.' Doyle keeping her eyes on the navy Punto across the square, the one Ray was sitting in, Doyle trying to guess which way Ray might jump now that the Amsterdam guy had Niko along. Doyle only now realising Niko was working undercover, stinging the Amsterdam guy, Johnny Priest. The sting being why Niko'd had to stay behind in Athens.

'That asshole, yeah,' Jade said. 'You didn't have him picked up?'

'Wasn't me.'

Jade shook her head, puzzled. She wiped listlessly at the table. 'You being on holiday, you're off duty, right?'

'Actually, I'm suspended.'

'No shit. What'd you do?'

'Got shot at, mostly. Why, what's up?'

Jade glanced over her shoulder into the café, then sat down and hunched in. 'It's a weird one. This girl gave me a note earlier, asked me to go to the cops if she didn't come back in this afternoon.'

'Go on.'

'See, I'm illegal here since July. I go to the cops, there's any kind of fall-out, I'll be on the next plane home.'

'What'd the note say?'

'I don't know, I didn't read it.'

Doyle hoisted an eyebrow.

'OK,' Jade said, taking the note out of the front pocket of her apron. 'It says she's meeting a guy owns the Blue Orange, this club up in the village. Says the cops should ask him where she is if she goes missing.'

'But you don't want to get involved.'

'Not if I don't have to. But I don't want this girl getting in any trouble either.'

'Noble. Where'd she say she was meeting this guy?'

'Over there.' Jade pointed across the port. 'The fish restaurant. See the big girl in the mustard sarong-and-pants combo?'

Doyle squinted against the glare trying to peer around the statue perched on the little marble roundabout. 'I can't see her right now,' she said, 'but she shouldn't be that hard to— Fuck.'

'What's wrong?'

'Give it five minutes,' Doyle said, slipping the note into her pocket, 'then come out and say there's a call for me inside. Can you do that?'

'Why, what's wrong?'

'Let's just say I'm in no mood for a reunion,' Doyle said, raising a hand as Niko ducked in under the awning. 'Hey, Niko! You finally made it, huh?'

Ray

What Ray didn't like about the set-up would've taken Homer a whole new book to say. The bustling port. Melody in the mix. The way the restaurant was open-fronted. Ray, parked in the Punto across the square on the shore road to Yialos Beach, got the crawls just thinking about trying a getaway in the crowded harbour.

Then there was the numbers. Johnny Priest being no moron, he'd arrived with muscle on the noon hi-speed ferry. Easy to spot, the only pair of suits disembarking amid a throng wearing shorts and T-shirts, brightly coloured wraps and baseball caps. Ray guessed the smaller guy doing all the talking was Johnny. The tall, beak-nosed guy was watching everything but saying little, nodding once in a while.

Ray had pretty much decided to take a pass, head back to the health centre to tell Pyle it was a non-runner, except then Johnny had sat down at a table with Mel. Ray grinning to himself, curious as to what kind of scam Mel might be running on a big-time coke dealer. He'd swung by the health centre after renting the Punto next door, this to check if they'd misfiled his passport and beg for some heavyweight painkillers, his arm starting to burn again. No joy both ways. Which meant he'd need to chat with Mel before she left the island, if only to eliminate her from his two-name list of suspects.

Still, Ray had decided on non-intervention, had already started up the Punto rental, when the tall guy stood up and left the restaurant, stalked across the port to the café where Doyle was keeping sketch. Ray figured it was some kind of sign, karma. He switched off and got out, left the Punto unlocked. Crossing the port, he diverted by the phone box, tapped Sleeps on the shoulder.

'Don't do anything stupid, Gary,' he said. He tugged up the front of his shirt, showing Sleeps the walnut butt of the .38. 'Tell Rossi I'll see him later. We'll talk then, pro to pro.'

'Where?'

Ray glanced at the number on the phone box. 'I'll ring you here, at eight tonight.'

'Don't let anything happen to Mel.'

Ray nodded. 'One last thing.'

'What's that?'

'The guy with Mel. He's Johnny Priest, right?'

Doyle

Doyle was wondering, with Johnny Priest wide open, what Ray was doing chatting with the fat guy at the phone box. What was he waiting for, Doyle to jump Niko's bones right there in the café? Niko half-listening to Doyle's earthquake story, sitting sideways on, still scoping the port.

'So you're stinging this guy,' she said, to grab Niko's attention.
'What's that?'
'The Amsterdam guy, piping in coke. You're undercover, right?'
Niko's eyebrows did a caterpillar conga. 'Who told you that?'
'Oh,' Doyle said, 'a little birdie.'
'A birdie?'
'This birdie,' Doyle said, 'mentioned the Dutch connection, the coke. I was the one twigged you're undercover. Because the birdie seems to think, for some reason, you're Johnny's guy, his muscle.'
'Fuck. Who's this birdie?'
'Oh, a guy I met last night, we were in a bar. I didn't catch his name.'
'This bar, it wasn't the Blue Orange, was it?'
'The, um, Blue Orange. Yeah.'
'Shit,' Niko said. He shook his head, then glanced around, a sly half-grin starting. 'You know how long it's taken me to get to this point?' he said. 'I mean, for people to start believing I'm Johnny's guy in the islands? Three fucking years.'
'Wow,' Doyle said. Christ, Ray was heading *this* way now? 'That's pretty impressive.' Doyle using her eyes, Ray coming on, to warn him off.
But Ray kept coming, Doyle realizing too late that Ray didn't know Niko was a cop. Ray knowing nothing at all about Niko, as it happened, Doyle believing Ray would be happier in his ignorance . . .
It took Niko a beat to register that Ray had slipped into the seat beside him. By then Ray had pulled out the .38 under the table and leaned in, placed it against Niko's knee.
'Hollow points,' Ray said. 'They'll take half your fucking leg with them.'
Niko did a double-take, glancing at Doyle and then back to Ray. 'Who the fuck is this?' he said.
'Ever seen a man gut-shot?' Ray said.
Doyle watched Niko's nostrils narrow. 'What happens,' Ray said, 'is the shit in your intestine gets in the wound. It's a horrible death. Takes days.'
Niko breathing heavy through his nose.
'Stand up,' Ray told Niko. 'But do it slow.'
Niko got to his feet slow.

'Nice and easy,' Ray said. 'The navy Punto, across the square. Smile like you're having a good time.'

Niko's face cracked like a dropped plate.

Ray

'**Y**ou're into something,' Niko said, 'you don't even know you're—'

'Save it for Karen,' Ray said.

'Karen?'

'This girl I know, who just happened to have her nose busted last night.'

Niko blanched. 'Now *wait* a fucking—'

'Just drive,' Ray said.

Ray sitting angled into the passenger seat, the gun on his lap pointed at Niko's thigh. The beach to their left, the Punto crawling along in second gear, Niko's knuckles white on the steering wheel. 'Where to?' he said.

'Keep going,' Ray said, 'all the way to the end. See the yellowy-blue sign, the Katina? There's a driveway to one side.'

Niko turned in.

'OK,' Ray said. 'Go down to the end, pull in under the pine.'

The village was dead ahead on the top of the hill, looking snow-capped, the hills to the left dissolving into the shimmering interior.

'Now switch off,' Ray said.

Niko turned off the engine. Ray said, 'You're fucking with the wrong people, man.' He touched the barrel of the gun to Niko's thigh, Niko edging away until he was wedged against the driver's door. 'I'm betting you don't even know who it is you're fucking with.'

'I'm going to take one guess,' Niko said, 'and say Sicilians.'

'Sicilians,' Ray said. 'Right.' He thought about that, realized it could only mean Rossi was involved somewhere along the line. Which meant the potential for everything fucking up was fast approaching critical mass. 'You carrying?' he said.

Niko pointed under his left armpit.

'Take it out,' Ray holding up a forefinger, 'using just that.'

Niko did as he was told.

'OK,' Ray said, 'we're going inside. One fucking peep and you won't hear the cavalry arrive. Now go.'

Sleeps

Sleeps watched the navy Punto crawl through the port and disappear out along the shore road, then rang Rossi.

'Sleeps?'

'It's me, yeah.'

'Thank fuck. I'm lost.'

'Shit. Where are you?'

'The fuck would I know? I'm lost.'

'Keep heading down. Let gravity do the work.'

'I'm trying, man. It's the Bermuda Triangle up here, I just saw Barry fucking Manilow driving the *Titanic* . . . What's happening down there?'

'Ray snatched Johnny's guy.'

'Jesus Willy Christ. Where's Johnny?'

'Over in the fish restaurant with Mel.'

'Any sign of our coke?'

'Johnny's coke. And no. But Ray says to sit tight, he'll ring later.'

'Ray's ringing us?'

'Yep.'

'You gave him my fucking number?'

'Nope.' Sleeps sighed. 'He said he'd ring the phone box.'

'What's he ringing for?'

'He wants to talk. Pro to pro.'

'About what?'

'He didn't say. But Rossi? He's tooled.'

'The Uzi?'

'Nope.'

'Fucking Wyatt Earp this guy.'

'So we talk to him, right?'

Rossi mulling it over. 'What d'you think – is he running a scam with Mel? On Johnny, like.'

'Let's just see,' Sleeps said, 'what the guy has to say.'

'First off, we want Mel, the coke. That's non-negotiable.'

'Forget about the coke, Rossi.'

'You shitting me? That's twenty fucking grand's worth Johnny owes me.'

'Us,' Sleeps said, 'he owes *us*.' Then, 'It's twenty now?'

'Johnny's fucking us around, Sleeps. So I made what they call an executive decision, we're double-bubbling every four hours. And that's including, the guy doesn't get his fucking skates on, while he's asleep.'

'OK, but here's the thing. You said Ray'd know where Karen is.'

Static on the line while Rossi thought about that. 'So you're saying, two birds, one bush.'

'Go back to the Triton. I'll meet you there.'

'You think I didn't try?'

'OK. Don't move, just sit down somewhere. I'll find you.'

'Make it fast. I'm getting looks up here from guys with wooden legs and three eyes. Fucking *Deliverance* it is.'

Sleeps hung up and turned around to find Johnny Priest just standing there.

'Hey, Fuckface,' Johnny said.

A woman came in behind Johnny, flipping a badge that glinted in the sun.

Sleeps felt his heart and stomach swap over.

Madge

Terry came back from the bathroom, ducked under the awning on to the terrace. He hung his jacket on the back of his chair and picked up the menu. 'See anything you like?' he said.

'Actually, I think I just saw a blond Ray,' Madge said.

'Ray? Where?'

'Over there, past those yachts. Bundling a guy into a car.'

Terry, eyebrows halfway up his bald spot, peered through the throng of backpackers, port officials, the hawkers with their laminated signs. He said, 'Bundling?'

'That's how it looked.'

'You're sure?'

'He was blond, but his arm was in a plaster cast. And he still has the quiff.'

'Karen wasn't with him?'

'No. But that guy over there, in the phone booth,' Madge pointed past the statue in the middle of the port, 'that's Sleeps.'

'Who's Sleeps?'

'Rossi's partner. He's the one treated me well up at the lake, after I fainted. Remember?'

Terry squinting into the glare of the noon sun. 'And that's Rossi, right? The guy about to floor Sleeps.'

'Him I've never seen before. But the girl beside him? That's Doyle, the cop I was telling you about, wanted to help with my alibi the day I shot Frank.'

'The Crazy Gang,' Terry said, 'all back together for one last reunion. What d'you think, should we send flowers?'

'Erm, excuse me?'

Madge looked up, shading her eyes. A large girl in a mustard sarong-and-pants combo was leaning forward from the next table along.

'Yes?' Madge said. 'Can we help you?'

'I couldn't help but overhear,' the girl said, 'you mentioning Rossi and Sleeps. You wouldn't happen to be friends of theirs, would you?'

Sleeps

'**W**here's *who* gone?' Sleeps said.

'Pull that Sicilian crap on me?' Johnny fuming. 'You don't even *look* Italian, man.'

'Who said I was?'

Johnny ducked in under the head-and-shoulders booth, crowding Sleeps, getting nose-to-nose. 'I won't ask again, Fat-Chops. Where'd they go?'

The stench of garlic caused Sleeps to rear back, but Johnny came on again. Sleeps couldn't resist. He faked another duck-back and then, as Johnny advanced, crashed his forehead into the guy's Adam's apple.

Johnny croaked once and went down hard, gurgling gravel.

Sleeps glanced at the woman cop. She shrugged, flipped her badge closed.

'Thank Christ for that,' she said. 'I'm Doyle. Who the fuck are you?'

Doyle

'Which way did he go?' Johnny said, sounding a lot like a frog gakking up hairballs.

'Thataway,' Doyle said, waving vaguely in the direction of Africa. 'Johnny? I really think you should get that seen to.'

'How come you didn't grab him?'

'You were choking,' Doyle said, 'right there at my feet. It was chase him or take care of you. And Niko, he was explicit, my number one responsibility is you.'

Johnny, sullen, sipped a few drops of iced water, wincing as they slid down. 'So what do they want?'

'The guy said to wait, they'd be in touch. With,' Doyle freewheeled, 'their full list of, y'know, demands.'

'Fucking Sicilians,' Johnny croaked.

'They'll be in touch,' Doyle reassured him. 'So all we have to do is wait and—'

'That car was a rental,' Johnny said. 'I saw the sign in the back window, Kosmos Rentals. All we have to do now is find—'

'You think that's wise? I mean the guy said, wait 'til they—'

'XRY three-seven-nine,' Johnny said. 'A navy Punto. They'll have the address, the details, of whoever rented it.'

'There's a rental place,' Doyle said, 'it's right there on the beach beside the health centre. So why don't we get you in there, just for a quick check-up. I'll scoot across to the rental place, see if they can—'

'Being brutally fucking honest,' Johnny said, getting up, 'right now I'm not really rating Niko's choice of back-up. So you got a lot to prove. And the best way to start is to do what you're fucking told.'

'OK by me,' Doyle said. She reached across and grabbed Johnny's wrist, giving it a twisty little turn yanking him back down into the seat. Johnny, stunned, just gaped. 'My orders,' she said, 'coming from Niko, are to keep you out of harm's way. Incognito.'

'Yeah,' Johnny said, massaging his wrist, 'but I'm the one who's telling Niko—'

'Being brutally fucking honest,' Doyle said, 'I'm not really rating Niko's choice of boss. So you got a lot to prove. And the best way to start is, shut the fuck up. And give me your phone.'

'My phone?'

'Triangulation,' Doyle said, describing a sloppy circle in the air with her forefinger. 'You start taking calls, they'll pin you down in seconds.'

'Who will?'

'The cops,' Doyle said. 'Niko didn't tell you?'

'Jesus, tell me what?'

'This sting they're running, undercover.'

'Fuck.' Johnny paled. 'Niko knows about this?'

'He does now.'

'That was the *cops*? Christ, I thought they were Sicilian.'

'They're still using that here?' Doyle, when you're in, you're in, was having a little fun with it. 'I'd have thought the Sicilian Feint was old hat by now.'

'You're saying, the cops are pretending to be Sicilians.'

'Sure. Unless it's the Reverse Sicilian Feint, when it's Sicilians pretending to be cops. It's rare, but it's a doozy.'

Johnny shaking his head, bewildered. 'So who told you?'

'This guy in the Blue Orange, last night,' she riffed. 'Said if I was a friend of Niko's I should let him know the score, how there's been these guys sniffing around asking for you, he reckoned they were bacon. Said he was wondering why they were so blatant, just walking in off the street.'

It took a second for the penny to drop but it came down hard. 'Now wait a fucking minute,' Johnny said. 'Those guys, I know them, they're doing me a favour for Chrissakes.' He sat back massaging his throat. 'Who told you this, Roger?'

'I didn't catch his name,' Doyle said. 'So these guys, you're vouching for them. I mean, you know them that well, they're cast-iron.'

Johnny thought about that. 'Shit,' he said. 'And I just set them up with some hot hardware.'

Doyle tut-tutted. 'That's what they call a schoolboy error, Johnny. Now give me your phone.'

Ray

Inside, in the room, Ray had Niko tear a sheet into strips then lie face-down on the bed, tie one of his wrists to the bedpost. Then he put a blanket over Niko's head and sat on that, got the other wrist secure. Checked the knots, then went out on the balcony and rang Pyle.

'I got him,' he said.

'Copacetic, man.'

'So what now?'

'There's an old Venetian castle the other side of the island, Paleokastro. I'll meet you up there at ten, it'll be good and dark. How's he looking?'

'A little confused. Seems to think we're Sicilians.'

'Yeah?' A chuckle. 'How'd that happen?'

'It's a long story.' Ray lit a cigarette. 'So, ten bells.'

'Watch the road, it's steep once you come off the main road, lots of S-bends. Come down slow. Flash your lights three times, then walk on up.'

'What happens if I only flash twice?'

'Why would you do that?'

'I'm the rebellious type. Put Karen on.'

'Right now she's out walking Anna, clearing her head.'

'Yeah? How'd those X-rays work out?'

'We haven't even been in yet, man. She was sleeping all morning.'

'Have her ring me when she gets back.'

'Will do.'

Ray hung up, ducked his head into the room to check on Niko while he searched his pockets for the number Mel had given him on the ferry, then rang it.

'Hello?'

'It's me, Mel. Ray.'

'Ray?' The sound of utensils clinking on china in the background, a muted hum of conversation. 'Hey, wow. Are you out of hospital yet?'

'Where's my passport, Mel?'

'Passport?'

'The money you can have. All I want is the passport.'

'But I don't have your passport.'

'No?'

'Why would I want your passport?'

'But you do have the money. The thirty grand that was in my bag when I got off the ferry.'

Silence. Then: 'I'm afraid I don't know what you're talking about, Ray.'

'That's a pity. Because you're owed ten grand by Rossi, right? So I was going to give you the ten gees, let you walk away, collect that ten-ski from Johnny Priest myself. Save you getting tangled up with scumbags.'

'Oh. Right.' Mel cleared her throat. 'The thing about that is, I have a deal now with Johnny for twenty.'

'Mel? Listen to me. You're in way over your head. My advice to you is take the ten and run, leave my twenty at the desk of wherever you're staying and go. Where are you staying?'

'Up in the, um, village. But Ray? This all sounds very messy. Wouldn't it be tidier all round if I just kept the thirty and you got it all back from Johnny?'

Melody

Mel came back to the table saying, 'OK, Dad, thanks for calling. I'll see you soon.' Then hung up as she sat down. 'Sorry about that,' she said. 'He's always fussing. Where was I?'

'Johnny,' Madge said, 'had just spotted Ray shoving Niko into the car.'

Mel nodding. 'I thought he'd explode. He was puce, his head swelling up.'

'This is when he goes running off,' Terry said.

'Telling me,' Mel said, 'to stay where I am, he'll be back in a minute.'

'Except then he spotted Sleeps,' Madge said.

'Not realising,' Mel said, 'your friend Doyle was watching Sleeps.'

'So,' Terry said, 'Ray has this Niko guy and Doyle has Johnny. And Niko and Johnny, they're trying to nail Rossi with what they're calling a hot rod.'

'That's certainly the impression I got,' Mel said, who had left out one or two pieces of the jigsaw she didn't believe were immediately relevant.

'So where's Rossi in all this?' Madge said.

'Right now,' Mel had to admit, 'I don't know. Although Johnny said he was up at the Blue Orange bar earlier, telling Johnny's guy he wanted twenty grand. Doubling up what he's owed.'

'As if he knew all along,' Madge said, 'he was being double-crossed.'

'He's crafty, this Rossi,' Terry said. 'Crazy like a fox.'

'I wouldn't recommend you overestimate him,' said Mel.

'You mean underestimate him,' Madge said.

'I know what I mean,' said Mel, who'd long ago realized she'd need to beef up Rossi for the movie, give him some of Sleeps' smarts, otherwise he'd look too dumb to breathe. Mel weighing her options, taking Ray's advice on board: cut and run, thirty grand seed capital to the good, a notepad already full of most of a movie.

Except what she didn't have was her ending, what Sleeps, Gary, had called her wop-boom-bam.

And then, yeah, Gary. The sleepy-eyed shaggy bear, still Javier Bardem in her mind but now more *Barcelona* than *No Country*.

'You know him, right?' she said to Madge.

'Who, Rossi?'

'No, Gary. Sleeps, I mean.'

And heard Madge tell how Sleeps had taken care of her that night up at the lake, showing a tender side she hadn't expected from such a rough-looking guy, Sleeps giving her his jacket to sleep on and explaining how Rossi's bark was worse than his bite, this contrary to any impression Madge might have formed about Rossi suffering a mild case of rabies.

'He's carrying a lot of weight,' Madge said, 'but I'm guessing a lot of it is heart.'

'He's too sensitive is his problem,' Mel said. 'Can't cope with being on the outside.'

'Go on,' Terry said.

'His plan,' Mel said, 'is to get back into prison, do what he calls soft time.'

Terry had a long sip on his wine. 'Seriously?'

Mel, who was carrying around more weight than she was happy with, nodded. Wondering if it wasn't too late, having already abandoned Gary once, to persuade him that she could offer a different kind of soft time.

Karen

From the porch, glancing down towards the sea as she locked her door, Karen could see stick-figures working at the blue beehives. Three, she thought, maybe four, shimmering in the afternoon heat. She strolled along the veranda towards Pyle's room, the courtyard deserted. Tapped on his door and heard, 'Christ, what is it *now*?'

She pushed on in. The room was the same shape as Karen's, a low desk where the second bed should have been. Pyle sitting at the desk where there was a radio transmitter with a large circular aerial on top. He swivelled when he heard the key turn, Karen locking the door.

'That's a big gun,' he drawled, taking off his headphones, 'for such a little lady.'

'Usually it's a Magnum .44,' Karen said, moving to the window to close the shutters.

'No shit.'

She crossed to the bathroom, poked her head in. 'Where's Anna?'

Pyle inclined his head. 'Out back. Why the hardware?'

'You tell me.'

'Tell you what?'

'Where that cop came from. Why I was doped, locked up. Why there's some asshole with a gun bringing me lunch.'

Pyle held his hands up, palms out. 'It looks bad, I know, but it's for your own good. Seriously. Those guys that were here last night, the ones who clonked you? We're expecting them back.'

'Pyle?' Karen waggled the .32. 'Trust me, you'll make a lot more sense with no holes in you.'

'OK,' he said, getting up. 'Like I told—'

Karen cocked the hammer. 'Sit back down. Put your arms out like you're an airplane.' Pyle obeyed, a cheesy grin starting. 'Now go,' she said.

Pyle, holding his arms out horizontal, told her about a hostile takeover bid, some guy from Amsterdam, a coke pipeline. Karen said, 'In that case I'll be moving on. I've got enough trouble.'

'If that's what you want. But Karen, these guys think you're with us now. They see you on your own . . .'

Karen looked at the .32, then back at Pyle. 'If all your crew are as good as the guy I left in the room, I'd be safer playing with snakes. Kneel.'

'Can I put my arms down?'

'No. Lie on the floor.'

Karen waited until he was spread-eagled, then patted him down. 'All right,' she said, satisfied, 'I want Anna and the bike.'

Pyle got slowly to his feet. 'I should probably mention,' he said, 'how Ray's helping out.'

'Ray?'

'He's just snatched the guy that's causing us problems.'

'Ray's retired, Pyle.'

'He thinks he's helping you. To stay here, I mean. You and Anna.'

'So if I run off, you lose Ray.'

'With you gone there's no reason for him to stick around.'

Karen considered. 'So this guy Ray just snatched, he's tied in with the cop bust my nose?'

'Yeah. But Karen, all we want is to spook him. And the guy's already spooked, thinks we're Sicilians.'

Karen groaned. 'Rossi, right?'

'Word is,' Pyle said, 'he's half-Sicilian, half-Crazy Larry.'

'He's all that,' Karen said. 'Only you won't be needing Rossi. I'll spook this guy plenty.'

Rossi

'And Doyle, she just let you walk away?'

Rossi, thank Christ, had finally made it back to base, the Triton. Out on the balcony now, overlooking the port below. His back hunched against the village, roaching a fat chillum, still shaky after wandering the maze. Sleeps slumped across the white plastic table, chin propped on his forearms.

'This so I could tell you,' Sleeps said, 'to quote-unquote, rev up and fuck off.' He flapped pudgy fingers at a bug buzzing around his right ear. 'Else she'll extradite you back home for capping Frank's knee and have put you away for, I think, attempted third-degree manslaughter.'

'It was Madge,' Rossi fumed, 'who pulled the trigger. Wasn't even my rod, it was Ray's, the Glock.'

'I'm only telling you,' Sleeps said, 'what this Doyle, the moxy cop, told me.'

'So that's,' Rossi counting them off, 'Madge, she's putting me in the frame. Then Mel runs off with the coke. And now Doyle, she's on my case too?' Rossi shook his head sadly. 'Fucking Janes, man, they're devious.'

'You're forgetting Karen.'

'Karen's different. Karen has her reasons.'

'Except it's not just the, um, Janes,' Sleeps pointed out. 'Johnny's fucking you too. And, it looks like, Ray.'

'Ray, to be fair,' Rossi conceded, grudging it, 'he's onside with Karen. The guy's just looking out for her, like you said.'

'Fair go. Only I got the feeling this Doyle was looking out for Ray.'

'Ray's a pro. No way he's hooked up with any cops.' Rossi sparked the doob, held the draw down. 'Here,' he said, exhaling slow, 'she flashed you her badge, right?'

Sleeps nodded. 'I said, "Aren't you out of your jurisdiction, officer?" She goes, "Put a tune to it, I'll sing along."'

'So what's she doing here?'

'Dunno. Looking for the ransom money back?'

'Yeah. But is she, y'know, working freelance? Scooping the pot for herself?' Rossi handed the joint across. Sleeps waved it away. 'Fuck,' Rossi said, 'maybe Ray *is* hooked up with—'

There came a rat-a-tat-tat on the door.

'Christ,' Rossi said, 'who the fuck's *that*?'

'Go look-see.'

'*You* go look-see.'

In the end, the rat-a-tats getting louder, Sleeps went to the door. He came back out on to the balcony saying, 'It's the guy from Reception. Has another note, except he got fifty for bringing it this far, wants another fifty to hand it over. Says it's what he was told to say.'

'You got a fifty on you?'

'Nope.'

'Fuck.' Rossi rifled his pockets, came up with twenty-three and change. 'See if that'll do it,' he said. 'He doesn't want to hand it over, get him to just read it out instead.'

Sleeps came back in with the note which looked to Rossi like it had been ripped from a notepad, the paper pale blue.

'*My dear Rossi,*' Sleeps read. '*That money you're owed is actually your inheritance, which is worth three-quarters of a million euro. I'll be at Sally Baba's this evening for dinner at nine o'clock if you'd like to talk about it. I checked, it'll definitely be open this time. Yours faithfully.*'

Rossi boggled. 'Say what?' he whispered.

Sleeps read it out again.

'Three-quarters of a *million*?' Rossi said. 'A fucking inheritance?'

'What it says,' Sleeps said.

'A grift,' Rossi said. 'Has to be. Some bastard setting me up.'

Sleeps thought about that. 'Well,' he said, 'it's not Doyle, she wants you gone. Same goes for Mel.'

'Karen?'

'You're the one chasing her. Why would she want a sit-down?'

'Like I said, a makey-up.'

'She came a thousand miles just to get away from you, Rossi. And now, you turn up, she has a change of heart?'

'So who? Johnny?'

'Not unless he's in cahoots with Doyle, who wants you gone.'

'Gimme that,' Rossi said. He scanned the note. 'Hey,' he said, 'there was a signature here. Right after it says, y'know, yours faithfully.'

'The kid,' Sleeps said, 'I gave him the twenty-three euro, he ripped the bottom of the note off and ate it. Said if we want to know who it's from it'll cost us another twenty-seven.'

Rossi with the overwhelming urge to stab some fucker in the heart. 'So what do we do?' he said.

'We?'

'Yeah, we. What, you're bunking out on me now? Doing a Mel?'

'Not walking into a trap, Rossi, that's not bunking out. That's basic sanity.'

Rossi had a long toke wiggling a finger in his good ear. 'What're you saying?' he said.

'We wait for Ray to ring, see what he has to say. Take it from there.'

'Except Ray's maybe hooked up with the cop.'

'On one side, yeah. On the other, Karen.'

'Plus he's got Johnny's guy.' Rossi thought about that, then frowned. 'So what's Ray want with us?'

'He had Johnny's guy,' Sleeps said, 'probably nothing. Except Ray thinks he has Johnny.'

'How come?'

'I didn't mention that?'

'Maybe you thought you mentioned it,' Rossi said, 'in some dream you had, on the nod again.'

'No personals,' Sleeps said. 'Like, how many times do we have to get into it?'

Rossi shook his head in despair. 'How's it help us,' he said, 'Ray holding Johnny's guy thinking he's Johnny?'

'Can't hurt,' Sleeps said. He flapped lazily at another bug. 'And the way things are going, that's the only positive I can see.'

'Look on the bright side,' Rossi groused. 'We keep going this way, you'll be back inside before it gets dark again.'

'Actually,' Sleeps said, beckoning for the jay, then waving it around like a joss stick to ward off the bug, 'that's something I've been wanting to bring up.'

'Fuck, no.'

'See, the time in Croatia? I could've taken a dive then. Except the guy would have taken you too, you with your pants down, I'm talking literally, taking a dump out in the scrub.'

'Appreciate it, yeah.'

'Then, with the cop earlier on? I could've just nutted her too, the way I did Johnny. Get myself done for common assault, some shit like that.'

'You nutted Johnny?'

'Guy was in my face, begging it. So I crunched the fucker.'

'But somehow neglected,' Rossi said, 'to nut the cop, she's just standing there.'

'A woman?' Sleeps shook his head. 'Anyway, things are different, man.'

'What? What's different?'

'Mel,' Sleeps confessed. 'I'm thinking I might give it a go, she ever sits still long enough to listen, with Mel.'

'Mel? The bitch ripped us off, man, ran to Johnny Priest with the coke.'

'The girl's got her reasons.'

'Fool me once, Sleeps, shame on you. Fool me twice, I rip your head off and shit in the hole.'

'I told you already, no one's slapping any women around on my watch.'

'*Your* watch?'

'Ray said he'd ring,' Sleeps said. 'So we wait, see what he has to say. Maybe, he's hooked up with Doyle, they'll put us in touch with Johnny. Maybe even Karen, for a parley.'

Rossi stuck a finger in his good ear, dug around until he came up with a decent ball of wax. He went inside to the bathroom and wiped off, came back out on to the balcony saying, 'Hey, Sleeps? Y'think maybe . . . shit.'

Sleeps with his head pillowed on his forearms, snoring gently. Rossi swore and reached across, plucked the joint from between Sleeps' fingers, smoked on.

The bug, persistent, finally landed on Sleeps' forehead. Rossi swore again, softly, then went back inside. Found the bug juice and brought it out, pumped it upward above Sleeps' head so the fine spray settled like a tiny-diamond rain.

Ray

The knock was a gentle tap-tap-tap but Ray on his feet and moving for the door at the second tap. He stood with his back to the wall, said, '*Vo ist das?*'

'Ray?' A whisper. 'It's me, Sparks.'

Ray let her in, locked the door. Sparks put a finger to her lips, pointed towards the balcony.

'What's up?' Ray said, angling himself so he could see back into the room.

'Doyle said to say you got the wrong guy,' Sparks said. 'That's not Johnny.'

'What?'

'It gets worse. He's a Greek cop undercover, his name's Niko. He's running a sting on Johnny.'

'Shit.'

'You get a chance, maybe during pillow-talk,' Sparks said, 'you might do me a favour and remind Doyle she's a cop too.'

'What's she saying we should do?'

'She's not saying a lot, Ray. Johnny thinks Doyle's hooked up with Niko, that she's right now looking out for Johnny's interests.'

'How'd that happen?'

'Doyle,' Sparks said, 'has a way with men when she needs to be believed.'

'Oh yeah?'

'One thing she did say, she's not handing Niko over to this Pyle guy like you're planning. They find out he's a cop . . .'

'Pyle wants Johnny. And we *have* Johnny.'

'Being precise about it, Doyle's the one has Johnny.'

'What's that mean?'

'It means, Ray, she's supposed to be handing over Johnny to this Pyle guy so Karen gets to walk away. Right?' Ray nodded. 'Except, when Doyle asked, just as a gesture, you wouldn't hand Karen up.'

'That was different.'

'It was a *gesture*, Ray. All she was asking for was something she could hold on to. Now she has it, all nice and Johnny-shaped.'

'That's bullshit. Where is she?'

'She can't talk to you now, it's a delicate situation she's got with Johnny. And there's no way *I'm* watching over him for any lover's tiff. I'm still an actual cop.'

'You're saying she wants me to go up there and meet Pyle with no Johnny, no this guy Niko you're calling him, and no back-up?'

'You don't have to go.'

'And just leave Karen twisting in the breeze?'

'What it all comes down to, I guess,' Sparks said, 'is Doyle's wondering who you're more worried about, her or Karen.'

Ray shook his head. He said, 'Say I don't go. What happens with Johnny and Niko?'

'Doyle didn't say. But if it was me, and I wasn't a cop? I'd have it on my toes, the nearest airport and the first flight out.'

'Only I can't go anywhere,' Ray said, 'until I get my passport back.'

'Your passport?'

'Yeah.'

'From who?'

'Possibly Karen.'

'Crap.'

'Exactly.'

'So what're you going to do?'

'You won't tell me what room Doyle's in?'

'No can do, Ray. Sorry.'

'That's all right, I can ring her. Although tell her, if it's not asking too much, that I'd rather talk face-to-face.'

Sparks said OK, only right now Doyle wasn't really in the mood for looking Ray in the eye.

'No problem,' Ray said. 'I'll wear a blindfold.'

'You keep your head in the game,' Sparks said. 'There'll be plenty of time for fun once this shit is sorted.'

Rossi

No way was Rossi strolling down into the port to wait for some call mightn't come, get trapped like a mole in a bucket.

'They've seen me, Sleeps.' He gestured at the suit. 'These threads, they get you noticed. That's the whole fucking point.'

'So I'm the one gets trapped like this mole.'

'The note,' Rossi said, brandishing the pale blue paper, 'starts off "My dear Rossi", not "My dear Rossi and anyone else needs a nosebag". You see what I'm saying.'

'What you said was the note's bad juju.'

'What, you think I'm just charging in there? I'll scope it out, see what's what.'

'Then, maybe this what works out as what, you scoop three-quarters of a million and bolt for Sicily, not stopping to rescue any moles in any buckets.'

That one hit Rossi where he lived. 'You're thinking *I'd* scam you? Me, the guy's been fucked four ways by everyone except you, you being the guy who volunteered, sure, took it back after, but offered to do my time if things fucked up?' Rossi was getting emotional. 'Last person I'm ever screwing over,' he said, 'is you. I mean, that fifty-fifty deal we were on up to now, that's out the window, we're talking my inheritance here. But if it works out it's bona fide, I'm cutting you in for a slice. No man left behind, Sleeps.'

In the end they compromised on a disguise, swapping clothes, although Rossi had to keep the belt from the suit, when he put on Sleeps' baggy shorts they dropped to the floor without even grazing his knees. He'd had to keep the two-tone shoes too, Sleeps taking a size thirteen. Rossi believed he'd need a tent-pole, guy-ropes, he was ever to wear the suit again.

Now, though, wandering around the Chora – the Whora, Sleeps called it, Rossi presuming it was on the basis the village fucked Rossi every time, no questions asked – draped in Sleeps' toga of a T-shirt, a Daffy Duck baseball cap tugged down over the turban of bandage, kids stopping to stare, Rossi took comfort in knowing the

cops'd never square him with the guy in the sharp Italian suit. As
a disguise it was—

'Oh, Rossi? Over here. Coo-ee. Rossi?'

'Fuck.'

Mel waving from the doorway to Sally Baba's in these pants that
looked like she was planning a getaway on Sally Baba's magic
carpet. Rossi, conned again by Mel but carrying no shiv, the darts
back in the room, guessed Mel had heard about Johnny's guy getting
snatched by Ray, Mel all of a sudden needing Rossi again, not
knowing which way Johnny might jump.

Rossi, with a sinking feeling, strolling across to Sally Baba's,
scaling down his expectations from three-quarters of a million to
twenty grand. Which, he made a mental note, would be forty grand
if Johnny didn't get the finger out in the next hour or so.

Except then he walks in and follows Mel to the table and Madge
is just sitting there.

'Hi, Rossi,' Madge said, her eyes bright. 'You're keeping well?'

Rossi was still trying to decide who he was forking first in the
eye, Madge or Mel, one stitching him up for Frank, the other for
swiping his coke, when the bald guy came back from the bathroom
adjusting his cuffs. The guy slowing now, appraising Rossi's threads
as he came on.

'Nice,' he said. 'Blending in, I like it.' The guy now putting out
his hand. 'The elusive Rossi, right? The Scarlet Pimpernel.'

Rossi eyed the outstretched hand. 'Who the fuck's this guy,' he
asked Mel, 'comes in here calling me a pimp?'

'That's Terry,' Mel said. 'Terry Furlong.'

'Although you might know him better,' Madge said, 'as Terry
Swipes.'

Sleeps

There was a queue when Sleeps got to the phone box. Which
in one way was good, he could blend in, just one more big
guy in an Italian suit about six sizes too small, waiting to
reverse-call Mom, let her know he hadn't yet succumbed to alcohol
poisoning or the clap, beg another loan to keep the party going.

Sleeps wondered what the protocol was, you were a gangster waiting at a call box, there was a queue. Uh, 'scuse me, I gotta take this call from a snatch artist, you mind?

Except – finally, a break – just as the last of the kids hangs up, the phone rings.

'Ray?'

'Who am I talking to?'

'It's me, Ray. Gary.'

'I was expecting Rossi.'

'Rossi's, uh, busy right now.'

'And that's why I'm talking to you?'

Sleeps, he was going to have to get into it at some point, said, 'You're talking to me now, Ray.'

'Not, you're saying, Rossi any more.'

'You got a problem with that?'

'The problem I have right this second,' Ray said, 'is I have a situation that needs another pair of eyes, a good head. A guy can handle himself.'

'And you were hoping for Rossi?'

'It was either Rossi,' Ray said, 'or some lummox who can't tell Johnny Priest from a Greek cop.'

'That'd be me, yeah.' Sleeps grinned. 'The guy's a cop?'

'Way I see it, Gary, you're the one put me where I need the extra pair of eyes. What d'you say?'

'I'll need, at some point, half an hour with Karen. A sit-down.'

'Where's Rossi for this sit-down?'

'In the corner, a pointy hat on his head.'

'I can't make you any promises, man. But I'll see what I can do.'

'OK.'

'You're in?'

'Where'll I find you?'

'Stay on the line.'

Ten seconds later the navy Punto eased up to the phone booth. Johnny's guy, the big-beaked cop, driving. Ray in the back nodding Sleeps on. Sleeps hung up, got in.

'The guy who unified Italy,' Ray said as Niko pulled off, 'was Garibaldi. You say it slow, it's Gary Baldy.'

'Except these days,' Sleeps said, 'people think he invented the biscuit.'

'What's that,' Johnny's guy said, 'some kind of Sicilian code?'
'You just drive,' Ray said.

Melody

Mel had seen her fair share of drama-rama, considered herself a connoisseur of the unexpected yelp or moan, the quivering declaration of undying love. But even Mel was a little shocked when Rossi dropped to one knee, took Terry's hand and kissed the guy's signet ring.

Terry a little embarrassed, heads turning in the restaurant. He hauled Rossi upright, gesturing for him to take a seat beside Mel across the table from Madge.

'I'm only here to ask you one favour,' Terry said. Rossi's eyes shining. 'Just hear Madge out, see what she has to say. Can you do me that one favour?'

So they ordered some more drinks, Mel wondering who Terry was exactly, Rossi dazzled by the guy's reputation, and then Madge went into her spiel, how she was Rossi's mother, his real name was Rossini. How his inheritance would come due once Frank's affairs were sorted, the insurance cleared, Madge finishing up with, 'Terry has agreed to help me prove it, he made a call earlier on to some guy he knows in the Births and Deaths office back home. We can have your birth certificate here tomorrow morning, or a fax version of it.'

'Three quarters of a million,' Rossi said, an expression on his face like a duck staring at thunder.

'The twins get half,' Madge said, 'you get half. It's only fair.'

'OK.' Rossi sipped on his Woo-Woo. 'Except what I'm hearing, the cop, Doyle, she wants me for Frank. Third-degree manslaughter, Sleeps said.'

'But *I* was the one,' Madge said, 'shot Frank.'

'Might be the best way to play it,' Terry said. 'Rossi gets pinched for Frank, Madge sews up the insurance, Rossi gets his half.'

'I gotta do *time* for that ratbag?'

'Worst-case scenario. You've done it before, right?'

'Sure, but—'

'Or,' Terry said, 'just thinking out loud, blue-skying, why not get Sleeps to do it? The guy says he'll do your time for you, he's practically begging for a reason. That's the kind of loyalty,' he told Madge, 'you just don't see any more. Not like the old days.' He toasted Rossi.

Rossi, morose, clinked Terry's glass with his Woo-Woo. 'He took it back,' he said. 'Guy's gone gaga for Mata Hari here. Reckons he has plans for her, she ever quits fucking him around, running off with other guys.'

'Really?' Mel said.

'That's sweet,' Madge said.

'Except,' Rossi said, 'the girl's poison. Like, first she's hijacking me and Sleeps, then she's on to Ray. Two seconds later she's canoodling with Johnny Priest. You see what I'm saying? She wants to make the *Guinness Book of Records* for being a back-stabbing tart and the only one who can't see it is Sleeps, the fat moron.'

'He's not fat, he's chunky.'

'The boy's a sumo superstar, Mel. And right now the fat fuck's down the port negotiating with Ray, putting himself on the line to get us back in touch with Johnny, mainly because you swiped Johnny's coke, ran off.'

'Easy, Rossi,' Terry said.

'Actually,' Mel said, wanting to get it out there while Terry was around, the guy a calming influence on Rossi, 'that's something I should probably mention. About the coke.'

'Do *not*,' Rossi said, 'tell me there's a problem with the coke.'

Melody cleared her throat. 'It's not so much that there's a problem with the coke,' she said.

Rossi groaned.

'It's more,' Mel said, 'that instead of any coke there's what Johnny's calling a hot rod. Which smells like it was recently fired.'

'Shit,' Terry said.

'Fuck,' Rossi said.

Madge cleared her throat. 'On the up side,' she said, 'there's still this three-quarters of a million inheritance we need to make a decision about.'

Doyle

'You know guys,' Sparks said, 'they say they'll ring, they think it's cool to leave it two or three days. So you can both pretend they're not pussy-whipped from the start.'

Sparks sitting on the low wall dividing the balconies, Doyle on her own balcony, smoking, watching the bathroom door of the room she'd rented specially in order to keep Johnny Priest stashed. Doyle wondering who she should charge the expense to.

'I have a hostage in my bathroom,' Doyle said. 'As in, Ray's hostage. So you'd expect him to make like he was keen.'

'Even if he's not.'

'Don't complicate it, Sparks.'

'Me? Listen, I'm not the one illegally detaining the big-time coke dealer from Amsterdam on account of this snatch artist I know somehow managed to fuck up and heist the wrong guy. This while I'm supposed to be a cop.'

'A suspended cop.'

'And you're thinking this is the best way to get your badge back?'

Doyle with a bad feeling. Not so much Ray and the little he knew about women, off rescuing Karen while Doyle sat home, barefoot and minding his fuck-up. Or even the way it might look if it all screwed up, Doyle holding Johnny Priest, the Amsterdam coke-dealer who believed Doyle was his temporary muscle. No, what was bugging Doyle was how she was at the mercy of all these unknowns, Doyle with no control, a sitting duck. Christ, at this rate she might as well be back home, at the desk right next to the corridor led to the holding cells, just sitting there waiting for the next clown to drop a case file on the desk, the latest dead fish to stink up the joint.

'I need to move,' she said. '*Do* something.'

'Where're you going?' Sparks said. 'No way I'm watching Johnny, if that's what you think.'

'I'm not asking you to do anything.' Doyle stubbed the smoke, thinking. 'Actually,' she said, 'I might ask just one tiny favour.'

Sparks groaned.

'Just give it five minutes,' Doyle said, 'after you hear Johnny flush. Then ring me. That's all I'm asking. Can you do that much?'

'Doyle,' Sparks said, 'you know as well as I do that I'm going to do anything you ask me. Because I know, it's a gut instinct, you won't ask anything that'll screw me over. Right?'

'Just wait for the flush,' Doyle said.

Ray

The Punto nosed up out of the village, the road snaking along the eastern flank of the valley's shallow bowl. The sky in pain, flaming orangey-red, half-torn scabs of violet cloud above hills turning mauve as night came on. By the time they got down and across the valley floor, started climbing into the hills again, it was almost full dark.

Ray said, 'You need to get tooled, right?'

'I'm not carrying,' Sleeps said, 'if that's what you mean.'

Ray leaned forward, gave Sleeps a little key. 'The glove compartment. There's a map in there too, if you don't mind doing co-pilot.'

'No problem,' Sleeps said. He liberated the gun, Niko's Sig Sauer, and the map. Ray talked him through the Sig's basics, the double-action pull, how Sleeps'd need to keep a stiff wrist to get one off or else the Sig would jam. Passing a village now, Pano Kambos, coming up on a fork in the road, a sign for Homer's Tomb in the headlights pointing off left.

'Where to?' Niko said, sullen.

'We're looking for Paleokastro,' Ray told Sleeps. 'You see it? Maybe a castle-shape on the map? I'm told Venetian.'

'It's here, yeah. Go right,' Sleeps told Niko. The road starting to climb steeply now, winding around short, tight bends.

'Hey, Gary?' Ray said. 'I don't by any chance suppose you know what Greek cops are carrying as standard these days.'

'Apart from bad breath, no idea.'

Niko stinking out the car with garlic. 'Think it might be a Sig?' Ray said. 'The P320, the kind you carry concealed, like in an ankle holster?'

'Could be.'

'But probably not.'

'This is what I'm thinking,' Sleeps said.

'So what's this Greek cop doing carrying a Sig?'

'Maybe he was off-duty.'

'Off-duty,' Ray said, 'and breaking bread with Johnny Priest . . . Niko? Feel free to jump in here, man, any time. Clear up a few details.'

Niko just grunted, gripping the steering wheel tight, knuckles pale under the olive tan. Sleeps said, 'Ray?'

'What?'

He pointed at the wing mirror. 'There's someone behind us. Since we turned off at that fork. Came down from Homer's Tomb direction, tucked in.'

'So?'

'So they're tucked in. Staying back, two or three bends behind. Apart from our friend here, he's under specific orders, how many Greeks have you seen with that kind of patience?'

'Not many on the road,' Ray said.

'Greeks,' Sleeps told Niko, 'have a lot of virtues, don't get me wrong. But patience isn't one of them.'

Niko, first time, took his eyes off the road. 'I'll wait for you,' he said. 'I'll do you last and slow.'

Ray sat forward, laid the barrel of the .38 alongside Niko's neck. 'Take the next turn-off,' he said, 'nice and easy. I want you in good shape for when you meet Karen.'

Karen

Karen, when the Punto swept by going right at the fork, the jeep's headlights flashing across it, glimpsed the unmistakable features, the beaky vulture nose.

'That's him,' she said. 'Pyle? The guy driving, he's the cop bust my nose.'

'Shit.'

'For him, yeah,' Karen said. 'Get after that car.'

'But the Chora's that way.'

'Screw that,' Karen said, pointing after the Punto with the .38.

Ten minutes later the road straightened out enough for Pyle to say, 'Fuck, where'd they go?'

'Down there,' Karen said as they passed a sign saying Neraki, a turn-off to their left. The turn-off, unpaved, dipping down into a wide valley, the sea glimmering way below, a beach white under the moonlight.

'You see them?' Pyle said.

'Nope. Get back there.'

Pyle pulled in, reversed back. 'Why'd you think they went down there?'

'They killed their lights, Pyle. Where's the sense in killing the lights, keep on going the same way, we're still behind them?'

'None, I guess.'

'So they're down there. Go down slow.'

'Giving them,' Pyle said gloomily, nosing the jeep into the turn-off, 'a better target, they're maybe pulled up somewhere in the bushes.'

'If I was you,' Karen said, 'I'd duck down a little. In the movies they always aim for the driver first.'

Sleeps

Niko went down through the hairpin bends in third gear, no lights, a sheer drop into the gorge on their right, the cliff's ruddy rock sheer on their left. Sweat coursing down Sleeps' back, the tight suit working like a sauna.

They came out of the last bend and cruised through a deserted village of tumbledown cubes, emerged on to an apron of sandstone. The beach curving away to their right, its far headland a vague looming half a mile away. A greeny-black sheen on the sea under a low and nearly full moon. 'What d'you think,' he said, 'back up into the village?'

'What about those?' Ray said, pointing at two shacks in the shadow of the near headland. 'That way no one sneaks up on us from behind.'

'I thought,' Sleeps said, 'we were the ones supposed to be doing the sneaking.'

Ray said, 'Niko? Cut the engine.'

In the silence Sleeps heard an angry gravelly whine. 'What're they driving, a tank?'

'I'd say a jeep. Get us over there, Niko. Behind those shacks.'

'What if we get stuck in the sand?' Sleeps said.

'Then we take their jeep. Niko?'

Niko eased the Punto down off the sandstone lip, ploughed into the soft sand. The car coughed twice, jerked forward, then stalled.

'Crap,' Ray said. 'Let's get over there.'

They crowded into the shack nearest the village and put Niko on his knees, hands behind his back grabbing his ankles. Ray took the handkerchief from Sleeps' breast pocket and balled it into Niko's mouth. Sleeps'd seen sturdier Wendy Houses, the shack more of a lean-to up close, built from driftwood, split cane and spit. They peered through gaps in the wall, watching as the jeep emerged on to the sandstone lip and crawled past the Punto, then bounced down on to the beach, revving hard and spewing up sand as it reversed into position, its headlights raking the shack as it came around to face back at the village.

'You see Karen?' Ray said, dazzled by the lights.

'I never met her,' Sleeps said. 'Wouldn't know what she looked like.'

'OK,' Ray said as someone hopped down out of the jeep, 'there she is. That's her.'

'What's she doing?'

'At a guess, nothing helpful.'

They watched as Karen half-jogged, crouching, towards a large boulder about halfway between the Punto and the jeep, something glinting dull in her right hand. 'Maybe she's taking a pee,' Sleeps said.

'Because we all take guns when we go for a wee.' Ray watched Karen get comfortable, the boulder between her and the shack, cutting off their escape route to the village beyond. Pyle positioned behind the jeep, no way of telling if he was tooled. 'Especially,' he said, 'when we're pissed with Ray.'

'Exactly how pissed,' Sleeps said, 'do you think she is?'

'Karen just gets mad, there isn't what you might call degrees.' Ray fumbled in his pocket, dug out his phone. 'Quick question – you ever shoot anyone?'

Sleeps, palm sweating, re-gripped the Sig. 'Never have, no.'

'Glad to hear it. Here, dial Rossi's number.'

Sleeps punched in Rossi's number, handed back the phone.

Karen called out, 'Hey, fuckface? I know you're in there.'

In the quiet of the shack the *brrr-brr* broke off. Ray said, whispering, 'Rossi? That you?'

He said, 'Ray.'

He said, 'Sleeps gave it to me.'

He said, 'A favour, man. One pro to another.'

Madge

R ossi hung up. 'That was Ray,' he told Terry. 'Guy's pinned down up north, needs the cavalry.'

'Is Karen with him?' Madge said.

'It's Karen has him pinned down.'

'She thinks Ray's a rat,' Mel said, 'for running out on her.'

'Ray ran out on Karen?' Madge said.

'The way Ray tells it,' Mel said, 'it was Karen who told *him* to go. But that didn't stop Ray, when Rossi was pointing the gun at him, telling Rossi she had gone to Crete.'

'You pulled a gun on Ray?' Terry said.

Rossi shrugged. 'It was empty at the time.'

'Partly,' Mel said, 'because Rossi'd already used one of the bullets on Ray's arm.'

'It was *you* shot Ray?' Terry said.

'And Anna,' Madge said.

'The wolf,' Rossi groused, 'was attacking *me*, it was self-defence. And Ray, the guy was coming on with a Glock. What am I s'posed to do?'

'This being the Glock,' Terry said, 'Madge used on Frank.'

'Correct.'

'So you have a wolf and Ray, both coming at you, you put them down. Then walk away with the swag.'

'Until the wolf catches up with me, yeah. Rips my fucking ear off. Then Karen strolls off with the money.'

'You should be in Nashville,' Terry said.

Rossi said, 'Mel? I'll be needing Johnny's gun.'

'You're going out there?' Terry said.

'Fucking A. Ray's got Johnny, says I can have him.'

'But he already told *me* I could have him,' Mel said.

'Get in line. Johnny tried to frame me with a hot rod, so I got first dibs. This is justice we're talking here.'

'I thought you said,' Madge said to Mel, 'that Ray has this Niko character.'

Rossi nodded. 'He says he's got Johnny too. Knows where he is, who's holding him. I'm guessing the cop, Doyle. Those two, they're sneaky.'

'What about my twenty grand?' Mel said.

'I'm owed,' Rossi said, glancing up at the clock over the restaurant's bar, 'forty gees from Johnny. Then there's Karen, who stole my money. There's anything left over after I get mine, you can have it all.'

'If it's the kidnap ransom you're talking about,' Madge said, 'this money Karen has, then technically speaking that's mine. I mean, I was the one kidnapped. And I was still married to Frank, still his beneficiary, when the insurance company paid out.'

'This much is true,' Terry said.

'OK,' Rossi conceded. 'But Karen, when I was inside, she stole my sixty grand stash, used it to keep the wolf in caviar and silk fucking pillows.'

'Fair point,' Terry said.

Mel put her hand up. 'There's one thing I'm not getting,' she said.

'You're not getting Johnny's rod,' Rossi said, 'still sitting there not going anywhere. That's what you're not getting for *me*.'

'This inheritance Madge is talking about,' Mel said. 'She's offering you three-quarters of a million, but you're still scuffling around after Johnny and Karen?'

Rossi considered that. 'It turns out I'm Madge's son, like she says, which I very much fucking doubt, then I still have to do time to get it, mainly because Sleeps is mooning around after you.' He sipped his White Russian, swirled the ice cubes. 'Johnny and Karen, though, they're here. Karen with a bag of cash where I'm due sixty gees, Johnny the double-crossing fuck just waiting out there for me to fork his eyes out I don't get forty grand and fast. You see what I'm saying.'

'Pragmatic, yeah,' Terry said.

'Then,' Rossi said, 'I dunno, maybe I put a round or two in Johnny's knees, from his own hot rod he tried to frame me with. For justice, like.' He said, 'Mel? Chop-chop, girl. If I know Ray, he won't stay pinned down forever.'

Doyle

D oyle tried the rent-a-car down on Yialos Beach first, Jacob's, the place closed and dark, open nine to nine. So they had to take the bus up to the Chora, Johnny bitching about how he hadn't taken the bus, for Chrissakes, since the last time he bunked off school. Doyle reassuring him it was counter-intuitive, no one expecting to see Johnny Priest on any buses.

Then, they find a place open in the middle of the Chora, the guy has all these forms to fill in, in triplicate, a spotty Irish kid working the counter on his own, nervous, not wanting to screw up and checking every last detail.

Doyle, finally, tucking the receipt into her back pocket, taking the keys, the free map, said, 'One last thing. Where's a nice place, somewhere romantic?'

The guy scratched his acne thinking. 'I dunno, Paris?'

'I mean on the island.' She jerked a thumb at Johnny, slumped down in the front of the four-wheel drive jeep she'd picked out on the way in. Johnny expecting, this being his compromise, Doyle to swing by the Blue Orange, Johnny touching base to see if Roger had heard from Niko. 'We're taking a few days out, not looking to be disturbed. Where's our best bet?'

The kid shrugged. 'Manganari, I guess. Down south, right at the end of the island. There's a village but it's quiet, just a few bars and restaurants. A nice beach.'

'How long will it take to get down there?'

'Depends how fast you drive,' the kid said.

'Say I'm driving normal.'

'A couple of hours, maybe. You don't know the road, it's dark – maybe three.'

'Thanks a lot,' Doyle said. 'You've been a huge help.'

'All part of the service,' the kid said.

Doyle hauled herself up into the jeep and said, 'Change of plan, Johnny.'

'Oh, you think?'

Doyle got the keys in the ignition, started up the jeep. 'We're skipping the Blue Orange. I got a feeling, call it a sixth sense, we should avoid it 'til we hear from Niko.'

'This sixth sense you got?' Johnny said. 'I'm thinking it's maybe on the fritz if it hasn't picked up on the guy in the back with the gun.'

Doyle turned. Rossi sat up showing her his gun and said, 'Last time, I was aiming to miss. This close I couldn't miss if I tried.'

'That's not strictly true,' Doyle said.

Rossi conceded the point. He said, 'Tell you what, though. You guarantee we got a truce until we get Ray sorted, I'll point the rod at the backstabbing fuck here, everyone's a winner.'

'Get *Ray* sorted?'

'Sure. Karen has him pinned down.'

'Karen?'

'Up north on some beach.' Rossi grinned. 'Man, that Karen. She's lively.'

'How come she has him pinned down?'

''Cos Ray hooked up with you.'

'Who told you this?'

'The fuck d'you think? Ray told me.'

'When?'

'Just now, he rang to say—'

'He *rang*?'

'Yeah. Said he needed back-up, someone to watch the road into the village, it's the only way in or out if you're coming from up north. Anyone other than Sleeps or Ray shows up, I'm following 'em, keeping sketch.'

'He rang *you*?' Doyle said.

Karen

Karen had left the pills in the jeep and was now in serious pain, her whole face pounding. The strain of listening for any kind of sound from the shack not helping. A good half-hour, maybe more, had trickled by. Karen wondering if the shack didn't have some kind of smuggler's trapdoor and tunnel built in.

A cicada chirred. The sea swush-swishing on shale.

'Pyle?' she called. 'You see anything?'

'Jesus Christ,' he hissed back, 'we said no names.'

'Yeah, well,' she said, 'you want to think about doing something useful? Like maybe circling out around on to the beach, see what you can see?'

'Are you insane?'

If I'm not, Karen thought, it'll do until the real deal kicks in.

'You broke my fucking *nose*, you bastard!' she bawled at the shack. 'Come on out and face me like a fucking man!'

Then, it was probably counter-productive, but Karen was past caring, she levelled the .32 at the roof of the shack, zinged one off. Waited until the echoes died away, then called, 'I'm counting to three. You're not out by then, I'm coming in shooting.'

No answer. Karen took a deep breath and bawled, 'One!'

Ray

The moonlight gave the landscape a platinum sheen pitted with black hollows. The only sounds were rustles and chirrups, the faint hiss of sand and breeze. And Karen.

'*One!*'

Sleeps, still ducked down, looking a little shaken even if the round had gone through the thatched roof a good three feet over his head, regarded Ray with some interest. 'You bust her nose?' he said.

'That's a bad case of mistaken identity,' Ray said. 'She's talking about you or him. And you're saying you never saw her before.'

They both looked at Niko. Ray said, 'Pyle tells me Karen got her nose busted last night. You wouldn't happen to know anything about that, would you?'

Niko, cheeks swollen around his makeshift gag, just stared.

'*Two!*'

'Whoa!' Ray called. 'Karen? It's me. We're coming out, OK? So no guns.' He said to Niko, 'Man, you better not be the guy she's looking for. It's way too nice a night for digging graves.'

Rossi

'See, if Ray hadn't gone up there in the first place,' Doyle said, 'Karen wouldn't have him pinned down anywhere.'

'What you have to understand about Karen,' Rossi said, 'is the girl's got spirit. I mean, she lives it real, y'know? Me and her, we first got it together, Christ, it was like Bowie and Keechie all over again.'

'Until she ripped you off.'

'You think I'm pissed at her for taking my stash?' Rossi shrugged. 'I was inside, the girl had to live. I mean, it wasn't easy for her, y'know? I'm on my third jolt, she's got the wolf to look out for. Except the issue,' he said, 'where it became an ethical matter, is when I get back out and she's not stumping up what I'm owed, the stash that'll get me back in the game, I'm not even talking any vig. So that's where me and Karen fell out. You see what I'm saying.'

'You're vouching for Karen?'

'Karen's straight up, all the way. Although,' Rossi felt obliged to add, 'not so much with me recently.'

'I could say the same,' Doyle said, 'about Ray. Taking off for this meet, he can't even do me the courtesy of a call.' She said, 'You know what I'm thinking?'

'What's that?'

'Me and you, we'd be the most to benefit if Karen went away.'

'Went away how?' Rossi said.

'Just, y'know, went away.'

'You're not talking about her doing time?'

'I'm on my holidays, Rossi.'

'And, you're saying, suspended.'

'That too.'

'I get my stash back,' Rossi said, 'the sixty gees, Karen can go anywhere she wants. I'll even buy her the fucking ticket.'

'What about Anna?'

'The wolf's different. The wolf can't just give me my ear back.'

'You think Karen'll stand for that?'

'That's between me and Karen.'

'It's just,' Doyle said, 'I'm wondering.'

'Wondering what?'

'Ray asked you sit out here, right? Keep sketch, you're calling it, to see if maybe Johnny's guy comes through on his own.'

'Perxactly.'

'What's in that for you?'

'I get Johnny. It was a favour Ray called, how I'd get—'

Doyle glanced meaningfully into the rear of the jeep.

'Oh shit,' Rossi said, 'yeah.'

'What?' Johnny said, his voice coming muffled. 'What *now*?'

Ray

'I tell you something, people,' Pyle said, 'y'all got a commendable appetite for hardware. You come out here to Ios, paradise in the sun, sleepy little island, and twenty-four hours later it's like Tarantino remade the OK Corral.'

No one answered, the four of them standing in a triangle on the beach, Pyle and Karen split wide, Ray keeping Niko close. Ray watching Karen, the girl dead-eyed, a busted nose and swollen bruise over her right eye, the crooked jaw set. Eyes on Niko.

Pyle said, 'How come, you don't mind me asking, you came down here?'

'We took a wrong turn,' Ray said, 'heading for the castle.'

Pyle pretended to shade his eyes against the moonlight, craning his neck to look up the coast. 'That castle way up yonder? You came down here to get up there?'

'We had the map upside down,' Ray said. Pyle talking too much, Ray when he had a gun in his hand preferring quiet to any possibility of insult or misunderstanding. Pyle now eyeing Niko up and down. 'So where's Johnny?' Pyle said.

'You'll get Johnny for this guy,' Ray said.

'Right. But what I'm asking is, where's Johnny?'

'He's safe.'

'Safe where?'

'Ray?' Karen said. 'You want to take that Johnny crap someplace else? Last thing I need right now is witnesses.'

Ray, generally speaking, the situation was any way normal, he'd have used Niko as a shield. But the way Karen was looking, he figured presenting Niko as any kind of target would be a bad idea. For Niko, first, sure. But for Karen in the long run. So he stood beside Niko, the guy on his knees grabbing his ankles, Ray with the .38 cocked and ready to go.

'Where's Anna?' he said to distract her.

Karen showed Niko the .32 and said, 'I've five left. Two for you, one in each ball.'

'Karen—'

'Back off, Ray. He's mine.'

'There's a queue,' Ray said. 'And Pyle got in there first.'

Niko, lids heavy, glanced from Karen to Pyle.

'All we're trying to do here,' Pyle said, 'is get Johnny back safe. OK? Everything else we can talk about.'

'Last I heard,' Ray said to Pyle, 'the point of the exercise was to get Karen safe. Now I see she's in one piece, just about, the rest is between you and Niko.'

Niko said, 'Pyle? How come something feels off here?'

'Nothing's *off*, man,' Pyle said. 'Ray here was just helping out, because the Sicilians have Johnny. Except there's no way we're trading you to any Sicilians.'

'Less of the "we" shit, Tonto,' Ray said. 'Me and Karen, we're out.'

'He got it right about not trading the guy anywhere,' Karen said. 'He's going nowhere 'til I'm done.'

'Guy's a cop,' Pyle said. 'You don't want to go shooting any *cops*, for Chrissakes.'

Karen swung the .32, pointing it now at Pyle. 'Tell me just once more,' she said, 'what I don't want to do.'

After, when he had time to think about it, Ray consoled himself with the fact that when you take an ankle gun off a guy, you never think he might be packing its twin on the other ankle. You did, you'd never put him on his knees leaning back to grab his ankles.

But that was after.

Niko, once Karen swung her gun away, came up fast, chopping at Ray's wrist with his right hand. The ankle gun, the second Sig, in his left. The .38 hit the sand, Ray rocking back and stumbling as Niko body-charged him out of the way, Niko already sprinting for the village. Not forgetting, the guy cop-trained, to loose off a couple in Karen's direction.

Ray, going down, heard a high-pitched scream, the sharp crack-crack of Karen's .32.

Sleeps

Ray, before he took Niko out of the shack, told Sleeps he'd try to pull Karen and Pyle as far over on the beach as he could, give Sleeps a chance to get around the back of the shack, sneak up along the headland in the shadows, take up a covering position near the village.

Sleeps had said, 'You're sure?' Hoping Ray wouldn't change his mind.

'Anything goes wrong,' Ray'd said, 'you're our ace in the hole, they won't be expecting you.'

Sleeps, ready to pass out in the tight suit, just nodded. Watched as Ray took Niko across the beach level with the shack, not up towards Karen and Pyle, then put Niko on his knees. Sleeps pulled the loose cane at the rear of the shack wide apart enough to struggle through, then crawled on his hands and knees to the nearest outcrop, started back up towards the deserted village. Hearing the murmur of conversation, not able to make out what was being said. He took up a position behind the boulder where Karen had been hiding and wiped his slick hands on the front of the suit. Checked Niko's Sig Sauer, making sure it was ready to go, and then nearly dropped it when the night blew up.

Sleeps peered around the boulder expecting carnage, and saw

Niko lurching for the jeep, Ray sprawled on his ass scrambling for his gun, Karen down and squirming in the sand. The wolf howling like a banshee from the back of the jeep. Ray, hampered by the plaster cast arm, got up on one knee and fired after Niko, sent two rounds whanging into the jeep. Niko, Christ, like a greyhound hitting the bend, changed direction fast to come sprinting straight towards Sleeps.

Sleeps froze.

He had a moment where he saw himself, like out-of-body looking down, this fat guy in a too-small suit about to, what, *shoot* a guy?

It was only a second, no more. But that was plenty.

By the time he'd started to bring the gun up, Niko, amped, caught the flicker of shadow and fired from low – still swivelling, not aiming, just squeezing one off. The percussive crack causing Sleeps' finger to spasm on the double-action trigger, get one away.

The last thing he saw was Niko, framed for a split-second in the yellowy-blue corona of the jeep's headlights, a killer in the sun.

Sleeps tottered, took one step, then collapsed on the sand.

MONDAY
Madge

M adge switched the phone from her left ear to the right, this to allow herself a hefty sigh, and said, 'It's just not that simple, Liz. I'm on standby but it's the height of the tourist season here, the place is full of Italians, they can't just yank someone off the plane because Frank is missing, cause a diplomatic incident . . .'

Sitting out on the balcony at the Triton hotel in a winged-back cane armchair, a potted palm behind. 'Say again, Liz? I've got a bad line here, I'm losing you . . .'

She had a sip of Cristal while Liz snuffled something incoherent down the line. 'Liz? Look hon, I could be on a flight within the hour, there's no way of knowing. But right now you need to be strong for your sister, you know she was always the dependent one. Oh, and Liz? Tell Bryan I said that if any newspapers are buzzing around, the TV, you've got my permission to talk to them. Especially the tabloids. Bryan'll work out the fee, don't worry about that. And if Bryan gets pissy about prejudicing the trial, some shit like that, tell him I'll sue for freedom of speech . . . What's that? No, I'm losing you again . . . I'll ring first thing in the morning, OK? Love to Jeanie. 'Bye.'

She hung up and said, 'Girl thinks she's distraught now, wait'll she meets Rossi, her brand-new brother.'

Melody leaned out of the other wing-backed cane armchair to top up Madge's glass from the chilled magnum in the silver bucket. Had herself a sip of her virgin Bloody Mary and said, 'Madge, there's something you really need to know.'

'What's that?'

'Ray and me, we got drunk on the ferry the other night. Well, Ray got drunk. I listened.'

'And?'

'Say someone was to hook you up,' Melody said, 'I mean, prove to you for sure who your son really is.'

Madge put down her glass of Cristal. 'Go on.'

'Like, say that someone was to show you Ray's passport that

says his real name is Israel Brogan,' Mel said. 'What d'you think, would that someone be due a finder's fee from this inheritance? I mean, nothing too outrageous. Ten per cent, say.'

Ray

Anna's howl had Ray expecting the worst. Which was why he made his second mistake in two minutes, realising too late Pyle wasn't tending to Karen, he was scrabbling around in the sand for her .32.

Pyle came up pointing at Ray, backing away, saying, 'Just put it down, man.'

Ray, still moving, dropped the .38 and went past him to Karen, hunkered down. A quick murmur for Anna, get the girl onside, Anna with this anxious whine as she butted Karen's shoulder, licked her face. A perfectly round hole in Karen's T-shirt just off-centre below her ribs, Niko cop-trained to aim for the biggest target, the torso. The girl white-faced, skin taut, twitching like she'd been electrocuted. Shock already wearing off, the pain now starting to burn.

'Karen? Just try to relax. Don't move.' Karen, teeth clenched, just nodded. 'I'm taking a look,' he said. 'Watch my eyes.'

Ray eased the T-shirt out of her jeans, gentle as he could, Karen sucking in a sharp breath as he pushed it up over her belly. The girl, Christ, more worried about her weight than Ray'd believed she would be, wearing some kind of corset, a sheet wrapped tight and knotted low above her left hip.

'How's she doing?' Pyle said from off to the side, Pyle like Billy the Kid, the .32 in one hand, .38 in the other.

Ray undid the knot in the sheet, pulled it away, then realized why there was no bleeding.

Pyle shuffled a little closer, grinning now, saying, 'Now that right there is not a sight you see every day.'

The slug just lodged there below her bottom rib, flattened against Karen's extra weight, half-buried in one of the bundles of cash she'd strapped to her stomach. Ray dug it out. Karen grimaced, the crooked jaw grinding hard. 'He's a *dead* man,' she gasped.

'We'll worry about Niko later,' Ray said. 'First we get you to a doctor.'

'Why's she need a doctor?' Pyle said. 'The slug's right there, no penetration.'

'She could be bleeding internally. And I'm guessing she'll have broken ribs, at least. Then there's general trauma, the shock.'

'If it's broken ribs, the doc won't be able to do anything. Meanwhile he's asking how it happened, the girl got this internal bleeding you're saying she might have.'

'She's seeing a doctor,' Ray said, 'fast as I can get her there.'

Pyle held up the .38. 'Sorry compadre, no can do.'

'He wasn't asking for no favour,' Sleeps said stepping out from behind the Punto, both hands braced on the butt of the Sig.

Melody

'Now I know you're shitting me,' Terry said. 'Ray is the kid Israel?'

Madge just stared, lying flopped back in the wing-backed chair.

Mel, nodding, said, 'I have his passport back in the room.' She considered. 'Well, three of his passports to be precise, Ray likes to keep his options open. But yeah, one of them says Israel Brogan. Be a bit of a coincidence if this Israel you're looking for wasn't our Ray. I mean, how many Irish kids were named Israel that year?'

'*Any* year,' Terry said. 'And it's definitely the right date?'

'The date I can't be certain about,' Mel said, 'but it's the right year, yeah. I mean, Israel Brogan – that one caught my eye.'

'And your maiden name,' Terry said to Madge, 'it's Brogan?'

Madge shook her head. 'That must be his adopted name,' she whispered.

Mel said, 'Anyway, this finder's fee we were—'

There came a knockity-knock-knock at the door. Terry went through and let Rossi in, Rossi parading Johnny out on to the balcony like the guy was Lord Lucan, saying, 'Johnny? I'd like you to meet a friend of mine, name's Terry Furlong. You might've heard of him as Terry Swipes.'

Johnny with a double-take, from Rossi to Terry in the wing-backed armchair. 'Oh shit,' he said, his jaw flopping around. He said, 'I didn't *know*. How could I *know*?'

'Don't worry about it,' Terry said. 'You know now.'

'You know forty gees' worth,' Rossi told him.

Mel said, 'Rossi? If you don't mind, we're right in the middle of—'

Except then Rossi's phone rang. Rossi checked the caller ID and handed Johnny the phone, saying, 'Here's this guy Niko wants to talk to you. Why don't you make it a conference call, huh?' Putting the CZ, 9mm Parabellum, in Johnny's face.

So Johnny took the call, hit speaker-phone. 'Niko?'

'Who's this?'

'It's me, Johnny.'

'You alone?'

'Sure, yeah. Where the fuck are you?'

'Where're *you*?'

'Up in the village, man. You get away?'

'Fucking amateurs he sent.'

'Who sent?'

'Pyle, the fucking hippy.' Niko taking a deep breath, letting it out with a hiss.

'You all right?' Johnny said.

'The fat guy, bastard clipped my shoulder.'

Rossi winked at Terry, gave him a thumbs-up.

'The fat guy?'

'The ex-fat guy.' Niko with an evil chuckle. 'Went down so hard there'll be quakes in Australia.' Rossi frowned. Mel put her fingertips to her lips. 'Johnny? You got serious problems with Pyle. He had me snatched by a guy who thought I was you, I think he's a pro hooked up with these Sicilians, working freelance. Told Pyle he had you someplace safe.'

'Bluffing him,' Johnny mumbled.

'What I thought, yeah. Where're you now, the Orange?'

'Yeah,' Johnny said, 'coordinating the, y'know, search. You coming in here?'

'Fuck no, are you kidding? Meet me at the place, a boat's coming in from Santorini to take me off, they'll be here in three, four hours.' Another slow hissing of breath. Niko swore.

'You need that thing seen to?' Johnny said.

'Shit, hold on – here's a car now. Johnny?'

'Yeah?'

'That boat's for me. You get off the island after you deal with Pyle.'

Niko hung up.

'The *ex*-fat guy?' Rossi said, not wanting to believe it.

Madge looked at Terry. Terry said, 'Where's this place he's talking about?'

'Up north,' Johnny said. 'Near Homer's Tomb.'

'How long'll it take to get there?'

'Half an hour, maybe more.'

'What's the read?' Rossi said.

'I'm thinking,' Terry said, 'if anything's happened to Ray—'

'Or Karen,' Madge said.

'Or Gary,' Mel said.

But Rossi only stared at her, stony-faced. 'You're a day late,' he said, 'and more'n a few dollars overdue.'

Sleeps

'How about this?' Sleeps said. 'I got one, you got two, Ray's got none.' Anna quartering the sand behind them, snuffling. 'You give him one, we all put 'em away, it'd be like a Mexican stand-off in reverse. Everyone knows everyone else is packing, who's likely to draw?'

This after Ray made the introductions, how Gary was the guy pulling the Sicilian's strings, Sleeps believing it was no time to mention how he'd fainted dead away when Niko opened up on him.

Pyle allowed he was agreeable to the gun-swap, Pyle handing Ray the .38 over Karen's protests, Ray insisting it was his before it was Karen's.

Ray said, 'Gary? You're a wheelman, right? How about you drive, me and Pyle'll sit in the back and admire how a pro does it.'

Karen huddled up, riding shotgun beside Sleeps, hugging herself. Anna was between her legs, Karen ducking left and right while Anna, seemingly puzzled at the discoloration around Karen's nose, tried to lick Karen's face clean.

'So where to?' Sleeps said, nosing the jeep up through the bends, the engine whining against the steep climb, the weight in the car.

'Back to the village,' Ray said, 'the health centre. Karen needs seeing to.'

Karen was shaking her head. 'This Niko guy first,' she said.

'We don't even know where the guy's gone,' Ray said.

'I've got a pretty good idea,' Pyle said.

Ray said, 'Gary? How do you want to play it?'

Sleeps considered. 'We get all the way up to the main road and we haven't passed him, it means he's behind us.'

'Then what?'

'We could turn around and come down slow. Maybe walking it, beating the bushes.'

'What's the other option?'

'We keep going, get Karen to the doctor. Then find this guy and kill him.'

'Kill him?' Pyle said.

Sleeps was still only realizing how close he'd come when Niko squeezed one off. Like the bullet, whining by so close, had punctured some cloudy bubble, leaving Sleeps staring up at the star-twinkling sky for the first time in his life, aware now of how much he'd had to lose, how fragile it all was.

It was this epiphany, he believed, that had induced his swoon. Although, thinking back, he couldn't entirely discount the narcolepsy either.

'Guy tried to kill me,' he said. 'It's open season now.'

'I'll dig you the hole,' Ray said.

Karen, cradling her ribs with one arm, got herself twisted around. 'Ray? We lose him now, we'll never find him again.'

'She's right,' Pyle said. 'And the fucker'll come back with an army, man.'

Ray said, 'Gary?'

'If Karen reckons she'll make it,' Sleeps said, 'then it's Karen's call.'

Karen gave a little shudder, an after-shock. 'I'll make it,' she said. 'Pull in.'

Sleeps pulled over to the verge. Karen opened the door and chucked at Anna, got the girl out. Ray leaned forward, tapped Karen on the shoulder, handed over a white rag.

'What's that?' Pyle said.

'What used to be Niko's gag,' Ray said.

'Christ,' Sleeps said, 'I could track him from that myself.'

'The boy likes his garlic,' Pyle said.

Karen waved the rag under Anna's nose, hissed in her ear. Anna's ears pricked up and then she threw her head back and howled again, Sleeps knowing he'd be hearing that sound for years to come in his bad dreams.

Karen shook her head, put a finger to her lips and then buried her face in the wolf's ruff. The wolf ducked around the open door, then took off at a steady lope up the road.

Sleeps put the jeep in gear, got going. He said, 'Ray? The hound being free and all, no muzzle, this might be a good time to put in a courtesy call to Rossi, give the guy a sporting chance if Anna misses out on Niko.'

Karen turned her head, slow, to raise an eyebrow at Ray.

'You're talking to Rossi now?' she said.

'It's a long story,' Ray said.

Rossi

Rossi took Johnny in the bathroom and had him stand in the bath and drop his trousers, bend over grabbing the taps. 'Ever see *Things To Do In Denver*, Johnny?'

'Listen, Rossi, I couldn't have known. If I'd—'

Rossi rammed the CZ between Johnny's buttocks. 'They've this thing in the movie, it's called buckwheats. Guy takes a round up the hole, it's a horrible death, lasts hours.'

'Rossi, for the love of Jesus—'

'I'd of thought,' Rossi said, cocking the CZ, 'you'd be more a Judas man. I mean, Johnny, you set me up with a hot fucking rod. So it'd be what they call ironic you were to take a round up the hole from your own hot rod now.'

Johnny with wobbly knees. 'It wasn't meant for *you*, man.'

'No?'

'You were supposed to hand off to Niko, let *him* take the heat.'

'Meanwhile,' Rossi said, 'I'm running all over with a smoking gun. For ten fucking grand?' He shoved the CZ a little further between Johnny's white hairy buttocks. 'I'm thinking, that forty gees you owe, it's maybe double-bubbling again.'

'Sure thing,' Johnny said. 'Anything you say.'

'Don't agree so easy, man. You do that, you're either fink all the way through or you're planning some other grift. Either way, I'm worried.'

'You got nothing to worry about, Rossi.'

'I got my main man down, Johnny, maybe bad, I dunno. Taken out by your guy Niko, who—'

'Whoa-whoa-whoa. Hold up.' Johnny peered back over his shoulder. He said, 'You think Niko's *my* guy?'

'You're saying he isn't?'

Johnny shook his head, said, 'I'm betting you don't even know he's a cop.'

Rossi let the CZ drop away. 'You're telling me,' he said, 'it was a *cop* took out Sleeps?'

Johnny like a toy dog in a car window, head bobbing.

'Jesus, Johnny.' Rossi shook his head. 'You're tied in with *cops?*'

'It's not what you think, man.'

'See, that's been my problem all along,' Rossi said, giving the CZ a vicious twist as he rammed it home between Johnny's buttocks, Johnny giving a little yelp and rising up on his tippy-toes. 'Too much fucking thinking.' He cocked the gun, slipped the safety off. 'Y'know the real beauty of buckwheats, Johnny? The whole body works as a silencer. Not a lot of people know that.'

'What do you want?' Johnny screamed. 'Just tell me what you *want.*'

'Blood,' Rossi said and squeezed the trigger.

Doyle

D oyle took the call and said, 'Hold on a sec,' none too comfortable negotiating one-handed through hairpin bends with sheer drops the other side of a low rail. She tucked the phone between her ear and shoulder, said, 'Ray? Go ahead.'

'What the fuck are you doing with Rossi's phone?'

'Rossi's a nice guy, Ray. Said he was expecting you to call, and thought you and me should talk once in a while. Plus I reminded him, if we were to swap, about all the gangster-type contacts he'd get from Johnny's phone.'

'Is Rossi there now?'

'Nope.'

'Where's Johnny?'

'Johnny, yeah. I gave him to Rossi too.'

'You gave him to—'

'I reckoned, you and Rossi being best buds now, you're telling him sad stories about you and Karen, that wouldn't be such a problem. I mean, maybe if you'd rang *me* when I still had Johnny, maybe then we could have—'

'Let me talk to Johnny, Doyle.'

'I don't have him.'

'Fuck.' A heavy sigh, Ray accepting it. 'So where are you?'

'Right now? Coming down the valley towards this beautiful beach, all moonlit and shit, *très* romantic. Does Karen still have you, y'know, pinned down?'

'Shit, Doyle – which fucking beach?'

'Neraki, the one where Rossi said—'

'Get out of there, Doyle. Do it now.'

'Don't you *dare* take that tone with—'

'Niko's loose, Doyle. We're coming up the road behind him, we don't know where the fuck he is.'

Doyle slowed down to make another bend, fumbling with the gear-stick, still coming to terms with it being on the right-hand side, Doyle half the time trying to change gear with her left hand and grabbing the window-winder. She came out of the bend saying, 'Shit, yeah, I think I can see his lights, way down—'

'That's us, Steph. Niko's on foot.'

'He's on—'

Niko reared up in the headlights, wild-looking, one hand holding up something shiny, the other pointing a gun at the Suzuki's windscreen. Doyle jammed on so hard the phone flew out from between her ear and shoulder and bounced back off the dashboard, Doyle following its general trajectory, her forehead cracking against the rim of the steering wheel. The Suzuki skidding to a halt about three feet short of ploughing Niko off the road and out over the low rail.

He came around the driver's side brandishing his badge, shouting something guttural in Greek, then hauled open the door and cut off, staring. '*Stephanie?*'

Doyle, her vision blurry, tears stinging, felt something warm and wet oozing from her nose. Niko said, 'What are *you* doing here?'

'Looking for you,' Doyle said. 'Niko, they have Johnny.'

Niko bundled her across into the passenger seat and sat in, tucked away his badge, the gun. Executed a fast three-point turn, then burned rubber surging back up the road, all the while watching the rear-view.

'Can you believe this shit?' he said. 'They sent a fucking *wolf.*'

Karen

'**W**here to now?' Sleeps said, the jeep climbing out of the valley on to the main road.

'Go right,' Pyle said. 'He'll head for the port or the coast, probably the coast. He needs to get out.'

Sleeps went right and pushed up a gear and said, 'Pity we didn't remind the wolf to stay on the road, not go tracking the guy cross-country.'

'Shssssh,' Ray said. Doyle, her phone still on, her voice crackling on Ray's speaker-phone, said, '*You want me to take a look at that arm?*'

'*It'll wait,*' Niko said.

First time she'd ever set eyes on Doyle, Karen had known the girl was trouble. Bad enough she was a cop, one with something to prove to the guys down the station, but then she starts batting the lashes at Ray, chasing the guy all over Christendom. No shame. Doyle had been the first time Anna ever got it wrong, cuddling up to the cop first time she met her, Doyle under the impression Anna, the two-time killer, three parts wolf to one part husky, was what Doyle called a wee dote.

Karen was starting to wonder, the way Anna'd taken to Pyle so fast too, if the girl's instincts weren't haywire. Then again, the way Anna had stopped Rossi's bullet with her forehead up at the lake, it'd be strange if that hadn't fritzed up her works just a little. Karen feeling all kinds of fritzed herself, in shock but buzzing, still kind of stunned but feeling electrified too.

Doyle, she wanted Ray, that was one thing. But if the girl tried to get between Karen and Niko, pull some mutual appreciation shit between cops, Karen'd go through her for a short-cut . . .

'*So how'd Johnny find out about the sting?*' Doyle was saying.

'*Fuck's it matter?*' Niko said. '*He knows. It's blown.*'

'*What happens now?*'

'*We get out. After that we worry about what happens.*'

'*We?*'

'*If I'm a cop, they'll think you're a cop too.*'

'*They didn't when they took Johnny,*' Doyle said.

The clink-flick of a Zippo. '*What happened?*'

'*Johnny, I couldn't put him off, he wanted to get to the Orange, said he was worried about you. I'm saying no, we need to stay out of sight, but he started wondering, I could tell, how come I'm giving all these excuses. So I thought I'd take him along, stick tight.*'

'*And someone hit you?*'

'*When I wouldn't back off.*'

'*Bastard.*'

Karen gritted her teeth. Sleeps said, 'Pano Kambos coming up fast. What now?'

'Shssssh,' Ray said.

'The Blue Orange bar,' Pyle whispered, 'back in town. You know it?' Sleeps nodded, stayed with the main road.

'*. . . paranoid as fuck,*' Niko was saying. '*I'm guessing Pyle, the way it sounded back at the beach, is planning a reverse takeover on Johnny, maybe cutting these Sicilians in. Or just using them for muscle, a flat fee, I don't know.*'

'*A reverse takeover on what?*'

'*This dope they're running, I told you in Athens, it goes out through the hippy commune.*'

'*And this is where you're meeting Johnny,*' Doyle said. '*The hippy commune.*'

'*Are you insane? If I go in there I'll come out horizontal.*'

'*So where?*'

'*This other place. Hey, is that your phone?*'

'*Yeah, shit. It must've fallen when I jammed on that time.*'

A scrabbling sound, then click-*brrrrrrrrr*.

'Shit,' Ray said.

'It's all right, I know where he's going,' Pyle said. 'Gary? Get back to Pano Kambos, go left.'

Sleeps pulled in, U-turned, got back on the road.

Karen said, 'Ray? When we get there, you best look out for Doyle. She gets in my way she's going down too.' She said, 'Which reminds me, who's got my gun?'

'That'd be me,' Pyle said, handing the .32 forward. He looked from Karen to Sleeps and back again, 'So that's both of you want Niko. Ray? You got a coin we could maybe flip?'

Ray

They came off a bend and over a small rise and straightaway Sleeps cut the engine, the lights, allowing the jeep to coast down slow into the parking area, tyres crunching on gravel. A Suzuki four-wheel drive parked to one side, a crazy-paved path leading away from the parking area to some kind of pagoda halfway up the hill, the black sea sparkling beyond. No one around. 'Think that's them?' Sleeps said.

'Why don't you just ring Doyle, Ray?' Karen, with an edge. 'See if she's out for a moonlight stroll with our boy Niko.'

'No need,' Pyle said. He pointed off to the right, the mouth of a ravine a jagged black chunk dug out of the silvery landscape. 'Guy thinks he can't trust us back at the commune, he's called a boat in here.'

'Back-up?' Ray said.

'Don't know if that'd make a whole lot of sense,' Pyle said. 'Like, he'll have a crew on stand-by, just laying off the coast ready to storm in?'

'There's prisons just busting at the seams,' Sleeps said, 'with guys who forgot how smart cops can sometimes get.'

'Like Doyle, say,' Karen added.

'Whoa.' Pyle glancing at Ray. 'This Doyle's a *cop*?'

'She's suspended,' Ray clarified. 'And getting out of the game.'

'This what she's telling you,' Karen said. 'Chased you all the way across a continent just to let you know she's retiring, how much her pension's worth.'

'You're saying,' Ray said, 'maybe it's female intuition, you know what's going on in her head.'

Sleeps said, 'Be fair, man. Doyle looked pretty friendly with Niko to me, the time you snatched Johnny.'

Everyone looked at Ray. Pyle cocked his head to one side. 'She's in with Niko?'

'She knows him from way back,' Ray said. 'Some kind of training programme, cops from all over the EU teaming up, sharing expertise. But that was—'

'She told you this?' Karen said.

'Yep.'

'And you're still here?'

Ray shrugged. 'Pyle had you,' he said. 'Trading you off for Johnny.'

Karen looked at Pyle, who said, 'That's not exactly the way it was.'

Karen, still staring at Pyle, said, 'OK, but now Pyle doesn't have me any more. How come you're not getting out?'

'Niko finds out Doyle's hooked up with me,' Ray said, 'she'll be in all kinds of trouble. And she bought in, Karen. I couldn't have come for you without her.'

Karen, with the busted nose and swollen eye, didn't need to try to look any more evil. She gave it a shot, though.

'Just out of curiosity,' Pyle said, 'is there anyone here who trusts anyone else even, y'know . . .' He brought his thumb and forefinger close together, squinted through.

Sleeps said, 'Let's just keep it simple. Hands up anyone wants to see Niko make it off the island.' He glanced at all three in turn. 'OK,' he said. 'So let's do this.'

Rossi

Lost *again*. Christ, this fucking island . . .

Sitting parked up at the fork in the road on a rusty bucket-of-shit moped, wiggling a finger in his good ear, one sign saying Homer's Tomb, the other Pakoto. Trying to remember Johnny's directions. Except Johnny hadn't been making much sense at the time, the guy in agony, blood spattered all across the porcelain bath, the white tiles.

Rossi with a serious jones for this guy Niko, the cop who'd taken down Sleeps. Rossi getting a little choked up whenever he allowed himself to think about the big guy, the only partner he'd ever had, who'd followed Rossi all the way to Sicily and was now lying out there somewhere in the dark.

He was already a little spooked, the place dead and bleak, this bluey light from the moon making it all ghost-like, when he heard the first faint howl.

He revved the moped, thinking, no fucking *way* . . .

Except it was. The wolf. There in the mirror, loping down out of the hills like a furry black fucking angel. Headed straight for him.

Rossi gave the scooter all the juice it had, back wheel skidding out as it surged forward. He got out ahead of the wolf but couldn't pull away from her, the road gouged and rutted, bad drops on the bends, a lot of tight turns. His good ear tingling, Rossi felt the hound's hot breath on the back of his neck, the bitch every second maybe half a stride off making a lethal leap.

Rossi wouldn't have minded so much, but he could've just as easily stole the helmet when he was taking the scooter. Safety first, he fumed as he banked into a long bend, safety fucking *first*.

It occurred to him, as he came off the bend and left the road going over a small hump, to wonder how many races Rossi, the Doc, would've won with a fucking *wolf* on his ass . . .

He went whining through the parking area scattering gravel, flashed past the jeeps, got a glimpse of Doyle's Suzuki, kept going out into the scrub, the moped bucking now on the rough terrain, slowing up, Rossi bouncing around rodeo-style.

Another piercing howl. Rossi turtled up, skin crawling, hearing a note of savage glee as the hound readied to—

Except the wolf hit the gas, the moped by Rossi's clock doing thirty miles an hour and it just went by him like he was standing still, headed for this ravine gouged out of the cliff, ears flat, tail streaming out behind.

Rossi hauled hard on the brakes, brought the moped slewing around in a clanking half-circle. Thinking, what the fuck . . .?

Then realized, shit, yeah. The wolf was tracking Karen.

Doyle

Niko stationed Doyle behind a low ridge where the soft sand of the beach dropped two feet to the hard-packed strand and told her to let fly if she heard as much as a bat fart, then took off his shirt, his tanned skin taking, Doyle couldn't help but notice, a nice sheen from the moonlight. The beach narrow between two high headlands that were virtually sheer, a long channel leading out to the placid open sea. Niko ripped off one of the shirt-sleeves, tore it into strips, then broke his Zippo apart and squeezed the spongy bit on to one of the strips, which he rolled in a ball and tucked into the shirt's breast pocket. Then he put the Zippo back together again.

The faint echo of a mournful howl came wafting down the gorge.

'You see that wolf,' Niko said, 'you shoot to kill.'

'Sure thing.'

'Actually,' Niko said, holding out his shirt, beckoning for the Sig, 'you signal the boat, I'll watch the gorge.'

'That's OK,' Doyle said. 'I'm cool.'

'I mean it. You ever shot to kill before?'

'Never, no.'

'Then give me the gun. Here.'

Doyle had a split-second to consider the options, one of which was to back off and hold the gun on Niko, hope Ray arrived before the boat. The problem there being that Doyle couldn't know if Ray had heard her conversation with Niko, or if it'd been any use to him if he had. If he hadn't, Doyle was looking at holding off Niko and a whole boatload with a gun she didn't know how many rounds it was packing, fighting a rearguard action up the ravine with, Christ, ten miles back to civilisation across an island she didn't know, this if she ever made it out. And nothing back at civilisation except a load of local cops curious as to why she'd unilaterally declared war on Greece.

She swapped the gun for the shirt and the Zippo.

'You hear the boat,' he said, 'see it pass across the top of the channel, then get—'

Another howl, this one louder, magnified by the ravine. More vicious than melancholy, Doyle thought, now that she could hear it right. Niko dropped to one knee and banged one off into the darkness of the ravine.

When the echoes died away, Doyle could hear a faint hum. Tinnitus, she decided, then realized it was the boat.

'Light the rag! *Light* it!'

Doyle held the Zippo to the pocket of the shirt and made a half-hearted attempt to flick the Zippo. What sounded like a small avalanche now tumbling down the gorge. Niko fired another one off, then thrust the gun at her and snatched away the shirt. Doyle let the Zippo drop on to the hard, damp sand.

'Fuck!' he said, snatching it up, flicking desperately. A thin lance of light shot out from the boat to probe the beach. 'We're *here!*' Niko bellowed, still flicking the Zippo.

Anna came around the final bend like a two-hundred-pound Fury, paws sliding out from beneath her as she skidded on loose shale, the one amber eye glowing in the dim shadows. Fangs bared and gleaming as she found her feet again, surged forward.

Niko yelped, dropping the shirt and Zippo as he turned to sprint down the beach and plunge into the water, waving wildly at the boat. 'Here!' he screeched. 'We're here!'

Doyle went down on one knee and gripped her gun-hand by the wrist, took a quick aim, loosed off three in quick succession. On the last one she heard a metallic plink as the bullet found metal.

The searchlight snapped off. An engine throttled up and then boomed, churning a phosphorescent wake as the prow angled up and the boat veered away in a wide semi-circle.

'Nooooooo!' Niko screamed as he ploughed deeper, thighs pumping but going nowhere fast.

Doyle pivoted on her knee to find Anna coming straight at her, two strides away, slavering drool, the amber eye fixed on the shirt at Doyle's feet.

Doyle dropped the gun and opened her arms wide, went to meet her.

Sleeps

Once Niko realized Doyle was down and busy wrestling the wolf, it was basically a sprint to see who got to her first, Niko sloshing up out of the tide and making for the Sig in the sand.

Sleeps was never going to win that race. Ray had the broken arm. Karen, even without the busted ribs and all, just wasn't a sprinter.

Niko came sliding in hard. Came up in a blur of sifting sand pointing at Ray.

Ray pulled up hard still ten yards short and overshot a little, bounced a couple of steps on his rigid left leg. Then he went into a slight crouch, the hands going up and out like a goalie facing a penalty kick. The .38 in his right.

Doyle by now lying on top of Anna, the hound in a half-nelson. Doyle murmuring something in her ear. Anna twitching, growling low in her throat and straining away from Doyle, the paws churning up sand.

Niko pointing at Karen.

'Easy,' Ray said.

Sleeps, outraged by the guy throwing down on a woman, said, 'Point that somewhere else.'

Niko didn't even glance his way. 'What happens now?' he asked Ray.

'I don't know. Any suggestions?'

'Everyone walks away. After that it's just detail.'

'I can work with that. Now point the gun somewhere else.'

'What about her?' Niko said. Karen with her .32 pointed at Niko's chest, Karen hunched over protecting her ribs.

'Karen?' Ray said.

'He shot me, Ray,' she said. 'Bust my nose.'

'Don't worry about it,' Niko said. 'You weren't much of a looker before.'

'Hey,' Sleeps said. 'We don't do personals.'

'Are you going to tell her,' Niko asked Ray, 'or am I?'

'You don't tell Karen anything,' Ray said. 'What you do is, you ask nice and hope she's in a good mood.'

'He's not leaving here, Ray.'

'Karen . . .'

And then Ray turned his head, cocking an ear to the ravine, hearing the faint hum grow louder, start to whine and snarl, become a rasping roar. This weird screeching wail floating above it aiming for a whole new frequency.

Ray glanced at Sleeps.

'Cometh the hour,' Sleeps said.

Rossi

R ossi was only twenty yards into the ravine, slowly slaloming between the boulders and outcrops, the slope starting to get steep, when he realized he'd hauled on the brakes a little too hard back at the parking area. This after one gentle tug sent the cable twanging free, pinging past his face. Rossi ducked under and watched the brake cable as it sprung back to flop out in front of the moped. Gave a low whistle, relieved.

Then the moped fell off the edge of the world.

The drop was only three or four feet but it was plenty. The moped bounced once on a sloping shelf of rock and shot forward, not so much rounding the sharp twists and turns as slamming into one wall and veering across to clang against the other, hot orange sparks blazing. Rossi dragged along in its wake, his hands at times the only contact he had with the screeching machine, the moped bucking and straining like it was possessed by the soul of Steve McQueen.

'Fuuuuuuuuuuuuuuuck!' he screamed as the moped glanced off the canyon wall and caromed out of the ravine on to the beach, Rossi only dimly aware of figures scattering, diving for cover, as he zoomed past. Then the moped whumped into the soft sand atop a small ridge and sailed out into the Greek night.

Rossi, without even thinking, let go the handlebars and twisted to clutch at the tall beaky guy, catching him under the chin with his forearm and practically decapitating him with a classic clothesline.

They went down together in an explosion of sand, a tangle of arms and legs.

Rossi kicked free and crawled away, rolled on to his back, already reaching for the CZ. Then realized the beaky guy was already on his knees, choking, one hand to his throat, the other – and Rossi couldn't help but admire the guy's balls – shakily pointing a gun at Karen. Doyle sprawled across the wolf.

'I'm guessing,' the beaky guy rasped, 'you're this fucking Sicilian I've been hearing so much about.'

Madge

'Except I'd already taken the bullets out,' Melody said. 'Even checked there wasn't one up the spout.'

'The spout?' said Madge, sitting on the toilet, smoking.

'That's what Ray called it, I don't know if it's a technical term.' Mel wadded another handful of toilet paper, began wiping down the sink, the girl with her sleeves rolled up. Madge, even looking at it, found it hard to believe one man could bleed so much, the bathroom not entirely unlike a Damien Hirst installation. 'Basically,' Melody said, 'it's when a bullet's ready to go.'

'So the gun was empty.'

'Sure. But Johnny didn't know that.'

'Did Rossi?'

'That I don't know.'

Madge made a sweeping gesture encompassing the blood-streaked tiles, the bath and sink. 'So where did all this come from?'

'According to Rossi, Johnny was up on his tippy-toes bent over and Rossi had the gun jammed up his wazoo. Then, Rossi pulled the trigger, Johnny toppled over or passed out. Anyway, he came down face-first on the taps.'

Madge grimaced, the Triton's taps being old-fashioned, the kind with spokes rather than rounded. Johnny, slumped in the corner with a strawberry-coloured pillowcase jammed against his face, moaned a little. 'How bad is he?' she said.

'Not sure. He won't let me touch him.' Melody indicated the little pile of teeth on the rim of the sink, some of them with lumps

of flesh still attached. 'But it looks like he came down on his upper
jaw, smashed the palate. I mean, he was still hooked on to the tap
when I got in here.'

'So what happens now?'

'Terry, when he finds a doctor, brings him back here, gets Johnny
stitched up. Although we'll have to strip him off first, make it look
like he was having a shower when he, y'know, slipped.'

'What if he tells the doctor what really happened?'

'With Terry standing there?' Melody shook her head. 'Besides,
presuming he can even talk with his mouth stitched up, his palate
busted all to hell, what's he going to say? He's a coke dealer out
of Amsterdam, got ambushed on Ios by you and Terry?' Melody
shook her head. 'No offence, Madge, but you don't exactly look
the criminal type.'

'None taken,' Madge said. She had a long drag on the cigarette,
let it out slow.

Melody dropped the bloody wad of paper into the wastebasket,
the sign above the toilet asking for no paper waste to be flushed.
Started unwinding another handful. 'So what're you going to do
about Ray?' she said.

'I honestly don't know. I guess he's entitled to what Rossi was
getting.'

'You don't sound convinced,' Melody said, hunkering down to
swab at the underside of the sink.

'I'm just tired,' Madge said. 'It's been a long week.' She shrugged.
'Maybe I'll just donate the money to charity, send him and the twins
a little card, let them know all the good works being done in their
name. Maybe,' she said gloomily, 'that way some good will finally
come out of Frank being a douche-bag.'

'Goats for Africa,' Melody said, 'that kind of thing?'

'Something like that, yeah. Although goats, I don't know about
you, they give me the willies.' Johnny moaned again, slumped a
little further into the corner. Madge said, 'What I'd like is if it went
to some kind of rehabilitation, where you could see it changing
people's lives. Maybe, y'know, education.'

Melody was nodding along as she swabbed. She said, 'You heard
about this new operation, FARCO?'

Karen

Rossi got up and dusted himself off and said, 'Sicilian, yeah,' then forked his fingers at Niko's eyes. Still staring Niko down, he said to Doyle, 'You OK?'

Karen thinking, Christ, first Ray, and now Rossi?

Doyle lying across Anna, talking her down like some kind of wolf-whisperer. 'I'm good,' she said.

'Whatever you do,' Rossi said, 'do not for the love of Christ let that hound go.' Then, to Niko, 'What you're going to do right now is take that rod and point it at your own fucking foot. And if I say blow a fucking toe off, don't go rushing in 'til I say which one.'

'Back off, Rossi,' Karen said. 'He's mine.'

Rossi, searching her out, saw Sleeps first. Did a little double-take. 'Shit, man – I thought you were down.'

'Nearly was,' Sleeps said, grim. 'The fucker's mine.'

Ray said, 'He's no one's, all right? Everyone's walking away, it's already arranged.'

'No way,' Rossi said. 'Guy's a cop.'

'We know,' Karen and Ray said together. Rossi raised an eyebrow at Ray, then glanced across at Karen.

Karen, she knew Rossi had his issues with her, but even at that she was a little shocked at the way his face darkened when he met her eyes. His own getting small and mean. He pointed at her, arm straight out, forefinger trembling.

'Who's the dead fucker,' he snarled, 'did that?'

'Niko,' Karen said simply. 'It's why he's mine.'

Rossi turned to look at Niko, his gun coming up to point at Niko's face. Except by now Niko, after the little exchange between Rossi and Doyle, was holding his gun about six inches from Doyle's head, Doyle still struggling with Anna, unaware.

The way Rossi grinned, Karen's stomach turned over.

'You shoot her,' Rossi said, 'I shoot you, the world's two cops better off. Everyone's a winner. So make your play.'

Ray

Ray said, 'Rossi? Doyle goes down, you go too. I shit you fucking not.'

Doyle, hearing her name, looking up and around, flinched back from Niko's gun. 'Jesus Christ,' she said. 'What the fuck, Niko?' Anna was whining harder now, wriggling around beneath her.

Ray, keeping it low, said, 'What I'm thinking is, the guy's a cop, we hand him up to Johnny, let Johnny do him. That way we all walk.'

'You're not getting it,' Rossi said, jaw set hard.

'I get it, yeah. Guy's a scumbag, broke Karen's nose. But you're going to do time for him, Greek time? He's not worth it, man.'

'See,' Rossi said, 'that'd be a plan, yeah, if Niko was Johnny's guy, not the other way round.'

'He's a cop,' Ray said, 'working undercover, stinging Johnny.'

'Not exactly,' Rossi said. 'Johnny and me, we had us a little chat.'

Sleeps said, 'Pyle, buddy?' Pyle backing off a step or two, a slow moonwalk aiming for the ravine. 'You leave now you'll miss the big finale.'

'What's Johnny saying?' Ray asked Rossi.

'He's saying he's Niko's guy.'

'Johnny's Niko's guy?'

'What he says. One of 'em, anyway. Says Niko's got guys, shit, all over. Marseilles, Bari, Barcelona, you name it . . . He's got this set-up going with guys in Crete, down the south coast, they've been smugglers since King Tut was knee-high to his midget mother. Niko's trafficking in from Morocco, out through the islands.'

'And Johnny's just one of these guys.'

'Correct.'

Ray, thinking it through, said, 'So if Johnny was to go missing, then Niko'd need to fill a hole in 'Dam. Someone he can work with, someone he already knows. Someone like, just for argument say, our old buddy Pyle who arranged for me to snatch Johnny.'

Niko was glaring now at Pyle.

'Sounds logical, yeah,' Rossi said. 'Hey, maybe whack Niko too while he's in the mood.'

'Putting Niko away,' Ray said, 'that'd be worst-case scenario, cause all sorts of confusion. I mean, it's an option, sure, if Niko doesn't play ball. Guy doesn't even have to know it's on the slate until he says no.'

'So Pyle here takes Johnny down,' Rossi said, 'and then Niko, he's maybe squiffy about internal promotion they call it, might or might not go too.'

'Pyle?' Ray said. 'If we're misrepresenting you, maybe slandering, you want to tell us where we got it wrong?'

Niko, still glowering at Pyle, said, 'Here's the deal. You give me Pyle, you get to run the island. Cut it up whatever way you want. I guarantee no one touches you.'

'Sounds tempting,' Rossi said. 'I mean, it's not Sicily, could do with a few street signs, but it's an OK place.' He said, 'Only thing is, if you're dying this horrible death for smacking Karen, what good is it us giving you Pyle?'

'No horrible deaths,' Ray said. 'Everyone walks, that's agreed.'

'Who agreed?' Karen said.

'Jesus, Karen – what're you going to do, execute a fucking *cop*?'

Niko, slow, reached into his pocket and pulled his wallet. Then he dropped his gun on to the sand and brought up his badge.

'You don't have any crucifix in there?' Rossi said. 'Some holy water, maybe?'

'I guarantee,' Niko said, holding the badge high, 'no one touches you.'

'Except you already did,' Karen said, bringing up the .32.

Ray, turning, lunging for her arm, knew from her tone he was already too late.

Sleeps

After, comparing notes, they worked out that Ray and Sleeps had the only guns packing ammo.

Pyle, explaining how he'd wanted Niko gone, sure, but

wanting Sleeps and not Karen to take the rap, had unloaded the .32 in the jeep before handing it forward.

Mel, Rossi confirmed, had long ago swiped the clip from the CZ, the girl a kleptomaniac, couldn't help herself.

And Niko, blazing away first on the beach at Karen, then at Sleeps making his getaway, then firing blind up the ravine at Anna, had left himself a few in the hole, which Doyle had blasted off at the boat. Which was why he'd dropped the gun and gone for the last resort, the badge, putting Sleeps in mind of Dudley Smith in *LA Confidential*, Bud White blowing Dudley away from behind . . .

Ray was packing but he was too busy rugby-tackling Karen, taking her out a split-second after the .32 went click, the hammer coming down dry.

Which left Sleeps, already pointing at Niko's torso, the biggest target, bracing a stiff wrist ready for when the guy came up from grabbing his rod off the sand. Except Niko, knowing his gun was empty, went for Doyle instead, hooked an elbow around her throat and started dragging her backwards down the beach, a hostage.

'Everyone drops their guns,' he croaked, 'or I snap her fucking neck.'

Forgetting, in his panic, about the wolf.

Which wasn't an issue immediately, the wolf coming up in a flurry of sand and springing for Ray, who was now rolling off Karen. Snarling, the jaws wider than Ray's head and about to guillotine him with one snap when Karen grabbed her collar and sicced her on Niko – or Niko *and* Doyle, Sleeps couldn't say for sure.

Niko, his bluff called, panicked again and started stumbling backwards down the beach, dragging Doyle with him, Doyle turning puce in the face, until she remembered what God gave her elbows for and sunk one deep into Niko's groin. His cheeks puffed out, eyes bugging, and then he toppled forward as Doyle tore away from his arm and pitched forward on to the sand.

The wolf took off from the top of the low rise, arcing out over Doyle and landing on Niko's chest, punching him so hard the guy flew a good three or four feet before touching down. His shoulders hit the sand first, the impact jolting his head back so that his throat lay open for the split-second the wolf needed. She ripped out his throat like so much warm marshmallow, then howled a moon-shivering glee and burrowed her snout again in the ragged hole.

She got in there so deep, the blood fountaining slick and black in the moonlight, that Sleeps for a moment wanted to believe the girl had struck oil. Then he lowered the gun and turned away, went down on one knee and quietly puked on to the sand.

Doyle

The first thing Doyle did when she got back to the Katina was take a long shower, trying to scrub away the feel of Niko's hands on her throat. Afterwards, Sparks listened in silence, chain-smoking while Doyle laid it all out. Then she said, 'He was still a cop, Doyle.'

'He probably would've walked away,' Doyle said, 'if he hadn't been trying to strangle me at the time.'

'So who was it pulled the trigger?'

'That's need-to-know.'

'But it definitely wasn't Ray.'

'Ray was there, sure.' Doyle shrugged. 'We all were.'

'You're saying, no tales out of school.'

'Who knows we were there?' Doyle shrugged. 'Far as anyone knows, Niko was in Athens. Why would they even look for him here?'

'And you're sure he won't be found.'

'Someone knows where to look, has access to a submarine, they might get lucky.'

Sparks nodding along. 'So what about Madge?'

'Madge? I don't know, I guess she was with Terry.'

'Exactly, yeah.'

Sparks, for once, sounding serious. Doyle leaned forward from the waist, shook out her hair, got it wrapped up tight in a turban. Made a beckoning motion. Sparks tossed her the smokes, the lighter.

'What do you want with Madge?' Doyle said, exhaling.

'It's more Terry, being honest.'

'Go on.'

'You told me, Terry was pulling Ray's strings in this kidnap scam.'

'So Ray says.'

'Ted likes Terry for having Frank put away, tying up any loose ends. Has that CCTV footage from the hospital car park, Terry Junior's guy bundling Frank into the Qashquai. Terry, if you squint real hard, he's in the frame.'

Doyle starting to see it now. 'And this is why you're here,' she said. 'Why you decided, just like that, to take a holiday.'

'Well, that and a tan,' Sparks said.

'Thinking I was hooked up with Ray and Terry.'

'Pretty sure you weren't,' Sparks said, 'but, y'know.'

'No, I get it.' Doyle with a sinking feeling. An anchor, maybe, crushing her guts. Realising she didn't have one single person from her old life she could trust, or who trusted her. 'So what happens now?'

Sparks crushed her smoke. 'Ray, he'd know where Terry's staying, right?'

'You think Ray'll just hand him up?'

For an answer Sparks stood up and went to her bag, rummaged around. Came back handing Doyle a sheet of paper, a black-and-white copy of an Interpol Red Notice for Terry Furlong, Terry looking Paul Newman-handsome even in the grainy picture, the offences listed including kidnap, extortion.

'Shit,' Doyle said.

'Ray plays ball,' Sparks said, 'he'll go a long way towards skating out. Especially if he gets a head start. Meanwhile,' she fanned herself with the arrest warrant, 'I'm standing there waving this around while the Greek cops slap the cuffs on Terry, I'm doing my promotion chances no harm at all.'

Doyle stubbed her smoke. 'So where am I in all this?' she said.

'You're the one tracked down Ray, put us beside Terry. All while you were suspended. That buys you a gold-star honourable mention, a cast-iron pension. I mean, you're still retiring, right?'

Karen

The deal Madge and Terry brokered was Karen stole Rossi's sixty grand while he was inside, OK, but seeing how Karen spent most of it on Anna, who'd belonged to Rossi before he went away, Karen only had to pay back half.

Rossi, already up the twenty grand Johnny Priest agreed to pay if Rossi didn't ring the Amsterdam cops about the hot rod, and well advanced into favourable negotiations about managing Johnny's Greek island operations, had finally agreed.

Karen's idea, that they strap the outstanding thirty gees to Anna and put her in a room with Rossi, was voted down three-to-one.

Now she sat perched on the edge of the bath in Madge and Terry's en-suite bathroom in the Triton counting out thirty large on to the toilet seat, ribs strapped, hissing every time she had to reach over into the bag. Rossi saying, 'You never gave me a chance, girl. Even before I got out you believed I'd be the same as going in.'

'Believing it,' Karen said, 'because you were the exact same coming out twice before. A deadbeat waste of space.'

'Three's the charm.'

'Rossi, you dug out Anna's eye with a fork. Charm that.'

'That was a long time ago, Karen. And anyway, she took my ear. Like it says in the Bible, an eye for, y'know, an ear.'

'You're saying you've changed,' she said, 'is that it?'

Although, even saying it, Karen had to admit she'd been pleas-antly surprised at the way Rossi'd stepped up for her with Niko, especially with an empty gun, no way Rossi was taking that kind of chance for anyone five years ago.

Except then Rossi had to ruin the moment by saying all he was talking about was a second chance, this on the basis that Karen didn't have any better offers coming in, Ray running off with his pet cop, Doyle.

'A *second* chance?'

'A fourth chance, OK. Let's not get hung up on detail here.'

'You're tripping,' Karen said. 'Is that it? Show me your eyes.'

'I haven't had anything harder than a beer in three days,' Rossi said. 'You don't believe me, ask Sleeps.' He said, 'This sober thing, I dunno, it's like a whole different kind of fucked up.'

Karen licked the ball of her thumb, finished counting out the thirty gees. Picked up the bundle and handed it across. 'Not a chance,' she said. 'You kidding me? Rossi, if you were the last guy on earth, I'd rip off my own arm and beat you to death.'

'Can't be Mills and Boon every day, right?' Rossi said, tucking the bundle away. He opened the door. Karen realized it might be the last time she'd ever see him.

'Rossi?'

He paused, looked back. 'Yeah?'

'Thanks,' she said. 'For, y'know, facing down Niko.'

Rossi shot his cuffs, colouring a little high up around his cheekbones. 'Sure, no problem. Hey,' he said, nodding at the holdall of cash at Karen's feet, 'you ever want to invest in FARCO, I'll cut you in on a sweet deal. For old times' sake.'

'FARCO?'

Rossi grinned. 'I never told you about FARCO?'

Karen, the guy was irrepressible, worked hard to suppress a smile. 'No,' she said. 'You never told me about FARCO.'

'Want to get a drink? I need to sit down with Terry and Madge now, talk over this movie about me Mel's trying to talk them into investing in. But after? I'll tell you all about FARCO.'

'So you and Madge, you're OK with the whole, um, inheritance thing.'

'Who can keep up,' Rossi said, 'with Madge? One minute you're her long-lost kid, the next it's Ray who's the prodigal son and you're down half a mill. Not good, emotionally speaking. What they call a rollercoaster.'

Karen felt a pang for what might have been. Ray, he ever lost the quiff, was a good guy.

The trouble there being, Karen needed more than just *good*. Karen needed an edge, the not knowing. The idea that tomorrow, no matter what it was like, wouldn't be the same as today.

'You're a rollercoaster yourself, Rossi. Anyone ever tell you that?'

Rossi nodded. 'Except with me,' he said, 'there's never a queue.'

Ray

They watched the ferry reverse in, its engines churning the sea to foam. Ray sipping a latte, Pyle with an ice-cold *frappé*. Already hot out there in the square, dazzling, the kids on the quay in their baggy shorts and baseball caps waiting to ship out like some defeated army, guys propping one another up, the walking wounded, others prone on the dock. Ray soaking up the heat in his bones.

'You just sit here hoping they won't come looking,' Pyle said, 'you're never going to know when they'll come at you. Am I right?'

'You got balls,' Ray said. 'I'll give you that.'

'Me? I'll be the good guy, I'm worried about Niko. I'm running around Athens going, "Hey, anyone seen Niko? He was due on the island, never showed."' He sucked up the last of his *frappé*. 'I mean, who saw him here except us?'

'You're not worried Johnny might squawk?'

'Who's he going to squawk to? And anyway, Johnny likes his little set-up in Amsterdam, playing the part, everyone thinking he's the guy. He's got his club, his dope, all the girls he can handle.'

'That wasn't enough for you.'

'It was,' Pyle said, 'until it wasn't.' He stood up, shouldered his bag. He said, 'Y'know, Ray, once I get it all straightened out, I'll be needing a guy to keep an eye on a few islands, can keep a lid on things without making too much noise.'

'Appreciate the offer, man. I'll think about it.'

'Do that.'

'I'm serious.'

'So am I.'

Ray ordered another latte and watched Pyle board the ferry. It was halfway out into the bay when Doyle came strolling into the square, shades on. Fresh out of the shower, it looked like, hair still damp and shiny. Ray remembered the luscious kiss on the beach that night, tasting in his memory the strawberry balm on his lips. He stood and waved until she saw him.

Ray got tingles just watching her cross the square, wondering if Doyle saw a future for herself in the Greek islands, but when she got in under the awning she turned her head, offering her cheek for a kiss, and then Ray saw her expression, her eyes when she took off the shades sitting down.

'What's up?' he said, and Doyle got straight into it, Interpol, the arrest warrant, what Sparks wanted Ray to do, how it was likely to fall if he said no. Then sat back, lacing her fingers behind her head. Leaving it up to Ray. Waiting, he guessed, for Ray to make some kind of gesture.

'So,' she said, 'what d'you say?'

And Ray shrugged. 'When you're out,' he said, 'you're out.'

Madge

Terry, in a split-cane armchair in the tiny bar across the hall from the Triton's reception desk, a potted palm behind, nodded along while Mel carved shapes out of the air with her hands, the girl in full spate as she pitched her investment idea, this movie she was making about Rossi and Sleeps, *Bonnie and Clyde* only with two Clydes.

'Like Butch and Sundance,' Terry said. Sleeps saying yeah, but what Mel had in mind – looking to Mel for approval, the pair of them taking up the entire couch – was more *Thunderbolt and Lightfoot*, buddy-buddy but with a serious touch. Then a wrangle started, Rossi angling more for *Kiss Tomorrow Goodbye*, a Jimmy Cagney vibe, this because they were washing Madge's cash through FARCO Productions, Rossi electing himself executive producer.

'What's it called?' Madge asked Mel.

Mel cleared her throat and held up her hands like she was framing the title. '*Beautiful Losers*,' she said.

'Nice,' Terry said. 'But you know what I like? *Crime Always Pays.*'

Madge, wishing Karen had stuck around so she'd have someone to roll her eyes at, had a sip of the Bolli that Terry had ordered from the kid at Reception, the kid nearly putting a hole in the low table plonking the bucket down, ice cubes rattling across the floor. 'So in terms of this budget you're talking about,' she said, making a mental note to tip the kid before she went back upstairs for an overdue siesta, 'how far would a million-five get you?'

'About halfway up Brad's little toe,' Mel said. 'But, you had that kind of seed capital, you'd open a lot of doors. Impress investors with your commitment, you're putting your own money on the line.'

'There's also,' Terry observed, 'the tax breaks. Like, you put up the first million and a half, suck some people in, by the time it all gets washed out you've staked half a mill, maybe less. A million back before the first camera rolls.'

'You've done it?' Madge asked Terry.

'Once or twice.'

'Really?'

'Sure. But if you don't mind me mentioning the vulgar subject of money, where's this million-five coming from?'

Madge reminded him about the insurance policies Frank had taken out, the twins' trust fund, how she'd be the one pulling the strings.

'OK,' Terry said. 'But that only works,' and here he looked directly at Sleeps, 'if someone takes your tumble, does whatever time is coming your way.'

'That's off the table,' Sleeps said. 'I told Rossi that already.'

Terry, his eyes still on Sleeps, said, 'Rossi?'

'What?' Rossi said. 'The guy's a dog, I just tell him to roll over?'

'I'm not telling anyone anything,' Terry said. 'All I'm saying is, if or when Frank finally turns up dead, someone needs to do time for Madge. I mean, the insurance company aren't paying out a million-five without an actual body. Fuck.'

Madge turned to look at where Terry was staring and saw Doyle standing at Reception with two uniformed Greek cops and a girl standing off to one side who looked to Madge like a punctured beach ball with frizzy red hair. The surly kid behind the desk taking his time tucking a twenty into his breast pocket, grinning now as he pointed straight at Terry, saying, 'Yeah, that's him.'